You've got

lily James ♥

HYPER SPEED
ASTRO SPACE LEAGUE #1

Copyright © 2025 by Lily James

All rights reserved.

No part of this publication may be reproduced, distributed, or transmitted in any form or by any means, including photocopying, recording, or other electronic or mechanical methods, including information storage and retrieval systems, without written permission from the author, except for the use of brief quotations in a book review.

No generative AI was used at any point during the writing process.

The story, all names, characters, and incidents portrayed in this production are fictitious. No identification with actual persons (living or deceased), places, buildings, and products is intended or should be inferred.

Book Cover by @leo.nor_art

Editing and Proofreading by S.J. Buckley

CONTENTS

Content Warnings	V
Official Playlist	VI
Team Index	VII
1. Over the Moon & Out of Orbit	1
2. The Stars Have Aligned... Poorly	8
3. Starman on the Grid	21
4. Keep Your Eyes on the Racing Line	35
5. Blood is Thicker Than Engine Oil	40
6. No Guts, No Glory, No Grid Position	45
7. Caught in Your Gravitational Pull	59
8. Beam Me Up, Hottie	67
9. Catch Me If You Can't	82
10. The Fast & the Flustered	94
11. The Need for Speed... and Something More	106
12. Houston, We Have a Big F#%king Problem	114
13. Out of the Pit Lane & into the Fire	121
14. Close Encounters of the Thirst Kind	135
15. Better the Alien You Know	147

16.	Burning the Midnight Rubber	161
17.	Don't Stop Me Now — I'm on Pole	175
18.	Speech Now or Forever Hold Your Peace	191
19.	Feeling Hot Under the Helmet	206
20.	Written in the Stars, Scrambled by Gravity	224
21.	Out of This World & Into Your Arms	236
22.	Full Throttle, Zero Inhibition	251
23.	Fly the Red Flag	265
24.	Don't Go Brakin' My Heart	278
25.	Steer Clear of Heartbreak	287
26.	Not Over Till the Checkered Flag Waves	294
27.	On the Right Track	305
28.	Heart Over Wheels	316
29.	All's Fair in Love & Track Limits	328
30.	Fast Track to Forever	346
31.	Epilogue	350
Afterword		357
Acknowledgements		358
About the author		359

CONTENT WARNINGS

Books should be a safe place for you to escape, and while I'll always promise a happy ending for my characters, there may be some bumps in the road along the way.

Please consider the content warnings before reading, because your mental health will always be more important than a book about queer aliens in space.

Trigger Warnings:

- Explicit sexual content

- Death of side character (on page)

- Motorsport crashes (on page, MC involved)

- Prejudice against certain species (affects MC)

- Absent parent and paternal abandonment (off page, childhood)

OFFICIAL PLAYLIST

1. Blinding Lights – The Weeknd

2. Dangerous – Sleep Token

3. Dancing in the Flames – The Weeknd

4. SPACE MAN – Sam Ryder

5. Von Dutch – Charli xcx

6. Sweettalk my Heart – Tove Lo

7. Harder, Better, Faster, Stronger – Daft Punk

8. Stargazing – Myles Smith

9. Dancing in the Moonlight – Toploader

10. Cosmic Love – Florence + The Machine

Listen to the full playlist on Spotify:

TEAM INDEX

Nexus Racing

Drivers:
- Kai Mercer (Human, Male)
- Jaxir Taal (Human, Male)

Zenith Nova

Drivers:
- Rev Arathiel (Iskari, Male)
- Zy'Lathrix "Zylo" (Itharan, Male)

Vortex

Drivers:
- Valen Dray (Vorkan, Male)
- Milo Serrano (Human, Male)

Nebula Shifters

Drivers:

- Cassiopeia "Cass" Lain (Human, Female)
- Kirok Tal (Morthian, Male)

Scorpion

Drivers:

- Corin Strax (Human, Male)
- Khalyss Rhau (Xivithian, Enby)

Eclipse

Drivers:

- Selena Vu (Human, Female)
- Aelra Vix (Jidran, Enby)

Pulse

Drivers:

- Ivy Juno (Human, Female)
- Varek Tholl (Zeltrathian, Male)

Vanguards

Drivers:
- Tarek Hanu (Human, Enby)

- Shaya Ritho (Korgathian, Female)

***Mum*,**
You may not be here to read this, but I feel you in every page.
You were always my loudest cheerleader, and you'll forever be my number one fan.

***Dad*,**
If you're reading this, you shouldn't be.
I'm your little angel, not the girl who writes alien smut.

The Cosmic Racing Federation required teams to submit this information every year. Every racer could see it, most using it to study their competitors before the season started. It wasn't anything new, and when I told Sam as such, he looked less than impressed.

"When was the last time you looked at it?"

"I dunno. Last week?"

"And how many racers were there?" Was he testing me? I'd expected something juicy, and instead, he was quizzing me on what I already knew. "How many racers did Zenith Nova have?"

"One. Zylo. He's racing alone, like always."

Sam brought Zenith Nova's roster up on the monitor. As expected, Zylo's smiling face sat above a brief description of his X-9 Stratos. Underneath it was—

Wait . . .

"Who the . . ." Jax trailed off, just as stumped as I was.

Sam smirked, stepping back so Jax and I could crowd the monitor.

"Revvak Arathiel." I read the name aloud.

"He's a rookie." Jax looked between Sam and me. "Zenith Nova hasn't taken on a new racer in years. Not since Xander Korr died."

"That's not even the best part," Sam said, bouncing on his heels.

"Smugness doesn't suit you, Sam," I mumbled, still reading the details of Zenith Nova's latest addition. I scanned the species field and blinked in disbelief at what had to be a mistake.

"*Iskari*?!"

Laughter erupted from Sam. "There we go."

I reread the details again. And again. "An Iskari is racing in the ASL?"

When I looked up, Sam nodded in confirmation.

"I questioned whether it was an error at first. Y'know, some daft intern rushing to submit the info last minute." He leaned forward, barely containing a smile. "But I was having a beer with one of Zenith's designers last night—"

"Did you fuck him?" I cut in.

"Is that relevant?" Jax glared at me in disapproval.

"What? It's polite to ask."

"Oh, is it?" he deadpanned.

"*Anyway*," Sam continued. "He was tight-lipped at first. But put a few beers in him, and he opened up like a moonflower on Nyxara." He winked, and we shared a high five while Jax rolled his eyes. "Turns out they signed the Iskari a few months ago, but kept it hush-hush. No one knew until they submitted two days ago, right before the CRF's deadline."

"Cheeky." I turned back to the screen.

His bio was fine, I guess. His success on the underground racing circuit was cute, but he'd never competed in any official league. Not like most of us.

How would he perform on the track? I'd never seen an underground race, but I knew they were dangerous. Full of reckless drivers hoping to be spotted by an ASL scout from a professional team. They weren't exactly legal, but the Unified Space Enforcement turned a blind eye.

I'd heard that the scouts didn't attend regularly, likely too scared of being spotted and booted from their well-paid positions. But if a racer's name made the rounds and impressed the right people, they were occasionally signed.

Vortex had signed Dray's teammate two years ago after scouting him. He was a mess at first, but he'd mellowed out, finding his place amongst the other drivers on the grid. He sometimes still pulled a careless trick, though, trying to prove he could play the game with the rest of us.

Would this new rookie be the same?

I stared at the blank grey square above his bio, missing the usual mugshot. "Where's his photo?"

"Dunno." Sam shrugged. "They're not mandatory; most just add them as part of the process."

"Maybe they didn't want anyone to know what he looks like," Jax suggested. "I mean, they waited until the last minute to add him to the roster. A secret from the press?"

OVER THE MOON & OUT OF ORBIT

Kai

There was nothing like the feeling of zero gravity. That moment when you're sailing along and suddenly the ship drops, dipping into a descent so steep that your stomach is still in your throat and your ass is up by your elbow.

For some people, it made them want to spew in a bucket. But me? I wanted to hoot like a child on a hyper coaster, my body thrumming with so much adrenaline I could shatter the shuttle's roof with raw power.

A look through the window showed a change from deep space to hazy yellow skies as we entered Ithara's atmosphere. A giant moon filled the horizon, bright enough to provide daylight for twenty hours a day, year round.

The planet was nice, with its wide-open spaces and miles of grassland. But there wasn't much to see. Not beyond the capital of Luminara.

I might've been biased, because nestled on the outskirts of the city was my favourite place—on this planet at least. And as the shuttle descended through Ithara's dust clouds, long cracks in the ground became visible, causing my heart to pump a little harder.

"Looks different from last year," my teammate, Jaxir, said from the row of seats across from me.

"It looks different every year, thanks to the windstorms," I replied.

But I couldn't take my eyes off the view, because we were approaching Vortex Canyon, the track for the first race in the Astro Space League.

"Welcome home, bud," Jax remarked, and I couldn't help but laugh. We both knew it wasn't home—not in a physical sense. But spiritually? My heart had always been wherever the race was. After six long months of downtime, I was ready for the season to begin, to shed the restless feeling of displacement that came with the off-season.

Even so, he wasn't wrong. The ASL was my arena. Everyone else was just passing through.

"Ready for the fun to begin?"

I peeled my eyes away from the window to grin at my best friend. "Always."

The shuttle landed in the dedicated spot for Nexus Racing, and Jax and I disembarked, followed by our team principal, Ailor. The winds were already blowing strongly, working overtime to knock us off our feet as we crossed the shuttle park towards the paddock.

At least, Jax and I were struggling. Ailor was a seven-foot-tall Trivorii with three tentacle-like legs covered in suckers that glued them to the ground. They were a walking, talking tripod.

The paddock was a hub of activity. Engineers ran back and forth, their arms filled with tools and tyres. Racers who'd arrived before us were admiring their new vehicles or leaning over screens and talking with their team. Some were already relaxing against the wire fence on the other side of the pit lane, enjoying the early morning sun despite the dust in the air.

I caught sight of Valen Dray, a Vorkan racer from the Vortex team. He wore a pair of tiny shorts and nothing else. Metallic-bronze skin gleamed as his genetically gifted, muscular legs—lucky bastard—propelled him down the pit lane at full speed. Hell, he wasn't even sweating. That shimmering sheen?

One hundred percent natural. Dray didn't even need to work out; the Vorkans were built for feats of strength. He was flaunting it, showing off in front of the competition.

Despite my jealousy, I raised a hand in a polite wave, and Dray nodded in return. But when Jax waved too, Dray's lip curled in a sneer, and he turned to run in the opposite direction.

Jax sighed, disappointed, and I muttered, "Still besties, then?"

He didn't reply, just pushed me towards the team garage where my baby was waiting for me.

"I hope you've been treating her nicely," I called out to Sam, a human engineer, who was leaning over the body of my HyperX Velocity.

He'd joined the team six years ago, during my rookie year, and we'd been working together for the last four. He was giving my vehicle a good rub down before the afternoon practice session, and she looked *beautiful*.

Sam looked up from polishing a thruster and smirked. "I've taken her out for dinner and complimented her. We've even cuddled after a good wax and polish."

Behind me, Jax snickered, while my face pinched. "Don't make it weird, you prick."

"Says the one who calls his vehicle a she," Sam shot back, raising a single eyebrow.

I envied people with that physical skill. Every time I attempted it, I looked like I was trying not to fart. As a result, my sarcastic quips never hit the mark like Sam's. And considering I had an entire arsenal of grade A remarks just waiting to be used, it was a great shame.

I wondered if I could still master it at twenty-eight...

"Kai." Sam's voice echoed through the garage. The elevated volume suggested it wasn't the first time he'd said my name.

"Huh?"

"I asked if you'd met any of the rookies yet, space cadet."

"Nah, not yet. Have you?"

He pressed the microfiber cloth he was holding to his chest and fluttered his lashes. It was creepy as fuck, like one of those weird baby dolls with the rolling eyes.

"Why would *I*, a humble engineer, have crossed paths with any of the other teams' rookies?"

"Because you're a nosy fucker," I hit back. "Come on, what's the goss?"

"Who said there is any?"

"Oh, come *on*," I whined. Placing my hands on the vehicle, I closed the distance between us. "Stop answering my questions with a question."

Sam snapped his cloth against my fingers to keep my oily palms from ruining his work.

I yelped and jerked back. "Hey! These are my moneymakers."

If I lost these hands, who would steer Nexus through another winning season?

"You're not a porn star," Jax scoffed.

"You don't know what I get up to in the off-season," I said, palming my crotch and waggling my eyebrows.

"Do you want the gossip or not?" Sam cut in, now standing up straight, arms crossed over his broad chest.

"Yes! I knew it. Just had to make you think I didn't care, so you'd crack open like a shoddy safe." I grinned. "I'm a genius in overalls."

Sam rolled his eyes and strode over to a nearby computer station. Jax and I trailed behind like little ducklings. A large curved monitor dominated the setup, while a holographic projection of my vehicle hovered just inches above the surface, rotating to display a full 360 degree view.

He swiped his hand through the hologram, making it disappear, and tapped on the monitor until a list of this season's racers appeared. It contained photos of each racer, a small bio, and vague details of their vehicle underneath.

Sam hummed in contemplation. "An Iskari racing in the ASL. Who'd have thought?"

Who *would* have thought?

Sam and Jax traded theories like it mattered. Like this rookie's name meant something.

I didn't care if he was an Iskari or the head of the Intergalactic Government. On the track, it wasn't about species or stories, it was about speed and skill. And no one outpaced me.

Revvak Arathiel could eat my dust with the rest of them.

THE STARS HAVE ALIGNED... POORLY

Kai

Practice went by in a blink, fast enough to leave me wanting more.

Meanwhile, the paddock couldn't shut up about the rookie who didn't bother to show. But his teammate Zylo was there, a big fanged smile pasted on his mint-green face as usual. By the end of the day, I had yet to set eyes on Revvak, so if he'd practiced, it was long after everyone had left.

The next morning, I arrived at Vortex Canyon for qualifying, pumped to get into my new vehicle. It was perfect, just like last year's, and the year before that.

But this time the designers had added a glove-synced system. It allowed me to adjust things like thruster output or shield intensity with a single hand gesture, giving me more leeway to focus on the track. On the competition.

Fuck, it drove like a dream.

The paddock was even busier than yesterday. Practice sessions always drew in a crowd and a tonne of press, but qualifying was where the race began. Especially the first one.

Racers' positions on the starting grid would set the tone for the rest of the season. As the reigning champion, I was determined to follow in last year's footsteps.

Once again, I disembarked the shuttle with Jax and Ailor, but today the press swarmed us.

"Kai, are you excited for today's race?"

"Kai, are you feeling pressure after three consecutive championships?"

"Kai, what are your thoughts on an Iskari in the Astro Space League?"

The last question made me pause in place. Jax, Ailor, and the herd of press stopped walking with me. The news had obviously broken regarding Zenith's recent addition. Maybe it came from the team, or a determined journalist had spotted him during his solo practice session.

Either way, I was just as curious as the masses were to see the mysterious Revvak Arathiel.

I pasted on my most photogenic smile—wide and dazzling enough to blind a drone lens—and leaned into the journalist's recording device.

"I haven't seen him race yet," I said, voice smooth as silk. "Hopefully he's got what it takes to keep up."

I gave them a cheeky wink for the perfect finish, and we continued walking. I answered more questions and smiled for the cameras without complaint, and when security held them back at the entrance to the paddock, I was almost disappointed that our time was up.

The media weren't allowed around the pit lane—too much of a health and safety hazard with all the extra bodies—but I wouldn't have minded if they were.

I was used to the fame, the attention . . . Stars, I fucking thrived on it. To me it was just another perk of the job.

"Ready for the day, boys?" Ailor asked, their tone smooth. Calm and collected, as expected from a Trivorii.

"Always." I was practically jumping.

Jax smiled, placing a steady hand on my shoulder. It grounded me amidst all the excitement. I loved racing season, and the best part of the weekend was still to come.

Ailor left us, stopping to talk to a CRF official, while Jax and I continued in companionable silence. I let my mind wander to tomorrow's race, the one that kicked off the entire season. To the roar of the engines, the heat of the asphalt, the smell of burning fuel and scorched tyres.

Races were where I came alive.

But this wasn't just another race. It was the start of my shot at a fourth championship title. No one had ever won four championships in a row, and this was my chance to go from champion to legend. This season, the stakes felt heavier, the eyes sharper, like—

SMACK!

Something hit my chest with a grunt.

No, not something. Some*one*. And I'd sent them falling to the dusty ground like a sack of bricks.

"Shit, sorry, I . . ." I trailed off when I looked down at the figure sprawled out on the asphalt.

Pale purple skin with a pearlescent sheen glittered under the morning sun, and inky black hair fell in waves past his shoulders, the top third tied up in a small messy bun. It wasn't truly black, though, and on closer inspection I caught glimmers of blue, green, and violet shifting in the light like oil on the racetrack.

But it was the void-like eyes that made my skin crawl, and right now they were twisted into a scowl that could sour milk straight from the udder.

There was something otherworldly about them, something that made my brain hesitate, as if it couldn't quite compute. And then the realisation slipped in like a whisper . . . This was the Iskari.

Jax cleared his throat, and I scrambled to hold out my hand, but the newbie was already getting to his feet without my help.

"Sorry about that." I tried to cover my embarrassment with a weak chuckle. "My mind was elsewhere."

He brushed off his racing suit with fine-boned hands. "Clearly."

His voice was quiet, a little raw, like it wasn't used very much. But there was an underlying intensity, a sharp edge that sounded like it could cut you off at the knees with only a few words. Those strange dark eyes continued to glower, but like his hair, they weren't simply black. Tiny flecks of light shifted and swirled deep in their centres, reminiscent of the stars scattered throughout the galaxy. Like the constellations I fawned over during the off-season.

I gave myself a shake.

Why was I waxing lyrical about a set of *eyes*? Even if I'd never seen a pair like his before . . .

Jax cleared his throat again, and I realised I'd been gawking, saying nothing while the Iskari glared back at me. Trying to save face, I stuck out my hand for them to shake. It was so aggressive, I almost jabbed him in the stomach.

"I'm Kai." There, that was polite. Seems my mum raised a boy with manners after all. "Kai Mercer."

His eyes dropped from my face to my hand, but he didn't take it, and the longer I waited, holding out my hand like an idiot, the more unsettled I felt.

Did the Iskari not shake hands? Was the gesture offensive, and I had no idea?

Shit. See, this is what happens when an endangered race takes part in an institution for the first time. Nobody has a fucking clue what to do.

When he still didn't take it, I dropped my hand and shifted on my feet.

Jax raised his own hand for a shake—which I thought was risky given the Iskari's reaction to mine. "I'm Jaxir, but everyone calls me Jax."

Surprising both of us, the Iskari took Jax's hand into his own and gave it a firm shake.

What the—

"I'm Revvak, but only my grandma calls me that. Call me Rev."

"You're Zenith's rookie."

The words slipped out, and Revvak—Rev—stared up at me with narrowed eyes. He was a few inches shorter than my six-foot frame. But the way he looked at me? I felt a fraction of that size.

"And?" He folded his arms, his words clipped.

"O-Oh. I was just, uh . . ."

He tucked a loose strand of hair behind a long pointed ear. It revealed a network of fine, raised silvery lines. Branching out like forks of lightning, they traced elegantly along his jaw before disappearing beneath the collar of his suit.

When he caught me staring again, the markings flared a vivid red. They flickered once before fading back to their previous muted hue, and my mouth hung open.

"Do you have a problem?"

"No, n-no problem." Why was my voice so *squeaky*?

"Kai's just a nosy fucker." Jax chuckled, slapping my back. He was trying his best to ease the obvious tension between us.

Rev took a step back.

"It was nice to meet you," Rev said, directing his statement at Jax. But before he walked away, he gave me a fleeting once-over, and those delicate lines glowed red once more. "See you on the track."

As I watched Rev walk away, some of the tension eased from my shoulders. His slender frame, clad in a dark racing suit, faded into the chaos of the paddock.

"What just happened?"

Jax snickered. "I dunno, man. But I quite like seeing your feathers ruffled."

"Fuck off," I breathed, giving him a light shove.

But that was the thing. I *was* feeling ruffled.

When people looked at me, it was with admiration, lust, or at the very least, envy.

Rev . . . he may as well have looked through me. To him, I seemed to be an inconvenience. An annoyance. He'd sized me up and decided I wasn't a threat. I was nothing.

And it shouldn't have even mattered. I knew that. But it did.

When we entered the Nexus garage, I pushed all thoughts of pearlescent skin and dark eyes from my mind. It was qualifying time, and I needed to get my head in the game.

We'd been on the track for what felt like hours, pushing as hard as we could to get the best possible lap time. Jax and I sailed through the first qualifying session, with me in first and my teammate in second.

The slowest six racers were eliminated, relegated to the back of the grid for tomorrow's race. Their final positions were based on their fastest overall lap time.

But while Jax and I had made it through with ease, so had Rev. According to Sam, who'd talked my ear off through the headset in my helmet, the rookie finished the session in sixth.

By the end of the second session, a further five racers were eliminated. Rev had slipped up into fifth, securing a position towards the front of the grid, and making it to the third and final session.

My current lap times were enough to sit pretty on pole position, but it was still all to play for. With five minutes left on the clock, Jax decided he was comfortable with his time and retired to the pit lane. His lead over the others—including his "bestie," Valen—was enough to secure second position, despite finishing early.

I decided to retire shortly after. Sam had already assured me it was almost impossible for someone else to snatch pole position.

Slowing down as I exited the stretch of canyons, I planned to divert into the pit lane, but as I approached the fork in the road, a vehicle I didn't recognise flew past me. Their speed made the hair on my arms stand on end. The team logo was a blur, but I caught the subtle blue and silver detailing—Zenith Nova's team colours.

It wasn't Zylo's vehicle, so only one other person could be behind the wheel.

With only a split second to decide, I passed the entrance to the pit lane and increased my speed to catch up with Revvak Arathiel.

Sorry, Sam. Turns out I wasn't comfortable with "almost."

"What are you doing, Kai?" Sam asked over the radio.

Rev was only a few yards ahead, and when a gust of wind blew along the straight, I flicked my glove to adjust the stabilisers. It angled the vehicle just right, to allow the wind to push me forward rather than off-course. The move worked well, carrying me ahead of Rev.

I grinned as I left him behind in a cloud of dust. "Trying to improve my time," I replied, navigating the sharp corner that would take me deep into the cracks of Vortex Canyon.

Of the ten tracks in the Astro Space League, Vortex Canyon was the easiest, but that didn't mean it came without challenges. Ithara's relentless winds and ever-shifting layers of sand and dust meant the track's layout changed every year. A single rogue gust could throw a driver off course, sending them straight into the natural stone walls lining most of the track.

Even Zylo, an Itharan native, sometimes struggled to grasp its nuances.

The road ahead dimmed as I made it deeper into the canyon, and light struggled to penetrate through the narrow cracks above.

The decreased vision meant I had to rely on the track's strategically placed lights to see fifty feet ahead of me. But they also meant I could see the vehicle coming up on my left, moving fast enough to pass my rear wing.

Rev accelerated hard enough to pull up beside me. When I chanced a glance at him, he was looking ahead. His hands were tight around the wheel, but they looked steady and in control.

"One minute left, Kai," Sam reported. "Remember, race day is *tomorrow*."

I grunted in confirmation, knowing better than to take irresponsible risks, and turned my full attention back to the track. The rookie and I drove side by side for a long time, and it was easy to forget there was anyone besides us in the competition.

The last corner before the pit lane approached—one of the sharpest on the track—I eased pressure off the thrusters to decrease my speed and nudged the wheel towards the wider racing line.

I expected Rev to do something similar, but instead of slowing down, he sped up. He barrelled towards the hairpin, tyres screaming, closer and closer to the track limits . . . too close.

I bit my lip, eyes locked on the wall creeping up fast. He hit the brakes at the last possible moment, and the car fishtailed wildly. I sucked in a breath, sure he'd smash straight into the rock.

But then, just like that, he caught it. Snapped the wheel to the left and drifted clean around the corner.

As he blasted down the straight, my heart hammered in my throat. "What the fuck?" I muttered, tuning out Sam's awed disbelief crackling in my ears.

This is what I was worried about. It's what everyone worries about when an inexperienced racer enters the professional league. Reckless, dangerous moves that could harm not only themselves but the other drivers around them.

That last corner was always a bitch to get around on race day. When there's a wall of other vehicles trying to hog the racing line, it's nearly impossible to overtake. Better to wait until you're back on the straight, in the open air and with the walls of the canyon behind you.

If Rev pulled a trick like that tomorrow, he could kill someone. He could kill *himself*.

As I rolled into the Nexus garage, my knuckles were pale against the console, and I still gripped the wheel. I jerked the vehicle to a stop, jaw tight, and the crew swarmed in before the engine had even cooled.

Shoving the cockpit open, I climbed out without a word, and when I yanked off my helmet, the dry Itharan wind slapped my face like a blessing. Sweat-slicked strands of hair peeled from my forehead as the breeze threaded through, cooling skin that had been cooking inside my suit.

Pulling off a glove with my teeth, I wiped the sweat off my forehead and headed towards Sam, sitting at his computer station with Jax. My engineer and teammate were watching a replay of the session—the part where Rev took the last corner at an eye-watering pace.

"Fuck, he's fast." Jax stared wide-eyed at the screen.

"And fucking reckless," I added, planting my helmet and gloves on the desk. Jax and Sam redirected their attention from the screen to me.

"You good?" Sam asked, likely confused about why I'd stayed out. But Jax's smirk told me he had a better idea. I ignored him and focused on Sam.

"Yep." I fell into one of the many rolling chairs scattered around the garage. "So?"

"So . . . what?" Jax cocked a damn eyebrow. Why could everyone do that shit but me?

"Where'd we end up?" I asked.

"Oh, fuck off." Sam chuckled, punching my shoulder. "You already know you're on pole."

"And I'm right behind you," Jax cut in. "But that's not what you're asking."

"What are you on about?" I scoffed, but I couldn't meet his eye.

The fucker had known me for far too long. It was a blessing and a curse, honestly. I sat back in the chair, legs spread and aiming for an air of nonchalance. It didn't work, and Jax's smirk widened. I was feeling unsettled, and the bastard knew it.

"The *rookie* . . ." Jax drawled, eyes narrowing. "Made fourth."

"Fourth?!" I squawked.

Sam grinned. "That risky move gave him just enough time to knock Dray down to fifth at the last second."

Ah, crap. I knew what that meant. "Dray's in fifth?"

"Yep." Jax stared down at his feet.

"Shit," I exhaled, raking a hand through my hair. I'd probably spiked it up in every direction, but there were bigger things to worry about. Like the fact Valen Dray—a seasoned racer who regularly made the top three—got bumped down to fifth by a fucking rookie. "Dray's not gonna take that well."

"Nope!" Sam crowed, clapping his hands. He missed the way Jax winced beside him, but I didn't. I didn't have the headspace to focus on that right now, though. "Dray stormed out of Vortex's garage before you even pulled up. And judging by the shouting, which half the paddock could hear, I'd say things aren't very peaceful in their camp."

Jax said nothing, just continued looking at his boots like they were the most interesting things in the galaxy. I couldn't blame him, though.

Despite their past, and their current rocky . . . well . . . relationship wasn't the right word. Whatever the situation between them, I knew Jax didn't like seeing Dray as anything other than the confident, arrogant bastard he was.

Cheering from outside pulled my attention away from the monitor, and beyond the wide doors of the garage, I saw Rev surrounded by crew from Zenith Nova. Zylo patted his new teammate on the back with vigour, his signature grin looking brighter than usual. Like he was proud.

However, Rev didn't smile back. He just stood there, his expression unreadable. It was weird. I mean, most rookies would be beaming after a debut like that—revelling in the attention—but Rev looked like he couldn't care less.

"Be right back," I muttered, jumping out of my seat.

Walking quickly, I exited the garage, and by the time I reached the group, the crew had gone back to their jobs. I caught the tail end of a conversation between the two drivers.

"You did good, kid," Zylo said. He squeezed Rev's shoulder in his meaty fingers.

"Thank you," he replied, cool as ever. But at least there seemed to be respect in the way he looked at Zylo.

Fair enough.

Zylo was an ASL legend, having been racing in the league for almost two decades with Zenith Nova. I'd looked at him with a dopey as fuck, "you're my hero" expression for my first two years with Nexus, and I still respected him—you'd be hard pressed to find anyone who didn't.

Though these days I saw him for what he was: a damn good racer, and someone I was worthy of competing against.

"Rev," I called out, and the dark voids turned away from his teammate.

My skin erupted in goosebumps under his intense gaze. Fuck. Every time his eyes were on me, I felt like he could see right into my core. Maybe he could. Little was known about the Iskari since there were so few of them left. It's not like I knew anything about the markings on his skin either.

"You're going to make your people very proud," Zylo murmured to Rev. Then he grinned at me, clapping a hand on my shoulder with such force I had to hide my grunt with a cough. "Good session today, Kai," he said, whipping his gunmetal-grey hair over his shoulder.

"Thanks, Zylo," I replied, offering a smile of my own.

"Looks like you're eager to get that fourth championship under your belt."

I shrugged, and my smile turned cocky. "We're neck and neck for the record, Zylo. I think I can beat you, old man."

Zylo threw his head back and roared with laughter. At thirty-eight, he wasn't old. Not really. But he was the oldest racer in the league, so I made damn sure to remind him at every opportunity.

"We'll see whether this *old man* can still whip your ass in the race tomorrow." Zylo dropped his hand and nodded at Rev, his grin softening.

He said his goodbyes and skipped towards Zenith's garage. He met up with his boyfriend, a Ymirithian called Saelix, at the door and disappeared inside.

Rev turned to me. "What do you want?" he asked, flat and direct.

"You came in fourth." The words came out as a statement rather than a question.

"Yes?" The markings on his face pulsed with a deep red light, and I wondered what they meant. Whether they turned any other colour on the spectrum. Whether the crimson was solely for me.

"Good session today," I replied, forcibly keeping my tone light.

"Right." Rev's expression didn't change. He stayed stony-faced, impassive. He didn't even say thank you. Rude.

"Uh. . ." I raised my hand to the back of my neck, attempting to squeeze out some of the tightness nestled in the muscles. It was the same tightness that had appeared the last time we'd spoken.

Conversation with a brick wall seemed to come easier than it did with him.

Rev said nothing, just moved to walk away, but I reached out to grab his wrist before he could get far. He sucked in a sharp breath and stared down at my hand, his top lip curled back like he might growl.

Where human canines would be, Rev had small, razor-sharp fangs, and unlike this morning, his hair was now braided away from his face, revealing pointed ears that twitched erratically. From irritation, maybe?

His markings pulsed red again, but the colour was darker—almost maroon, like a finely aged red wine.

"Your last manoeuvre was dangerous, Rev." I released his wrist when he tugged back. "I know you're used to the underground circuit—"

"You know nothing about me," he snapped. Then he stepped back, putting distance between us, like he was scared I'd try to grab him again.

My jaw tightened, a scowl tugging at my mouth. "You could hurt someone if you pull a trick like that during a race."

Didn't he get it? This wasn't an illegal street race. This was the Astro Space League. There were rules to follow, penalties to be had. It was more than just your average game, and you had to play it properly.

"Thanks for the feedback. I'll take it on board." His words dripped with sarcasm, which only annoyed me further.

"You know you could kill someone, right?" I bit out. "We're not a lineup of hacks. We're *professionals*, and that means—"

"I know exactly what it means," he hissed. "You think I don't know what kind of opportunity this is?"

"Exactly! It's a huge fucking opportunity." I threw my hands up, exasperated. "So don't blow it for the rest of us with fucked-up moves that could run someone off the track."

"Save your 'I'm better than you' attitude for the track, hotshot." This time, when he turned to walk away, I didn't stop him from walking towards Zenith's garage.

But because I was a stubborn prick, I couldn't let him get the last word in.

"We'll see who's better than whom when it matters—in the race, *rookie*."

Rev stopped in his tracks and glared at me over his shoulder, dark eyes narrowed and both ears flicking. The marks on his face glowed a colour so dark it looked black from this distance.

He said no more, but neither did I. He just stood there, chest heaving, expression seething.

We glared at each other for a few more seconds, a battle of wills to see who'd break first.

But as if he didn't want to waste any more of his precious time on me, he broke the connection and stormed away, disappearing into Zenith's garage.

What a fucking prick.

STARMAN ON THE GRID

Rev

I woke up far too early. My watch read four a.m., and the sun illuminated my hotel room despite the blackout blinds. I don't know how Zylo coped growing up on Ithara with its twenty hours of daylight throughout the year.

Though, as an Iskari, I gravitated toward the dark—it was easier on my oversensitive eyes.

The city of Luminara was quiet this early in the morning. Better than the constant hub of noise it would be in a few hours' time. Ithara was mostly empty grassland, and Luminara was one of only three cities on the entire planet. As the capital city, and the biggest, "overcrowded" was an understatement. This wasn't my favourite planet.

Though I suppose I didn't have a favourite at all.

None of them were my home.

The Iskari didn't have one anymore.

Iskanya had been destroyed centuries ago, pillaged by a neighbouring planet filled with warmongers. Given our peaceful nature, it wasn't a surprise to anyone when we lost that fight and the Iskari were all but wiped out.

Now there were less than a few thousand of us spread across the galaxy. We could go our entire lives without seeing another beyond the hub of our families. Hell, we weren't even recognised as an independent species anymore.

We were displaced.

Endangered.

Weak.

I was determined to change those perceptions, and despite my aversion to people, the Astro Space League was my chance. My opportunity to remind the galaxy that we were still here. That we were still struggling.

I rolled out of bed, deciding that now was as good a time as any to get up. Even if I didn't have to be at the track for another six hours. It was race day. My *first* race day—in the Astro Space League, at least.

I'd been racing for years on the underground circuit, determined to make a name for myself. To get to where I was today.

Yes, it was dangerous and illegal. And *yes*, Mum and Grandma were less than impressed upon finding out I'd been taking part.

But karting from an early age before climbing through the lower Intergalactic Racing Leagues—the usual, more official route—was brutally expensive if you wanted to do well. Far beyond what my parents could afford on their meagre salaries. There were sponsors to be had, sure, but no major corporation was going to risk its money on a scrawny little Iskari, diversity quota or not.

It meant I'd had to take matters into my own hands.

My watch pinged with an incoming call. I tapped the screen, and a hologram of my mother hovered in the air above my wrist. I crossed the bedroom and opened the blackout curtains so she could see me better, and she gave me a beaming smile, her ears twitching affectionately.

"Hi, *zyli*!"

Despite a groan at my childhood nickname, a sense of warmth filled me and the lines on my skin flared gold. She'd started calling me her "shooting star" when I was a kid.

After Dad had brought home a beat-up kart he'd salvaged from the scrapyard he worked at. I practically lived in the thing, racing up and down the hallway outside our cramped two-bedroom apartment. The only times I wasn't in it were when I was at school, asleep, or being dragged to the bath—usually by Grandma, who had to force me into the tub. Like any other kid, I'd thought bath times were a full-on mutiny against my comfort.

"Hi, Mum," I said through a yawn. Hearing her voice soothed the nerves I hadn't noticed bubbling away in my stomach. "You're calling early."

Zyphar, the planet where we lived, was three hours ahead, and given it was my parents' day off, I hadn't expected to hear from her until later.

"Sorry, love. Forgot about the time difference. I was just so excited for my baby's first race!" I felt those pesky nerves flare up again, and when I smiled, it probably came out more like a grimace. Mum's gaze was as sharp as always, not missing a thing. "What's wrong?"

"Nothing, I'm—"

"Nope," she cut me off, eyes narrowed. "If you say 'fine,' your grandmother will be on the next shuttle there to knock some sense into you."

The words died on my lips at the image of Grandma whacking me over the head with her favourite wooden hairbrush. I knew Mum well enough to know her threats were never idle. She'd do it if she thought it would help.

"I'm just nervous," I mumbled.

Mum's face softened. "Nerves are natural, *zyli*. This is a huge opportunity for you. Something you've worked so hard for, even if . . ." She trailed off, but I knew what she'd left unsaid.

"Even if your grandmother and I don't agree with how you got there."

But the mention of opportunity had Kai Mercer's face appearing in my mind. The way his square jaw had tightened as he ripped into me for the move I'd pulled during qualifying. His condescending tone, like I was some clueless child.

The memory had me seething. Sure, I was a rookie, but I wasn't a fucking idiot.

I *knew* it was a stupid risk. Stars, if I'd lost focus or second-guessed my instincts for even a moment, I'd have been an Iskari-shaped smear on Vortex Canyon's walls.

Of course, I wouldn't pull that stunt during an actual race. No, the only reason I'd risked it was because it had been only the two of us on the track. Also . . . a small, like *teeny* tiny part of me wanted to show off in front of the league's previous champion.

There'd been more than enough room between us to pull off the move I'd perfected while in the underground circuit. And it had given me just enough of an edge to push the legendary Valen Dray down to fifth place. It had earned me a starting spot in fourth today—three places behind that cocky bastard, Kai Mercer.

Hearing Mum say my name, I tuned back into the tail end of the conversation. There was more soothing and motherly love before we said our goodbyes.

I headed to the hotel's gym and did a quick workout—just enough to get my heart pumping since I didn't want to overexert myself. Racing was hard on the mind and body, and I needed a minor boost without zapping all my energy.

Iskari weren't naturally physical, and it showed in my lean frame. But still, the exercise cleared my head of thoughts related to that infuriating prick.

By the time I'd finished my cooldown on the treadmill, I was feeling pretty zen. Calm. In control. That was what I needed to be to get through this competition. To show the galaxy that the Iskari were anything but weak.

No. We could do anything we wanted, given the opportunity.

By the time I'd left the gym, showered, and eaten breakfast in the hotel restaurant, it was only eight a.m. The race started at noon, and the team shuttle was picking us up at nine.

Sigh.

It was going to be a long day.

The paddock was . . . hectic.

I wasn't used to this level of activity on race day. We didn't have qualifying sessions or even practice on the underground circuit. News of a race spread through the grapevine, then you'd turn up with a vehicle and race. It was simple. Just make it from start to finish however you could.

You didn't have a team either. Some turned up with friends or an entourage, but that was more about showing off. No one had ever accompanied me before. I didn't have anyone to bring. But now I had an entire team at my back—engineers, crew, strategists, the team principal.

I even had a *teammate*. The underground could be a lonely place, so I was still getting used to having people I could rely on, and who'd rely on me in return.

There were two championships within the Astro Space League: the Drivers' Championship and the Constructors' Championship.

The constructors built the vehicles, and the drivers raced in them, and while we drove alone, fighting for individual points and a place on the podium, we also had to work as a team for the constructors. For the people behind the scenes who put in the work to build a vehicle worth racing.

My name was now on the ASL's constantly shifting points table. Sitting at zero, just like everyone else's. For once, I was an equal—at least for today.

I followed Zylo off the team shuttle, my personal coach Zha'reen, or Reen for short, marching along beside me. She was a feisty Vorkan woman and built like a brick shithouse. I'd never had a personal coach before, and it wouldn't be a stretch to say she had dictatorial tendencies.

But after working with her in private over the last few months, I couldn't deny that my driving skills had improved.

We'd barely made it two steps when the press surrounded us. Reen tried to scare them off with her snakelike eyes and sharp tusks, but these journalists were relentless, flashing cameras like vultures circling a fresh kill, all hungry for the next big scoop to cash in on.

Microphones and cameras jabbed inches from my face. I clenched my jaw, fingers twitching to swat them away.

"Revvak, how does it feel to be the first Iskari driver?"

"Revvak, do you feel pressure to succeed?"

"Revvak, what does this mean for the future of the Iskari?"

Nina, Zenith's publicist, had already advised me to keep my mouth shut. So I stayed silent, ignoring their constant questions. I kept my face blank, back straight, and chin held high. If I showed them nothing, there'd be no risk of a ridiculous story just because I looked at someone funny.

When we walked through the entrance to the paddock, the press held back by security, the tightness in my chest eased. But I waited until we were safely in Zenith's garage to exhale and let my shoulders slump, knowing their cameras were on me until the last possible moment.

I knew that talking to the press was par for the course in this job, even if I didn't enjoy interacting with others. I'd received extensive media training as part of my signing, and Nina had prepared me for many questions and scenarios. So if a journalist cornered me, I had a Rolodex of ready-made answers I could throw their way that wouldn't negatively impact me or the team.

What irked me most was how the journalists' questions fixated on my species instead of the season ahead.

I understood it to some degree. I was a novelty, a shiny new toy. More than just another rookie. But in the end, I was more than just my heritage—endangered or not. There were plenty of species that'd never driven in the ASL before. But I could guarantee everyone would scrutinise their skills, not their origins.

"Revvy!" Zylo's low voice reverberated through the garage, and I tried not to cringe at my unwanted nickname. We'd only met a few days before the practice sessions. Nina had explained that they'd wanted to keep my signing under wraps until the last possible moment, but Zylo was notoriously bad at keeping secrets.

Like me, Zenith wanted the spotlight to be on my racing skills. It was why I'd agreed to race with them when Tavoris approached me. Vortex Racing had also offered, but they'd have been happy to milk my heritage dry if it brought the team more money and attention.

In the end, my final decision had been easy.

More experienced drivers would kill to be on a team with a six-time galactic champion. I knew how lucky I was, even if our personalities were like night and day.

From the beginning, Zylo had taken me under his wing. His advice and feedback had been kind yet constructive, and unlike with Kai Mercer, I was more than happy to listen to what Zylo had to say.

He skipped towards me—yes, skipped—and dropped a heavy arm over my shoulders. "Ready for your first race?"

I'm shitting myself.

But I couldn't tell him that. I didn't want to let him down . . . or for certain dickheads to overhear and think I couldn't handle the pressure. So instead of being honest, I just nodded. "So ready."

If I said it enough times, manifested it, I was sure I'd believe it.

If Zylo saw through my bullshit, he didn't say. He just placed his hands on my shoulders and squatted until we were eye to eye. "It's okay to be nervous, Rev."

The words were quiet, meant only for the two of us. A warm, friendly smile spread across his face. I wanted to tell him yes, I was nervous. My bones felt heavy with it, and it had nothing to do with the gravity on this planet.

But I was used to masking my weaknesses.

"I'm fine."

Zylo didn't push. He just grinned wider and slapped my shoulders, hard enough to almost buckle my knees. Because he was so strong and tactile, Zylo may have forgotten how puny I was.

He cupped the back of my neck in a supportive gesture and led me to where our team principal and strategists were waiting. We spent ninety minutes analysing data from practice and qualifying and discussing strategy. Then I tested my reflexes with Reen.

Time passed quickly, and with ten minutes before lights out, it was time to get ready. I approached the starting grid, dressed in my racing suit, helmet under one arm. Rows of sleek, roaring machines lined the asphalt like predators ready to pounce.

Drivers settled into their cockpits, helmets locked in place, visors shielding their eyes as they prepared to start the race.

I spotted Kai and Jax at the front, chatting away while admiring each other's vehicles.

Jax's vehicle was burnt orange, almost bronze, with yellow accents along the nose and thrusters. Kai's was an obnoxious metallic red with over-the-top gold accents, fading to black at the rear wing. The design made it stand out on the track. Perfect for a man who obviously needed to be seen.

Sensing my eyes on him, Kai looked up from his drooling and met my gaze. Jax followed suit and waved. In contrast, Kai glared, his jaw tight, and I could hear the tense words he wouldn't say . . . *"Don't blow this for everyone."*

I was grateful when Zylo dragged me away.

Eventually, we climbed into our vehicles and started a slow circuit around the track, before stopping back at our assigned spot on the starting grid.

I did a comms check with the team, made final adjustments, and then there was nothing to do but wait. My heart thundered in my ears, drowning out the roar of engines, as the five stoplights above flickered red, counting down to go time.

I pushed all thoughts of annoying journalists, nerves, and Kai Mercer from my mind. The spectators in the grandstands were loud, but I couldn't hear them, my focus reserved for the low rumble of my thrusters, the empty stretch of road ahead.

The race was all that mattered.

Four lights . . .

Three . . .

Two . . .

One . . .

Lights out.

Time to move.

I pulled away quickly, but Valen Dray was quicker. Before we'd even made it off the straight and into the canyon, he'd pushed me down into fifth. Frustration bloomed in my chest, but I ignored it.

The Astro Space League was all about the long game, and there were still fifty laps to go.

Even after months of endurance training, this would be my longest track session yet—underground races usually had a ten lap limit—so I knew strategy would be better than impulse. Mostly. Because both underground and ASL races were unpredictable.

Sometimes you had to let your instincts take over.

"You good, Revvy?" Zylo's voice appeared in my ear.

Engineers weren't the only ones who could speak to drivers. Teammates and competitors could communicate on a dedicated frequency. Taunting was part of the game, and if you riled up a rival enough to make a stupid mistake, it was a win.

Plus, viewers at home could listen in, and they *loved* hearing a shouting match between drivers. Dray's creative insults were infamous. Whether it was a racer who'd cut him off, or his own engineer for a last-minute strategy change, no one was safe from his wrath.

"All good," I replied, taking the first corner with precision as we entered the canyon.

Towering walls loomed on either side, making the already narrow track feel even tighter. It was my first time on a track with this many racers, and although I was loath to agree with Kai's assessment of yesterday's manoeuvre...

It had been fine when we were alone, but with at least five of us fighting through the corner at any one time?

Yeah, not happening.

The first fifteen laps were uneventful. I spent a lot of them fighting with a Morthian driver from Nebula Shifters, constantly switching between fifth and sixth. Fortunately, a blown tyre forced him to retire on lap thirteen. For now, I was doing well and keeping calm.

If I continued as I was, my lead ahead of the other Nebula driver would be too big to close without a serious fuck-up on my part. I'd even crept up to Dray occasionally. The fucker was fast, though, and I struggled to find a moment to overtake him.

Kai pitted on lap twenty-seven, desperate for a tyre change if his massive reduction in speed was any indication, and when he re-entered the track, he ended up behind me. I thought I'd have a chance to hold him back, but unfortunately, Kai had a trick up his sleeve.

Winding through the canyon's twisting pathways, he took advantage of a short straight to use his superior acceleration and fresh tyres to overtake me, leaving a cloud of dust in his wake.

His voice crackled through the comms, sharp and cocky, laced with a smugness that made my teeth clench. "Getting comfortable back there, rookie?"

"Just letting you clear the debris for me."

Kai cackled. I momentarily switched off the radio, only allowing contact with my engineer if required. With the increasingly rough winds howling through the canyon, the last thing I needed was that infuriatingly casual tone slipping into my ears like a static that wouldn't turn off.

Lap forty-five was when everything changed. I'd clung to fifth place, even after a pit stop for fresh tyres a few laps prior. Their reinforced material, built for endurance over short bursts of speed—a feature unique to Zylo's vehicle and mine—meant I could push on for longer without another stop.

"Reports of debris on the track in sector three," Kileen, my engineer, announced over the comms. "Not sure of the extent yet, so just be cautious."

I was just entering the sector when Zylo roared, *"ROCKSLIDE!"*

He was in third, with a significant gap between himself and Dray, who wasn't that far ahead of me. In his wing mirrors, he'd clearly noticed the large chunks of rock that were now tumbling down the walls and straight onto the track.

"Be careful, Rev," Tavoris, Zenith's team principal, warned over the radio.

I wanted to panic, to brake hard just like Dray was doing in the face of the enormous boulders now slamming onto the track.

But this was an opportunity... While Kai was skilled in speed and overtaking, my forte was risky manoeuvres and dodging obstacles. If I did this right, I could overtake Dray and climb up into fourth.

I'd been good this whole race, sticking to strategy and playing it safe.

Perhaps it was time to show the competition what an Iskari could do.

Instead of slowing down, I sped up, flicking a switch on my steering wheel to activate the dynamic hull. It allowed my vehicle to adapt to certain conditions, becoming more compact during narrow turns or wider on open stretches for maximised stability and speed. It wasn't meant for narrow gaps between tumbling pieces of rock, but I figured it could work all the same.

I sped towards two lumps of stone, each bigger than my vehicle and enough to squish me if this all went wrong.

"Revvak, slow down! Hard stop!" Tavoris ordered.

But I ignored his command.

"I got this," I urged, taking a deep breath.

I pressed another button at the last possible second. The body of my vehicle contracted, switching to a second set of thrusters for better stability, and my car slipped through the narrow gap between the boulders with seamless precision. They didn't even graze the bodywork.

I let out a victorious hoot while Kileen and Tavoris responded with an exasperated laugh.

"Fucking hell, Rev," Kileen wheezed.

"Well done, Revvak," Tavoris added. "But let's try to stick to strategy now."

A flicker of guilt crept in. I'd ignored Tavoris's instructions and pulled a risky move, living up to Kai's expectations.

But this time, it paid off.

And when I passed the checkered flag in fourth, I couldn't resist sending a silent *"fuck you"* to Kai Mercer.

After the race, there was no time to rest.

As soon as I pulled into the pit lane, Nina dragged me to a quick press conference before the podium. Reen took my helmet, while Nina shoved an ASL-branded ball cap onto my head. Someone directed me to stand next to Zylo, Jax, and Kai, and we each received a microphone.

Ben King, the presenter from Cosmic Sports Network, introduced us to the viewers at home and then began his questions. He directed those questions primarily towards the top three, which I appreciated.

Despite the media training I'd had, I wasn't used to public speaking, and I tried extra hard to make sure the markings on my skin didn't flare a pastel green with embarrassment, just in case someone watching at home actually knew what that colour meant.

After covering Kai's win, Zylo's time in the league, and my rookie introduction, I'd expected it to be over. But Ben surprised me.

"Kai, Rev's overtake on lap forty-five was, let's say . . . bold. Some might even call it reckless." I bristled at his choice of words, knowing Kai would inevitably have something to say. "As one of the more experienced drivers here, what's your take on it?"

"Well, Ben." Kai leaned in, mouth tipped up in a smirk. "You can call it bold all you want, but I'd agree that it was reckless. It was a miracle he didn't end up crashing into the canyon walls."

I didn't want to respond. I really didn't. But something about this prick just made my blood boil, and I cut in before Ben could respond.

"I didn't realise taking risks was such a crime in racing. Sorry I'm not content to just follow the pack, Mercer."

His cocky smile remained, but I saw the way his hand tightened around the microphone, knuckles white against the dark plastic. "If you keep pushing your luck like that, eventually it won't go your way."

"And yet here you are, first place and still rattled. Guess luck's working just fine for me," I remarked, one eyebrow raised.

Kai turned away from Ben and narrowed his eyes at me, fixated on my cocked brow. "I'm not talking about the *result*; I'm talking about the way you race." Jax and Zylo stood awkwardly between us. "You're lucky the move paid off. Next time, that stunt could cost you more than just fourth place."

I snorted, flicking my hair over my shoulder. "We'll agree to disagree. But I am sure about one thing."

"Oh?"

"Yeah. Next time, you can watch me up ahead, not just glance at me in your wing mirrors."

Kai scowled, and Jax struggled to hide his smile. Zylo, meanwhile, straight up guffawed and slapped me on the back.

"Dream on, *rookie*," Kai bit out. He snarled the word like it was an insult, and I felt the marks on my skin heat. A quick glance at my hand confirmed they were glowing a vivid red, my annoyance on show for the galaxy to witness.

Kai's scowl vanished, replaced by his trademark smirk, all too satisfied with the reaction he'd provoked. The tension lingered as the cameramen exchanged wary glances, and Nina stared at the sky as though begging the stars for patience.

Eventually, Ben cleared his throat before turning back to the cameras.

"Well, it's clear the track will be heating up in more ways than one. Will Rev's bold moves pay off next time? Or will Kai's strategy keep him ahead as we begin the race for the championship?"

Kai flashed the camera a blinding smile that made my stomach churn, while Ben finished up.

"That's all for today, folks. It's goodbye from Vortex Canyon, and we'll see you at the next race!"

KEEP YOUR EYES ON THE RACING LINE

Kai

Two weeks after the race in Vortex Canyon, I was alone in my top-floor apartment on Zyphar, still watching the replay of Rev's manoeuvre on lap forty-five. I'd watched it more often than my go-to porn clips, and for once my right hand was getting a break.

Every few days, I opened the recording on my TV, and skipped through the race to watch that moment. My heart beat faster each time, my breaths came quicker, convinced he'd crush himself under the rockslide.

Obviously, I knew he wouldn't. Knew his cocky little ass had made it through, just to snipe at me during the press conference.

But watching Dray slam on the brakes while Rev sped up, my gorge rose. My stomach churned as I watched the structure of his vehicle narrow, my gut in knots as he slipped through the minutest gap between boulders, only slightly wider than his car.

And I hated to admit it, but it was impressive . . . brilliant, in fact.

But it was also reckless. He was a rookie with no sense of self-preservation, pulling tricks some of the most seasoned drivers wouldn't dream of.

The worst part? He didn't even break a sweat.

I'd listened to his radio—to Zylo yelling about a rockslide, his team principal ordering him to brake—and all the while, Rev's breathing didn't even quicken. Didn't stutter. Unruffled, he calmly passed through the gap, overtaking Dray in the process.

All he said was, "I've got this."

Dray had been furious, of course. The rookie had bested him in qualifying, and then he'd lost out because Rev had the balls to do what most of us wouldn't.

There was a reason for that.

What if his timing had been off? A split second either way and he'd have been history before his career had even got off the ground. Wouldn't look great for Zenith, would it? They finally replaced the driver who'd died on the track with another who met the same grisly fate.

I'd warned him against his impulsive behaviour, and I thought he'd listened. Rev had driven like a top-tier Astro Space League racer. He'd held his own against drivers from Nebula Shifters, and he hadn't batted an eye when a swirling dust devil materialised on lap twelve.

But then he had to do *that*.

Coupled with the jabs we'd shared during the press conference, the fans were eating it up.

"Next time, you can watch me up ahead, not just glance at me in your wing mirrors."

Like hell I'd let that happen. Rev may be good behind the wheel, but there were still nine races to go, each one more difficult than the last. The ASL was about endurance—the long game—and I wasn't sure how long Rev would last if he pulled stunts like that on the harder tracks.

My watch pinged, the holo-screen showing Jax at the front door of my apartment building. "Let me in, dickface."

"What do you want?" I groaned. I wasn't in the mood for company, but I could never say no to my best friend.

He held up a white paper bag. "I brought the dumplings you love."

I sighed. The twat knew just how to win me over, so I buzzed him in without another word. He knocked on the door, and when I opened it, Jax presented the bag like a rare jewel. "For you, good sir."

I chuckled. "You're such a weirdo."

Then I snatched the food before he could take it away. He followed me through the open-plan living room into the kitchen, and I grabbed two plates while he plucked beers from the fridge.

He nodded towards the TV across the island. "Why are you watching that?"

The screen was paused on a close-up of Rev in his vehicle. Although an iridescent blue visor hid his face, Rev's raised fist showed his jubilation at having slipped through the rockslide.

I shrugged. "Nothing else was on."

We crossed the room and took our usual seats on the black leather sectional in front of the TV.

"You're partway through at least five films on SpaceFlix, yet you're watching this?"

I paused with my chopsticks halfway to my mouth.

"Have you been using my account again?" He didn't outright confirm it, just winked, and I nudged him hard in the thigh with my socked foot. "Get your own, you freeloader."

"Why, when I can leech off you for the rest of my life?"

"So you're the reason my watchlist is filled with romcoms and true-crime documentaries."

He raised a single eyebrow. "Who else would it have been?"

"Dunno," I mumbled through a mouthful of dumplings. "An ex, or something?"

"You need to stop giving out your password."

"I didn't give it to you!"

"No, you left it logged in the last time you passed out on my couch."

With a growl, I lurched forward, chopsticks raised to steal a dumpling from his plate. "Hey!"

He tried to snatch it back, but I shoved the whole thing in my mouth. "Daz paymen fuh uzin' my SpaceFix aggound."

Jax glared at me but continued eating his food, clutching his plate against his chest. "So why *are* you watching a replay of the race?"

"I told you. Nothing else to watch."

"You've found something that's piqued your interest." He eyed the shot of Rev. "It *was* pretty impressive."

"It was dangerous."

"Yeah, but *racing* is dangerous." He tilted his head to the side. "It just helps if the danger is fun once in a while."

"What are you on about?" I leaned forward, placing my empty plate on the wooden coffee table.

"I'm just saying." Jax rested his chopsticks on his plate and set it on his lap.

He had one dumpling left, and my eyes were on it. Knowing what I wanted, he put his plate on the couch beside him, far away from my greedy fingers.

"You're always at the front," he continued. "Which isn't a bad thing. You're good at what you do. But while you're up ahead, the rest of us are fighting to keep our position, so playing it safe isn't always an option."

His lips curled into a wistful smile, full of fond memories of the track. "Besides, being reckless after forty-odd laps spices things up a bit. Makes it more exciting."

I could see his point.

When you reached the front of the pack, the race became a game of calculated caution. Pushing just enough to secure a better result without risking it all. Focus shifted to making it past the checkered flag in one piece. Locking in points for yourself and the team. Keeping the championship in sight.

Anything less than perfection wasn't an option. One wrong move could turn a comfortable lead into a race-ending disaster. A blown tyre, a failed thruster . . . just like that, you're out.

But that didn't mean the race wasn't fun, right?

"I have fun," I argued, my pout doing most of the talking.

"I'm sure you do, champ." Jax patted my shoulder with the exaggerated care you'd give a sulking toddler. "But you should join the fight once in a while. Gets the blood pumping."

"Maybe I will join the fight sometime . . . if anyone is ever good enough to overtake me."

Jax snickered. "Okay, cocky. I can think of *someone* who might give you a run for your money."

"Who? The rookie?" I scoffed, folding my arms over my chest.

My gaze dropped back to the abandoned dumpling. If he didn't eat it soon, I was kidnapping it and holding it hostage in my tummy.

Jax held up his hands in surrender. "I didn't say a word. But it sounds like Rev has taken up some prime real estate in your head."

Fucking stars.

If only Jax knew how right he was.

BLOOD IS THICKER THAN ENGINE OIL

Rev

After the first race, my family decided it was the perfect time to throw a party, so here we were in my childhood home on Zyphar, the most populated planet in the galaxy. We'd squeezed around the small dining table to enjoy some *luzari'eth*—my favourite dessert.

I might've moved out after signing with Zenith, but that didn't stop me from making the twenty-minute walk to their apartment for Grandma's cooking several times a week.

I'd already been here for a few hours by the time we got around to talking about the race. Mum and Dad had watched it live on CSN, but they still insisted I share my account between mouthfuls of luzar fruit, velvety cream, and sweet nebula honey.

"I can't believe you finished fourth!" Mum gushed, spooning more dessert into her bowl.

The party might've been in my honour, but this was a treat for everyone. The ingredients were pricey, so we only had it on birthdays or during *Liora'shenn*—the galaxy-wide festival of light and remembrance.

"I can," Dad said. He smacked my back hard enough that I almost deep-throated my spoon. "Our boy was made to race in the ASL."

As he dived into an analysis of my "quick thinking," his tone swelled with pride, like it was the best thing he'd ever seen. Warmth crept up my neck. The markings on the back of my hands glowed amber-gold, drawing attention to my mild embarrassment.

I wanted to brush it off, act like it was nothing, but the subtle violet gleam threading through the markings gave me away. A quiet admission that I liked it. That I craved the praise from those who mattered most.

Then Grandma clocked me on the head with her heavy-duty copy of *Galactic Expectations*.

"What was that for?" I whined. The spot on my skull pulsed with a dull throbbing sensation, and I was sure a lump was already growing.

She tossed the book aside, the cover slapping against the floor with a flat smack. "You could've died, *va'tari*!" Her pet name for me—"star-born spirit"—was sweet, but it did nothing to ease the pounding in my head.

"But I didn't . . ."

"There are so few Iskari left in the galaxy." Grandma's words came low and firm, sharper than any shout. "And you want to risk dropping that number further because of a silly trophy?"

"No, but—"

"And how can I flaunt my grandson to the knitting club if he's busy being a smear on the road, huh?"

I didn't bother arguing, just sighed, knowing she'd never understand.

I understood her concerns, but I'd chosen not to tell her the real reason I was desperate to be in the league. As far as Grandma knew, my reasons were superficial—a need for fame, fortune, and trophies on a shelf. She had no clue I was fighting for our people. Battling to improve the lives of my family.

I looked down at my lap, noting the shame-filled coral glow on my arms. "Sorry, Grandma," I muttered, my bowl of *luzari'eth* forgotten.

No one spoke, and the tension hung heavy in the air. It changed what should have been a celebration into something awkward.

Grandma cupped my face, urging me to look at her. I tried to resist, but she pinched my cheek until our eyes met. Hers were dark and full of stars, just like mine, and the coral glow of my markings faded as if her soft touch had eased away my shame.

"I may not agree with all your choices, *va'tari*, but I will always be proud of you." Then she pressed a soft, wet kiss against my temple.

"Love you, Grandma," I whispered.

"I love you too, my little supernova." She reclined back in her chair, spooning up a mix of cream and fruit. "Anyway, I'm glad you put that arrogant wanker, Kai Mercer, in his place."

Dad choked on his mouthful of dessert, while Mum brought a hand to her mouth, trying and failing to hide her smile.

Grandma may be old, but she'd hung onto her colourful vocabulary. "Who does he think he is?" She huffed. "Calling my grandson reckless! The nerve of him."

"*You* just said I was reckless, Grandma." If she noticed my side-eye, she didn't comment on it.

"I'm your grandma. I can say whatever I want." Because of course, old-lady logic always won.

"I think we can all agree he was fantastic," Mum said, turning the conversation back to lighter topics.

"Not too shabby, my boy." Dad nudged me. "You're going to be a nightmare for the rest of the season."

I smiled at him, flashing a honey-covered fang. Fourth place *felt like* a victory. Way better than I'd expected for my first race.

But I hungered for the top spot, and a certain egotistical prick was standing in my way.

"You held your own out there, *zyli*. Even after the drama with the press conference . . ." Mum trailed off. She glanced at Grandma, who was too busy licking her bowl clean to comment. The woman loved *luzari'eth* just as much as I did. "Maybe a little less drama next time, yeah?"

"Can't promise anything," I tossed back with a crooked grin.

"You always have to make things harder than they need to be, don't you?" She sighed, but her answering smile was fond, full of motherly love. "I think you get it from your father."

Dad scoffed and flicked a piece of luzar fruit at her head, making her giggle like a teenager.

"Nah, I think I get it from Grandma." The woman in question sent a cheeky wink my way.

"You know," Dad drawled, resting his elbows on the table. "I didn't think I'd be saying this so soon, but I could get used to this 'famous racer for a son' thing. I can't believe how many times I've seen your name in the news over the last two weeks."

"Great. Guess I should get used to the reporters and paparazzi following me around."

"Racing's not all bad, huh?" Mum teased. "Next they'll be writing about your skills rather than your recklessness."

"Not if Kai Mercer has anything to say about it," I mumbled, slipping a spoonful of cream into my mouth.

The conversation slipped into a more comfortable silence, and we all finished our desserts. By the time I finally dumped my spoon into the empty bowl, I was bloated and convinced I might fall into a sugar coma.

"When's the next race?" Dad asked, breaking the quiet.

I looked across the room at the calendar hanging on the wall in my parents' kitchen, and my chest tightened with anticipation. "Next weekend."

Grandma narrowed her eyes at me. "No more chasing boulders this time."

"I promise. Wouldn't want to give the old man a heart attack." Dad burst into laughter. He flicked the tip of my ear, making it twitch, while Mum collected the empty bowls.

We spent the rest of the evening immersed in casual conversation, talking about everything and nothing at all, laughing at the time I shredded the carpet in the hallway when my old kart's axle snapped. Warmth and laughter filled the room—two things that always made everything feel right.

And as I sat there, surrounded by those who loved me, I felt a deep sense of gratitude.

But even with the comfort of home wrapping around me, my mind drifted to the next race. The anticipation buzzed beneath my skin like static. I still had something to prove, not just for myself, but for all the Iskari. To show them we weren't weak, that we could stand toe to toe with the best. And if I was going to do that, I'd have to pass Kai Mercer.

Something told me he wouldn't make it easy.

NO GUTS, NO GLORY, NO GRID POSITION

Kai

Horizon Rings was one of my favourite tracks. It wasn't just about driving wheels to the ground. There were stretches of zero gravity as you circuited Solara 9, a gas giant on the far side of the galaxy.

Horizon Rings was all about flying, and there was no need for pit stops. There was more room for high-speed manoeuvres, flips and tricks, and a shit tonne of fun.

Rev would be in his element.

I'd never admit it, but I'd watched the replay of Vortex Canyon at least a dozen more times since Jax came over. I watched Rev's vehicle the entire time, fascinated by how easily he navigated the track. There were other rookies in the league this year, but Rev blew them all out of the water. Hell, he was even better than some of the seasoned pros.

I'd never tell him—couldn't risk inflating his ego even more—and I stood by the fact that it didn't pay to be reckless just for the sake of it. Jax could preach that a bit of danger made for a fun race, but fucking around didn't get you the win.

No, it took focus. Determination. Precision.

Flying around Horizon Rings was my kind of fun. I'd just win all the points while I was doing it.

The Nexus shuttle took us from Quorath—the nearest inhabitable planet to Solara 9—and dropped us off at the floating space station slash paddock.

The surrounding gravity barrier provided a breathable atmosphere, so it felt like any other paddock on the ground. Bright lights made everything visible, and beyond the paddock's ledge, you could see the floating rings of ice and debris that gave the track its name.

The shuttle trembled as we passed through the barrier, accounting for the sudden change in g-force, and then we landed.

Disembarking ahead of Jax and Ailor, I skipped across the asphalt to the team garage.

I was excited. Sue me.

"Gonna have some fun today?" Jax asked.

"I always have fun," I replied with a grin. "But today I'm gonna have *more* fun."

After settling into the garage, we followed the usual routine—analysing last year's data, reflex training, and a quick scan of the track itself. Drones had followed the route prior to our arrival. They painted a picture of the course we'd take on Sunday, creating a holographic diorama that teams could use to refine their strategy.

Given the rings constantly moved, the track layout often changed. Even in the twenty-four hours between qualifying and race day, the route could end up completely different. We also had to consider the changes in gravitational force. If you weren't paying attention, they could pull you off course and push you in the wrong direction. Plus, thick clouds of gas decreased visibility in certain sectors.

Unlike Vortex Canyon, this track was wider and not caged in by stone walls on either side. Instead, deep space surrounded you. A blanket of stars that you could fall into if you lost an ounce of focus. I'd driven here multiple times.

But as I watched the hologram spin, the same rush of exhilaration I'd felt in my rookie season made my blood fizz.

When my turn came to head out for practice, I snatched my helmet from Sam and jumped into the vehicle. From my position, parked in front of the garage, I could see Rev chatting with a Zenith engineer.

He'd pulled his multicoloured hair into a low, messy bun, the pointed tips of his ears visible through the strands, and I watched as he brushed back some pieces that had fallen to frame his face, revealing the fine lines on his neck and jawline. They currently glowed a fiery gold.

"Ready to go?" Sam asked over the comms.

I confirmed before pressing a button on my steering wheel, and a transparent dome of glass closed over my head. Fresh oxygen flooded the cockpit, sharpening my senses. Another button brought the electromagnetic thrusters to life, lifting the vehicle a few feet off the ground, and the whirring noise that followed let me know the tyres had retracted to be concealed in their dedicated compartments.

I directed the vehicle towards the edge of the paddock. "All good."

"Get a move on, Mercer," Dray snapped via the drivers' radio, his vehicle appearing in my wing mirror. It seemed that Vortex were practicing too, so just to fuck with him, I crawled along at a snail's pace.

"Lovely day for a leisurely drive," I chirped.

He growled, low and rumbling, and swerved to the left, attempting to overtake me. But I cut him off at the last second, enjoying the stream of curses he sent my way. Instead of responding, I cackled and pressed down on the accelerator, zooming onto the track.

Other than Dray, I was alone on the track. Jax hadn't started yet. I flew through the first floating ring, narrowly avoiding a rogue chunk of ice that was trying to break away from the pack. Then I switched to my custom thrusters, built for maximum acceleration, and pushed my vehicle to the limit.

The straight opened up before me, stars streaking past in silver blurs. My pulse kicked up with the speed—fast, faster—until the speedometer was almost at its limit. I gritted my teeth and held the line. A corner surged into view. I slammed on the brakes and pulled hard, the g-force biting deep into my chest as I drifted clean through the next ring, inches from the edge.

It reminded me of Rev during qualifying, and I tried not to imagine his smug expression if he knew I was doing something similar. But at least there was no one around for me to harm. That was the difference between us.

The gap between me and Dray had grown rapidly thanks to the thrusters, and he'd disappeared from the view in my mirrors. My AI navigation system alerted me to the incoming gravitational pull, so I hit the throttle again, twisting the steering wheel to the right.

Instead of veering off course as one might expect, I tilted in a smooth anticlockwise arc. The momentum carried me into a corkscrew turn, and I released an excited *whoop* as I blasted through the next ring.

Five laps later, I returned to the paddock, parking up with just enough time to watch Jax head out, Zylo close behind him. My gaze skimmed the rest of the lineup, but Rev was nowhere to be seen.

Not that I was looking for him.

My eyes just had their own ideas, apparently.

Sam watched from the garage door as I lowered my vehicle to the ground. "How was it?" he asked once the glass dome had retracted.

I pulled off my helmet and grinned. "Absolutely perfect."

He smiled back, taking my helmet while I climbed out of the vehicle. "I saw your little twirl on the feed. Have fun?"

"Everyone's asking me that lately." Frowning, I brushed strands of sweaty hair off my forehead. "I always have fun."

He nodded, and I followed him into the garage. "I'm sure you do. Today just seemed like . . . more."

"Has the rookie been out yet?" I asked. If he noticed my sudden change of subject, he didn't call me out on it.

"Not yet." He didn't have to ask which rookie I was referring to, and I couldn't tell if that irked me or not. "I think all the rookies are planning to head out at the end, once the pros have finished."

I hummed. It made sense. There were only a couple of zero-gravity tracks in the lower racing leagues, and I doubted the underground circuit had one. A track like this could be intimidating, despite being one of the easiest. When I was a rookie, I'd practiced towards the end too.

But Rev was ballsy, so I was surprised he hadn't raced on the track with the pros to show off his supposed skills.

When Jax returned, we ate lunch, comparing the bland, protein-packed lunches our personal coaches had put together. I was the kind of guy who'd never leave a meal unfinished. I loved food, and as a growing boy, nothing came between me and my breakfast, lunch, or dinner—even if it *was* just a plain piece of chicken and salad.

So tell me why, when Sam announced the rookies were heading onto the track, I abandoned half of it to watch the feed.

"Feeling full?" Jax smirked. Of course he'd noticed something was off.

"Yep . . . so full." I dumped the rest of my lunch in the bin, power walking to the other end of the garage before he could say any more.

Ailor was already there, studying the live feed as rookies began leaving the paddock. On the desk was a tablet, full of annotations I didn't understand. They routinely watched the other teams during practice and qualifying—analysing their decisions and reactions, seeing how they could play into our team's race-day strategy.

I pulled up an empty chair, settling in to watch as high-speed drones followed the rookies around the track.

"You don't normally watch the other teams practice," Ailor stated.

Their eyes didn't leave the feed. Scaly fingers rapidly tapped the tablet's screen as Ivy Juno—a human driver and former Pulse Racing engineer—misjudged her braking while taking a sharp turn through one of the floating rings. She skidded off-course and crashed into a chunk of rogue ice.

My shoulders jerked up, teeth gritted tight, like I could feel the shudder of impact in my own bones.

"That'll be a difficult fix," I remarked.

Ailor scrolled up, reviewing notes from the previous race at Vortex Canyon. "Juno also hit the wall in her first practice session. She's solid on the straights but struggles to judge braking distance ahead of tougher turns."

"I'll keep it in mind if she's nearby."

"Yes, but it's unlikely. So far, her average times won't make the top ten. Still, you'll probably lap her, so stay alert."

We watched the rookies in silence, the only sound being the steady *taptaptap* of Ailor's fingers.

"You still haven't answered my question."

I was so engrossed in the feed that their words made me jump. "What question?"

"You don't normally watch the other teams practice."

"Still not seeing the question, boss." I gave them some serious side-eye.

Ailor smiled. It was small, but enough to reveal a set of needle-like teeth. If I didn't know Ailor well, they'd unnerve me, but our team principal was nothing more than a huge softy, all wrapped up in a yellow-skinned package.

"The question was implied," they muttered. "You haven't done this for the last two seasons, at least. I've told you before, Kai. You can't outrun what you don't understand, and studying your competition is—"

"The first step to beating them," I cut them off. "I know, I know."

They finally looked up from the screen, grey eyes locked on me. "And yet here you are for the first time in a while. What's changed?"

I wanted to tell them that nothing had changed, but a black vehicle with blue and silver detailing diverted my attention, and I couldn't focus on anything else.

"Ah." Ailor spoke, their words barely louder than a breath. "I see."

"What do you see?" I couldn't look at them, scared of what I'd find there.

I focused on Rev's vehicle as he blasted through the first ring. His speed left the other rookies in the dust, on par with the more seasoned racers—quicker, even.

Of course, it didn't count until qualifying, but the way Rev chewed through the seconds, creeping closer to my best lap time, had me on the edge of my seat.

"You feel threatened."

Okay, that took me off guard.

My head snapped to the left, and I frowned at Ailor. "I'm not threatened by a *rookie*." I regretted the words as soon as they left my mouth. They made me sound way cockier than I'd like, and I cringed when the ridge above Ailor's eyes rose on one side.

They didn't even have proper eyebrows, and they could still do what I couldn't.

"He may be a rookie, but he's still your competition, Kai. Revvak Arathiel is on the same level as you and Jaxir. The same as Zylo and Valen. If Zenith signed him, then that boy has earned his place here. You'd do well to remember that."

Feeling scolded, I dropped my gaze to the desk. I hated getting told off by Ailor, even when I deserved it. They'd never raised their voice, not once in the five years I'd been on the team. I didn't think they were even capable of speaking above a certain decibel. But they gave off those "I'm not angry, just disappointed" vibes.

So if I pursed my lips, pouting like a baby, that was my business.

"I seem to remember another rookie who shook things up with their talent," Ailor continued. "And when others dismissed him because he was new, do you know what he did?"

"What?" My teeth sank into my bottom lip, trying to fight the smile pulling at my mouth.

I looked up to see them watching me, eyes overflowing with fondness. "He proved everyone wrong, showed them what he was made of."

My mouth stretched wide, curling up at the corners, unable to be contained any longer. "I heard he won the championship three years in a row, so I bet that helped too."

"Absolutely." Ailor huffed a quiet laugh. "But don't forget. He wasn't just handed the title. He had to make everyone eat their words first."

I turned my attention back to the screen. Rev took the turn where Ivy Juno had careened off course, navigating it with ease before zooming along the straight. "Guess I'll have to follow in those legendary footsteps, huh?"

"That's the spirit. You've fought for that title three times before. Now you'll have to do it again."

"Sounds like a challenge." The familiar fire I'd felt so many times before burned in my chest. "I'm used to those."

Rev stayed on the track far longer than the other rookies.

I watched the entire session with Ailor until Rev returned to the paddock. I hated to admit when I was wrong, but Ailor had a point. Watching could be helpful, especially when anticipating the decisions my competitors would make on race day.

But Rev was an enigma, and with every lap completed, his approach shifted. One lap, he'd brake early before a turn, and the next, he'd push it to the last possible second. Sometimes he'd take a wider line. Other times he'd hug the inside curve, testing every way to shave time off his run.

I couldn't predict what he'd do next, and considering how easily I could read the other drivers, that scared me. It was usually second nature to me, allowed me to expect their moves so I could stay ahead when it mattered most. Even with the rookies, it only took a few laps to predict their next move before they made it.

But Rev was a blank slate every time he crossed the line. With each prediction, he'd prove me wrong.

It impressed me. I mean, how could it not? Most drivers fell into patterns, giving in to predictability. Year after year, the pros settled into tried-and-true strategies for each track, sticking to what worked. If it got you over the finish line in one piece and racked up a solid number of points, why change it?

But it was also unnerving.

What if I were ahead and Rev appeared beside me? With his speed and agility on the track, he'd proven that was at least a possibility, and after our last conversation, I wouldn't put it past him to cut me off and send me straight into the wall. If we were battling for first, I feared I wouldn't be able to predict his moves.

And maybe Ailor was right.

Maybe I was feeling . . . threatened.

Not that I'd ever tell them. If Ailor knew they were right about *this*, I'd see their smug "I told you so" face for the rest of the season—the rest of my career.

When Rev returned to the paddock, we were the only two drivers left behind. Jax had returned to his hotel hours ago, and I'd waved him off without a glance. I was leaning against the wall between garages, arms crossed and one leg pressed into the brick, when Rev pulled up.

His dark eyes found me as soon as he removed his helmet, the fine lines around his jaw flickering crimson. Knowing that the sight of me got under his skin made me laugh. The sentiment was mutual.

Though while he was probably plotting my untimely demise, he left me feeling off-kilter. And despite feeling . . . threatened, I refused to let him throw me off my game. I was a three-time galactic champion, for fuck's sake. I wouldn't let some newcomer screw up my chance for a fourth.

"Rookie," I said, a cocky smile plastered on my face. My only defence against the way he unsettled me. "Enjoy your drive?"

"What do you want, Mercer?" Rev stuffed his helmet under his arm. "Come to yell at me again before the race? Newsflash, you're early. Qualifying isn't until tomorrow." He was a sassy little shit. It made the blood boil under my skin, and it took an immense effort not to snap back like he wanted me to.

Rev approached the door to Zenith's garage like he knew where he was going. He was too damn confident for a rookie still trying to prove himself.

"Nope," I replied, lifting my shoulders in easy dismissal. "I was just enjoying the show on the screens. You were good out there. Too bad you're slow on the corners."

Rev turned, one eyebrow cocked, with the look of someone bracing for round two.

"It's cute how you think you're ready for the pros. Maybe you should come back next year when you're not holding everyone up." I knew I was being a prick. But there was something about his arrogance, something that made me ache to knock him down a peg or two.

Why? Fuck knows . . . I'd book myself in for a psych evaluation later.

The lines on Rev's skin pulsed like an angry red beacon, but he didn't rise to the bait. He just shrugged, casual as anything.

"Is that how it is?" His voice was low, steady, the glitter in his void-like eyes swirling. "Look at you, the high and mighty Kai Mercer. Think you've got it all figured out, just because you've got a few titles under your belt?"

My cocky facade faltered, just for a second, but the way his lip twitched told me he'd noticed. I bit my tongue, tamping down my urge to retaliate, and the tang of copper flooded my mouth.

And just like a shark salivating over blood in the water, he said, "Maybe you could use a little reminder of what it feels like to be tested."

A spark ignited beneath my ribs, burning me from the inside out. Maybe it was Rev's insinuation that he could beat me. Or maybe it was the urge to prove myself, despite having done that for the last three years.

Either way, I wasn't about to back down now.

"You wanna race, rookie?" I cocked my head, mouth stretching into a wolflike grin.

Rev just stared, face expressionless, but the challenge in his dark eyes was clear. When he hesitated, I wondered if he'd crumble under the weight of his bravado.

Then he smirked. All confidence, none of it earned. And it irritated me, because while I knew it was a mask, it lit up his androgynous features. Ones I'd only seen scrunched into a scowl.

"Why not?" He put on his helmet and lifted the visor, revealing dark voids that threatened to suffocate me if I wasn't careful. "Hope you're not a sore loser, Mercer."

I pushed away from the wall, closing the distance until we were chest to chest. Rev had to crane his head back to meet my gaze.

"Wouldn't dream of it. Just don't cry when I lap you," I retorted. We stared at each other for a beat, tension thick as tar between us. "Track's clear. Let's see what you've got, *rookie*."

Without waiting for a reply, I turned on my heel and marched towards my vehicle, ignoring Sam's questioning stare from the pit wall as I climbed inside.

Time to remind Revvak Arathiel who he was up against.

"Five laps. First one to cross the line wins."

"Confirmed," Rev replied over the radio.

We sat on the starting grid, waiting for the signal. Sam and Ailor had asked what I was up to, but I couldn't explain *why* I planned to race the newest rookie around Horizon Rings, just that I was.

So instead of explaining, I switched off the comms and prayed I wouldn't get into too much trouble. I wasn't sure what Rev had told Zenith, but that wasn't my problem. I was just certain that we had to get it out of our systems.

What *it* was, I wasn't sure. Competition? Ego? All I knew was that I was determined to win. And if it put Rev in his place in the process? That was a whole other victory.

Again, I knew I was being a dick. Psych evaluation still to come.

The five red lights illuminated one by one, pulling my attention back to the matter at hand. When they disappeared, Rev and I shot forward, neck and neck down the straight. The first corner loomed, and I slammed on the brakes early.

But Rev didn't. He waited until the last second before cutting the turn tight. The move made my stomach drop, and I fought to catch up.

He zipped through the first ring with smooth precision. A few turns later, I edged past him, feeling the rush of the lead, but he stuck to my tail, almost bumper to bumper, and I gritted my teeth in frustration.

On lap three, I tried Rev's late-braking trick. I failed miserably, my turn too sharp, and gravity tugged at the vehicle, pulling me close to the edge of the track. My heart beat against my ribcage, panic turning to vexation when Rev surged past, cool and steady. I recovered—barely—and returned to the racing line, cursing my arrogance as the gap between us increased.

But on the penultimate lap, something shifted. I wasn't just chasing the win anymore. No, I was chasing Rev. Pushing harder, taking risks I never would have before. His lead didn't bother me as much anymore. How could it when the chase was so *thrilling*?

Adrenaline mixed with the blood in my veins, driving me to dig deeper, to up my game.

Stars, I hadn't felt like this in a while.

"Enjoying my exhaust fumes, Mercer?" Rev asked.

And instead of getting annoyed, I laughed.

Rev pulled further ahead when we entered the last lap. This little competition wasn't going the way I'd planned, but I couldn't deny that I enjoyed racing by his side. His out-of-the-box decisions caused me to think on my feet and try something new.

Sure, he still irritated me. But he was *good* at what he did.

"A real race is ten times the length of this, rookie. Five laps doesn't prove you're built for longevity." I fired off the words, more reflex than fury.

On the final straight, I gave one last push, attempting to overtake Rev at the last second, but it was impossible. His vehicle narrowed to reduce solar wind resistance, leaving me wide-eyed as he stormed down the track.

Half a second later, my vehicle crossed the line.

"Feeling sore, hotshot?" Rev sounded smug, and annoyingly, he had every reason to be. I'd instigated the challenge, insisting I'd beat him by a mile, but he left me trailing behind as we drifted back to the paddock.

His win surprised me, the gap between us more so. But what caught me off guard was the eerie calm I carried beneath it all. I was used to coming in first. Used to doing everything I could to stay ahead and take my place on the podium. Today I'd made mistakes, tried new things. I'd learned that maybe being predictable wasn't always a good thing.

I'd wanted to teach the rookie a lesson, and he'd schooled me instead. Not that I'd ever tell him. He was still unpredictable, and any decision to go off-piste could take someone out with sixteen of us on the track. But . . . maybe I could shake up my strategy from time to time. Maybe tried and true wasn't always the best.

"You're good, rookie," I begrudgingly admitted.

"Just having fun, Kai."

Hearing my name on his lips surprised me, too used to hearing my surname or his derogatory "hotshot." Which I deserved since I called him "rookie" like it was something unsavoury.

But it meant nothing. Today meant nothing. Rev was still the arrogant newcomer, and I was still a three-time galactic champion—albeit one who'd apparently had a brain transplant in the last few weeks.

We were rivals, and I was going to beat him when it mattered.

I grinned as I parked up in the paddock, watching Rev disappear into Zenith's garage without even glancing my way.

The battle may be over, but oh, had the war just begun.

CAUGHT IN YOUR GRAVITATIONAL PULL

Kai

"Do I have to go?" I whined from my couch in the living room.

I hadn't moved all day, too busy watching reruns of *How I Launched Your Mother* on SpaceFlix. After finishing two full seasons, I didn't want to end my marathon now.

Jax just rolled his eyes. Even through the holo-call, I could tell his vast well of patience had runneth dry. I was whining like a baby, but I didn't fucking care. I really, *really* didn't want to go out tonight.

"Savannah has already RSVP'd. Said if you don't go, she'll sign you up for at least three charity marathons in the off-season."

Savannah was Nexus's publicist, and a complete and utter bitch. Okay, she wasn't. Except when we didn't "follow her vision," and I'd rather be spaghettified in a black hole than find myself on her bad side.

"I'm a driver, I'm—"

"Not built for running," Jax finished. "So you'll just have to go, then, won't you?"

"But I don't *wanna*." I felt like screaming and rolling around on the floor.

Jax was no longer paying attention to me. He was at the edge of the holo, rooting through his wardrobe for something to wear.

It was one of our weekends off. Horizon Rings had ended with Dray, Zylo, and me in third, second, and first. Dray had shoved Jax off the track in the penultimate lap, and he'd collided with a chunk of debris that forced him to retire. He'd fumed about it ever since, so tonight Dray would be first in line at an all-you-can-eat buffet of icy glares.

The event was a party for the league's newest sponsor—CosmoCharge: the ultimate fuel in the galaxy. Basically just another bog-standard energy drink packed with sugar and preservatives.

Sam had called me twice already, speculating whether his favourite porn star would be there. Wasn't sure what kind of party he thought it was, but I wasn't in charge of the guest list. Maybe CosmoCharge had a more . . . progressive approach to sponsorships.

All I wanted to do tonight was veg out in front of the TV and become one with my couch. Maybe jack off a few times.

Unfortunately for me, tonight's attendance was mandatory—for *every* driver. Including a certain rookie who'd finished fourth once again. The thought of Rev scowling his way through a sea of celebrities and execs, forced to make nice and play the game, lifted my spirits.

Huh. Maybe tonight wouldn't be a total dud after all.

I wondered what he was like when let loose in the wild. Did he smile? Or was he grumpier than usual? I didn't even know where he lived. Would he crawl out of some rocky cave to begrudgingly network with the masses? And what would he wear? I'd only ever seen him in his racing suit.

"What's the dress code tonight?" I asked Jax, who was ironing a floral shirt. "Clearly not black tie."

He flipped me off without looking up, making me snicker. "The invite says 'galactic chic,' so interpret that how you will."

"And you think *that* screams chic?" I eyed the shirt as he draped it over a hanger.

"I don't even know what 'chic' means," he snarked. "Maybe everyone will be in florals, and you'll stand out like a sore thumb in one of your thousand and one identical black T-shirts."

"I'm not wearing a black T-shirt."

His brow quirked. "Oh?"

"Nah," I smirked. "It's blue."

"Fuck off, you bellend," Jax chuckled. "You changed your tune."

"It's either buck up and go, or run some fucking marathons. And if Sam's vision is accurate, I'd rather be stuck with celebrities, porn stars, and an open bar."

"Not sure where he got the porn stars from." Jax entered the bathroom and placed his watch on the vanity, reaching to the left and turning on the shower. Steam billowed through the room, distorting his image.

"Is everyone going?" I asked, aiming for casual.

The smirk tugging at Jax's mouth told me I'd missed the mark. "I'd assume so. Attendance is mandatory, isn't it?"

"Oh, so Dray will be there."

His expression soured, and I burst out laughing as he grumbled goodbye and told me to get ready.

There were forty-five minutes before I needed to leave. I leaned back, my head hitting the couch, and let out a groan that sounded too loud in the stillness of my apartment. With *every* driver in attendance, I suppose it was only polite to make sure I looked good.

I gave my comfortable couch cushions one last mournful look before dragging my sorry ass to the bathroom.

Time to fucking primp.

The theme "galactic chic" became obvious when I arrived. Guests' sparkling outfits rivalled the stars twinkling beyond the windows of Nebula, a cocktail bar built into an abandoned space station floating just beyond the planet Tyrus.

The outside looked like a rusted hunk of metal, but the interior was the kind of place that made you stop and stare the moment you stepped inside. It'd been transformed into a blend of industrial grit and celestial beauty. The walls bore remnants of the original metallic framework, but unlike the outside, they gleamed under soft ambient lighting accentuated by shifting panels of iridescent glass that mimicked the swirl of distant galaxies.

A circular bar sat at the heart of the space, the counter sculpted from polished obsidian, with veins of luminescent blue that pulsed in time with the low, sultry music playing in the background. They reminded me of the fine lines on Rev's skin.

I looked past the suspended tubes that held vibrant, shimmering liquors, definitely not hoping to spot *his* signature scowl in the crowd. I met the eyes of Jax instead, who was chatting with Zylo at a high table in the corner.

"Is this chic enough for you?" I asked on my approach, adding a twirl to show off my outfit.

I'd chosen a form-fitting leather jacket embedded with LED piping that flickered between red and gold, the colours of my vehicle. Underneath I wore a textured undershirt and slim, tailored trousers that shimmered under the low lighting. A pair of black fingerless gloves and iridescent loafers that shifted between black and indigo tied the outfit together.

In contrast, Jax had paired his garish floral shirt with a pair of ripped grey skinny jeans and white high-tops. "Alright, alright." He waved me off, sipping his drink.

"Bit underdressed, mate." I ruffled his hair, ignoring his complaints, and grimaced when my fingers came away sticky. "How much hair gel have you got on?"

"Oh, fuck off. Do you know how hard it is to style these ringlets into something manageable?" He stared at the shiny mirrored wall, attempting to fix his mop, but there wasn't much he could do to tame his wild curls.

I'd perfected the "I just woke up like this" style in my teens. I'd been a lazy shit who always wanted ten more minutes in bed before my early morning karting sessions, so now, with a touch of wax and a run of my fingers, my hair looked perfect.

"I'd still fuck you," Zylo announced, just as his partner, Saelix, arrived in a lilac shift dress that hung prettily over his lean frame.

"Who are you fucking?" he asked, smiling at the three of us.

"Jax," Zylo deadpanned, revelling in the way Jax choked on his luminous pink drink.

"N-no," he spluttered. "We're not, I swear. I—"

I cut him off with a solid whack to the back, while Zylo and Saelix snickered across the table. "They're taking the piss."

Zylo put his hands in the air and shouted, "Revvy!" I followed his eyeline to see a stranger standing at Nebula's entrance.

Except, it wasn't a stranger.

Rev shifted from foot to foot, arms wrapped around his waist, sharp teeth nibbling his bottom lip. He looked out of his depth, but hearing Zylo's voice, he replaced his trepidation with a mask of indifference. His arms dropped to his sides, and he strutted through the bar, oblivious to the eyes on him as he moved. If I didn't know him, I'd have said he was a vision.

The top of his dark hair was tied into its usual messy bun, while the rest hung loose down his back. The strands shifted between deep shades of blues, purples, and greens under the recessed ceiling lights, and his pale pearlescent skin glittered like the surface of a moon.

A thin silver chain dipped between his pecs, while matching chains hung between the piercings lining his ears. His sheer midnight-blue shirt stopped just above his waist, showcasing the smooth but toned skin of his stomach. The top three buttons were undone, revealing protruding collarbones and the way the delicate lines around his face extended down his body before dipping into the waistband of his trousers.

I wondered how far down they went.

His leather trousers moulded to his long, slim legs like a second skin. They were tight enough that a semi would be obvious to passersby, so fitted they were almost indecent. And curled around his thigh, gripping the limb, was a . . . fucking stars, it was a tail.

Polished, heeled boots added a few inches to his height, their steady clip echoing as he arrived at the table. Up close, I noticed a dusting of periwinkle eyeshadow framed his dark eyes, and the subtle shimmer made the galaxies in them seem infinite. A tiny star-shaped silver stud glinted in his nose, while a thin ring pierced his septum.

His plump lips glistened with a clear gloss, and I wondered whether they'd feel soft or sticky to the touch.

"Can I help you with something?"

"Huh?" I grunted. My eyes snapped up from Rev's lips, meeting his glare.

"You were staring," Rev said, and the corner of his mouth twitched.

My cheeks burned with my embarrassment at being caught. "Not staring." I lifted my chin. "Just surprised to see that you clean up so well."

The ghost of his smirk fell away, replaced with his usual scowl. Returning to our normal back and forth made me feel steadier. More balanced.

"It's nice to see you again, Rev," Saelix cut in. He rested a slender hand on the rookie's bicep. "You look lovely."

Rev dropped his eyes to the table and shrugged, but his skin pulsed with an amber-gold glow, the flickering obvious under his sheer shirt. He was like a walking light show. It was mesmerising. "Attendance was mandatory," he muttered, almost shyly. "So here I am."

"We're glad you're here!" Zylo added, dropping his thick arm around Saelix's thinner shoulders.

When Rev looked up, there was a tiny smile on his lips, and he softened while looking at the pair. Seemed a few pleasant words could make the icicle thaw.

"Do you want a drink, Rev?" Jax had finished his cocktail and was preparing to get another.

"You didn't offer to get me a drink," I grumbled.

"You're big enough and ugly enough to get your own."

To my right, a snicker made me turn my head, and I caught Rev trying to cover the sound. Caught, he cleared his throat and dropped his hand. He replaced his arrogant mask before turning to Jax. "I'd love one, thank you."

"Anything in particular?"

Rev shrugged. "Surprise me."

"Careful, Revvy." Zylo twirled a glass of sparkling liquor in his thick fingers. "They look pretty, but they're strong as fuck. Kind of like a certain Ymirithian I know." Saelix giggled when Zylo nipped at his jaw.

I pretended to gag. "You two are sickening."

"Don't worry, Kai." Saelix trailed a hand down Zylo's broad chest. "You'll find your partner in crime soon enough."

I scoffed, waving him off. "No way. I'm a lone wolf. Bachelor for life, and all that."

"More like too infuriating for a single person to put up with," Rev mumbled.

I turned to him, narrowing my eyes. "Bold words from someone who looks like he'd rather be launched into deep space than have a meaningful conversation."

Rev flicked some hair over his shoulder with his delicate fingers. "And yet, here I am, suffering through this event just like you."

Zylo roared with laughter. "He's got you there, Mercer."

"I'm here to support the league's newest sponsor. And it was mandatory." The last part was muttered, but Zylo heard well enough.

"Savannah threatened you again, didn't she?"

I waved him off before turning back to the rookie. "That's neither here nor there. I'm here for my team, not to make small talk with people who think they know everything about racing."

Rev narrowed his eyes, gaze sharp. This little fucker knew he was getting to me. "You sure about that? You seem pretty engaged." He rested his elbow on the tall table, appearing relaxed as ever. The lines on his body flickered sunshine yellow.

"Only because you keep running your mouth," I shot back.

"Oh, please. You love it." He tilted his head, his void-like eyes calculating. "Probably get off on it."

My jaw tightened, and heat crept up my neck. The worst part was that he wasn't even wrong. The back and forth between us, the constant challenge he presented . . . it was infuriating, but it made my pulse quicken.

If he were anyone else, I'd have dragged him to the bathroom and ravaged him in a cubicle like the classy fellow I was. The fact that my dick was twitching right now was nothing more than a biological reaction to his sass—the need to tame a brat and have them begging on their knees.

My treacherous appendage had to get with the programme, because Rev was *not* someone I wanted to fuck until he cried. He was a snarky little shit whose neck I wanted to wring.

Repeatedly.

Jax returned to the table, a drink in each hand. He passed one to the rookie, who thanked him before taking a sip, then Rev circled around me, starting a conversation with my best friend.

Saelix leaned across the table, humming in amusement. "He's getting under your skin, Kai."

I stepped away from the table. "You know what? I need a drink." I turned on my heel, ignoring the amused looks from my friends—and the knowing smirk on Rev's face—and headed to the bar.

Point to you, rookie, I thought. *But just you wait. The game is on.*

BEAM ME UP, HOTTIE

Rev

Nebula got busier and busier as the night went on, filling to the brim with guests in designer clothes. We listened to speeches from CosmoCharge's CEO, and servers drifted through the crowd with trays of finger foods. Drinks flowed, and I knocked them back like I was dehydrated.

Zylo was right; they were strong as fuck.

Nebula was fancier than any place I'd been to. It catered to the elite, and until Zenith swooped me up, I was used to being broke as shit. Thankfully, CosmoCharge had gone all out on the infinite bar tab.

I begrudgingly made small talk with important people, and even exchanged words with Dray. Jax sent him glares from across the room the entire time—so fiery I half expected Dray to burst into flames. His hostility was palpable, and even drunk, I knew better than to ask.

Nina, Zenith's publicist, had checked on me a few times, and Tavoris praised Zylo and me for our performances so far. Given the rosy tint to his cheeks, it seemed like even the team principal was letting loose tonight.

I mainly stayed at the table with Zylo and Saelix, doing my best to ignore Kai as he spoke with Jax nearby. But his voice was just a little too loud, and his hands gestured a bit too wildly. The cocky smile he wore so often, the one that always pissed me off, never left his face.

Now and then, I'd hear his obnoxious laugh from across the room, only to get more annoyed when the sound sent a shiver down my spine. He was just so . . . carefree. Like nothing could bring him down. Even in an overcrowded room surrounded by strangers, he looked at ease.

Oh, to enjoy the privilege.

Kai revelled in all the shoulder slaps from people he didn't know, the congratulations from everyone he spoke to. He was a commodity to everyone here, and he knew it. A natural at holding court with his admirers, he ensured everyone felt the weight of his attention, leaving no one out, while his harem hung on his every word. They laughed at his jokes—which weren't funny—and complimented him for existing.

Meanwhile, I was content being a wallflower, fading into the background. But occasionally, I'd feel a prickle of awareness, and looking around the room, I'd find Kai's eyes already on me.

Each time, the frown he wore would fade away, replaced with a smug grin. I'd hold his stare for a moment, letting him know he wouldn't get to me. That I refused to let him bother me. Then I'd sip at drink one hundred and whatever, and return to my previous conversation with Zylo.

I was grateful when the bar got busier and I lost track of Kai in the crowd. I was listening to Saelix and Zylo chat about their holiday plans for the off-season when someone approached my back.

"Hi there."

I turned to see who'd spoken, meeting a pair of upturned eyes with slitted pupils and golden irises. The newcomer was a stranger, and a handsome one to boot. He was tall, with viridian skin dappled with scales shining like polished gemstones. His smile revealed a mouth filled with pointed teeth, which should've been intimidating, but the shyness of it made him endearing.

"Hello." My face stayed blank. I could've smiled, but I rarely did with the people I liked, let alone a stranger. At least it was a step up from a frown.

"Revvak, right?" He held out his hand, dwarfing mine as we shared a handshake. Despite the scaled skin, his palm was soft and warm.

"Rev. Only my grandma calls me Revvak."

He chuckled. "I'm Nery." Dropping my hand, he ran his fingers through his grass-green buzz cut. "My nana full-names me too—Nerytharion—so we've got that in common."

His genuineness surprised me, so I smiled. Just a small one. "I guess so." I gave him a once-over. "You don't seem like the formal type."

Nery bit his lip, cheeks darkening. "Not really. Life's too short for formalities, don't you think?"

I sipped my drink, feeling much more relaxed, but I couldn't tell if it was Nery's calm presence or the strength of the liquor in my glass. "I'm thinking you might be right."

Orange light danced across the markings on my skin, and his gaze drifted to my exposed stomach before rising, lingering on my lips. I tipped my head back and finished my drink, feeling the weight of his stare on my throat. When I finished, Nery smiled again, his mouth closed this time.

He pointed at the empty glass in my hand. "Could I get you another drink?" Then he ran a hand through his hair again, and I expected it was a nervous tic. "If you're, um, you know, not too busy?"

"Sure," I replied, gifting him a proper smile. "That sounds great." I tried to keep my tone casual, but the words came out a little faster than intended. No one had ever approached me in a bar before. I couldn't help but be a little excited.

Nery's face lit up, but before he could respond, a loud voice cut through the moment like a rusty guillotine.

"Revvy!" Kai yelled from across the bar.

Zylo's nickname for me on Kai's lips made me shudder, especially when it drew the attention of those around us. I ignored it, keeping my eyes on Nery, but a muscular arm curled around my neck, resting gently on my shoulders and demanding my attention.

Kai's arm.

I caught a whiff of his cologne. There was a spicy undertone—cardamom, maybe—wrapped in the deep, earthy richness of worn leather. I sent him a disapproving look and shoved his arm away. He let it fall to his side and smiled down at me, charming and cocksure, but there was a slyness to it. Unnoticeable if you didn't look closely.

"What do you want, Mercer?" I hissed.

Undeterred by my harsh tone, Kai's smile seemed to stretch wider. "Came to find you, silly." He sounded strange. Far too cheerful. "Tavoris wants a word."

Then he *booped* me on the nose.

What the fuck was happening?

I blinked once, twice, three times before registering his words. "Why?"

"I dunno. Some Zenith business probably." He waved off the question, turning to look at Nery. "Alright, mate?"

I wasn't sure what Kai was playing at. Nery shuffled from foot to foot, awkwardly observing our conversation from the sidelines. I went to speak, but he just smiled at me in apology.

"Looks like your friend needs you," Nery said.

Naturally, I wanted to argue. To set him straight. To tell him that Kai Mercer was *not* a friend. He was more like an annoying itch that wouldn't disappear, no matter how hard you scratched.

I wanted to tell him not to leave. That I'd enjoyed his presence. Enjoyed being around someone who treated me like I was normal.

But curiosity got the better of me, and I needed to find out what this prick, Kai Mercer, was up to. So instead, I sighed, and looked up at Nery in apology. "Maybe next time?"

Nery gave me one last smile before disappearing into the crowd. I shoved Kai in the side, desperate to put some space between us, and glared up at him.

"The fuck was that, Mercer?"

"I don't know what you mean." Kai cocked his head to one side, feigning innocence.

"Why would Tavoris send *you* to find me?" I asked.

He patted me on the forehead like I was a dog, and I shoved him again, even more annoyed because his non-answer said more than words.

He was fucking with me.

"You're such a prick." The lines on my skin flared a vicious, deep red through my shirt, and my tail uncoiled from my thigh, flicking behind me.

"That's not very nice, rookie. You'll wound my ego."

"A battering ram couldn't make a dent in that thing," I snapped, turning on my heel and storming towards the bar.

Maybe I'd find Nery while I was there, but I doubted it. He was probably keeping his distance from this silly circus act, and I couldn't blame him.

"I was saving you from a boring conversation," Kai called after me.

"The only boring conversation is this one," I hissed over my shoulder before following Nery's example and disappearing into the crowd.

I needed to put as much distance as possible between myself and Kai. If I didn't, I'd be looking at jail time.

For the next hour, whenever I spoke to someone who wasn't Jax, Zylo, Saelix, or even Valen, Kai was there. It didn't matter where I was in Nebula—by the table, on the mezzanine, or even in the conservatory—Kai found me and ended whatever conversation I was in.

At first, it was just ridiculous excuses.

"CosmoCharge's CEO wants to meet the rookies."

"A journalist wants a chat with you and Zylo."

"The CRF wants a photo of the racers in the lounge."

When they stopped working, Kai changed tactics, upping his game to fuck with me.

I was on the mezzanine, making small talk with a D-list soap actor I'd never heard of. I wasn't even interested in the conversation, just killing time while Zylo and Saelix were off fucking somewhere.

The more they drank, the less capable they seemed of keeping their hands to themselves. I'd watched them maul each other at the table, feeling like a voyeur, when Saelix abruptly announced that they were going to get some air. I wasn't sure what air they'd find behind a "Staff Only" door.

So I'd wandered, getting caught in the net of a mind-numbing conversation about this actor's extensive collection of vintage spoons. I think they were handcrafted on one moon or another, but I was only half listening.

That was when Kai appeared.

Again.

Why was he doing this?

Why me?

What did he want from *me* of all people? Was this a game to him? Another ego trip? Was I a new toy to prod and poke and crack open for his own amusement?

I didn't get it. There were other rookies in the league this year, and other admirers in the room who hung on his every word. So why keep bothering the one who refused to play nice?

I wasn't sure if it was his fucked-up idea of fun, or if he was trying to rattle me before the next race. But whatever it was, it was working.

And I hated it.

I didn't react to his presence, too used to his antics and insufferable presence by now. He was like a barnacle on a rock, and it would take a jackhammer to pry him off.

But unlike his previous attempts, the excuses never came. Instead, he leaned in until the tip of his nose brushed my neck, his warm breath tickling my skin. His scent—so annoyingly appealing—flooded my nostrils, and my breath caught when I heard him inhale through his own.

I was stunned, unsure how to react. Even my skin stayed dark, my brain offline because of shock, confusion, and . . . something else. I remained still, barely breathing to avoid another lungful of cardamom and leather, until he pulled away and nudged my temple with his nose.

"Hey, baby," he purred, the words deep and sultry, with a teasing undertone meant only for me. "I missed you."

If it were anyone else, I wouldn't mind the way goosebumps bloomed over my skin. I didn't have any experience with flirting—or sex in general—but Kai's voice made my pulse quicken, and heat crept up my neck.

Again, if it were *anyone* else, the rough tone would've sent me to my knees.

Thankfully, my brain rebooted before I could embarrass myself and do something stupid. Like whimper. I elbowed Kai in the stomach, hard enough for him to double over.

"What the fuck?" I snarled.

The actor, who I'd otherwise forgotten about, was staring at us from across the table—eyes wide, mouth hanging open.

"Just c-coming to see you," Kai wheezed. He was bent over, arms curled protectively around his abdomen. "My n-nebula babe. The sun at the c-centre of my galaxy."

I pressed my lips against his ear and hissed, "I hope that fucking hurt." He held up his thumb in confirmation.

"This ain't worth a hookup," the actor mumbled, rising from his chair before power walking away from the mezzanine.

"It was never going to be a hookup!" I yelled after him. "Have fun with your stupid spoons!"

Kai straightened up and rubbed his stomach. I hoped he'd get a painful bruise to remind him of what a twat he was.

But a million and one thoughts rushed through my head. Was he drunk? Was he bored? Was he trying to get into my head? Why the fuck was he messing with me of all the people in the room?

With his breathing now steady, his cocky grin returned to its usual spot, and he raised his hand to his head in a stupid salute. "Success."

Kai was playing some sort of game, and I wasn't in the mood to entertain him anymore. "Stay away from me, wanker." I turned away, hurrying to escape his fuckery. But I could travel to a distant galaxy, and Kai would find me just to piss me off.

Descending the stairs, I re-entered the main area of the bar. My legs trembled, and I stumbled as I passed some crew members from the Pulse Racing team. With Kai behind me, the adrenaline of our encounter was wearing off, and I realised how drunk I was.

I hadn't meant to get this inebriated, but each time Kai popped up, I'd run to the bar. It was a quiet moment where I could take a breath and let my anger levels come down from scorching to just a simmer.

Zylo and Saelix stood at the bar, looking a little rumpled. When Zylo spotted me, he waved me over and ordered a drink. It went down too easily, but fuck it, I was already drunk, so another replaced it.

I couldn't even say whose bright idea it was to do a shot of Voidka.

"Let's dance!" Saelix yelled, words slurred. He was just as drunk as I was, so he pushed through the crowd, dragging me behind him.

The dance floor was in the conservatory, lit up by shifting bands of light that rippled in the sky above the domed glass ceiling. Waves of violet, emerald, and cerulean pulsed and flowed, casting a dynamic glow over the gyrating bodies. It made everything feel more electric.

I was drunk enough that I didn't refuse Saelix's offer to dance, letting him lead me to the middle of the throng. Men and women, humans and aliens, danced and ground their bodies together in a steady rhythm.

As a general principle, I didn't dance—had never even been to a club—but the evening had been a car crash thanks to Kai, so I closed my eyes, let go of my inhibitions, and moved.

My hips swayed with the music, slow and effortless, and my arms rose from my sides as if they could think for themselves. My head dropped back onto my shoulders, and I no longer cared who was watching.

There were no arrogant racers to throw me off, no stupid excuses to ruin the moment. It was me, the pulse of the beat, and the stars beyond the glass. My fingers stretched towards them, as if I could pluck them straight from the sky.

I didn't know if Zylo and Saelix were nearby. The room could've emptied, leaving me dancing by myself in the centre of the room, and I wouldn't have noticed. Wouldn't have cared. I just wanted to *feel*—the vibration of music I didn't recognise, the fizz of alcohol buzzing through my veins.

Was this what Kai felt like, floating through life without a care?

Knowing all eyes are on you, but not giving a damn what people think. What they see.

The heat of the room left a thin layer of sweat spread across my skin. Bodies moved me from side to side, but I didn't care where I ended up. My eyes remained closed, and I stayed in the moment, my own tranquil little bubble.

A firm body pressed against my back, but I didn't flinch. I barely acknowledged them, just continued to roll my body. Backwards and forwards, side to side, I demanded their body move with my tide. Otherwise, they could step away and let me be.

But in the end, my new partner found my rhythm. They pulled me closer until our bodies were joined, from my head resting on their shoulder to our feet. Warm, calloused hands touched my hips before sliding upwards. They roamed over the bare skin of my stomach, leaving a trail of sparks in their wake. Fingertips traced my slightly defined muscles, drifting back down to my waistband. My tail curled around their thigh, pulling them even closer. It was enough to feel their hard cock against my ass.

I rolled my head on their shoulder, my hair falling away to expose my neck. I felt a puff of warm air as they dragged their lips along my shoulder, over my throat... They ended at my ear, sucking the lobe between their blunt teeth, and I shivered, exhaling a shaky breath. The stranger chuckled, low and raspy, and I got a whiff of something spicy.

Was the mystery dancer Kai? Fuck, I hoped not. I felt so good, and I didn't want to ruin it with a confirmation. Because if it was him, I would have to shove him away. To ask what the hell he was doing, just like I'd done all night.

I didn't want to open my eyes.

But I had to know.

So I let the world in, eyelids fluttering from the sudden change in light. It wasn't Kai I was dancing with, because Kai, the thorn in my side, was watching me instead.

He leaned against the wall on the other side of the room, arms folded over his chest, ankles crossed. He looked casual, but the more I watched him back, the more I saw beyond his cocky facade. His jaw tightened, the muscles flexing as he grit his teeth. His eyes were almost pitch black, devoid of their usual hazel. Jax stood beside him, his stare piercing and furious.

But Jax wasn't glaring at me. He glared at whoever stood behind me.

I tilted my head, startled to see Valen Dray. His hands still roamed my abdomen, lips pressed against my jaw, but he stared at Jax, mouth curled in a smirk. When I looked back, Kai was nowhere to be seen. Jax was seething by himself while Dray continued to grind against me.

I was wondering where Kai had disappeared to when the man himself burst from the crowd, tugging me from Dray's embrace. I stumbled, falling into Kai's hard chest. His spicy scent surrounded me, and my drunk mind wanted to bury my face against him. To get high on the smell and breathe it in until I was dizzy.

Get a grip on yourself, Rev.

I looked up to see Kai scowling at Dray, but Dray didn't seem bothered by Kai's ire. He just curled his arms around another dancer, replacing the one he'd lost.

"Don't be a dick, Dray," Kai snapped.

Dray chuckled mirthlessly. "Mind your business, Mercer."

I waited for Kai to snap back, but he turned his anger onto me. "What are you playing at?"

"Me?" I scoffed, crossing my arms over my chest. "What the fuck did I do? You're the one who's been stalking me all night. You're like a rash I can't get rid of."

His brows shot up, the corners of his mouth twitching. "A rash? That's cute. I was going for charming."

"You're about as charming as a concussion," I shot back, heat rising to my face. "What do you want, Mercer? You've crashed every conversation I've had tonight like it's some kind of competition."

"So I need a reason to speak to you now?" He stepped closer. Close enough that I got another whiff of cardamom and leather beneath the pulsating lights in the sky. "Maybe I just like pissing you off."

"You've got it down to an art form," I growled.

"So touchy." He laughed, sharp and bright like a live wire. "Look at you, all flushed and fuming. It's adorable."

I clenched my fists. "Keep pushing, Mercer."

His smirk dropped. "And what?"

"And you'll find out I hit back."

"Oh? You want to fight?" The challenge in his eyes was clear. "Let's go then, rookie." He spun on his heel and stalked off into the crowd without warning. And like a fool, I followed.

Thanks to the alcohol, my steps were less than steady. I stumbled, but before I could hit the ground, Kai caught me, his hand circling my wrist. We stopped in front of a "Staff Only" door. The same one I'd seen Saelix and Zylo slip through earlier.

"Where are we going?" I huffed.

Kai didn't respond, and when he opened the door and pushed me over the threshold, I squawked like a chicken. My tail whipped towards him, annoyed by his manhandling, but Kai just sidestepped it. He paced back and forth, as if he was gearing up for the promised fight, and I leaned against the wall, waiting for him to spout whatever bullshit was running through his head.

I wanted to give him a piece of my mind, but before I could speak, Kai was there, caging me in.

His hands rested on the brick, on either side of my head. We were chest to chest, with barely a lick of space between us, and the only sounds were our heavy breaths and my tail as it smacked against the wall. My skin flared crimson, enough to illuminate his face in the corridor's low lighting. It exaggerated the shadows under his eyes and cheekbones, creating a sinister picture.

His breath was a warm caress on my lips. I couldn't be sure if it was the alcohol or a residual effect from Dray's groping, but my skin burned with each one of his exhales.

"What the fuck were you doing with Dray?" His voice was low, an edge of something sharp coiled beneath it.

I forced myself to smirk, not wanting him to know that my insides were fizzing like a firework preparing to explode in my stomach. "Dancing, Mercer. You know, the thing people do at parties?"

One hand left the wall as he brought his index finger to my lips, not quite touching, but enough for me to feel the thrum of anticipation. Kai closed the gap, his fingertip lightly brushing my lower lip, and I hated the way my breath hitched. His eyes dropped to where we connected, just for a second, before rising to glare at me once more.

They were dark, overtaken by his blown-out pupils.

"With Dray?" he scoffed, spitting the name like it tasted foul.

I noticed the way his chest heaved. The way his eyes continued to flick between my eyes and my mouth. The way they tracked the movement of my tongue when it crept out to lick my lips.

"And?" I watched him through narrowed eyes. "What's it to you? Jealous, hotshot?"

"No, I just don't enjoy seeing you with him," Kai huffed, returning his hand to the wall. Heat radiated from his muscular body, and while I should've pushed him away, I couldn't.

I let his fierce gaze pin me in place.

"You've butted into every conversation I've had tonight. That's how your stupid little game works, right?" I laughed, more sarcastic than joyful. "Yet dancing with Dray is where you draw the line?"

"That wasn't dancing," Kai growled. "That was soft-core porn."

Kai could say he wasn't jealous until he ran out of breath, but his poker face was terrible. Envy was written all over his expression, which made me wonder. Had he spent the night cockblocking me because he wanted to annoy me, like he insisted? Or was he cockblocking me because . . . because he wanted me?

Well, two could play that game.

I leaned forward until the tip of my nose brushed his. "Did it turn you on, Mercer?" I purred, enjoying how the muscles in his jaw twitched. "Does it make you jealous when I get attention from someone else? Someone who isn't you?"

"Please," he scoffed, cheeks turning a beautiful shade of pink. "If I wanted you like that, I'd have you."

His arrogance cut through the heat swirling in my gut, and my skin glowed red with irritation. "You seriously think I'd submit to you?"

"I know you'd melt the second I touched you."

"You've already touched me, and I'm still in one piece. Alive to tell the tale."

Speaking of tails . . . I whipped his leg with my mine, but he didn't react. Like he barely felt it because his focus was solely on me. My body vibrated with the same energy, just begging to be released. To shove him away. To punch him. To explode.

But I tamped it down, letting the tension stew. I raised my hand and dragged my fingers down his chest, feeling the way his muscles twitched. Kai's breath hitched before he could catch himself, and he forced an unimpressed glare, as though daring me to call him on it.

Naturally, I obliged.

"What's wrong, Mercer? Feeling a little flustered?" My index finger moved back and forth along his waistband, teasing the hem of his shirt.

He smirked, but it was mostly for show. And when he spoke, his voice was rougher, deeper than before. "You wish."

"I don't have to wish." My finger slipped under the hem of his shirt, trailing over his heated skin. I pushed up onto my toes—because even in heeled boots I was a good two inches shorter than him—and pressing my lips to his ear, my breath tickling his skin, I whispered, "You're burning for me, aren't you?"

Kai turned his head until our cheeks brushed. It was a stupid, fleeting thing, but it sent a thrill straight through my core. One of his hands left the wall, curling around my back and sliding under the sheer material of my shirt. He stroked the bumps of my spine, moving down, down, down until he reached the base of my tail. He rubbed with firm yet gentle circles, and electricity coursed through my veins, my limbs, my cock.

And I fucking whimpered.

"You'd like that, wouldn't you?" he growled.

His free hand gripped the back of my neck, pulling me in until there was barely an inch between our lips. He breathed in every one of my exhales, and I did the same with his, sharing this little pocket of air. We said nothing, just stared, brushing each other's skin until Kai was panting and I was pressed up against him. The smallest movement would close the distance, would bring our lips together so we could devour one another.

I didn't move, and neither did he. It was like we were waiting to see who'd crack first. And when he squeezed the base of my tail, making me whimper *again* ... Fuck. I worried it might be me.

But I wasn't about to lose to Kai Mercer.

Not at this.

So I let the moment stretch, just long enough for him to think he had me. To think I was right where he wanted me.

Then I grabbed the front of his jacket, pushed forward, and twisted our bodies, so that Kai ended up being the one against the wall with my palm pressed against his chest. I felt his accelerated heartbeat, and I arched my hips forward, pressing my groin against his. His hardness answered mine, both of us feeling the effects of the last few minutes, and he stared down at me, eyes hooded.

He opened his mouth to speak, but I beat him to it. "I don't play games I can't win, Kai." My hands wrapped around his throat, thumbs pressed against his pulse point. "And I'm not playing yours."

Without another word, I shoved away from him and returned to the bar, ignoring the way my skin still burned where he'd touched me.

CATCH ME IF YOU CAN'T

Kai

A month had passed since the party, and with it, two race weekends. Titanium Falls had been great, and once again I was on the podium in top spot. But I hated the course at Crystal Barricade—the dazzling lights that refracted off gems alongside the track fucked me over every year, and it showed in the results.

The lights had blinded me on a turn, and while swerving to avoid another driver, I'd locked up my wheels, sending my vehicle off the road. It had pushed me down to fourth, but I'd overtaken Jax in the penultimate lap and finished third. Zylo had taken the win.

And in second place? Fucking Rev. His strategy had been unpredictable as ever, and he was fast as a whip. Try as I might, I couldn't close the gap.

It was my first loss of the season, because anything below first was a loss in my book, but Rev had achieved his highest finish so far. He'd climbed the drivers' overall standings to fourth, sitting between Jax in third and Dray in fifth.

The gap between the three of them was minimal. If the rookie continued as he was, Jax's position in the top three was at risk. Though as long as Jax beat Dray, wherever he was on the table, he'd be ecstatic. The competition between the two of them had been going on for years. It was the reason for their very public breakup three years ago, and since then, they'd continued to wind each other up.

On the podium, Zylo had been the only one smiling. I'd tried, but based on the photos posted online, the most I'd been able to muster was a grimace. Rev had maintained his usual calm and detached expression.

Yet under the bright lights of flashing cameras, I'd seen the way his eyes sparkled. The way the stars in their depths had swirled and burst like a supernova. I'd expected him to rub the result in my face. Had waited for a snarky comment about losing my edge or some shit.

But it never came. There was no scowl, no glare. He'd just stepped off the podium and walked away, without even acknowledging my existence.

Thinking about it, I'd barely seen him throughout that entire race weekend. The same could be said for Titanium Falls.

When I had seen him, I'd thrown out some teasing jibes. Again, the usual. Picking at his driving skills, his penchant for being reckless, and calling him "rookie" in my most condescending tone, just because he hated it.

And he'd heard me, because the lines on his skin flared a bloody red whenever I so much as breathed in his vicinity. But he'd never outwardly reacted. He'd just turned in the other direction, hid in Zenith's garage, or put in some headphones to block me out.

Why was he avoiding me?

It's not like anything had happened between us at the bar. Not really. Just the usual insults, some cockblocking, and mutual awkward boners.

So, yeah . . . nothing.

I'll admit, watching him dance had stirred something in me. Well, more specifically, in my groin. Rev had looked different from his normal grumpy self—hips rolling seductively to the beat, neck straining, head tipped back—and if I'd had a semi just from watching, I couldn't imagine how Dray had felt being pressed up against him.

And that was when things had got weird. Because when Dray had draped his body over Rev like a cheap pair of curtains, I'd . . . seen red. I'd wanted him off the rookie and somewhere far away. Another room. Hell, another galaxy.

Jax had been just as annoyed beside me, watching the way Dray's lips trailed along the rookie's slender throat. I wasn't sure what had made me react the way I did, but all I knew was that I didn't like it.

I hadn't expected to find myself pressed against Rev in a dimly lit corridor, close enough to share the same air, to feel each other's skin, and . . . yeah, I guess that's when we arrived at mutual awkward boners.

"I don't play games I can't win, Kai."

So yeah, I guess he was avoiding me.

But again, *why?* Rev had reacted just as viscerally, and we *both* knew it. His breath had hitched, skin burning beneath my fingers. And when I'd looked deep into the voids of his eyes, he'd been just as wrecked as I was.

His desperate whimper would play on a loop in my head until I died. It lived there rent free now. Couldn't be evicted. And every time I saw him—before he ducked out of sight—it echoed through my brain while images of his body, pressed against the wall and damp with sweat, played on repeat. A short film with a singular soundtrack.

Vibrations interrupted my internal brooding, and not the fun kind. I looked down at my watch, groaning at the words flashing on the screen.

"Savannah calling."

The vibrations stopped, before starting again almost instantly. *Sigh.* I should answer. I *had* to answer. The longer I waited, the more inevitable those goddamn off-season marathons felt. The damn woman knew how to manipulate me into doing whatever she wanted. You tell her once you hate running, and she stuffs it in her box of ammunition, ready to use against you later. If Savannah weren't a publicist, she'd be an amazing supervillain.

With a huff, I answered the call. But I'd somehow hit the option to make it a holo-call, so imagine my surprise when the image of a scowling Savannah flickered to life above my wrist.

"Are you still in bed?!" she screeched, making me wince.

"No..."

"Do not lie to me, Kai Mercer. I can see your rumpled sheets, and as much as I never wanted to, your naked torso in fucking HD."

"Who hasn't seen my half-naked body these days?" I forced my trademark cocky grin. "I've done a spread for Galactic Sports Weekly at least twice. And there was that calendar for Cosmo Hunks..."

"Yeah, well, I avoided them. And seeing it up close just made me gayer."

"Do you want something, or did you just call to give me a complex?" I snapped.

"I was making sure you're on your way to Varkos 2."

"Why would I be on my way to Varkos 2?"

"The PR day, Kai!" Savannah's face grew red with frustration. If this were a cartoon, she'd have steam bursting from her ears. "You're supposed to be at Karting for Kids with the other drivers for the sports day, giving underprivileged children a day to fucking remember."

"Shit," I hissed, tossing my covers back.

Savannah had planned this months ago. All drivers had agreed to spend the day at Karting for Kids, a galaxy-wide charity that offered children from low-income homes the chance to get into the sport. Most of us started in kids' karting competitions before moving up to the lower leagues.

But like most sports, it was expensive as fuck. It took up a lot of time and effort, not just for the child, but for the whole family. There were relays to travel to, protective gear to pay for, and don't even get me started on the karts. They could cost a small fortune if you wanted one that was decent.

Programmes like KFK had emerged as the ASL rose in popularity. It offered grants to families for the gear, and they had a warehouse full of secondhand suits and helmets to choose from. There were karts for the members to share, and corporate sponsors donated brand-new, high-spec versions to be used at competitions. There was also a shuttleload of volunteers who took kids to competitions when their families couldn't.

As the son of a single parent with no other family to speak of, KFK had opened the door for my career, and I'd be damned if these kids didn't have the best day ever.

"If you're not en route to Varkos 2 in ten minutes, I swear on the celestial gods, Kai," Savannah yelled as I ran into my en suite. "I will sign you up for every damn marathon I can find in the off-season."

"Threat received. Bye, hot stuff!"

"Kai—"

I hung up, cutting off her screeching. Then I hopped in the shower, having the quickest wash of my life.

By some miracle, I was washed, dried, and dressed in under ten minutes, then flying in my two-seater shuttle towards the edge of Zyphar's atmosphere. Varkos 2 was an hour away via the nearest registered wormhole, and with my thrusters pushed to their limit, I arrived only a few minutes behind schedule.

I spotted Savannah as I parked up, deep in conversation with the other teams' publicists. A short distance away, the drivers posed for photos in front of the KFK campgrounds entrance.

During school breaks, they hosted week-long camps for young racers. But today it was overrun with professional, hyper-competitive drivers and their no-nonsense publicists, all geared up for what would be an intense sports day.

"About bloody time," Savannah muttered, giving me a once-over. "At least you look presentable."

"I always look presentable."

"Debatable." She brushed a strand of hair from my forehead. "Now, get over there with the rest of them, and smile."

"Yes, boss." I gave an over-the-top salute, ignoring her glare, then I walked over to join the group of drivers.

"Great job, guys!" The ASL's official photographer, Tov, waved his arms, directing from behind the lens. "Jaxir, stand next to Valen. Yep, that's it. Can you move a little closer? A bit more... great. Revvak, can you try to tone down the... uh... scowling?"

My snicker drew Tov's attention. Rev's too. And the weight of it felt heavy after a month of going without.

"Kai! Great to see you." Tov lowered the camera and strolled over, extending one of his six hands towards me.

I took it in mine, giving it a firm shake. "Alright, Tov? How's the wife?"

"Oh, she's great. Pregnant with twins if you can believe it, and—"

"Can we get this over with?" Dray cut in. He'd put some space between himself and Jax, and my teammate was glaring daggers at the side of his head.

"Yes! Y-Yes, sorry!" Tov stammered, gesturing for me to join the group. "We'll put Kai in the centre of the group."

"Of course," a voice muttered to my left.

Pure delight filled me as I realised I was next to Rev. "Problem, rookie?" I whispered, while Tov continued to position the others into the perfect tableau around us.

"Just that your colossal ego will overshadow everyone else."

I lowered my head, close enough to whisper in Rev's ear. "The last time we were together, you didn't seem to mind my *colossal* ego."

Red and orange rippled across his skin, his ears twitching with agitation. "Fuck off, Mercer."

I straightened up, chuckling under my breath. It was easy enough for Rev to avoid me when we were both busy with race-day preparations, but today we'd be in close quarters. Besides, I'd missed the way we clashed, and the way his skin would light up when we did.

So no, Rev wouldn't be avoiding me today. I was going to make the most of our forced proximity.

Fuck, it was going to be so much fun.

KFK had set up multiple sporting events—like a kiddie Olympics. The idea was to evoke teamwork and camaraderie. We formed eight teams, each with two drivers and four children, and points were awarded after each event. The overall winners would then stand on a mini podium at the front of the campgrounds.

We were professional racers—the thrill of victory was our lifeblood; we craved the challenge—and just like any other race weekend, standing on any spot besides number one wasn't an option.

With the kids . . . obviously.

They paired Zylo with Cassiopeia, a human driver for Nebula Shifters, and I don't know who Jax had angered in a past life, but he ended up with Dray. And call me a terrible friend, but when Elyn, one of KFK's volunteers, had called their names, I'd almost busted a gut trying not to laugh.

But while the stars were fucking with my teammate, they were on my side, because I was paired with my favourite grumpy gremlin, Rev.

He wore the same closed-off mask as always, but his posture stiffened, and a brief pulse of red flared across his skin. I realised how hard he tried to fake indifference, but when you looked at the finer details, he was more transparent than he liked to believe. By the end of the day, I expected to be able to see through him like a pane of glass.

"Ready for a fun day?" I teased while we waited to meet our four pint-sized teammates.

"The only fun part of this day will be going home," he mumbled.

"Oh, come *on*." I reached out and ruffled his hair, smiling when he smacked my hand away. "It's gonna be great. All for the kids, remember?"

He pulled an elastic band from around his wrist, tying his hair in a bun at the base of his neck. "If it weren't for the kids, you'd already have a black eye."

"Ooh, we'd be twinning."

Rev sneered at me, his little fangs peeking out between his lips. I wanted to poke them with my finger, to see how sharp they were. How would they feel against my neck? Teasing the skin of my—

"Hello."

The voice of a child popped the balloon of my inappropriate fantasies. Because it was inappropriate to be thinking about Rev like *that*, and around children no less.

The source of my turmoil crouched in front of three kids. One was a human with red hair, green eyes, and freckles dotted across his skin. Jeremy—according to his name tag—was holding the hand of Vaeri, a Trivorii with yellow skin and white hair that shone in the sunshine. Next to them was Lyla, a human girl with ebony skin and dark brown eyes. Beads jingled like bells at the ends of her braids when she moved.

"You're Kai Mercer!" Vaeri gasped, bouncing on their three tentacled legs.

My hands went to my hips, and I pretended to look confused. "Am I? I thought I was Valen Dray."

Their laughter chimed like music, light and infectious. Even Rev had a reluctant smile creeping onto his face. Before he ruined it with a frown.

"Shouldn't there be four of you?" Rev's eyes flicked between the three of them, as if checking he hadn't miscounted. But he was right; there were only three.

Lyla's hand shot into the air, waving back and forth like she was desperate to answer his question. Rev nodded once, encouraging her to speak, and Lyla leaned in closer. She didn't answer right away, just looked into his eyes, losing herself in the voids.

It happens to the best of us, kid.

"He's coming," she whispered. "But he's shy." She looked over her shoulder, and that was when I noticed the child standing on his own a short distance away.

His pale skin seemed to sparkle, while his black hair shifted with blue, green, and purple hues when moving in the breeze. He looked at the ground, wringing his hands together against his stomach, and a thin tail whipped back and forth behind him, just long enough to dust the blades of grass.

After a few moments of silence, he looked up from the ground, revealing a pair of large black eyes. Eyes that were so similar to the man crouched beside me.

This boy was an Iskari, just like Rev.

Rev rose to his feet and slowly approached the child. Lyla and Vaeri took my hands, while Jeremy held onto Vaeri, and we followed behind, stopping far enough away that he wouldn't feel surrounded. Rev dropped to one knee, meeting the small Iskari at eye level.

They both seemed shocked, surprised to see another of their kind. It was sweet, but also a little sad. Humans, as a species, dominated the galaxy, so I was one of many. A drop in the ocean of billions of humans.

In comparison, I couldn't imagine a species so scarce that meeting someone you weren't related to felt like a once-in-a-lifetime event. And yet here it was, a miracle unfolding in front of me. For Iskari, living life surrounded by those who don't understand your culture or its nuances must be lonely. Isolating. Feeling like you never belonged . . . always something *other*.

Rev was a novelty in the ASL. The first Iskari ever to take part. Yet he kept to himself at the edge of the group, even though Zylo, an Itharan—one of the more abundant species in the galaxy—always tried to include him. Rev was polite, embracing his teammate's advice and mentorship, but he seemed to keep Zylo at arm's length, like he couldn't quite bring himself to embrace their friendship.

Was Rev lonely?

His soft words pulled me away from the edge of the rabbit hole I risked falling into. "What's your name?"

The child dropped his eyes once more, intimidated by Rev's attention. He stared at his battered trainers while his tail curled around his thigh, just like Rev's did. Was it a comfort thing?

The silence stretched, and I thought he might not answer, but Rev smiled, bigger than I'd ever seen before. It wasn't the smirk or wry smile he used when riling me up; it was soft, encouraging, and friendly.

Beautiful.

"Korvithan," the child whispered, and Rev dipped his head in quiet acknowledgement. "My m-mama calls me Korvi."

Rev tilted his head to one side, like a curious puppy. "My name's Revvak, but my mum calls me Rev."

"That's a nice name."

"So is yours." He glanced over his shoulder to where we stood before turning back to the child. "Can we call you Korvi?"

The four of us gave a quick wave, our smiles meant to reassure. Korvi glanced between us and Rev, but he nodded once. It made Rev smile again, which made the markings on Korvi's skin pulse with molten gold light.

It didn't matter that the rest of us had no idea what it meant, because Rev and Korvi did.

Rev stood up and held his hand out for Korvi, who took it and held it tight, and when they joined us, Rev introduced him to the group, like we hadn't heard every word of their exchange.

Almost immediately, Lyla, Vaeri, and Jeremy started yapping a mile a minute, making sure Korvi was included in their conversations. He joined in as much as he could, offering quiet responses here and there. Rev and I watched on until Korvi looked overwhelmed.

I clapped my hands, getting everyone's attention. "Right, who's ready to dominate the competition?"

"They're kids, Kai," Rev quietly chastised. "It's not all about winning."

"But winning is fun!" Vaeri cut in, and the kids nodded so hard I thought their heads might pop off.

"We're gonna be number one!" Lyla added.

Jeremy pumped his freckled little fist in the air, like he was ready to deliver a war cry. "Let's crush 'em into the ground and dance on the bodies of the losers."

Lyla and Vaeri grinned, looking a little too feral. Even Korvi's tail swung faster, and the lines on his skin glowed emerald green.

Rev and I looked at each other and then at Jeremy with wide eyes.

"I like the spirit, Jer-Bear, but let's pull it back a little, yeah?" With a shrug from the kid and no signs of imminent violence, I pulled everyone into a tight huddle. "Okay, team. Let's get out there and win—" Rev cleared his throat and glared at me. "*And* have a shuttleload of fun, yeah?"

"Yeah!"

"Okay, hands in."

I put my hand in the middle of the circle, and Lyla, Vaeri, and Jeremy followed suit. My heart swelled when Korvi placed his on the top of the pile, but there was still someone missing.

The kids must've thought the same, because we all looked up at Rev. He frowned, clenching the hand that wasn't in Korvi's at his side.

"Come on, rookie." I said. "You with us?"

Rev opened his mouth, but before he could speak, Korvi tugged on the hand he was holding, making Rev look down.

"Let's crush them into the ground," he whispered.

It was so quiet, so at odds with his innocent appearance, that a sharp laugh burst out of me before I could stop it. It did the trick, though, because Rev laid his free hand over the others.

"That's the spirit!" I quipped, tossing him a wink.

"Don't push it, Kai." But he couldn't hide the way one side of his mouth twitched.

"Okay, on three, everyone shout 'winners' as loud as you can. One . . . two . . . *three*!"

"*WINNERS!*" they yelled, raising their hands to the sky.

We broke the huddle and walked towards the first event. I glanced over at Jeremy, watching as he discussed intense war strategies with Vaeri.

Better keep an eye on that one . . .

THE FAST & THE FLUSTERED

Rev

The first event was an egg-and-spoon race.

Eight at a time, one kid from each team would run to the finish line, hoping to earn the maximum number of points. Unlike the ASL, it didn't matter if you finished first or last; there were still points to be won.

While the volunteers distributed plastic spoons and foam eggs, Kai gathered our team into another one of his stupid huddles. He waved at Korvi, encouraging him to come closer. The little mouse being glued to my side meant I had to go too.

But while Kai annoyed me, I didn't mind joining in for Korvi's sake. He reminded me of myself.

I'd never met another Iskari beyond my family, and seeing one at Karting for Kids was unexpected. When I'd seen him standing alone, segregated and wary of connecting with others, it had shifted something inside me.

I was looking at a mirror image of my childhood.

I'd always wanted to join KFK, but I'd never been brave enough. My parents had offered to sign me up when they'd seen how obsessed I was with the busted-up kart my dad brought home.

But school was rough enough. I'd been the weirdo, mocked by my peers and called a freak when my skin lit up. That's the way it was when your species was basically nonexistent. They dropped you from the history curriculum, and didn't teach your classmates about your differences. Instead, they filled in the blanks with cruelty.

I turned down each one of my parents' offers to join KFK. Not because I didn't want to go, but because the thought of something I loved being tainted by bullying and name-calling made me sick.

At least I could do what I enjoyed at home. Love surrounded me in that space, regardless of who I was. So I'd found solace in driving up and down the hallway in a rusted metal kart until the carpet beneath it gave way.

But Korvi was different.

I guessed we'd shared similar experiences, because while our group had been accepting, he still kept some distance between himself and others. Yet here he was, brave enough to do what I couldn't. I hoped Korvi had a family who loved him, and friends he could turn to.

Seeing Jeremy, Vaeri, and Lyla fuss over him, I had no doubt Korvi would settle in just fine.

"Okay, gang." Kai placed his hands on Jeremy's and Lyla's shoulders. "We've got the egg-and-spoon race, and I know what you're thinking . . . go as fast as you can."

Jeremy bobbed his head, like that's exactly what he planned to do.

"But the foam egg is light. If you go too fast, your hands will shake or there'll be too much wind, and the egg will fall off."

They hung on Kai's every word, eyes wide with rapt attention. You'd think he was revealing the secrets of galactic peace instead of explaining the ins and outs of an egg-and-spoon race.

Annoying as he was, I had to admit he had a way with kids. Probably because half the time he still acted like one.

"Move quickly, but not so fast you can't hold it steady. Got it?"

The kids ran to grab equipment from the volunteers, and Jeremy approached the starting line.

"I figure if anyone's gonna stumble, it'll be Jeremy," Kai murmured. "He's too excitable. But at least he'll show the others what *not* to do."

"Kind of like you do from the front of the race," I retorted, shoving my hands into the pockets of my gym shorts.

"I never fu—" Kai glanced down at where Vaeri, Lyla, and Korvi stood close by watching Jeremy give himself a pep talk. "Fudge up." Then he smirked. "But you're right."

I raised an eyebrow. "About what?"

"I'm usually at the front of the pack."

"Of course you took *that* from the insult."

"Ready?!" Elyn, the head volunteer, shouted from the starting line. She held up an air horn, and the piercing sound rang through the open campgrounds.

The other kids bolted forward, and I'd expected Jeremy to do the same. But just as Kai suggested, he held back, moving quickly yet holding his hand as steady as he could.

Foam eggs hit the ground, and kids dived to catch them before chucking them back on the spoon. In their haste, some dropped them again almost instantly, while others made it a few more steps before their egg fell.

Jeremy's egg stayed perfectly in place. He watched it with rapt concentration, as though commanding it to stay with his mind. Most importantly, he remained calm while his competitors stumbled around him.

Unlike his teammates, who screamed like a pack of monkeys.

Lyla and Vaeri jumped up and down, bellowing their support as Jeremy edged closer to the finish line. Korvi's grip on my hand tightened as he watched with wide eyes, wiggling on the spot while his tail flailed through the air behind him.

Even Kai was clapping his hands, yelling like a pageant mum with a toddler on the stage.

When Jeremy crossed the finish line first, our team's screams almost burst my eardrums. But when Jeremy yeeted the egg and spoon so he could pump his freckled fists in the air, I couldn't fight my smile.

I nudged Kai in the side. "So much for your assessment."

It was barely loud enough to carry over the commotion, but Kai still heard. He didn't argue back, though, just shook his head and stared at Jeremy in awe, like a proud parent.

"He did good. That's what matters."

"And that they have fun, Kai," I pressed.

"Yeah." He nodded. "But if we can help them win, that's even better."

"Save the competition for the track, Kai," I replied with a sigh.

Jeremy had a hero's welcome when he returned to the group, receiving hugs and pats on the back. But there were three other kids to go, and it was Lyla's turn to stand at the starting line.

The air horn bellowed, and Lyla started moving. She was doing well, following Jeremy's example. Even when she dropped the egg, she stayed calm and placed it back on her spoon.

With the kids distracted by the race, Kai turned to me. "Or we could keep it between ourselves."

I frowned, keeping my eyes on the race. "Huh?"

He leaned in to whisper in my ear. "We could engage in another friendly competition . . . just the two of us."

"I know your ego's massive, but I didn't realise you'd dumped all your common sense to make some room." Now it was Kai's turn to frown, so I clarified. "We're on the same team, you idiot."

"So?" He shrugged. "We can still play a little game. See who comes out on top."

He purred the last word, making goosebumps burst across my skin. The lines on my body pulsed a dusky shade of pink before I could stop it. Kai might not know what it meant, but his wolflike grin said he had an idea.

Prick.

"No," I hissed, pointing to where Korvi and I remained connected. Thankfully, the child in question was ignoring the adults, focusing on Lyla finishing second. "We're here for the kids, Kai."

He held up his hands in surrender. "Fine, fine."

Knowing Kai, though, he wouldn't let it drop. He was the type of person who always wanted things his way. But that wasn't happening today.

I returned my attention to the competition. Vaeri followed in Lyla's footsteps, finishing the race in second.

And then it was Korvi's turn.

Convincing him to release my hand so he could compete took some gentle persistence. He eventually relented, approaching the starting line like a prisoner would the gallows—extremely slowly. I walked by his side and crouched beside him when we made it.

As he placed the egg on top of his spoon, it shook in his trembling grip. Korvi looked at me with big black eyes that matched my own, tail flicking back and forth.

His skin flared emerald, a sign of nerves in Iskari. "What if I fall?"

My heart ached for him, because it was obvious he wasn't afraid of losing; he was terrified of embarrassing himself.

When you were already so different, the last thing you wanted was to draw more attention, and the prime way to do that was by fucking up in front of a crowd.

Other kids would fall and get right back up, laughing at their stumble. But for Korvi, I imagined falling over would feel equivalent to an award-winning actor forgetting their lines on stage. Or a seasoned professional racer making a rookie-level mistake.

"You might fall." I gripped his bony elbow, stopping his hand from shaking. "But what if you win?"

"I won't win," he replied vehemently.

"How do you know? You could be the best egg-and-spoon racer in the galaxy." Korvi giggled, which loosened the tension in both our shoulders. "But you have to try so you know what you're capable of."

"What if they laugh at me?"

"If they do, get up and smile *so big* that you show off your fangs," I said, stretching my mouth wide, my own fangs glinting in the sun. "Laugh along with them, because if they're laughing with you, they're not laughing at you."

Elyn asked if the competitors were ready, and I looked at Korvi, who bobbed his head. He still looked nervous, but at least he'd stopped shaking. The specks in his eyes swirled with what I thought was determination.

"You've got this," I whispered, and jutted my chin towards the finish line. "I'll wait at the end, so if you get nervous, just look for me. Okay?"

"Okay."

I patted him on the shoulder. Before Elyn could blow the air horn, I jogged along the track, stopping at the end of Korvi's lane. I sent him an encouraging smile, which he returned with a weary one of his own.

Kai watched me from among the sea of children, brows drawn. I guessed he wondered what I was up to, but my focus was elsewhere—on the child about to race.

"You've got this," I mouthed, giving him a double thumbs up.

The air horn blew, and the race began.

At first, Korvi didn't move. He remained in his spot like a statue.

Beside him, his competitors rushed forward, dropping their eggs one by one. Korvi's brain seemed to reboot. He gripped the spoon, his little knuckles white with tension, and I worried the plastic might crack. But to his credit, it remained steady, even as he paced down the track. Even his tail was still, coiled tightly around his thigh.

And the egg?

It didn't even tremble.

Korvi overtook one competitor after another, as more and more dropped their eggs, fumbling to return them to their spoons. I could hear Kai's booming voice, encouraging words floating through the air towards Korvi. Even I was yelling.

Telling him how great he was.

To stay calm.

To keep it steady.

But he didn't need our advice. He was leading the way.

Our team erupted when Korvi crossed the line first, louder than the entire crowd combined. He dropped the egg and spoon and fell into my arms, gripping me around my waist. The others joined us, surrounding the winner and patting him on the back.

Kai scooped Korvi up and put him on his shoulders. His black eyes widened, but he giggled, the sound free and exhilarated. A total one-eighty from the nervous loner we'd met just over an hour ago.

I looked up at Korvi's smiling face.

This was why I'd joined Zenith Nova. Why I'd wanted to join the ASL.

Because if one little Iskari boy felt seen—felt like he belonged—then maybe others would too. Maybe one day, we wouldn't be an endangered species. A curiosity for others to gawk at.

We'd be remembered.

Recognised.

Respected.

There were perks to being a champion—the trophies, the fame, and the fortune.

But for me, racing professionally was more than glory. It was making a name for my people. Carving out the possibility of a better, more comfortable life.

For people like my family. Like Korvi.

And thanks to this moment, I was even more determined.

🏁🏁🏁🏁🏁🏁🏁🏁

The kids enjoyed a quick water break while the volunteers totted up the scores.

And while they were resting, it was the professionals' turn to race. But unlike the kids, all of us would go at the same time. All sixteen of us.

So while Kai and I were on the same team today, only one of us could finish first.

We lined up, receiving the same equipment as the kids—a plastic spoon and a foam egg. I stood between Jax and Kai. Zylo was on Kai's right, and Dray was on Jax's left.

Dray and Jax argued fiercely, exchanging wild gestures and hissed words. I couldn't hear their words, though. The kids' excited squeals drowned them out. I also didn't particularly care.

I was too preoccupied with the annoying presence on my left—Kai, who stood in his lane, twirling his spoon like a bat and flicking the egg into the air with an infuriating little flourish.

The kids on our team let out a chorus of awed squeals while taking bets on which of us would come first.

"I think Kai's gonna win," Jeremy bellowed, overenthusiastic as ever.

Vaeri agreed, while Lyla remained on the fence. Kai didn't care, though. "Don't worry, guys. I'll prove to you why I'm a three-time galactic champion."

"I want Rev to win," Korvi whispered. The lines on his face glittered with amber when all eyes turned to him. "Because he's cool."

"He may be cool, little K . . ." Kai puffed out his chest, unable to help himself. "But I'm the best of the best."

I picked at a hangnail on my thumb, trying to appear disinterested. "Tone it down, Mercer."

"You know I'm right, rookie."

"I know nothing of the sort."

Kai grinned. "I'd say you're scared of losing to me, but you're used to that by now."

The kids released a collective "ooh," like Kai had just delivered the final blow in an interstellar rap battle. I dared a glance, only to find him grinning at me like the cocky bastard he was.

I didn't know how he had any energy left to function, when he seemed to burn so much of it keeping his ego inflated.

"I won't lose to you, Mercer," I drawled, checking my nails. Couldn't let him think he was getting to me.

"I bet you say that before every race. Keep manifesting, boo. It might happen."

The sarcastic endearment made me bristle, and I recalled what he'd said earlier. From the corner of my eye, I noticed Elyn preparing to start the race.

I turned to face Kai, mouth curled into a smirk of my own. "We could engage in a little friendly competition . . . just the two of us."

He blinked, lips forming a perfect O as surprise hit. He quickly schooled his expression, nonchalantly bouncing the egg on his spoon.

Seemed I wasn't the only one who masked my emotions.

"We're on the same team, Revvak. Besides, we're here for the children. It wouldn't be appropriate."

"We can still play a little game," I continued, repeating his words back to him. "See who comes out on top."

The egg stilled as I mimicked him, purring the last word. His eyes caught mine, pupils dilating just for a second. "Unless you're scared."

This time, the kids' juvenile "ooh" filled me with satisfaction.

Now I was the one with the cocky smile. I knew Kai was loath to turn down a competition—a chance to best me, like I'd done to him a few weeks ago.

Except now we'd have an audience.

I'd tried to play the grown-up card earlier, but Kai was frustrating, so sure he was unbeatable. I was dying to remind him that when you'd made it to the top, the only way left to go was down.

I was sure I was losing my mind, but it was too late to back down without looking like a coward. And when Kai's jaw popped, the muscle twitching under his skin, I knew I had him right where I wanted him.

"I'll bite, rookie. Let's make this a fun competition between *friends*."

The term was obviously used for the sake of the kids. I was under no illusion that Kai and I were anything other than rivals. We were competitors who couldn't resist riling each other up, so why not do what we did best?

Compete.

"You're on, *friend*."

Elyn broke the tense bubble surrounding us. "Is everyone ready?"

None of the drivers said a word, because this is what we did for a living.

We were ready to race.

Elyn raised her arm, and the sound of the air horn kick-started our bodies' engines. Kai and I moved before anyone else even registered the sound. Someone laughed from behind us, most likely Zylo dropping his egg because of his massive hands.

But I didn't look, too focused on keeping mine steady.

"This might be the first time you've followed my advice," Kai teased from beside me.

It annoyed me that I was in fact taking his advice, and it annoyed me more that he'd noticed. I moved quickly, as gracefully as I could, all the while keeping my spoon balanced. His advice turned out to be helpful, but I'd never actually admit it.

I'd rather go streaking around an icy track with my balls hanging out.

"Careful, Mercer," I snapped back. "Don't want to trip over those huge championship shoes you're always trying to fill."

Kai didn't respond, just bit his lip, trying to fight the smile that threatened to burst through.

Unfortunately, the sight of his perfect teeth sinking into that plump, rosy skin took me off guard.

I missed a clump of grass on the ground, and my toe caught it like a dart searching for a bullseye. It sent me ass over tit, and my egg tumbled to the ground, while I ended up with a mouth full of grass.

Of course, Kai laughed, the sound carrying over his shoulder as the gap between us grew. I scrambled to pick up the egg, plonking it back on the spoon. By the time I was moving again, Jax had almost caught up. But he didn't overtake me.

Still, when I crossed the finish line in second place, Kai was waiting with that maddening grin that set my nerves on fire.

"Told you, rookie." His hazel eyes sparkled, the gold-flecked irises flashing like first-place medals in the sun. "I don't lose."

I panted as if I'd finished a marathon, every muscle wound tight. Taking a few grounding breaths, I forced my shoulders back, spine straight. My expression settled into cool composure, belying the chaos simmering just beneath the surface.

"It's only the first event, Mercer. Plenty of time to kick your ass."

I waited for him to call me out on my false bravado. Stars, part of me wanted him to. Wanted the surge of adrenaline that came from a verbal spar with Kai.

But he didn't. He just looked down his nose at me, the corner of his mouth turned up. Kai leaned in, closing the distance until the tip of his nose brushed mine.

"We'll see, rookie," he whispered, so close I could taste the sweetness of his breath. "I'd rather spank yours, though."

Air snagged in my lungs, and when I tried to speak, the words refused to come. Colour pulsed across my skin, illuminating Kai's annoying, smug face. Red gave way to a rosy pink as I stared, speechless, trying to process Kai's words.

He was crass.

He was vulgar.

He was—

"I like making you speechless." Kai's laugh was soft, almost teasing. "Maybe I'll make a habit of it."

"Fuck off, Mercer," I growled, clenching my teeth while my mask of indifference continued to crack.

Naturally, it just made his grin stretch even further.

I shoved him aside and stormed away, following the kids to the next event. I clenched my jaw, balled my fingers into tight fists, and tried to patch up the holes that Kai had made in my veneer.

Behind me, I heard Kai's low chuckle, the sound happy on the surface with dark promises hidden underneath.

And I just knew . . . that sound would haunt me for months to come.

Completely smug, completely insufferable, and unfortunately, completely unavoidable.

THE NEED FOR SPEED... AND SOMETHING MORE

Rev

The egg-and-spoon race was only the start of the competition between Kai and me.

We watched the kids compete, playing the professional mentors. We hyped them up, offered our strategic advice, and celebrated no matter what. Because we had a talented team, we celebrated quite a lot.

But when the kids were done, it was the drivers' turn, and Kai and I went head to head.

If someone asked me about the others' performances, I wouldn't know. My sole focus was Kai. No . . . my sole focus was *winning*. Kai was just an obstacle I had to pass along the way.

With every event, the pair of us ignored the confused and amused looks we got from the adults. Jax asked what was going on, if everything was okay, but we waved him off with shoddy excuses, not caring whether he believed them.

Our only priority was proving which one of us was best.

The kids thought it was hilarious and had taken to making bets beforehand, using their snacks as payment. By lunchtime, Jeremy had two pockets stuffed with fruit bags and cookies, which he graciously shared with the team anyway.

On the plus side, Kai and I were raking in points for our team, and combined with top performances from the kids, we were dying to know the overall total—even if we'd be checking our individual scores with Elyn later.

Kai won several events, like the meteor dash, where we had to hop across an obstacle course in a metallic anti-gravity sack. I'd almost beaten him, but the sacks would randomly jolt, making it hard to balance, so Kai used one of my stumbles and a well-timed jolt of his own to overtake me and cross the line first.

I still had my fair share of wins, though. I'd crushed Kai in the laser ring toss, which involved throwing magnetic rings onto robotic targets that moved. It looked easy enough when the kids did it, but Elyn upped the speed for the adults, and we had our work cut out for us. It was thanks to extreme focus and pure luck that I hit all the targets—the only driver to do so.

Kai went at it with his usual cockiness, but a big head and a "championship attitude" doesn't always bag the win.

He missed about ninety percent.

He seethed, embarrassed by his poor performance, even if he forced a smile for the kids' sake. I'm sure he expected me to rub it in his face, but I stayed silent, smiling wide like the professional I was.

The rouge tint of his skin and the murderous glare were satisfying, though.

The last event was a three-legged race.

I had no idea what our team's score was, but I was confident we'd done well. Turns out Jeremy, Lyla, Vaeri, and even Korvi were extremely competitive. They each stormed ahead whenever it was their turn, leaving their competitors in the dust with every first and second place finish.

So, yeah. I was confident. But we still had one more race before we'd find out.

Korvi and Lyla went first, finishing in second place behind two of Zylo's kids. Then it was Vaeri and Jeremy, and because Vaeri had an extra limb, they had to keep it curled up so things were fair. It meant their balance was a little off, which then affected Jeremy. They crossed the line a solid fourth, and our team didn't waste a second making sure they knew just how well they'd done.

But then it was the adults' turn, and Kai and I realised our competition was over. When we stood at the starting line, ankles tied together with a glittering yellow cord, it dawned on me.

It wasn't a rivalry anymore. It was something worse.

We had to be a team.

"This is a terrible idea," I muttered.

"I think you mean *brilliant*." Kai cracked his knuckles. "You're lucky I'm on your team, rookie."

"I'm two seconds away from gnawing through this rope and crawling to the finish line by myself."

His breath brushed my ear as he dropped his voice to a whisper. "I think I'd like to see you crawl."

I elbowed him hard in the ribs. "One more word and I'm disqualifying us for violence."

Elyn raised the air horn, and Kai readied himself to move. "Left leg first. You can tell your left from your right, can't you, rookie?"

"Shut up."

"On three."

"Wait, are we going *on* three or *after* three?"

"How are you so bad at this already?" Kai complained. "Just follow my lead."

"Like hell."

The air horn blew, so we took a synchronised step . . . and immediately stumbled.

"Ow! What the—lift your leg!" I gripped Kai's arm for balance, trying to pull myself up.

"I did lift it. Your long fucking limbs got in the way."

"You're taller than I am!"

"Stop talking!"

We lurched forward, half hopping, half dragging each other.

"You are the *worst* partner—"

"Because I don't want to lose!"

"You're making us lose!"

"Just *MOVE!*"

In my frustration, I shoved him, forgetting that we were tied together. We tipped sideways, landing in a heap on the grass as dust rose around us. Lying flat on his back with my face smushed into his hard stomach, Kai burst out laughing.

I growled, the sound muffled by his T-shirt. "I hope you choke."

He laughed harder, so I lifted my head and glared. Kai plucked a leaf from my hair. "As much as I wanted to win, losing was worth it to get you on top of me," he teased, pumping his eyebrows.

I shoved off him, enjoying his grunt when I caught his ribs with my knee, and untied the rope with jerky fingers. The kids and volunteers thought it was hilarious, and the other drivers cackled from beyond the finish line.

Turned out we'd lost.

Spectacularly.

Because it was impossible for Kai and me to work together.

Without helping him up, I turned away, stomping across the grass towards our team.

"At least we almost made it to the halfway point!" he called out, running after me. I just rolled my eyes, taking a few calming breaths before I reached the kids.

"That was . . . so . . . funny!" Vaeri wheezed, tears in their eyes.

Lyla giggled, giving her friend a nudge. "Even Vaeri made it to the finish line, and they've got an extra leg."

"I still thought you were good," Korvi said, voice soft and sincere, sunshine yellow blooming across his skin as I ruffled his hair.

"Thanks, kid," I replied, holding out my fist. When he bumped it, the yellow glow on my skin matched his.

"You were *terrible*!" Jeremy bellowed, never one to mince his words.

Kai gripped his stomach, as if he'd been mortally wounded. "Woah, tone it down, Jer-Bear. We're a team, remember."

The kids continued to snicker as we strolled to the mini podium for the final results. Everyone sat on the grass, while Elyn stood at the front of the crowd with a microphone, waiting for us to settle.

"Well done to all of our Karting kids, and the Astro Space League drivers!" she said, making everyone cheer. "Winning's great, but it means nothing without teamwork and kindness. All of you showed up and took part, and that's where every champion begins."

"I still think we're the winners, though," Kai muttered, and three of the kids bobbed their heads in agreement. Korvi kept his eyes on Elyn, fingers crossed in his lap. I didn't even think he was breathing.

I whispered in his ear, making him jump. "Even if we don't win, you were still brilliant today."

He turned those starry eyes on me, and the smile he gave tilted my world off its axis. It was the brightest I'd seen from him all day, and knowing I'd helped bring it out made me proud.

"Okay, let's hear some results!" The crowd quietened until you could hear a pin drop. "In third place . . . Jax and Valen's team!"

Cheers and claps filled the campground as the group of six stood up and walked to the podium. They were all given a bronze KFK medal, with an additional toyshop gift card for the kids.

"In second place . . . Zylo and Cass's team!"

Zylo gave a mighty cheer, and the kids dog-piled him. Then they scrambled to the podium, red-faced and laughing, to receive their prize. Zylo, being the legend he was, beamed at his teammates and shook their hands, congratulating them for their hard work.

But there was still one award to be announced.

"Here's the one we've all been waiting for. In first place . . ." The campgrounds were silent, and the kids held their breath. So did I. So did Kai. "Despite a mighty tumble, it's Kai and Rev's team!"

Our team screamed with joy, Kai louder than all the kids combined. My ears rang as they jumped to their feet, tugging Korvi and me up with them. Kai pulled us into a group hug, and seeing them all so ecstatic, I couldn't find it in me to complain.

Our gazes met over their heads. "Told you we'd win," he mouthed with a smug glint in his eyes.

I rolled my eyes, half-heartedly at best, but a smile snuck through anyway.

When I glanced at the kids, I spotted Korvi's tail whipping with excitement, the lines on his skin flaring in every colour of the rainbow, like a living fireworks display. The sight warmed my chest. Iskari adults rarely lit up like that; they'd long since learned to temper their emotions.

But for a child? It meant pure, unfiltered joy.

When the event was over, and the kids had been collected by their parents, Kai and I looked for Elyn. She was putting away the rings from the laser toss when we cornered her.

"Thanks for a great day with the kids, Elyn," Kai said, ever the charmer.

"No problem!" She beamed at him. "You two were great. I've never seen Korvi so comfortable with the other kids." Elyn looked pointedly at me, and I couldn't help the way my skin flickered bright orange.

"He just needed a little encouragement, you know?" I shrugged as if it were nothing. "To feel like he belonged."

She nodded. "Well, I'm glad he got that from you. And from his new friends."

"He's a great kid," I mumbled, not sure what else to say.

For once, I was grateful when Kai stepped in, commandeering the conversation. "Actually, Elyn, we had a quick question."

"What's up?"

"Well, we were just wondering if you'd recorded our individual scores?"

Elyn frowned in confusion. The day was about teamwork, so why would we want to know our individual scores?

But Kai barrelled on. "We were curious to know how we did. I mean, we spend a lot of time working on our own, so we're used to hearing our individual scores, you know?"

He was rambling, but it seemed to appease Elyn, because she grabbed the clipboard from a nearby shelf. "Yes, of course! Just give me one . . ." She flipped through the pages. "Ah, here we go! Huh."

"Is everything alright?" I asked, concerned.

"Sorry," she chuckled. "I was just shocked."

"Why's that?" Kai's smile faltered, just a smidge.

Were we thinking the same thing? Were our scores wrong? Maybe one of us lost remarkably compared to the other, and she didn't know how to tell us.

"More surprised. Your scores were identical." She looked up at us with a smile, but we just stared in return.

"Identical?" I asked, sure she was wrong. Must have miscounted somehow.

"Yep." Elyn passed us the clipboard, and there in black and white were our scores. Identical, just like she'd said.

"You both did great," Elyn said. "You blew the other drivers out of the water! But isn't it cool that you finished up with the same score?"

"So cool," I muttered, eyes glued to the paper.

"Yep," Kai bit out. "Fascinating."

When Elyn left us, telling us to keep the scoresheet, we continued to stare at it, shoulder to shoulder. Neither of us spoke, and the silence stretched.

Growing uncomfortable, I cleared my throat, looking anywhere but at Kai. "Guess that makes us evenly matched."

"Guess so," he replied.

Another beat passed, and the usual tension crackled between us, tight and sparking like a live wire.

"This doesn't mean we're equals," I snapped, quicker than I meant to.

Kai turned to me with a smirk.

"No, rookie. It means next time, I'm gonna bury you."

I snatched the scoresheet from his hands, resisting the urge to crumple it and throw it at his forehead. "In your dreams."

He stepped in close, voice low and smug. "You'll look so good in my dreams."

And with that, he sauntered off, whistling a jolly little tune as he went.

HOUSTON, WE HAVE A BIG F#%KING PROBLEM

Kai

I lay in bed, staring at the pile of laundry on top of the chest of drawers.

They were the clothes I'd worn for the KFK event, and I'd had to wash them three times before the grass stains came out. The white T-shirt still had streaks of green, though, so it'd have to go. At least I had a dozen more tucked away in a drawer.

The stains were a result of the three-legged race, when Rev and I had spent more time rolling around on the ground than we had on our feet.

When laundry time came, a part of me hadn't wanted to wash them away because it felt like I'd be washing away the memory. The greater, more logical part of me knew I *should* want them gone. They were a reminder of our failure, because we hadn't even finished the race.

Sure, we'd won the overall competition, but I hated losing anything. So why would I want to keep something that reminded me of that?

Even if the aftermath was hilarious.

Days later and it still made me chuckle.

The way Rev had scrambled to untie us before running away. The way his ears had twitched in frustration and his skin had glowed with fiery hues. The way his body heat had seeped into mine from where he'd lain on top of me, his face pressed into my stomach just above the waistband of my shorts, and his thigh pressed between my legs applying the slightest friction to my cock.

I couldn't shake the image of his eyes—deep, shadowed things lit with diamond-bright sparks—and my dick twitched beneath the covers. I stared down at it in horror, because I was not chubbing up over thoughts of *Rev*.

It'd been a while since I'd got laid, but was I really that hard up?

Absolutely fucking not.

But it seemed my dick was feeling neglected and choosing violence.

The horny part of me controlled by my hindbrain begged me to pet it . . . maybe stroke it a little to say how sorry I was. Pretty sure it was my dick sending subliminal messages to trick me into something I'd later regret.

Alas, I was a man of integrity—sort of—and it wasn't going to happen.

I needed a distraction.

I opened SpaceFlix on the TV, deciding on a generic action flick. Explosions, high-speed chases, damsels in distress . . . the perfect way to take my mind off thoughts I shouldn't be entertaining.

I settled against the headboard, letting my body sink into my pillows while the screen bathed the room in a golden glow. But thirty minutes in, and I couldn't tell you a single plot point. I didn't recognise half the actors either, although it had promised a stacked cast.

Instead, all I could think about was pearlescent skin, a long tail, and pointy fucking ears.

That psych evaluation I mentioned? Yeah, it needed scheduling. Like yesterday.

What grated most was that our scores had been identical.

I could've taken a one-point loss—for him, not me, obviously. But equal? I couldn't think of anything worse. If I'd tied with Jax, I'd have laughed it off. We'd have shrugged it off and shared a drink afterwards.

But with Rev, it didn't feel like a tie; it felt like a loss in disguise. Like he'd still won somehow. And then he'd had to get in one last insult, his voice like a blade wrapped in velvet.

"This doesn't mean we're equals."

No shit, it didn't.

Because I *was* better, wasn't I?

The season stats proved it. My three championship wins proved it. With every event, Jeremy and Vaeri had been certain I'd win. Even when I hadn't earned it, they'd looked at me like I was their hero.

The same way Korvi had looked at Rev.

And Rev had smiled at him—warm, genuine, and soft around the edges. The moment was stuck in my head, immortalised like a photograph.

The entire day, Korvi had lit up whenever Rev so much as glanced his way. Literally too, because his skin had pulsed with yellow light. He'd clung to every word the rookie said, as though sharing a quiet understanding the rest of us weren't privy to.

And it was infuriating. Unsettling.

And worst of all? It was hot.

I was used to Rev being unreadable, covered with a mask of indifference that gave nothing away. Locked up tighter than a high-security prison. On the surface, it seemed like nothing got under his skin.

But some things did, as proven by the luminous lines decorating his skin. The way they pulsed and shifted, lit up like a silent language only the Iskari could understand.

I may not have figured out the pattern, but I knew it wasn't random. It couldn't be. Not when his skin lit up in shifting shades of red every time I got close—scarlet, crimson, ruby—like a slow burn barely held in check.

With every pulse of colour, something in me came alive. The urge to test his limits, to chase every hue he had to offer, to see just how bright I could make him shine. It was like a challenge, a siren song to my competitive heart.

How far could I push until his surrounding fortress crumbled?

As infuriating as he was, I couldn't deny that Revvak Arathiel fascinated me. Not because he was Iskari, but because of everything beneath the surface. I wanted to lift the hood and dig into the engine. Strip him down to his atoms, figure out what made him tick. What drove the polished exterior, and who he became when it cracked.

What would those dark eyes look like stripped of restraint? Wide with raw, unfiltered desire? I'd seen a glimpse in Nebula. His body pinned to the wall, plastered against mine. His breath hitching whenever my fingers skimmed the base of his tail. Broken whimpers, soft and helpless, caught between fleeing and surrendering.

When I'd mentioned spanking his ass, he'd been flustered, all scoffs and narrowed eyes before storming away. But I hadn't missed how the specks in his eyes had swirled like a freshly shaken snow globe, or the delicious pink glow of his skin.

Those plump purple lips had formed the prettiest O, and in a split second of madness, I'd imagined them wrapped around my cock, his tongue out, ready for me to slide in and fuck that smart mouth quiet—

A loud groan ripped from my throat.

Between a fight scene I wasn't watching and the thought of Rev's mouth doing wicked things, my hand had wandered down, traitorous and eager, stroking without hesitation.

A ragged "fuck" slipped out as my hips surged upwards, chasing the heat coiled in my clenched hand. My conscience begged me to stop. Thinking was impossible. All the blood had drained to my cock, now flushed and iron-hard in my fist, demanding release.

Gun to my head, I couldn't recall a time when my dick had been this hard, at least not without a partner. I'd been reduced to nothing more than a mindless beast searching for pleasure, and if I didn't come soon, I was afraid I'd combust. A spontaneous human disaster, reduced to ash and regret.

My lizard brain conjured the image of Rev, on his knees with tears streaming down his face, drool on his chin. He was always full of snark, wearing a blanket of arrogance to cover his nerves.

The vision of him on his back, too busy crying out in pleasure to remember his name—let alone a snide remark—was enough to have me dancing along the knife's edge.

But horny Kai wanted to drag this out.

I loosened my grip, easing the pressure around my cock as I drew in slow, steady breaths, grateful when the tingling at the base of my spine ebbed, inch by inch. My thumb caressed the tip, spreading the pearly drops of precum leaking from my slit. I dragged it down my shaft, and the smooth glide made me shudder. My back arched off the soft mattress when I cupped my neglected balls in my free hand.

And the hornier I got, the clearer my version of Rev became. It was easy to imagine his lithe, naked body crawling up my bed, straddling my hips.

Would his cock be short or long? Thick or thin? None of it mattered, not when the image of him pressed against me had me growling into the silence, feral with want.

I recalled the way he'd moved in Nebula, hips rolling in a hypnotic rhythm, fingers trailing sweat-slick skin with teasing precision.

How would he look above me, grinding down, our cocks sliding together, slick with precum and heat? Would he like it if I held his hips, urging him into a rhythm I controlled? Would he whine and writhe if I pinched his nipples? Would he chew his lip raw, fighting back the wrecked, needy sounds threatening to break free?

Or would he be lost to it, moaning my name as skin slapped against skin, each echo a hymn to something wicked?

The tingling in my spine returned, and now I was fucking my fist in earnest. My cock leaked a river of precum, my fingers covered in it. My window was cracked open, the cool air caressing my damp skin.

I was hurtling towards the finish line, but my conscience was cockblocking me, desperate to hold me back from rapture. Horny Kai was stronger, though, and dying to fucking come.

I focused on the Rev in my mind. The one who straddled my hips, tail coiled around my thigh, looking almost wrecked with pleasure.

That Rev would press down to my chest, lips whispering against my ear . . . and I was so lost I could almost feel his heated breath on my skin.

He'd whisper, breathless from the exertion, rough from his whines and moans. "You can't stop thinking about me, can you?"

And even knowing he wasn't really there, the word "no" came out in a low, desperate whine.

"Let me hear you, hotshot," he'd purr. "Come for me, Kai."

So I did.

Imaginary Rev vanished with the wind as my hips bucked one final time.

I screwed my eyes shut, giant stars exploding behind my eyelids, and ropes of cum shot from my cock. They covered my stomach and chest, some even hitting my chin. My heart pounded, threatening to burst through my ribs, and my lungs burned.

"Fucking hell."

My limbs twitched with the aftershocks, but my eyes stayed closed. Because while I knew he'd been a figment of my imagination, I worried that when I opened them, the rookie would actually be lying next to me.

The devil on my shoulder whispered that they wished it had been real, and I shut that thought down fast. Wanking over thoughts of my rival was one thing, but fucking him?

Nah.

If that ever happened, I'd find the nearest black hole and dive right in, spaghettification be damned.

Spaghetti Kai-bonara. Bon appétit.

When the twitches subsided, I felt brave enough to open my eyes, and as expected, I was alone in my bed. Just me, my perverted thoughts, and the sticky reminder of how fucked up I was.

A reminder that was drying and making my pubes itch.

Before I could spiral over what had happened, I forced myself out of bed and into the en suite.

And if behind closed shower doors I gave in and tugged another one out?

Well . . . that was no one's business but my own.

OUT OF THE PIT LANE & INTO THE FIRE

Kai

Race weekends were my idea of heaven, though as constant hubs of activity, others might think they were a nightmare.

Everyone was always on the move. Whether it was crews working on vehicles, strategists working out plans for the weekend, or drivers working with their personal coaches.

Then there was the pressure to perform. From the moment you arrived on Friday morning, all eyes were always on you—your team, your competitors, and the spectators who paid a lot of money to be there. Practice sessions were an exhibition for the other teams to see how you managed the track. Qualifying was a competition in itself, because your performance determined your starting position for the race.

There was never a dull moment, and rarely an opportunity to rest.

Yet I was like a diamond—pressure formed the best parts of me, and I sure as hell loved showing off. I was self-aware enough to know I was a cocky bastard, so being watched and performing at my best in front of the crowd and my competitors was right up my alley.

But while I was an exhibitionist on the track, the love of being watched hadn't followed me to the bedroom. And stars help me if anyone ever discovered what now lived rent free in my wank bank.

Ever since my little self-love session, I hadn't stopped thinking about the rookie—in ways that weren't safe for work.

The man had starred in fantasies so filthy, I was convinced at least three positions violated intergalactic law. One of them required flexibility I'm not even sure he had, and I'd spent far too long picturing how his stubborn ass might prove me wrong.

I'd refused to wank in my bed since that night—not while perverted thoughts of Rev were running rampant in my mind—but that meant I was running up my water bill, because every boner sent me straight to the shower to knock one out under the spray.

I mean, if there was no evidence left behind, did it really happen?

Of course it fucking did.

Mentally, I was a mess.

Physically? Immaculate.

And I'd gone through a bottle of body wash like it was holy water, just days after restocking.

Don't even get me started on the lube.

Thank god I had a race to distract me. So when I stepped off the shuttle at the start of the weekend, my mind was firmly in race mode.

For about five minutes.

I'd avoided Rev for most of the weekend, hiding inside Nexus's garage when I wasn't on the track.

To the team, I probably looked more determined than ever, and Jax assumed I was trying to make up for my previous third-place finish at Crystal Barricade.

I let him believe it, because what was I supposed to say?

"Sorry, mate, been furiously jerking it to the rookie all week and now I don't trust myself to make eye contact."

No, that wouldn't go down well.

I might not have seen Rev in person, but he was still everywhere. A glimpse of him on the highlights reel and I was half hard. Someone mentioned his name, and my cock perked up like it'd been waiting. A few too many wanks and I'd developed a Pavlovian response to the word "Rev."

So imagine my horror when I finally bumped into the fucker an hour before the race.

I was hyped up for lights out after a successful qualifying session the day before. I'd snagged pole position without even breaking a sweat, out-qualifying Dray by only a tenth of a second. He'd put up a good fight, and I expected he would today too.

But after a poor performance in the last race, I was glad to be back at the front of the pack. Plus, I'd obliterated last year's lap record, setting a new personal best that had Ailor beaming like a proud parent.

I was visualising the track in my mind when Rev strolled out of Zenith's garage.

His dark hair hung loose around his shoulders, and even under the smoggy skies of Thrylon Prime, it shone with blue, purple, and green highlights as it fluttered in the breeze. The pointed tips of his ears peeked through, as did the fine lines that illuminated whenever I wound him up.

My eyes drifted down the length of him, remembering the way they decorated his upper body, currently covered by his racing suit.

"Do I have something on my face?"

Rev's voice jolted me out of my daydream, and I realised I'd been staring. His ears twitched under my attention, and the lines I could see pulsed a bright tangerine colour.

Faced with awkwardness, it seemed my brain felt the safest option was to power down.

So instead, I grunted like a caveman.

He frowned, but his dark eyes sparkled. "Bash your head too hard in qualifying, hotshot? Maybe you need a new helmet."

"Huh?"

Okay, so words were still beyond my current capabilities.

Still, the faint twitch of Rev's lips told me I'd dented the armour of his usually unshakable composure.

"Actually, keep your current helmet," he went on. "With your head that scrambled, I might just bag a win."

My brain chose that moment to restart, his snark forcing us back into our usual routine. Verbal sparring was our baseline, and after he'd weaselled his way into my brain, this put me back on even footing.

"I could beat you even on my deathbed, rookie."

"At least I'll outlive you, old man. That's some comfort." He scowled, crimson streaking the markings I'd imagined following with my tongue.

"You're only four years younger than me," I scoffed, shaking off my inappropriate thoughts.

"That's four more years of peak performance than you'll ever manage."

"You're ridiculous."

"Bite me."

"You'd like that, wouldn't you, rookie?" I purred.

Rev exhaled, and when the lines on his skin glowed red with threads of pink, I smirked. Stars, I may not know what the colours meant, but that one *had* to mean arousal.

He growled, eyes narrowed and ears twitching under his hair. "Fuck off, Mercer."

When he stormed into Zenith's garage, out of sight yet not out of mind, I chuckled.

That was more like it.

I didn't see Rev again.

Jax and I had a last-minute team meeting with Ailor, while the crew performed their final checks. When we headed to the grid, I was high on the smell of burnt rubber and biofuel. Spectators packed the grandstands, their roars deafening.

We lined up for Thrylon Prime's national anthem, and three fighter shuttles zoomed through the smog overhead in a triangular formation, leaving a trail of red and orange clouds in their wake.

With the pomp and circumstance done, it was time to race. Jax and I exchanged fist bumps by my vehicle before he walked off to fourth position.

Dray smirked at me from under his helmet. "Here's hoping for a repeat of the last race, eh, Mercer?"

I flipped him off with a sneer, and the smarmy prick laughed before flicking his visor down.

I put on my helmet and surveyed my competitors, spotting Rev in fifth. He took his helmet from one of the Zenith crew, and our gazes met as he turned to face his vehicle.

The sea of noise on the track faded away as I lost myself in his dark eyes. I gave him a single nod, enjoying the way he scowled in return, then he donned his helmet and climbed into the vehicle.

Get your head in the game, Mercer.

I tore my eyes away from his lithe form, ignoring the way it moved under his fitted racing suit. My focus had held all day—mostly—and now wasn't the time to explore my dirty fantasies.

A whisper from the devil on my shoulder promised *later*, and with a quiet growl, I hauled myself into my vehicle.

"Comms check," Sam said over the radio.

"Confirmed."

"We're aiming for Plan Alpha, but we'll revert to Plan Bravo if necessary."

Plan A was a one-stop strategy, where I'd only need to change tyres once throughout the entire race.

The track temperature at Solar Flare Speedway had remained steady, so the tyres shouldn't deteriorate too quickly. We planned to go as long as possible, building a big enough lead before entering the pit lane in the latter half of the race. It meant the crew could change my tyres fast enough for me to rejoin the race without being overtaken.

Plan B meant two stops. Something we only did when necessary. I treated my tyres well, so they usually lasted a while before I had to replace them, but some things were beyond our control. Like when the track got too hot, or I had to push harder to stay ahead. It meant I had to stop again, and if I didn't, I could risk my position.

I refused to fuck things up because of sheer stubbornness, so if Ailor ordered Plan B, I'd do it. I followed the rules, listened to my team.

Even if there were times I argued in the heat of the moment. All drivers did, because we thought we knew best. Frustration and focus, combined with adrenaline, made it easy for us to lash out.

But Sam and Ailor saw what I couldn't—the finer details of my vehicle and my competitors'. They had screens full of numbers, weather reports, track temperature, and so much more.

If they told me to do something, I'd whine and pout, but I'd stick my metaphorical tail between my legs and do it.

I wasn't reckless.

Unlike some people.

"Conditions?" I shifted in my seat, getting comfortable and powering up the vehicle.

"We're expecting strong flares around lap thirty-two, but Plan Alpha remains in place."

"Noted."

I flipped down my visor, watching as the crew removed the blankets covering my tyres, and before long, the track was clear of everyone but the drivers. We started our formation lap, and I made some mental notes while I drove.

Solar Flare Speedway got its name because of Thrylon Prime's two massive suns. Smog clung to the sky from the planet's relentless industry, but the suns' searing flares sliced through it like a knife through butter. The flares illuminated the whole track, leaving you blind until they passed.

Plus, they were really fucking hot, and the smog trapped the heat like a greenhouse. The track could go from manageable to molten in minutes, and what should be a straightforward race could turn brutal.

If you missed the chance to pit and swap to heat-resistant tyres, your treads would melt onto the asphalt, leaving you glued to the spot with no way forward.

On top of that, the flares' electromagnetic disruptions fucked with the vehicles' power systems, and if your built-in heat shields failed, it was like driving fifty-plus laps in an oven on full heat.

I'd seen drivers pass out because they refused to retire. Last season, Jax's vehicle caught fire because the coolant system didn't kick in. He was lucky to walk away with nothing more than singed eyebrows and wounded pride.

Weather reports could warn us to a point, but the twin suns were temperamental, and the flares could be unpredictable. An unexpected surge of heat could come out of nowhere, leaving the teams scrambling to alter their strategies.

Narrowed down to the track itself, the race was straightforward. But the planet's conditions and unpredictable variables made it a nightmare.

At Solar Flare Speedway, strategy wasn't just important.

It was everything.

We returned to the starting line, free of early casualties and ready to race.

As the first red light blinked overhead, the crowd fell silent, leaving only the low, pulsing hum of our engines. I watched as the second and then the third red light appeared, and I counted down in my head, holding my breath until all five lights glowed.

Then they disappeared.

Go time.

At the first turn, Zylo crept up, drawing my focus. I didn't see Dray until he slipped through on the inside, stealing the apex with perfect timing. I cursed under my breath.

On the next straight, I flicked to secondary thrusters, and surged ahead, Dray's vehicle shrinking fast in the mirror.

The next twenty laps blurred into routine. I held the lead easily. No threats, no drama. Just an empty track stretching out in front of me.

After the chaos at Crystal Barricade, I should've been grateful, but halfway through, boredom crept in, and I craved a challenge—something, anything, to stir the blood.

It reminded me of what Jax had said at the start of the season.

"Being reckless after forty-odd laps spices things up a bit. Makes it more exciting."

That race at Horizon Rings with the rookie had been electric. He'd beat me—and yeah, I'd hated it—but having someone to fight had made it all worth it. On the track, off the track, with him, every second was a battle.

Racing Rev, just the two of us, I'd pushed myself harder, took risks I'd never dared to before.

Reckless, just like I'd accused him of being at the start of the season.

But you couldn't afford to be reckless with sixteen drivers on the track all at once. God forbid your reckless stupidity ended in a crash that left someone broken—or worse, dead.

Zylo's last teammate, Xander Korr, was killed when a Vanguard racer sliced in front of him, forcing him into the barrier. Overwhelmed by guilt, she'd had a breakdown and been forced to withdraw from the rest of the season, and eventually the ASL.

Last I heard, she couldn't board a shuttle bus without having a panic attack.

I wasn't asking for carnage, though, just a little competition. Something to liven things up.

Instead, I was out front alone, cruising like it was a Sunday joyride.

No threats in my mirrors. No pressure in my gut. Just silence in the cockpit and a calmness that made me itch.

I hated that it made me sound like a smug asshole, but I wanted another race like the one Rev gave me. Tight turns. Smack talk. That sharp edge of not knowing who'd come out ahead.

Turns out, the universe listens. Just not in the way I'd hoped.

"Unpredicted solar flare detected," Sam snapped, voice sharp with tension and static.

"Shit," I muttered, watching the sky ignite above the clouds, knowing blindness was imminent. "Things are about to get hot."

"Box on the next lap to change to heat-resistants."

"How are the tyres?" I asked.

"Looking fine for now," he replied. "Push as much as you can without burning the tyres too low. We need as much distance between you and the ground as possible."

"Confirmed." I stepped on the accelerator.

Sunlight blasted through my visor and blurred the track ahead. I forced my speed down. At least it was a straight and not a sharp turn in the blind.

Sweat pooled at my neck, and heat crept inside the cockpit. Systems were holding for now, so I flipped the heat shield on, kicked the cooling system into gear, and sucked down water through the straw in my helmet. The cockpit cooled just enough to ease the burn.

It wouldn't last long, though.

"Jax is out," Sam reported. "The flare blinded him at turn five and he ended up in the barrier."

I gripped the steering wheel so hard it creaked. I wanted to shake things up, but not at the expense of Jax.

"Is he okay?"

"He's fine." Sam replied, and I exhaled a long sigh of relief. "The medical shuttle already picked him up. Nothing more than a mild headache from the light."

"Big baby," I chuckled.

I glanced in the wing mirror. No sign of Dray, just empty space. The light was still harsh but dimming fast. I'd slowed more than I meant to, so someone should've caught up by now. My lead couldn't be that big.

Could it?

"Where's Dray?"

"He got glued. Ran his tyres too hard and they melted," Sam explained. "They're peeling the vehicle away but should be gone by the time you pit."

"Anything else?"

I pressed harder on the accelerator. The heat pushed back, rising fast. Dray hadn't pitted before he DNF'd, so his tyres were probably in a similar state to mine.

Five turns until I could pit. I was determined not to get stuck before I made it.

"Shit," Sam hissed.

"What's wrong?" I gritted out.

"There's another solar flare."

"Already?!" I barked. A second one rarely came that quickly. "How long?"

"Sixty seconds. Zylo's engine died, so he's out. Rev is coming up behind you."

Rev's vehicle grew larger in my mirror, creeping closer with every second.

Another burst of light cracked across the sky, brighter than before. My eyes burned. I flinched, blinking hard, then eased off the accelerator. For a moment, I drove blind. Just a breath. Just a prayer.

When the glare faded and I looked again, Rev was still behind me. But barely.

"How the fuck is he still moving so fast?" I snapped.

A red light blinked on the wheel—cooling systems were failing. Not ideal, but as long as the heat shields held, I could keep going. Still, the cockpit was stifling. The air pressed against my skin, heavy and hot, sweat clinging like a second suit.

"He was the first to change tyres," Sam said. "Pure luck that he was by the pit lane when the first flare warning came through."

I shook my head, clearing the beads of sweat dripping into my eyes. "Lucky bastard."

I hit the button for my additional thrusters, hoping to gain some speed.

Nothing.

My stomach dropped. "Second thrusters have gone!"

Sam grunted in confirmation, and Rev kept closing the gap. I pushed as hard as I dared without tearing my tyres to shreds. But his were fresh and heat resistant, while mine were half melted and slipping.

At the next turn, he dived in for the overtake. Somehow, I held him off. The tyres fought back as I exited, no grip left, almost locking up.

I flicked to driver comms. "Nice try, rookie."

"I've got all the time in the galaxy, Mercer." Rev's voice, calm and controlled, sent a chill down my spine despite the heat. "Your tyres look a little glossy."

"They're fine," I snapped.

Though we both knew that was bullshit.

He hummed, smug as hell. "Fine and sticky."

Just as Rev's voice cut out, my pressure sensors lit up red. I didn't need the warning; I felt it. As I hit the penultimate turn before the pit lane, a robotic voice echoed in my helmet.

"Warning. Surface integrity compromised."

My rear tyres fishtailed. The track shimmered with heat, warping the air. From the groan of the wheels, they sounded like they might rip clean off. I kept going. No choice.

Rev pulled up beside me. On the last turn, he went for it again, and this time, he made it.

His vehicle pushed me wide, skating the edge of the track. Not illegal, but damn close. As he cut in front, I caught a flash of his gloved hand flipping me off.

Then the world spun sideways.

He'd been so damn close his rear wheel clipped mine, and I was gone, spinning off the track toward the barrier. I fought, desperate to pull it back, but the tyres were finished. They peeled apart under me, melting and shredding like confetti.

Then—

SMACK!

The wall hit hard. Everything jolted. Smoke curled around the vehicle, thick and slow, cloaking me as the systems went dark.

I was out.

DNF.

"Ka . . . okay . . . medi . . . it's . . . right . . ." Sam's broken words crackled through the comms, tangled with the high-pitched ringing in my ears.

I climbed out of the vehicle, every movement stiff, the heat clawing through my suit. Thank fuck I'd kept my gloves on. The metal was molten.

Track stewards sprinted over. One yanked me back while another unloaded foam onto the flames licking the vehicle's nose. Smoke billowed. The fire hissed. My pulse hammered in my throat.

My poor baby was going to need some serious TLC before the next race.

A couple of stewards grabbed me, pulling me back as the others fought the stubborn flames. The heat made the air shimmer, too dry for quick work. They'd need the full fire crew to finish the job.

A medical shuttle touched down nearby, its white cross stark against the haze. A medic jumped out, clutching a portable first aid kit like a lifeline.

"Mr Mercer," they said, raising the visor on my helmet to see my eyes. "Did you hit your head?"

"I took a couple of whacks, but my helmet bore the brunt of it."

They shone a small torch into my eyes. I winced, but the absence of any shooting pain through my brain was good. Right?

"No sign of concussion," they confirmed, and I removed my helmet.

Sweat glued my hair to the sides of my face, and I could feel it dripping down my body. It was pretty swampy under my suit, and I was dying to go home and get into bed.

A pity party was just what I needed. But it wasn't in the cards just yet. No doubt I'd have post-race interviews to do, followed by a check-in with the team and Jax.

And . . . the podium. Where Rev would likely stand in first place after running me off the track.

Once the medic gave the all-clear, they hauled me back to the paddock, but after that everything blurred, my vision clouded with anger.

If the rookie hadn't pushed so close, if he hadn't pulled that borderline dirty move, I would have made it to the pit lane. I would still be out there, choking him out with my exhaust.

There'd be no penalty, of course. I could already hear the officials spinning it. They'd say it was just bad luck. An accident. Maybe his wheel brushed mine. But with my tyres gone, I could have clipped him too. There was no way they would pin it on Rev.

And that made me furious.

The logical part of my brain told me the officials were right. But the fury was louder.

When the podium came, I refused to go, because I was stubborn. But Jax dragged me with him against my will. Something about being a good sport and clapping for the top three, not just the winner.

So I stood beside my team, wearing a fake-ass smile and clapping a little too aggressively.

The top three climbed the podium. And right in the middle?

Rev.

He didn't smile when the planet's president handed him a trophy, because of course he didn't, but a hairline fracture appeared in his cool exterior the second an unfamiliar melody filled the air.

"What's the music?" I asked Jax, because he knew everything.

"Iskanya's national anthem," he replied. "Word is, the CRF dug through galactic archives just for him."

Rev's dark eyes turned glassy under the floodlights, his expression softening with something raw. I'd expected them to play Zyphar's anthem—his current home, just like mine and most of the other drivers'.

But the melody that rose was older, sadder. A song from the Iskari's ruined homeworld that no longer existed.

And yet, he still didn't look happy. Even after the lengths the league had gone to to include him. He just stood there, mask in place, like celebrating his first win was beneath him.

Fuck him.

Rev was an ungrateful bastard, and I'd make sure he knew it.

Right after I took a damn shower.

CLOSE ENCOUNTERS OF THE THIRST KIND

Rev

The drivers' locker room at the paddocks wasn't anything fancy. Just some metal lockers, a cubby with fresh towels, and some wooden benches down the middle. At Solar Flare Speedway, a glass door in the corner of the room hid a set of four showers.

The rooms were clean enough, but people seldom used them for more than a quick change. Unless you were Zylo, who regularly dropped trou in the middle of Zenith's garage. I'd become desensitised to the sight of his cock and balls on display, but I don't know how Saelix wasn't walking around bow-legged.

Unlike Zylo, I didn't whip my equipment out in public, so I joined the handful of drivers who chose the locker room. I'd bumped into Jax a few times, and we'd talked about this and that while getting ready, but never Kai.

He probably demanded a private space at the rear of Nexus's garage, complete with a solid gold toilet to shit in. Probably had one at all the tracks, so his highness didn't have to mingle with the peasants before a race.

I'd seen him in the crowd from the top of the podium. He'd smiled, but it had seemed strained, almost crazed.

It was his eyes that had given him away, and I wondered how many looked beyond the surface to realise it. Flames had danced in his hazel eyes, and they'd looked like molten gold under the sky's solar flares. He'd looked like a celestial demon, and if looks could kill, I'd have been obliterated.

Knowing Kai, it was only a matter of time before he'd corner me, to rage about his DNF and place the blame on my head. After all, he was the professional, and I was just an ignorant rookie.

In reality, I'd been close to him on the track, but not enough to shove him off. Nexus had asked for an investigation, and Tavoris had reviewed the footage with the officials. By the time the race was over, they'd all come to the same conclusion.

It was pure bad luck on Kai's part. His tyres had melted in the heat, just like many other drivers', and he'd started skidding just as our wheels touched. A complete accident. So Kai would have to put his big boy pants on and deal with it.

Entering the locker room, I was still in a daze.

I'd just won my first race in the Astro Space League.

It had been tough with the heat, but Iskari regulated heat differently than other species. For me, the track had just felt like a warm day in the summer, even at its hottest. Thankfully, the solar flares had settled towards the end of the race, and the track had cooled down enough that we hadn't been at risk of getting stuck.

Afterwards, various people had pulled me from pillar to post—interviews, chats with officials, and photo ops. When Zylo had managed to get to me, he'd scooped me up in a crippling bear hug. He'd had tears in his eyes when he told me how proud he was, and considering how closed off I was, it had been strange to see someone wearing their emotions so freely.

When he'd congratulated me, misty-eyed and snotty-nosed, I hadn't smiled.

My skin had pulsed orange and violet, but Zylo had no clue what that meant, and he hadn't asked. I'd never told anyone before. Had never felt comfortable enough. Because to do so meant revealing something intimate. Iskari wore their emotions on their skin, the glowing lines shifting with every feeling, but with so few of us left, almost no one knew how to read them. Most mistook them for scars or tattoos until they lit up, and when colours flared, people were too stunned to ask what they meant.

I'd spent too many years playing the role of the freak with light-up skin. Showing my emotions on top of that only made me vulnerable. Made me look weak. The rest of the galaxy already saw us that way, and I refused to prove them right, so I locked everything down. Kept my face blank. Indifference became my armour. My skin still betrayed me, glowing like a neon sign whether I wanted it to or not, but at least no one understood what the colours meant.

I'd probably looked like a stiff prick, but Zylo wasn't one to be deterred. He'd just clung to me tighter, like he could squeeze the feeling out of me. And maybe he had, because my lower lip had trembled, much to my horror. I hadn't cried in public since I was a child, and this big lovable buffoon had just come along and made my eyes leak.

After weeks of working together, Zylo was used to me by now. He'd said more than once that he loved my *prickly* side. *"Even the sharpest cacti need a little love and affection, Revvy,"* he liked to say.

And even though only my family and Zylo had ever given me that kind of care, some stubborn part of me wanted to believe he was right.

I'd just climbed out of the shower, towel knotted at my waist, hair dripping down my chest, when my watch vibrated with an incoming call. I needed to get dressed, but I smiled and answered anyway, because I knew who it would be.

A few taps later, the image of Mum, Dad, and Grandma hovered over my wrist.

"There's our superstar!" Dad bellowed, voice echoing around the small room.

"You were tremendous, *zyli*," Mum gushed, resting her head on Dad's shoulder. "We watched it all from start to finish."

"Where's my grandbaby?"

Grandma shoved her way between my parents, leaning in way too close to the screen, so I could see up her nose. We were always telling her to wear her glasses, but she complained they made her look old. She was in her eighties, but the woman was still sprightly.

And if something made her look her age? It was going into the bin.

"Hi, Grandma," I chuckled while the three of them shoved at each other, trying to squeeze into view.

"Ma, you don't need to push!" my mother squawked, and my dad grunted as he got an elbow to the stomach.

"Let me in. I'm old," she snapped back. This time I laughed a little louder, because she was only "old" when it suited her.

"It's fine. I can see all of you."

"Are you all in one piece, *va'tari*?" Grandma asked.

I held up a hand, wiggling my fingers. "All fingers and toes accounted for."

"Good. You're small enough. You can't afford to lose any part of you." I opened my mouth to complain, but she'd already moved on, discussing the race like she hadn't just insulted me. "You were quick. I was thrilled when you pushed that silly Mercer boy off the track."

"Ma," Mum warned, but Grandma rolled her eyes and waved it off. Behind them, Dad tried to tamp down his smile.

"What? He thinks he can come after *my* grandchild and I won't say anything? At my age, I can hold a grudge till I die."

"Won't be long, then," Dad muttered. Mum gasped while Grandma pinched the tip of his ear, pulling him down so she could tell him off.

I cleared my throat, trying to get their attention before the call devolved into chaos. "I didn't push him off the track. The officials agreed it was just circumstantial."

Grandma smiled wryly, tapping the side of her nose. "Don't you worry, *va'tari*. Mum's the word."

"No, Grandma. I—"

A loud thump on the door cut off my protests. I was the last driver here, so I'd locked the door for a bit of privacy, just in case anyone was still lurking around. Maybe it was a cleaner needing to check the room before heading home.

I turned back to my family. "Listen—"

The thumping started again, a little louder this time. To avoid someone breaking the door down, I said a quick goodbye and promised to come over for dinner the next day, then I approached the door and flicked the lock.

The door flew open before I could reach the handle, sending me stumbling backwards onto a bench. I was grateful the towel was big enough to cover my dick, since I was suddenly sprawled across the wood.

And when I looked up, searching for the culprit, I met the narrowed eyes of Kai Mercer.

He loomed over me, chest heaving. His hair was damp, droplets falling onto the white T-shirt that hugged his chest. He'd showered somewhere, and for a second I wondered whether he really did have a private changing area.

"What the hell is your problem?" I snapped, gripping the towel tighter around my waist. Kai's gaze flicked down for a second before returning to mine, his hazel eyes burning with anger.

"*My* problem?" he bit out. "My problem, *rookie*, is that you cost me the goddamn race."

I pushed to my feet, but he was still taller, and I hated that he could literally look down at me.

"You DNF'd because your tyres melted, Mercer." The marks on my skin pulsed a deep merlot, illuminating his shirt. "Maybe next time don't ride them into the sun."

"You knew I'd go wide on that turn." He stepped closer. "You knew I'd oversteer."

"You're blaming *me* for your fuck-up?!" I scoffed at his audacity, my resulting laugh dark and void of humour. "Of course you are. God forbid the great Kai Mercer makes a mistake."

"You think you're so clever, don't you?" His voice dropped lower, darker, with the promise of . . . something. This time, when he took a step forward, I took one back before he could close the gap between us. "Just because you got one win—"

"*Earned* a win, you mean," I cut in, shoving his chest to stop his approach. But he didn't budge. "You're not the only one who knows how to drive, Mercer."

Kai continued to stalk me, like a predator eyeing its prey, while I retreated, attempting to put distance between us. Our respective movements continued until I felt the cool metal of the lockers against my back.

I had nowhere left to run. His jaw clenched, and this close, I could see the twitch of muscle under his skin. His hands flexed at his sides, as if he didn't trust them. Like they might do something unwise.

And then they did.

One slammed into the locker beside my head, making the door rattle. It took everything in me not to flinch, and I wondered if he'd dented it.

"Admit it. You just *love* to get under my skin," he growled, leaning in until our noses brushed.

When I tilted my head back, my lips brushed against Kai's, his stubble tickling my freshly washed skin. He was so close that when I exhaled, he could feel the heat from my breath. Feel the moisture on his lips. His tongue flicked out, slow and deliberate, as though trying to steal whatever trace of me lingered there.

"Maybe I like seeing you unravel, hotshot," I murmured.

The air between us was heavy and thick, like the static before a storm. My heart pounded against my ribs, hard enough to leave bruises under the skin. It was so loud in my ears, I worried Kai would hear it too. That he'd call me out on my nerves, on my false display of confidence. Each heaving breath forced his T-shirt to brush against my chest, and the contact made my nipples pebble.

We didn't speak, just stared, locked in a silent standoff. Our eyes were twin pools of fury, yet worlds apart.

One black, one hazel.

One alien, one human.

I thought Kai would push away and storm out. But he didn't.

He just murmured, "Fuck it."

And then his lips were on mine.

He crashed against me—angry, desperate, *filthy*. One hand gripped my damp hair, while the other wrapped around my throat. His grip wasn't so tight that it cut off my air, but it was enough for me to feel it. Enough to pull out a moan that Kai swallowed down as if it was meant for him.

His tongue invaded my mouth, battling with mine and invading every inch, as though he was desperate for a taste. The feel of them intertwined made me shiver, and I gripped his T-shirt in my fingers.

When Kai pulled away, I chased his lips for more. I knew I'd be mortified later, but for now, I didn't have to worry. He didn't go far, just kissed along my jaw, his teeth scraping over my skin. The sensation had heat flooding my system, and I could feel my cock thickening under the towel. He pressed his thigh between my legs, adding just the right amount of pressure, and I couldn't help but groan.

I'd jerked off countless times. I was a healthy young guy with a standard sex drive, after all.

But I'd never been touched by anyone other than myself, and the unfamiliar sensation lit me up from the inside—literally, if the way the markings on my skin flared pink was anything to go by. Stars, it was bright enough to drown out the ceiling lights.

"Still think you earned it, rookie?" Kai rasped against my throat, his lips dragging fire across my skin.

"Still mad you didn't?" I shot back.

He released my throat and hair in exchange for my hips, and my breath hitched as he ground against me, his cock just as hard as mine in his grey sweatpants. He held me tightly, thumbs pressing against my prominent hip bones. I'd have bruises if it weren't for the towel cushioning his fingers, and it worried me how much I wished he'd move it.

"You're infuriating," Kai snarled, low and hungry.

He kissed, licked, and nipped my skin, marking me as he trailed down towards my collarbone, then even lower. When his lips covered my nipple and sucked, I cried out, my hips bucking against his thigh. My tail thumped against the locker behind me, the rhythmic sound matching the racing beat of my heart.

"That's it," he whispered against the swollen nub. When I dared to look down, his eyes were on my face, dark with lust, the pupils blown out.

Then he straightened, hand gripping my jaw to tilt my head back. His other hand stayed firm on my hip, guiding my rhythm, urging me to keep grinding against him. His face hovered above mine, our lips a breath apart. I sucked in every one of his exhales, like his breath was the only air I needed. My mouth was slack, open, spilling desperate, broken sounds I didn't know I could make.

"You're like a comet." Kai brushed his nose against mine. "Dazzling from a distance, until you get close enough to burn. Hot enough to scar. And still... people look up and make a wish anyway."

"What was your wish?" I choked out.

Kai let out a low, wicked laugh, grazing his calloused thumb along my lip. "If I tell you, it might not come true."

A tingling feeling began at the base of my spine, and it felt like I was just waiting to fall. To fly. To dive into the great unknown, or submerge myself in a lake of heat that I wasn't sure I'd survive but desperately wanted to feel.

Then he stepped away, and I fucking whimpered.

Kai grabbed the edge of my towel and pulled. The material gave way, leaving me standing completely naked and vulnerable, my tail wrapped around my thigh. Before I could cover my leaking dick, he reached back and tugged off his shirt, distracting me.

There were miles of golden skin, sun-kissed and stretched over muscles that shifted like waves with every slight movement. His body should've made me feel less than, given my lean frame and lack of definition, but I was too captivated to care. My gaze roamed over him, greedy and unashamed, drinking in every line and curve, burning him into my memory.

This moment wasn't meant to be repeated. It couldn't. I knew that.

So I let myself have it.

Just for now, before my rational mind caught up and buried it deep in the vault where no one would ever find it.

"Like what you see, rookie?" he drawled, voice dripping with smug satisfaction. The kind that wasn't unwarranted.

If I looked like that underneath my clothes, I'd be insufferable too. He dragged his hand down his chest, over muscled pecs and a set of washboard abs that made my mouth water. If I thought I had control of my limbs, I might have raised my hand to check I wasn't drooling.

But I was too busy watching the way his fingers brushed through the treasure trail of sandy hair that led to the bulge in his sweatpants.

XL marks the spot.

"Fuck off, Mercer," I croaked.

My mouth was dry as he hooked his thumb under the fabric and pulled it down. He wasn't wearing any underwear, so the movement revealed the base of his cock, nestled in a trimmed patch of pubic hair. His other thumb joined in on the action, lowering his sweatpants enough for his thick, uncut cock to spring up, smacking him in the stomach with a wet thud. The action left a glistening patch of precum on his stomach, and I had to force myself not to drop to my knees and lick it clean.

Didn't stop my tongue from flicking over my lips, or the traitorous pulse of fuchsia from lighting up my skin. Kai noticed, of course, smirking as he stepped closer, like he already knew he had me right where he wanted.

His body pressed mine against the lockers, and the contrast between the cool metal and his warm skin was maddening. My palms rested on his pecs, and he was so close, I couldn't be sure where one of us ended and the other began. He thrust his hips forward, and our cocks made contact.

The firmness of another dick against mine was a new yet amazing sensation. My eyes rolled upwards as he began a slow grind, and I bit my lip, trying to contain the noises desperate to escape.

Kai cupped my chin, tugging my lip free with his thumb. "I want to hear what I do to you. The man you can't fucking stand," he mused. "Don't hold back, little comet."

I whined at the ridiculous pet name. Definitely *not* at the pleasure coursing through me when he picked up the pace. My fingers dug into his skin, nails leaving little crescent-shaped indents on the otherwise unblemished surface.

His hands went back to my hips, urging me to move with him. Our combined precum eased the friction, both of us leaking, as Kai leaned in and nibbled on my earlobe, his warm breath making goosebumps rise across my skin.

Noises poured out of my mouth like a waterfall, and when it became too much to handle, I thrust my hands into his light brown strands, pulling his face to mine.

Our lips moved as if in sync, tongues clashing. I bit his bottom lip, catching it with my fangs. The coppery tang of blood hit my tongue, and when I licked over the wound, sucking his lip between my own, Kai grunted and released a deep groan.

We moved faster and faster, our skin slick with sweat, cocks wet and hard. The fizzing in my spine started up again, building steadily.

But I needed...

"More," I moaned into Kai's mouth, tugging on his hair as I rutted against him like a bitch in heat.

One hand released my hip, slipping into the tight space between us. When his rough fingers wrapped around both of us, I let out a high-pitched mewl, hips jerking as he dragged his fist upwards.

"Fuck," he panted, dragging a thumb over my slit and swiping through the sticky mess.

The symphony of sex—breathy moans, ragged gasps, and the sharp rhythm of skin against skin—reverberated through the room like a hymn sung in reverence of our combined pleasure. I climbed higher and higher, rising to my toes as my climax crept closer.

My tail tightened around my thigh, threatening to cut off my circulation. It could've snapped my femur and I wouldn't have cared, because Kai clung to me, knocking my back against the lockers behind me with every thrust.

The end was in sight. My vision grew fuzzy around the edges as my orgasm came close to cresting. But it remained just beyond my reach, like I couldn't quite—

Kai's free hand curled around my back, fingers caressing the base of my tail.

And I fucking lost it.

I screamed, throat stinging as my cock erupted between us, covering Kai's fingers and slicking his prick. Stripes of it coated my stomach and his, matching masterpieces only we would ever see.

He continued to stroke us together, my hips spasming with the aftershocks, and just as I hit my limit of oversensitivity, Kai followed me over the edge with a roar.

The warmth of his release on my skin was almost calming, soothing the rapid pounding of my heart. My forehead rested against his shoulder, our heavy breaths the only sound.

For once, the marks on my skin were dark, with no light to be found thanks to my post-nut haze. My brain felt like it was stuffed with cotton wool, and I wasn't sure which way was up.

I closed my eyes and lifted my head, leaning it back against the lockers.

When Kai's hands left my body, I kept them closed, even as the distance between us increased and the air grew chilly.

Even when I heard a rustling sound, which I assumed was him putting on his T-shirt, I kept them closed. Even when I heard his footsteps approaching the door, pausing as though he wanted to speak, I kept them closed. Even at the sound of the door opening—which we'd forgotten to lock before mauling each other—I kept them closed.

It was only when I heard it shut that I dared to open them. And when I did, Kai was gone.

I was alone again.

It was only the evidence of our combined release, still warm and wet against my cooling skin, that made me believe the entire thing had happened at all.

Grabbing a fresh towel from the cubby, I stepped back into the showers. I let the warm water rinse away the evidence of a secret tryst between two people who could barely tolerate the sight of each other.

No matter how good it had been, no matter how badly my body ached for more . . .

It would *never* happen again.

BETTER THE ALIEN YOU KNOW

Rev

Hazel eyes had carved themselves into my thoughts ever since that night in the locker room.

It'd been a week, and still, every time I shut my eyes, I saw them—molten gold, seething with lust and rage, seared into the core of me like a brand. And worse, I could've sworn his scent lingered. Cardamom and leather, warm and sharp. Comforting but dangerous. A contradiction I couldn't seem to shake.

No matter how many times I showered or how hard I scrubbed my skin, I could still feel the heat of our joint release on my stomach, the rough pads of his fingers caressing my body, my face, my tail. I'd almost rubbed my dick raw over the last seven days with how much I'd wanked to the memory.

I'd even tried putting myself on a ban. Absolutely no touching my dick while Kai Mercer feasted on my brain like a flesh-eating bacteria.

I'd lasted two hours.

In the middle of the night, I'd woken up with a boner so solid it could have been used for structural support. It had its own heartbeat. Stars, I'm pretty sure it was trying to form a band and start a drum solo. All because my subconscious decided to stage a midnight rerun of *The Locker Room Incident: A Tale of Two Dicks*.

I'd compromised by rutting into my mattress like a teenager. Horny me figured if I didn't use my hand, then I hadn't violated the sacred terms of my no-touch treaty.

So tell me why, thirty minutes later, I was coming all over myself with a treacherous hand around my cock?

"Are we okay to continue?"

Shit. I blinked, and the fog of my mighty mistake cleared. I was back in a conference room, the bright lights and white walls feeling all too real after where my mind had gone. A journalist sat opposite me, separated by a wide wooden table.

Nina had locked in the interview at the start of the season—an exclusive with ThrottlePoint, the biggest name in motorsport media across the galaxy. I hadn't jumped at the idea, but she'd insisted it was the perfect way to bring attention to the Iskari people. To bring us one step closer to official recognition.

From day one, I'd told the team that was my goal, and Tavoris didn't hesitate. He'd promised they'd back me and then handed the reins to Nina to make it happen. If there was anyone you wanted in your corner for managing the press, it was her.

The journalist smiled, finger poised over her watch, ready to stop the recording if need be. I couldn't even remember her name. Was it Loren? Lorna? Lola?

"Sorry," I mumbled. "Was in my own world for a minute."

"No problem. I imagine you've had a bit of a busy season. It must be tiring, especially for a rookie."

I bobbed my head, grabbing the pitcher of water from the centre of the table. I filled my glass with the ice-cold liquid and downed it in one go. Then I settled back in my seat, giving Lottie a look that said I was ready.

Plot twist: I wasn't ready.

I shifted around in my seat, cringing with every loud creak it made. My posture felt unnatural, like I'd borrowed a body that didn't fit, and I was hyperaware of my body language.

Was I sitting like a normal person? How did *normal* people act? Was it weird to have my hands in my lap, or should I put them on the table? Was that sweat on my lip, or was it water? Was I breathing too loudly? Was I scowling like I usually did, or was it too aggressive?

The whole point of this was to talk about myself, but it was hard to talk about myself when I'd been nothing but a mystery for years. I'd spent most of my childhood trying not to be seen, blending into the background, praying no one looked closely enough to realise I didn't quite fit.

That wasn't the angle we were going for today.

"So," the journalist started. "Can you tell me a bit about your upbringing?"

I blew out a breath, staring blankly at Lorelei. How did I answer this without sounding like a sob story or a statistic? Louise kept smiling, unaware that I was short-circuiting over how utterly unequipped I was for basic human interaction.

"Well, uh . . ." I cleared my throat. "I um, lived with my parents and my grandma."

"Awesome," Lois replied, smile broadening. "My grandma lived with my family when I was a kid too."

I guessed we had something in common, at least.

"Yeah, it was pretty cramped."

Her eyes lit up with interest. "What do you mean?"

"Well—"

Before I could continue, a knock sounded at the conference room door. Without waiting for either of us to respond, it opened, and in walked the bane of my life.

Kai strolled in like he'd arrived straight from a fashion shoot. Camo cargo pants slung low on his hips, spotless designer trainers, a light-wash denim jacket, and a black T-shirt stretched across his chest like it had something to prove. His hair was its usual tousled mess, like he'd just rolled out of bed and raked a hand through it. Maybe he had. The mirrored aviators covering his eyes gave him that extra layer of untouchable cool, and I hated how easily he pulled it off.

Hated it even more when my brain stalled as he looked in my direction, my flushed face staring back at me in the lenses' reflections.

"Sorry," he replied, not sorry at all if his usual grin was any sign. "Am I interrupting something?"

"Yes," I snapped, at the same time Lorraine said, "No."

She glanced between Kai and me, confused and maybe a little uncomfortable. I didn't want to fuck up the interview any more than I already had, so I forced a very small, very fake smile onto my face.

"No," I said, forcing my jaw to unclench. "It's fine." Kai raised an eyebrow, but ever the professional, he didn't call me out in front of Lisa.

"It's my fault," she cut in. "I was running late this morning, and I forgot to call you to push our time back."

"It's all good," Kai replied like it was no big deal. "I can come back in a bit."

"Don't be daft. Just take a seat at the end." Leanne motioned to the empty chairs before turning back to me. "If that's alright with you, Rev? It might make you feel less nervous having someone else in the room. Someone you're well acquainted with."

I could've laughed at the accuracy of her statement. She didn't know just how well acquainted I was with Kai—specifically, his naked body.

But having Kai in the room wouldn't make me feel less nervous. Irritated, maybe.

"Aw, you feeling nervous, Revvy?" he drawled, voice syrupy sweet and dripping with condescension. "Interviews are easy. Just open your mouth and let it all spill out."

Were his words supposed to sound so filthy?

He sat down, slipping off his sunglasses with a practiced flick. It revealed the mischievous gleam in his eyes, and I had to bite down on my tongue. The fucker was teasing me, trying to rattle me.

"So, Rev," Lucy said, pulling my attention away from Kai. "You said your home was cramped?"

I took a deep breath, doing my best to ignore Kai when he turned his chair in my direction. How he sprawled out like a king on his throne, his right ankle resting on his left knee. The way one arm of his sunglasses rested against his plush lower lip, right beside the red mark left by my teeth.

"Yeah," I started, my voice rougher than before. "I grew up on Zyphar, and we lived in a two-bedroom apartment. My family still lives there; they just don't have me camped out on the sofa anymore."

"You didn't have your own room?" Lynette frowned. From the corner of my eye, I saw Kai sit up straighter, listening intently.

"We couldn't afford a three-bed, and landlords aren't lining up to rent to a family of Iskari. I guess they thought we'd go extinct before the end of the lease." I tried for humour, but it landed with a thud. The silence in the room was so heavy I could hear muffled conversations drifting up from the hotel lobby.

"That sounds . . ." Loretta started, trailing off.

"Rough," Kai finished. I couldn't discern the tone of his voice, but I also couldn't look his way to confirm.

I was scared of what I might find. I wasn't sure what would be worse—his eyes gleaming with amusement at my rocky childhood, or brimming with pity.

"I didn't have a difficult home life or anything, not really," I blurted. I didn't want them to think I was neglected. "My family worked as hard as they could, but it's difficult for the Iskari."

"Can you explain how?" Kai asked.

This time, I felt brave enough to look, and the earnest expression on his face surprised me. He wasn't being nosy, asking me to justify myself.

No, it sounded like he wanted to understand.

What was that about?

"Well, after the destruction of Iskanya—way before my time, obviously," I added with a dry huff of laughter, hoping to cut through the tension with a bit of levity. "Iskari numbers were lower than ever. They've climbed over time, but they're still low enough for us to be classed as critically endangered. I mean, I'd love to see us upgrade to just endangered, or even vulnerable, in my lifetime, but since we're spread so thin across the galaxy, some Iskari go their whole lives without meeting another who isn't part of their family."

"That's heartbreaking," Lily whispered, and I returned my gaze to hers.

"It is. But in a way, it's also incredible." I leaned back in my chair. "Let's put it this way. You're human, right?" I gestured to Lucinda.

"Yes."

"Could you imagine the possibility of never meeting another human who you're not related to?"

"Honestly," she started, eyes wide. "I couldn't."

"Exactly," I continued. "I don't think people understand how it feels to be so . . . isolated, especially when you're different from everyone else. How lonely it can feel when you don't have someone who can relate to you.

"Like during puberty, when your whole body lights up like a damn billboard, flaring with emotions you don't understand. There's no one around who looks like you, feels like you, or has any idea what it's like. Just your family, and it's way too awkward to ask them why your skin won't stop glowing because someone you have a crush on sat a little too close. So instead, you keep it inside. You pretend it's fine, hoping like hell it'll stop."

"Have you ever met another Iskari?" Lennon asked. "Someone who wasn't your family?"

"Once." Kai sucked in a breath. He knew who I was referring to. "Recently, in fact."

"Can you tell me about it?"

I smiled when I thought of Korvi. The joyful way his skin had pulsed in every colour of the rainbow when our team won. "It was during an event at Karting for Kids. I was just as surprised as anyone to see another Iskari there, so to have two of us in the same place who didn't know each other? That was some kind of miracle."

"Were they a volunteer?"

"Nah, one of the kids," I explained. "Probably the bravest kid I've ever met, to be honest."

Lucia's smile was soft, and when I chanced a glance in Kai's direction, it looked like he was remembering Korvi as fondly as I was.

"You should tell her about him," Kai said, voice tender.

"His name was Korvithan." I huffed out a laugh, wondering if he'd go wild at seeing his name mentioned in an interview. "He told me his friends called him Korvi, and I was lucky enough to be among that group."

"I loved that little dude," Kai said. "He thought you were cooler than me, though, so he's a poor judge of character."

This time, the laugh that escaped was fuller. Genuine. And when it did, I caught the slight widening of Kai's eyes, like he hadn't expected the sound from me.

I suppose I hadn't expected it either, not in his vicinity.

"Knowing he was part of Karting for Kids told me he was brave. My parents had offered to send me for years, throughout my childhood, but I never went. I think my fear stopped me."

"Fear?" Huh, seemed like Kai was taking over this interview, but from the interested look on Lolita's face, she didn't seem to mind.

"Yeah." I shrugged. "I didn't have any friends, and I ate my lunch in the bathrooms throughout my entire school career. Kids don't do well with anything 'different,' and Iskari history isn't a hot topic on the curriculum. I don't *blame* my peers for giving me a rough time. I think they just didn't understand. They probably still don't."

"That's no excuse for bullying, though," Kai snapped, a scowl twisting his features. There was heat there, but not the sexy kind. No, it was... protective. Like he wasn't angry *at* me.

He was angry *for* me.

And I didn't know what to do with that.

"No, it's not," I agreed. "That's why I'm doing this. Why I wanted to race in the Astro Space League. I want to help people understand, so that any other Iskari kids—like Korvi—can have a much easier time than I did."

"You want to help the Iskari as a whole?" Lara asked, and to be honest, I'd forgotten she was in the room.

"Yes." I scolded myself for forgetting why I was here, even if she'd just reminded me. This wasn't a chit-chat with Kai. This was a *professional* interview with... whatever her name was.

"We're no longer recognised as an independent species, and it has a real impact on our lives. We don't have the same rights. Like, my grandma's eighty, right? But she's not entitled to a pension, so she makes money by selling homemade herbal creams on Astrazon. It's not much, but it's enough for her to get by.

"My parents both work full time, but they're paid far less than everyone else. If employers don't have to pay them a minimum wage, they won't. My mum's a cleaner for a major supermarket chain on Zyphar, but I won't say where, and my dad works at a scrapyard. He's the one who got me into karting."

"Ooh!" Luna's eyes lit up. "Yes, I'm excited to hear how you got into motorsport."

"I suppose we got heavy there, didn't we?" I grimaced. "Sorry."

"Sometimes it's good to discuss the tougher stuff," Kai said. "It makes the rest of the story more important."

Hearing him say that threw me off, because I didn't expect it. I'd expected him to come in and take the piss—to mock me—but here he was telling me to share the good, the bad, and the ugly. He was listening to me, taking it in, and talking about what I'd said like he cared.

My parents cared, and that was great, but they were endlessly optimistic, always trying to see the brighter side.

Sometimes I just wanted someone to say, *"You're right, Rev. That is shit."*

With Kai . . . he gave me this *look*, and it just seemed like he got it. *Him*, of all people. Like he'd been through some "tougher stuff" of his own and it was okay to share. And for the first time in a while, I didn't feel like a freak, like no one would understand.

I didn't feel so alone.

And it felt weirdly validating.

It was then I realised I hadn't felt the nerves in a while. Not since Kai had entered the room. I was relaxed in my chair, and I wasn't fidgeting or focused on the volume of my breathing.

I felt *normal*.

It might not have been much to anyone else . . . to Kai. But to me? It was everything. And it made my chest feel a little lighter.

"My dad came home from work one day," I explained. "He walked in with this beat-up piece of metal, and my mum almost made him throw it straight back out again. But he was determined to show me.

"So he calls me over, and it's a rusty old go-kart, like the kids use before they graduate to proper vehicles. Six-year-old me was mesmerized; I'd never seen anything better. Since we lived in a high-rise downtown, I couldn't take it outside—can't exactly kart in a dodgy alley—so I used the hallway outside our apartment instead. And I swear I zoomed up and down there for hours after school."

"I'm sure the neighbours were pleased," Leighton chuckled, and I couldn't help but laugh along with her.

"They didn't mind. The maintenance guy was a whole other kettle of fish, though, especially after I wore the carpet down to shreds."

Kai barked out a laugh, and I snapped my head towards him. His smile was genuine, softer than his usual cocky grin, like he was remembering something from his own past, something we might've shared.

For a moment, it was like we weren't so different after all.

"When I turned eleven, my parents surprised me with a trip to a real karting track. They'd saved up for months, and I drove around that track for hours. Turns out, though, while I was driving my mum had a chat with the owner—this Vorkan called Alvoth. She offered to clean for them on weekends if I could come with her and drive around the track."

"Seriously?" Kai's expression was one of disbelief.

"Yep. I went with her every weekend until I turned eighteen. Alvoth was pretty cool. He helped me upgrade that rusty kart my dad brought home and showed me some vehicles he'd built. He raced in the underground circuits, and when I finished school, he paid me to help him build. I tried to give the money to my parents, since they'd done so much for me, but they told me to keep it, to put it towards my future career.

"I don't think my grandma was thrilled. I mean, I know she wasn't. Still isn't. She's a worrier, y'know?"

"That's grandmothers for you," Leslie giggled. "When I told mine I wanted to be a writer, she asked why I couldn't be a doctor instead."

"Right?" I let out a soft, amused exhale. "When she found out I was racing in the underground leagues, I swear she nearly cut my tail off. Actually threatened to at one point. But I think she's changed her tune these days, especially now I have a win under my belt."

I glanced at Kai from the corner of my eye, a smirk tugging at my lips. His expression was unreadable, lips pressed into a tight line, but I caught the flash of something in his eyes—maybe amusement, maybe something else.

Whatever it was, it made the air between us feel a little too charged, like there was more to this conversation than I'd intended.

"What was it like racing in the underground circuits?" he asked.

I raised my eyebrows, shocked he didn't know.

"You've never been?"

"Nah. Not sure it's my scene."

I scoffed. "I mean, they're more dangerous than the ASL. They're not regulated, and there's no medical shuttles on hand to patch up every little graze." I cocked my head, pretending to think about it. "Huh, I guess you're right. It isn't your scene."

This time it was Kai's turn to scoff. "I can handle *dangerous*, rookie."

"I don't think you can, Mercer."

"I drive alongside you, don't I?"

"Only when your tyres aren't melting."

"Or when you're not pushing me off the track."

"It was an accident," I argued. "The officials said—"

"You guys are hilarious together."

We both turned to Liz, who was looking at us with a wide smile, eyes glittering. Kai cleared his throat and sat back, making me realise we'd started leaning towards each other as we'd bickered. The marks on my hands had glowed red, just like they always did around Kai.

But as the colour faded, I caught a subtle hint of amethyst.

What the *fuck?*

I was twenty-four, and I'd never seen my skin glow that colour before.

"Sorry," I mumbled, settling back in my seat like a scolded child.

"No problem," Lotus said. "Just a few more questions, then I think you and I are done!"

I exhaled a sigh of relief. The interview hadn't gone as terribly as I'd thought. At least I hoped so. I'd find out when it was published and Nina either praised me or killed me.

Thankfully, the rest of the questions were a doddle. I explained how I hoped to help the Iskari get officially recognised again, my experience with Zenith

Nova, and my thoughts on the other drivers in the league. Kai almost fell off his seat when I admitted to Lilith that, despite everything, he was a decent driver.

"You might drive me up the wall, Mercer," I replied with an eye roll. "But I'd be a fool if I said you're not good at what you do."

Kai pressed a hand to his chest, the over-the-top expression of awe completely fake. "Aw, thanks, rookie. I'll turn you into a fan yet."

"There's a better chance of Iskari extinction," I deadpanned. Kai's responding chuckle was low and knowing. Like he didn't disagree, but he'd make it happen anyway.

"Well, I have everything I need," Lex announced, tapping her watch to turn off the recording software. She rounded the table and held out her hand to me with a big smile. "It was great to meet you, Rev."

I shook her hand. "You too . . ." Shit. What the *fuck* was her name?

"Steph." She smirked.

Of course, the marks on my skin chose that exact moment to flicker bright orange with embarrassment, and my ears twitched. I wanted the ground to open up and swallow me whole.

Steph turned to Kai, who was hiding behind his hand, but his grin was too wide to be concealed. "Do you mind if I take ten to grab a drink and a sandwich?"

"Sure."

Then she left, and it was just the two of us.

Alone.

"I—"

"That was a good interview," Kai said.

I searched his face for any evidence that he might be making fun, but I found none. He seemed sincere, and not for the first time in the last hour, Kai had thrown me off-kilter.

"Thanks."

"I'd like to see the underground circuits sometime."

"So go." I frowned. "You don't need an invitation, and the details are easy to find online."

He shrugged, glancing down and fiddling with a loose thread on his jacket. "I know. I just thought it'd be more fun to go with an expert."

"I don't think there's such a thing as an expert in the—"

"Look, will you go with me?" Kai stared at me, his expression earnest and somewhat . . . desperate.

But there was something else.

"Are you nervous, Kai?" I teased.

"What?! No!" he spluttered. "Why would I be nervous?" With all the times he'd thrown me off balance today, I couldn't help but enjoy seeing *him* flustered for once.

"It's okay if you are."

"I'm not," he bit out.

I heaved a great sigh, as if it were a hardship. "I guess I'll take you."

To be honest, a small part of me was excited to show him the underground circuit. Show him where I'd come from, the place I'd made a name for myself.

"When?" Kai perked up.

If he were a dog, he'd have a fluffy tail that would be thumping. Like the half-naked werewolves I read about in my spare time.

"Not sure," I replied, like I wasn't mentally scrolling through the schedule I'd already seen online. I turned to the door and pulled it open. "Text me and I'll let you know."

I was halfway down the hallway, heading for the lobby, when he left the room and yelled after me.

"I haven't got your number!"

"Guess you'll have to find it, hotshot," I called over my shoulder as I walked, a smirk pulling at my lips.

And I had a weird sense of faith that he would. Because if anyone could annoy someone into bypassing data protection laws, it would be Kai Mercer.

The silence that followed was thick with something unspoken, but I still didn't look back. Yet the sound of his voice echoed in my ears.

"You're impossible, rookie!"

I couldn't help the laugh that escaped me.

BURNING THE MIDNIGHT RUBBER

Kai

I found his number.

I bet the little shit doubted me, but I fucking found it. Well, Savannah found it for me, but I'd set the wheels in motion.

As soon as I'd finished my interview, I'd called Savannah and used my best puppy-dog eyes. Of course they hadn't worked, because she's immune to my charms, and I'd had to resort to negotiation. I'd agreed to represent Nexus at one charity marathon in the off-season, but it'd be worth it to wipe the smug smile off the rookie's face.

At least I'd thought so, until Jax rained on my parade.

"Why didn't you ask Zylo?" he said after I explained Savannah's conditions during a phone call.

I'd neglected to mention what had happened in the locker room. As far as Jax knew, I was just looking for another way to wind Rev up. And while my bank of dirty fantasies had evolved, I would always take any opportunity to jerk his chain—and his cock, apparently.

"Why would I ask Zylo?"

"Because he'd have Rev's number, and then you wouldn't be running a marathon dressed like Sparx."

Sparx was the Nexus mascot: a humanoid fireball with bulging eyes and a manic grin. Apparently, Savannah would milk my desperation for all it was worth, and her terms included running the marathon in a ridiculous full-body suit.

I was already dreading the chafing.

I shook my head. "He wouldn't just hand over his teammate's number."

"Mate, Zylo lives in sunshine and rainbow land. He's dying for the drivers to be a big circle of besties. He'd have handed it over in a heartbeat, and because he's so nice, even Rev wouldn't be mad about it."

The idea hadn't crossed my mind, but now that I thought about it, the solution was obvious.

Fuck.

Damn you, Savannah, you beautiful wicked witch.

"Have fun training for your marathon," he teased before hanging up.

It took everything in me not to call Savannah back and have a tantrum. But I was a man of integrity, so I didn't. I'd have my tantrum in private instead.

After lamenting my life choices, I used the number I was sure had been secured by violating at least one privacy law.

> **Kai**
> When are you taking me to this mysterious underground race circuit of yours?

> **Rookie**
> Who's this?

> **Kai**
> Oh, so it was just pillow talk.

Kai: Also, you know who it is.

Rookie: Bold of you to assume there were pillows involved, Mercer.

Kai: Locker room talk, then. Better?

Rookie: Fuck off.

Kai: Still waiting on a date, rookie.

Rookie: You'll be waiting a long-ass time.

Kai: Just tell me when!

Rookie: Are you always this impatient, or are you that desperate to spend time with me?

Kai: Can't help it. You glow red, and I lose all sense of dignity.

Kai: So? When?

Rookie: Tomorrow, 11 p.m. Meeting point is the old Nebula Goods shuttle park, just off the I-9 on Solveth.

I frowned. Solveth was two planets over from Zyphar. Compact and densely populated, its single megacity stretched across most of the surface, packed with high-rise towers, multi-tiered transport grids, and a nightlife powered by more neon than sense. It was loud, fast, and always switched on. A suitable location for an underground race, I supposed.

But why were we meeting at an abandoned supermarket?

Ten years ago, the chain went bust, and the building had remained abandoned ever since. For whatever reason, no one had purchased the land and upgraded it to fit Solveth's aesthetic, so I couldn't fathom why he wanted to meet there.

Was he luring me there to commit murder? *My* murder?

Nah, he wasn't that kind of guy . . . right?

> Kai
> Are you planning to kill me?

> Rookie
> It wasn't on my bingo card this week. Maybe next. Why?

> Kai
> No reason.

> Rookie
> You're so fucking weird, Mercer.

Charming.

At least I could sleep better knowing he wasn't plotting my demise. And despite the possibility of being murdered in the future, I still cracked a smile.

The rookie had agreed to see me . . . off the track . . . just the two of us.

Why was I so happy about it?

I was surprised when the SpaceNav announced my arrival. It wasn't the abandoned Nebula Goods I'd expected. The building was old and dilapidated, yet the shuttle park overflowed with people.

I nabbed an empty parking spot towards the back of the lot, and a crowd moving like a raging river immediately engulfed me. Excitement crackled in the air, sharp and electric, raising the hairs on my arms. People recognised me, calling out my name, so I waved and smiled while being jostled by the crowd.

But while it was chaos, we seemed to move towards something.

I knew when we'd reached our destination—right at the edge of the car park, by the exit to the highway. The people in front of me shifted, splitting off to gather around a lineup of vehicles. They weren't the kind you'd see cruising down a city street, and my heart kicked up a gear just looking at them.

Unlike racing vehicles in the ASL, drivers constructed these for short-term speed over longevity. They came in all shapes and sizes, each one rough around the edges but crafted with purpose. There was a handmade quality to them, which only made them more impressive—raw, personal, like each one had a story under the hood.

The drivers were different too, especially their outfits. While we wore thick, well-fitted, flame-retardant suits in the ASL, here, most were wearing T-shirts, jeans, and chunky leather boots. The professional in me worried how they'd fare in a crash, but I had to remember, this *wasn't* the ASL. And these drivers weren't professionals.

Though . . . one of them was.

Scanning the lineup of vehicles, I spotted none other than Rev, standing beside an impressive looking vehicle. He'd dressed simply—just a plain black jumpsuit that reminded me of my early years at the karting tracks. And based on the "Kosmic Karting" logo on his back, I realised it was a karting suit.

At least it would offer more protection than standard casual wear.

He was chatting with an enormous Vorkan, arm curled around a battered helmet tucked against his side. Like the suit, it was plain black, but on closer inspection I noticed hand-drawn veins of lightning etched across the surface, mirroring the markings on Rev's skin, shimmering like prisms under the floodlights.

I walked over, and Rev ended his conversation with the Vorkan.

"Mercer," he said with an up nod. The galaxies in his eyes sparkled, like they often did before a race. He was excited, and that reminded me . . .

"Where's the track, rookie? Can't imagine you're doing fifty laps around the shuttle park?"

Rev rolled his eyes, and his friend chuckled, a rich sound that rumbled through my chest like thunder.

"One, it's only ten laps," the stranger said, smile full of sharp teeth, similar to a shark. "And two, you've already driven on it."

I must've looked confused, because he jerked his chin towards the highway.

"You can't be serious?"

"As a heart attack," he replied with a casual shrug. "The highways make for some great racing. Better than the sewers, am I right?"

Rev hummed. "Definitely smells better."

I raised my hands in surrender. "I can't tell if you're taking the piss right now."

His friend laughed again, and Rev sighed as if I was testing his patience. I noticed he did that a lot around me.

"This isn't the ASL, Mercer. We take what we can get," he countered, chin lifting just slightly. "The race starts late because the I-9's dead this time of night. Everyone's either at home or partying in the city. We've got the road to ourselves for a few hours."

"And it's worth it for the unobstructed view of Solveth's neon skyline," the Vorkan mused, gaze fixed on the glowing cityscape.

"Didn't expect you to be racing today," I commented, nodding at Rev's helmet.

His friend dropped a heavy hand on his slim shoulder, and Rev grunted on impact. I winced in sympathy. Vorkans were stronger than most, and other species looked like weaklings in comparison. A heavy gust of wind could easily sweep Rev away.

"Course he is. Might be all fancy now, rubbing shoulders with the pros," they said, gently conking Rev on the top of his head with a fat fist. "But our little Supersonic is still the fastest thing to come out of this crew."

"Supersonic, huh?" I smirked, and the markings on Rev's skin glowed burnt orange.

I could've made fun, because it was funny as fuck when he got embarrassed, but I didn't want him to regret bringing me here. Seeing it firsthand, experiencing the atmosphere, I wanted to come again if he'd let me. So as he shuffled from foot to foot, obviously feeling awkward, I turned back to the Vorkan.

"I'm Kai, by the way."

"I know who you are, Kai Mercer." He took my proffered hand, giving it a firm shake that almost pulled my shoulder from the socket. But I felt how he tensed, like he was holding back. My curiosity was piqued; I wanted to see what he was truly capable of. "I'm Alvoth, but everyone calls me Al."

Alvoth.

Rev had mentioned him during his interview, the stories a mixture of heartwarming and heartbreaking. This was the man who'd taken the rookie under his wing, given him an outlet while his mum worked for free on the weekends.

In my periphery, I saw Rev worrying his bottom lip, star-filled eyes watching me. He said nothing, but I could hear his unspoken words.

Please don't judge me.
Please don't pity *me.*

I wanted to dive in with questions about their relationship, about Rev's past. What was Rev like as a child? Had he been as closed off then as he was now? Was he a natural talent, or were his skills learned from hours on the track?

But Al wasn't the person to ask, so I kept them to myself.

I'd felt how much it had cost Rev to open up during his interview, especially while I was in the room. He'd meticulously built his take-no-shit attitude, each barb and glare a brick in the fortress designed to keep people out.

So letting his guard down, revealing so much of himself . . . it didn't seem to come naturally. I imagined he'd felt untethered afterwards. Vulnerable. And I didn't want him to feel like that again, not because of me.

Being here must have helped him feel like himself again. More in control. It was something familiar, rooted in who he was, and I realised how *monumental* it was that he'd invited me.

I'd asked him to bring me along, but he could've said no—told me to fuck off into the nearest sun like he usually would—and yet he hadn't. He'd told me I could come, shared the correct details, without knowing how I might react to it all. He'd lowered his guard just enough to let me in.

Despite everything between us, Rev had allowed his two worlds to collide with no safety net.

He'd been adamant that Korvi was brave for putting himself out there. For doing what the rookie hadn't been able to do in the past. But right now?

I thought Rev was pretty fucking brave too.

Given our usual state of play, I wasn't sure how to feel about that.

The tension in Rev's shoulders eased when I grinned at Al. "Great to meet you, mate." I gestured to the vehicle behind him. "You build that?"

It looked similar to the standard X-9 Stratos we drove in the ASL, but there were a few interesting additions.

"I sure did." Al circled the vehicle and started pointing out the features. "Added some mag-thrust boosters for an extra surge on the straightaways, *and* it uses a dual-ion fuel mix."

"Isn't that dangerous?" I asked, brow furrowed. "It has a major burnout risk."

"High risk, high reward, my man," he laughed. "You've gotta be careful. Too much can overheat the engine quickly, but used at the right time, the burst of speed is *insane*." Al nudged Rev, whose lips curled up in a smirk. "How do you think this one got his nickname?"

"So this is where you inherited your death wish," I remarked. "Duly noted."

"You'd cream your pants if you could use it in the league, Mercer." He tapped Al's chest with his knuckles. "Tell him about the rest."

"Rev's is pretty similar." Al pointed at a second vehicle. "Same fuel mix, similar thrusters, but it has chameleon paint, which reacts to the surroundings. It can mind-fuck the competition when you disappear from behind and reappear up ahead." He waved me closer, pointing to the cockpit. "The best part is the Holo-HUD with a RaceNet tap-in—"

"What's RaceNet?"

"Live analytics for the race, only accessible by the event organisers. It's like what your engineers see, I guess, because you can view everyone's positions and vehicle conditions . . . but only if you can hack your way into it." He straightened up and folded his thick arms over his chest. "Very black market, but not against the rules. In the underground, if you've got the means to get it, you can have it."

"That doesn't seem fair."

"It's an illegal underground racing league." Al cackled, like I'd told the galaxy's dumbest joke. "Fairness isn't part of the rule book."

"Touché." I looked back at the vehicles. "You built both of these beasts?"

He bumped his hip against the first vehicle. "Nah, this baby's mine. But this one . . ." He laid a hand almost reverently on the rear wing of the second. "This one's all him."

I looked at Rev. His ears twitched, skin glittering with a mixture of orange and yellow. He kept his eyes fixed on the floor, as though the concrete was more interesting than our conversation.

"You built this?"

His head snapped up and he grew defensive. "You don't have to sound so surprised."

It stung that his first thought was that I'd rip it apart. That I'd zero in on the flaws and dismiss the rest. But thinking back to how I'd treated him early on—and even recently—I couldn't say he was wrong to expect it.

"Rookie, it's—"

"I don't want to hear it, Mercer."

"Wait, hang on—"

"*No.*"

"Will you let me sp—"

"Don't say anythi—"

"It's fucking brilliant, you asshole!" My yell cut through the ambient noise, loud enough that a few heads turned our way.

I didn't care, though, because Rev had his dark eyes fixed on mine.

"What?"

"It's brilliant," I said, softer this time. "I'm impressed."

"You're . . . impressed?"

"You don't have to sound so surprised," I teased, repeating his words back to him.

His mouth opened, then closed, then opened, and then closed again. Maybe I'd broken him. Either that, or he was doing a wonderful impression of a fish.

"You know," I drawled, trying to get us back to normal—or at least somewhere on the spectrum. "I said I enjoyed seeing you speechless, but I didn't think it'd happen without a single innuendo involved."

He made a strangled noise, somewhere between a scoff and a cough. "Al helped with the frame and the paint," he squeaked. Before tacking on quickly, "Not that I need your approval or anything."

Al looked between Rev and me with an amused smile, eyebrows up to his hairline. "You racing as well, Kai? Slumming it with the petrol heads?"

He was teasing me, but the idea that I was "slumming it" made me uncomfortable. It only took one glance at the vehicles here to see the hard work and passion that each driver put in.

The ASL had the money, the skill, and the tech to build vehicles that were fast as fuck, but I couldn't tell you who'd built mine. I couldn't imagine how it felt to create your dream vehicle from scratch—no rules, no red tape, just adding whatever parts you could get your hands on, strategy be damned.

That's why I was so dazzled by Rev's creation. Even if Al had helped, that didn't make it any less impressive. I wasn't such a shithead that I couldn't appreciate actual skill. Rev had been hanging around Al since he was eleven. He was twenty-four now, which meant he'd had plenty of time to hone his craft. If I tried to build something like that, it'd fall apart before it even left the garage.

He was a skilful driver, and even when I'd disliked him, I couldn't deny the fact. But what gave him an edge was that he didn't just race the machine; he understood it to its core. And based on the telltale twitch in my jeans, I was getting a semi.

I couldn't tell if it was Rev's skill on the track, or the mental image of him in nothing but a tool belt, but something was setting me off.

"Nah," I croaked in response to Al's question. "I don't have a vehicle."

"Mercer wouldn't last five seconds in the underground chaos." Rev's smile was sly. "He's a big fan of rules and structure."

"If I had a vehicle as cool as yours, I'd run rings around you, Revvy."

"It's dangerous out there, Mercer. *Reckless.*"

I scoffed. "I can be reckless."

"Please." Rev's answering chuckle was dark and wicked. "You wouldn't know reckless if it bit you on the ass, mister three-time galactic champ."

"Why don't you bite me, and we'll see?" I grinned, narrowing my eyes. "On the ass this time, since you've mauled my lip already."

"You're such a child." He glanced at Al to see if he'd heard, and based on the smile he was failing to stifle, he had.

"You can use my vehicle, Kai."

We turned to Al in perfect sync.

"I'm not dressed for it." I plucked at the collar of my white T-shirt. Based on what others were wearing, it seemed like a weak excuse, and of course, Rev homed in on it.

"What's the matter, hotshot? Scared you won't be able to 'run rings' around me like you promised?" He looked far too pleased with himself, and I couldn't have that.

I lifted my chin in defiance, turning back to Al. "I hope you've got a smaller jumpsuit and helmet with you. If you hand me yours, I'll disappear like a magic trick."

He laughed and slapped me on the shoulder. "I've got a few in my shuttle. I'll go grab 'em."

Rev put a hand on Al's enormous arm.

"Are you sure about this?" he muttered, just loud enough for me to hear. "You were excited about this race."

"And I'll be just as excited for the next one." He tapped beneath Rev's chin with his knuckle—a soft, almost fond gesture. "Now wait here while I grab the gear, and try not to kill your boy while I'm gone."

Then he disappeared into the crowd, missing the way Rev grumbled, "He's not my boy."

But I heard it.

The devil on my shoulder didn't like it, so I shook *that* off before it could sink in. Rev was right. We weren't each other's anything. Just two rivals who had seen each other's dicks.

And touched them.

Well, I'd touched Rev's.

And his tail.

Rev turned away from the crowd, and I caught the moment his mask slipped into place, like shutters slamming down behind his eyes. He'd reverted back to the character he usually played. One I recognised all too well.

When did I start hating it?

Was it because I'd had a peek at what hid beneath? The *real* Rev. The one buried under so many layers of indifference. He'd proven he could be expressive, even open, but only if he let it happen.

I'd been given a tease in the locker room when his walls had cracked. Watched his eyes transform from calm to chaos as he writhed in pleasure, moaning up a storm, completely unfiltered. Witnessed him *feel* for the first time.

Something towards me.

Something that wasn't annoyance or disdain.

And perhaps the mask was growing too small. Or maybe it wasn't as opaque as it used to be. Despite his lack of expression, the stars in his eyes shimmered, galaxies swirling in anticipation. Because right here, Rev wasn't the rookie. He wasn't an outsider.

Instead, he was a household name—someone impressive—and he was in his element. If his tail wasn't tucked into his jumpsuit, I imagined it'd be lashing back and forth with excitement.

Rev turned to me and puffed out his chest, growing by an inch yet still barely reaching my chin. "Ready to lose, Mercer?"

He was cocky, arrogant, and so fucking sure of himself.

To my surprise, I found it sexy.

"Those be fightin' words, rookie."

"I think you'll find *you're* the rookie today, rookie."

A surprised laugh fell from my lips. I couldn't even argue, because he was right. This was his turf, and I was the newcomer. Our roles had flipped, and he wore the advantage like a second skin.

Here we stood, eye to eye, sizing each other up like we had most weekends this season.

Familiar, but different.

And when the ghost of a smile tugged at his lips?

Yeah . . . that might have felt better than any race win.

DON'T STOP ME NOW – I'M ON POLE

Rev

Al had come through with a helmet and suit for Kai. It didn't drown him, but it might've been a bit too small. My lizard brain wasn't complaining about the way it cupped his ass and stretched across his chest, though there was a gap of a few inches between the cuffs on the legs and his trainers.

If you ignored his ankles peeking out, Kai looked like a walking wet dream.

I could see why people drooled over his photoshoots in Galactic Sports Weekly.

I'd taken a peek at his InSTARgram, not that I'd ever admit it. His feed was a mixture of promo pics for race weekends, candid shots from his travels, and selfies with his friends. The comments were the real entertainment, though, each post filled with simpering men, women, and enbies.

I'd laughed at the constant requests for him to father someone's children, but the flare of jealousy that followed his flirty replies to models and minor celebrities?

That was new.

Unprecedented.

"Last chance to back out, *rookie*."

Kai rolled his eyes before placing the borrowed helmet on his head, visor open. "You've called me rookie four times in the last few minutes. No need to keep reminding me who the pro is today, *hotshot*."

His use of a nickname I only reserved for mocking him made me shiver. I put it down to the anticipation of racing in an environment I knew so well. Not because I liked it or anything . . .

I set my helmet on my head and lifted the visor.

"Just keeping you in check, rookie." Oops, that was number five. "Just making sure you remember who's number one."

Kai glared, but there was no heat behind it, only a playfulness I saw from Jax at the paddock. I'd never been on the receiving end of that attitude before, and this novel exchange with Kai threatened to throw me off balance.

So I reached up and snapped his visor shut, knocking the side of his helmet with my fist. The gesture was light and teasing—not something I generally was, and definitely not with Kai.

"Good luck, rookie."

Kai's head dropped back onto his shoulders, and he groaned towards the sky. "Stars help me, I've created a monster."

The laugh that burst out of me was sudden and unfiltered. Somewhere between a giggle and a squawk, high-pitched and mortifying.

Kai straightened, startled by the noise.

And honestly? So was I.

I couldn't see his eyes, but I could feel them on my face, my skin tingling under their attention.

"Yeah," he replied, voice deeper than before. "You too, Revvy."

Again, a nickname reserved for teasing, but instead of bristling, I shivered. Because the soft, almost reverent tone made this ball of . . . *something* burst to life in my chest.

At the edge of my vision, the marks on my hands glowed, unhidden by my gloves. Amethyst. That one colour I'd never seen before. I raised a hand to my face, trying to get a closer look at the colour that left me so confused. Maybe even concerned.

Was I broken? Was there something wrong with me?

I couldn't dwell on whether I was dying, because Kai placed a hand on my shoulder, and the heat from his palm seeped through the fabric of my racing suit, spreading to all my extremities. When he *squeezed*, I had to fight like hell to contain the whimper that wanted to break free.

I was grateful when he said nothing and just walked past me towards Al, who waited next to his vehicle—Kai's vehicle, just for tonight.

He was starting behind me, in second position.

The underground circuit differed from the ASL, but not only because it was illegal. The lack of a full weekend for practice and qualifying led us to base starting positions on past-race stats. I hadn't rejoined the circuit since I'd signed with Zenith, not wanting to bring negative attention to my new team, but even after months away, my numbers were miles ahead of everyone else, so I'd kept my position at the front.

So similar to Kai, yet still so different.

Al's stats weren't far off mine, and since it was *Kai Mercer* driving in his place, the organisers agreed to let him keep his spot. The idea of corrupting the ASL's golden boy with an illegal street race probably thrilled them. And once the ASL fans found out, they'd only fall harder for him.

Nothing like a bit of rebellion to give a poster boy some edge.

If the books I read were anything to go by, everyone loved a bad boy.

I climbed inside and powered up the vehicle. The engine thrummed, and the Holo-HUD lit up with RaceNet's interface. At the push of a button, the thrusters began warming up to prepare for lights out. Al and I had filled the separate tanks with standard fuel and the dual-ion mix in the shuttle park, and there were no red lights on the dash to signify any problems.

In my wing mirror, I saw the top of Kai's borrowed helmet. He sat in Al's vehicle, and the big guy loomed over him, pointing out the different buttons and switches. I hoped Kai took it in, because I'd hate to see him blow up the engine with a fuel-boost overload if he mixed it up with the thrusters.

At the start of the season, it wouldn't have bothered me—even a few weeks ago, I might've felt the same—but something had changed after Kai barged into my interview. An understanding had formed between us. Some kind of truce.

But we were still rivals, even if we had seen each other come, and our competitive fire wouldn't fade; we were both too stubborn for that.

Maybe we could keep the fights to insults and barbs, without trying to kill each other—though I was sure I'd always have some urge to kill him; he was annoying as fuck on the best day. But at some point, the homicidal urges had eased, and I couldn't decide if that was growth or cause for concern.

Still, there wasn't an "us."

Sure, he'd been the first to touch me. Had made me come harder than ever. But that didn't flip my whole opinion of him.

He was still Kai. Still annoying. Yet somehow, I found him a little easier to tolerate.

"You good, sonic?"

I jumped at least a foot out of my seat, and I realised I hadn't heard Al approach. I'd been busy staring into the middle distance, thinking about the way Kai had touched my tail.

"Yep, all good," I squeaked. Then I cleared my throat and repeated it, forcing my voice into an octave deeper than usual. "All good."

"You've got this, kid." He thumped me on the back so hard I could've sworn I felt my heart get poked by a rib.

I nodded, and Al melted into the crowd of spectators dotted along the edge of the highway.

"Ready for this, hotshot?"

Kai's voice came over the radio unexpectedly, and I jumped out of my skin for the second time in a matter of minutes. I'd forgotten that Al and I had connected our vehicle's comms, using a specific frequency to talk with no one overhearing. Kai wouldn't have known, so Al had must have shown him to fuck with me.

I sighed. "Get off the comms, Mercer."

He cackled but said nothing more. A drone hovered above the starting line. Attached to the base were five red light bulbs, hanging from thin cables that swayed in the wind. It was a crude impersonation of the lights used in an ASL race, but I watched them just as closely.

My breathing slowed as each bulb illuminated.

One . . .

Two . . .

"See you at the end, Revvy," Kai whispered.

Three . . .

Four . . .

"Good luck, Kai," I breathed, just as the final bulb shone.

Then they darkened.

Engines roared. The crowd cheered. And we were off.

I surged ahead, blasting a quick burst of dual-ion fuel to pull the gap. Only Kai stuck close, tucked into my slipstream, watching every move. Neither of us knew the track, but I'd raced before in a handbuilt rig. Some drivers raced every week, so I knew who to watch if they came too close.

"Nice launch, little comet," Kai remarked.

Hearing the name he'd only ever used once—voice rough as he'd breathed it in my ear, the damp heat of his firm, sweaty body pressed against mine—almost made me swerve off the road.

And that tiny fuck-up was all Kai needed. Right before the highway exit, the one where we'd loop back for the next lap, he sped past me.

"See ya later, alligator."

I huffed down the mic in my helmet. "Watch your thrusters, starboy. They're looking a little hot."

I passed him on lap two when he locked up a turn. Like at Horizon Rings all those weeks ago, it was the two of us trading first and second. The rest were so far back it felt like another private race.

On lap three, Kai pulled up beside me, inches from my side pod. Our wing mirrors nearly kissed at two hundred miles per hour. I glanced over, picturing that cheeky grin under his helmet. It made me want to return the favour.

"Flirting on the straight? Risky move, Mercer."

"Call it foreplay," he retorted, laughing as I used my booster to pull ahead.

I couldn't respond because my mouth was dry, and I regretted not putting a drinks system in.

A few laps later, Kai caught up again.

I didn't hit the booster this time. I stayed beside him. He waved, and I flipped him off. One hand left his wheel and tapped his helmet where his mouth would be. Then he flicked it towards me in an over-the-top gesture. It took me a second to realise he was blowing me a kiss.

What a knob.

Wheel to wheel, I forced my focus back to the asphalt as we hit my favourite stretch. It was a long service tunnel lined with glowing billboards, and they pulsed with animations—roaring solar flares, glittering meteor showers, and imploding supernovas.

Kai and I tore through the neon glare, perfectly matched, neither willing to pull ahead. Light ricocheted off our panels, turning both vehicles into twin streaks of colour, like two shooting stars knifing through an artificial cosmos.

"Something, isn't it?" I breathed, soaking in the wash of cosmic light.

"Yeah," Kai answered, his voice thick. "It is."

I risked another glance his way, only to find he wasn't watching the tunnel at all.

He was watching me.

"Eyes forward, rookie," I said, letting the slightest grin slip.

Then I pressed on the accelerator, leaving Kai as nothing more than a flicker in my wing mirror.

For several laps we kept to the rhythm, swapping places, neither giving an inch. Then, on lap six, Kai flicked the switch for the dual-ion fuel mix. I focused on the distant glow of Solveth, its lights shimmering like a jewel against the endless black of space.

A low rumble behind me shattered the calm, growing louder with every second. Before I could react, Kai blasted past, a blur of speed and fury, his engine's roar crashing through the silence like thunder following lightning.

"Holy fuck!" Kai shouted over the comms. "This is insane!"

He sounded like a kid on his first hyper coaster at the theme park—pure, unfiltered exhilaration. A few days ago, I might have found it irritating. Might have rolled my eyes and flicked an insult his way.

But tonight, after everything that had shifted between us, I realised it came down to one thing.

Jealousy.

I envied how he owned the world, the golden boy of the Astro Space League. The guy who melted crowds with a grin and a cocky wink.

No walls. No fear. Just Kai.

Always at the centre of everything.

The complete opposite of me.

His excitement was contagious. It spun around me like a whirlpool, tugging harder with every mile. Something inside me whispered, begging me to stop fighting the pull. To let myself sink into the bright current of Kai's joy.

And with no one else to witness it but Kai, I gave in.

I let myself laugh, loud and free.

It flowed from some place deep inside, as though Kai had played the right notes and coaxed it straight from my core. And when he joined in, his laughter threaded through mine, turning it into a melody only the two of us seemed to know.

"I like your laugh, rookie," he mused, and I felt my cheeks heat under my helmet. "You should let it out more."

I didn't know how to respond, so I defaulted to deflection. "Careful, Mercer. You're the rookie tonight, remember?"

"Whatever you say, hotshot." His voice was so smug, I could almost hear the wink. But as I pulled closer, I noticed his exhaust was smoking, and my heart climbed into my throat.

"Kai, you need to ease off the fuel mix," I warned.

"Are you trying to trick me, little comet? Playing dirty just to get ahead?"

He could joke, but this was dangerous. This was what Al had warned him about, and why it wasn't used in the ASL. Kai was aware of the dangers, but was so captivated by the boost of speed, he'd forgotten the risks.

If he wasn't careful, he wouldn't be alive to claim the reward.

"I'm serious, Kai," I snapped, accelerating until we were wheel to wheel. "Your exhaust is smoking. If you keep going, the engine will explode."

"Wait, what?" He turned his head to glance in the wing mirror, spotting the dark cloud in his wake. "Shit. Fuck!"

"Relax—"

"What do I do?"

There was genuine panic in his voice, something I'd never heard from Kai. He was a ball of bulletproof optimism, the human equivalent of my parents' relentless cheer. Nothing had ever seemed to rattle him.

Until now.

"Fuck, I need to pull over."

His speed bled off as fear muscled its way past the adrenaline. The reckless driver who'd barrelled past me thanks to an illegal fuel mix was gone, replaced by someone desperate for something solid, predictable, safe.

"Kai!" I barked. "You can keep going."

"I can't. The car will blow!"

"Mercer," I said, trying to stay calm. He wouldn't respond to my anger. Would think I was being combative rather than trying to help. "Switch back to your main fuel tank and press the button for 'water.' It'll let some coolant into your engine and lower the temperature."

"No way, I'm—"

"*Kai*," I urged. "Trust me."

I heard him exhale over the radio, and I wondered if he'd do as I said. If he'd trust me like I asked. I hadn't done anything to earn it, but I didn't want to see Kai leave the race.

Holy supernova. Things had changed.

"I swear to fuck, Rev," he growled. "If I die, I'm coming back just to take you down with me."

"Don't threaten me with a good time, starboy," I snapped back. "Now do it before we have to deal with each other for eternity."

The sound of water sizzling over a smoking engine was loud, cutting above the usual noise of a vehicle built for racing. But the black smoke cleared, replaced with pure white clouds of steam, and I breathed a sigh of relief.

"Oh my god," he exhaled.

"Told you," I mumbled.

"That you did, little comet. That you did."

The last few laps passed without a hitch.

Kai stayed in front, and I took the chance to show off my chameleon paint. Sliding in close behind him, just within his wing mirrors, I flicked the switch on my wheel. The paint sprang to life, colours shifting and shimmering like a living aurora across the bodywork. I knew it was only a matter of seconds before—

"Where the fuck did you go?"

I shimmied in my seat, grinning wide as my tail wriggled with glee in my trouser leg.

The paint was one of the first things I added when Al showed me how to build a vehicle. It worked insanely well, no matter the track or the time of day. It had taken us a while to get the right ratio of ingredients, and it wasn't quite as effective in the beginning...

But once we'd cracked the code, it was perfect, and it was a component I was most proud of.

I'd let Al use some for his vehicle too, since he'd helped me mix the paint until our hands were ready to fall off. Given the feature wasn't unique to my vehicle, it amused me to know that Al hadn't told Kai he could use it himself.

The Vorkan may have wanted us to race, but I had no doubt he wanted me to win.

"Catch me if you can, starboy," I teased, using a boost from the fuel mix to speed past him.

He whipped his head from side to side, trying to spot me. But the paint was too good, and I was invisible.

"You little fucker," he yelled, but there was no anger, only amusement.

"Two laps left, Kai. Better catch up!"

I pulled in front of him and pushed the button on my wheel, revealing myself in the lead. It was satisfying to surprise him, especially when he swerved with an, "Oh shit!"

No one gained on us until the last lap, and of course it had to be Quorik, a Hessirian with a year's worth of notoriety.

He was infamous for pulling last-second, do-or-die manoeuvres just to edge ahead. In my last race before joining the ASL, he'd pushed his thruster too hard and almost sent me into the sewer wall on Zyphar.

I wasn't sure how he'd closed the gap, and there was an unspoken rule that you didn't ask the other drivers what went into their vehicles. Every component was a guarded secret, and like fuck I'd ever reveal my tricks, even if I never raced in the underground circuit again.

Only Al knew, and now Kai.

Quorik's reptilian eyes were in view, glowing a bright yellow, even under his tinted visor. He edged closer to Kai's vehicle, and my heart pumped faster.

"Watch out for him, Kai," I warned, my eyes flicking between the road and the view of Kai in my mirrors. "You think I'm reckless, but he's something else."

"Confirmed," he replied, like he was replying to an engineer on race day.

It told me he was focused—too focused to talk, because he'd seen how close Quorik was, and our instincts were screaming the same thing.

Danger.

We blasted into the tunnel. A spark from Quorik's vehicle hit the wall, and the billboards blinked out. Darkness swallowed everything. Only Quorik's yellow eyes cut through the black. My enhanced sight helped me see, but Kai? He was driving blind, so he couldn't see Quorik preparing to ram him into the billboards on their left.

I triggered the chameleon paint since Hessarians could see in the dark better than Iskari, and vanished into the shadows. I dropped back, sliding right behind them. Quorik zeroed in on Kai, oblivious to the sudden gust of wind as I slipped past.

"Keep going, Kai."

"Keep going?! I can't fucking see."

He was pissed. He'd already had a scare with the engine, and now he was about to be slammed into a wall by an oversized lizard.

"I know, but I can," I reassured him. "Just keep going straight. I've got this."

"What are you going to do?" He sounded wary, but also curious.

"Just focus on you, hotshot. I've got you."

"Okay, little comet," Kai whispered. "I trust you."

I released a shaky exhale. This would be the second time tonight that Kai had put his trust in me. But this time I'd fucking earn it.

The tunnel exit surged closer. Quorik pulled away from Kai's side, gearing up for a hit. Then I saw my chance.

I hit the fuel-mix boost and shot through the gap. My rear tyre brushed his nose before he even swung. With one sharp flick of my wheel, Quorik's vehicle fishtailed hard, skidding straight into the tunnel wall in a shower of sparks.

It was just what he'd planned to do to Kai, and as we exited the tunnel, Quorik's vehicle burst into flames.

"Fucking hell!" Kai screeched as I appeared alongside him. "Is he okay?"

"Just keep driving, Kai," I replied, panting from the adrenaline. "It's all part of the game."

"We need to check if he's okay!"

"No we don't. People crash here all the time. This isn't the ASL with stewards and officials to enforce the rules. If you wanna play dirty, you've gotta be prepared for others to do the same."

For a moment, he said nothing, and we drove alongside each other in silence. But Kai being Kai, it didn't last for long.

"I quite like it when you're dirty, Revvy."

Once again, my laugh was genuine.

The race was a photo finish.

On the last straight, Kai and I maxed out our boosts, utilising the last of the dual-ion mix. We hit the line neck and neck, my front wing crossing just 0.04 seconds ahead.

The LED board at the side of the highway announced the result, and Kai let out a colourful string of profanity. Then he spent the cooldown lap laughing like it was the best loss he'd ever taken.

And perhaps it was, because tonight had been a shit tonne of fun.

Back in the shuttle park, we stopped side by side, close to where Al was waiting for us. "That was epic!" he boomed as we climbed out, pulling Kai and me into a bone-crushing hug.

Seriously, I think he cracked a few ribs. And by the grunts coming from Kai's mouth, he wasn't faring much better.

"It was fucking brilliant," Kai wheezed when Al put us down, trying to catch his breath. He tossed his helmet into the vehicle and turned to me. "*You* were brilliant."

I pulled off my helmet, revealing lines that glowed with an orange hue. Kai traced the lines with his finger, a soft smile on his face.

"Why don't you two head to my shuttle and change? I'll get everything packed up." Al patted the rear wings of both vehicles, eyes glittering as he looked between us. "I'll meet you there in ten."

"Okay," I mumbled, my eyes still on Kai.

"Shall we?"

He gestured for me to lead us, so I did. I steered him through the knot of bodies, our progress slow as every other bystander stopped us for a congratulatory slap on the back.

As expected, people swarmed Kai, and he met each well-wisher with his trademark grin and easy banter. What I hadn't counted on was how many people stopped me too.

In the past, I'd slipped away the second the checkered flag dropped. I told myself it was to avoid the stares, to dodge the novelty of being the lone Iskari.

But tonight, their greetings were genuine, the excitement aimed at both of us. And for once I didn't feel like a curiosity to gawk at. Just a winner.

When we finally made it to Al's shuttle, we both reached for our respective clothes. Kai had seen me naked in the locker room, but considering how much had changed in such a short amount of time, I was nervous to undress in front of him.

The last time had been a spur-of-the-moment thing. I hadn't had time to think, because Kai had decided for me, ripping my towel away before I could blink.

Apparently, Kai didn't have the same qualms.

He unzipped the suit and peeled it away from his body, like a snake shedding its skin, and stood in the public space in only his boxers and designer trainers, golden skin glowing under the floodlights.

I hadn't expected to see him this way again, and the sight made my mouth water. All I could do was stare at the chiselled set of abs, the firm pecs topped by perky pink nipples, and the trail of dark hair that disappeared into his underwear.

Fuck, was I drooling?

Kai cleared his throat, catching me gawking. I ripped my gaze away from his body and landed on his face, where his eyes sparkled, crinkled around the edges thanks to his huge smile. It was often cocky and smug, but now it was pure joy, with a hint of tiredness. The race-related adrenaline was wearing off.

"You okay?" he asked, and I nodded.

"Yeah. You?"

"Yeah," he replied. "Yeah, I'm great."

We stared at each other—Kai half naked, and me fully clothed. Once again, he traced the lines on my face with his finger. The feel of his rough skin against mine made me shudder, and this close, I could watch the way his hazel eyes darkened.

He licked his lips, taking a deep breath before speaking.

"Are you gonna . . . ?" He looked at my racing suit, still zipped up, and I bit my lip.

"I, um . . ." How could I tell him I was nervous?

It turned out I didn't have to.

My skin glowed orange *again*, and while Kai didn't know what it meant, I think he had an idea. His expression softened into something almost fond, and he cupped my cheek, stroking his thumb over my skin.

What was happening right now?

His mouth opened, and he seemed to lean towards me. And I leaned towards him too.

But then he blinked and stepped back, dropping his hand.

He dressed quickly, keeping his eyes on me the entire time, and I relaxed once he'd covered his Adonis-like body, leaving us both clothed. Once again on an even keel.

"You were fucking brilliant out there, rookie."

"I told you, Kai." My voice was quiet, scarcely a whisper. "You're the rookie today."

"Race is over now, little comet," he said with a wink. "You're back to being my rookie."

Not *a* rookie, or *the* rookie.

My rookie.

"I still beat you, starboy."

He didn't call me out for my deflection. Just smiled his usual smile, wider than I'd ever seen it.

"Hell yeah, you did."

The words landed warmer than I expected, free of any mockery or teasing. He gazed down at me, and pride shone in his eyes, like my win mattered to him almost as much as his own.

It pressed against the armour I wore around my ribs, around my heart, and I felt something loosen inside me. Something I wasn't sure I wanted to fix.

Kai took a step backwards. "Thanks for inviting me, Revvy."

"Better luck next time, hotshot."

"Will there be a next time?" He asked the question, vulnerability and yearning lacing it, as if he was hoping I'd invite him back.

"Yeah," I replied, and his posture relaxed. "You'll have to build your own vehicle, though."

He threw his head back and laughed at the night sky, easy and unguarded. When he dropped his chin to his chest, he looked at me from under his eyelashes.

"Will you help me?"

I scoffed. "Obviously. Al wouldn't trust you in his garage unsupervised."

"Figured as much." He winked before melting into the crowd.

As I watched him disappear, I wondered how the fuck we'd ended up here . . . and where did we go next?

SPEECH NOW OR FOREVER HOLD YOUR EACE

Kai

"Which shirt makes my eyes pop?"

"The green one."

"There is no green one, you wanker," Jax complained.

We were both in Jax's hotel room, getting ready for tonight's event. Well, *Jax* was getting ready. I'd dressed in my room before heading to his.

Now I sat on his bed, playing holo-games on my watch and trying not to text Rev for the hundredth time this week. All the while, my best friend had been agonising over his outfit choices.

For an entire fucking hour.

"Kai!"

When I lifted my head, I saw there was in fact no green shirt.

"Find a green one, then," I shot back, returning to level twenty-three of *Planet Popper*.

"It's either white or cream."

"They're the same."

"They are *not*," he snapped, throwing both shirts onto the bed with a huff.

There was another party tonight; hence, his reason for stressing.

The Cosmic Racing Federation dinner was an annual event, and one of the most important in the racing calendar.

Well, at least for the officials.

For the drivers, it meant squeezing into stiff tuxedos and getting paraded around like prized show dogs.

Every year, I waited for someone to grope my arms, comment on the sheen of my hair, and peel back my lips to inspect my teeth, before finishing off with a pat on the ass and a condescending "good boy."

After losing the game for the third time in ten minutes, I switched over to a brief message thread on my watch.

Our last exchange was a week ago, when we'd talked about the underground circuit. Since I'd left him at Al's shuttle, I'd hovered over the reply button more times than I could count. Typed messages, deleted them. Thought about calling, then chickened out.

I wanted to reach out, but I held back, afraid that one wrong move would send him running.

Rev was like a feral stray, hissing and growling if you got too close. All prickly fur and sharp edges. And the moment you reached for him, he'd go wide-eyed, stiff as a board, then bolt like a flash into the shadows. Probably to sulk behind a bin somewhere, licking his wounds and pretending he hadn't even wanted your attention.

The idea of Rev with cat ears and tufts of fur on his tail made me grin like a loon, but I tamped it down before Jax could notice and call me a psycho. Lucky for me, he was still comparing the same two shirts he'd been poring over for the last twenty minutes.

At least he'd narrowed it down from six.

With a sigh, I powered down my watch and rose from the bed. I grabbed the hanger holding the white shirt and shoved it against my teammate's chest. He glared at me, but I only smiled in return, knowing it'd piss him off.

"Go with the white. It's a classic," I encouraged. "But hurry the fuck up or we'll be late."

Jax glanced at his own watch before springing into action, shoving his tanned arms into the shirt's sleeves. Thankfully, the material wasn't creased, though I guessed that was because he'd spent ages ironing all six shirts before tossing the rejects back into his suitcase.

A *suitcase*.

For a one-night stay.

"Sorry for caring about my appearance," he complained, shoving the shirt's tails into his silver-grey trousers.

I waved him off, leaning against the wall by the door. "It's a dinner with a bunch of stuffy old dudes from the CRF, not a fashion show."

"Says the one looking like he walked off the catwalk and onto a billboard ad for aftershave."

I batted my eyelashes. "Are you saying I look pretty?"

He flipped me off before grabbing the bow tie and slinging it around his neck. "I hate these things," he huffed, trying and failing to tie it correctly.

After the third attempt, I walked over and smacked his hands away.

"How do you get yours to look so perfect?" he complained.

"Well." I grabbed the ends of the black fabric and twisted them into place. "First off, I'm incredible at everything I do. And second . . ." I leaned in, lowering my voice like it was a secret. "It's a clip-on."

I flicked him under the chin, smug satisfaction curling in my chest when he cursed me out.

Jax grabbed his jacket, and I stepped towards the door of the hotel room, yanking it open. "Move it, brother. There's an open bar with our names on it, and I intend to drink it dry."

The dinner was being held in the hotel's ballroom, and by the time we arrived, it was packed.

Large circular tables with ten place settings stood around the room, framing an open space I assumed was a dance floor, which would fill up after the food and speeches. Because if there was one thing these dinners were never short of, it was fucking speeches.

Clips from the season were being projected onto the large screen behind a small stage at the front of the room. On the stage was a single table, filled with decorative glass awards to be presented later, and 360 degree holograms of team vehicles, both current and past champions', decorated the walls. A few legends would be in attendance tonight, but unlike ours, their attendance wasn't mandatory.

We approached the bar, and Jax placed his hands on the marble top. "This round's on me, so what are you having?"

"They're free, you asshole." I nudged him in his ribs. "But since you're offering, I'll take a whiskey sour."

"Coming up, squire," he replied, waving down a bartender.

I turned to face the room and spotted Ailor. They were stuck in what was sure to be a boring conversation with the CRF president, Aetha'riel Lunvara.

The Thalorii was ancient. Like, well over a hundred, with one foot in the grave. And based on Ailor's glazed expression, Lunvara would be taking them down with him.

"What are you looking at?" Jax passed me a small tumbler filled with golden liquor, and I took a sip before nodding towards Ailor.

"Old man Lunvara is sending Ailor to sleep."

My teammate chuckled, and I joined in when Ailor looked over, mouthing what looked like "save me." But the last thing I wanted was to spend an hour listening to Lunvara make it through a single sentence.

So because we were bastards, we just shook our heads in condolence.

Apparently Ailor was also a bastard, because they pointed in our direction, trying to divert the old man's attention, but before he could take a decade to turn his head, Jax and I downed our drinks and ducked into the safety of the crowd.

I pushed past guests whose faces I knew but couldn't remember, offering polite smiles as I went. "That was close," I called over my shoulder, but there was no response. When I turned to look for Jax, he was nowhere to be seen. "Where the fuck did he go?"

The room was getting busier, if that were even possible. Someone had dimmed the lights for ambience, and jazz music played in the background. Once the alcohol flowed and the dance floor opened, the DJ would switch to trashy pop hits and classic bangers.

Servers in waistcoats roamed the room, balancing large trays of canapes. I was almost decapitated more than once when they got too close and I wasn't paying attention.

The smell of food made my tummy rumble, and the posh snacks looked tasty despite being tiny. I grabbed a handful, knowing they wouldn't touch the sides, to keep myself going until dinner was served.

Eventually, I made it to the lobby, where I could take a full breath.

The bar here was much quieter, and I took a seat on one of the high stools, ordering a second whiskey sour from the bartender. The nearby lift pinged as I received my drink, and when I turned to see if it was someone I knew, my mouth went dry when Rev walked out.

He'd tied his long hair in a messy bun at the back of his head, revealing his long neck and sharp jaw. Strands fell loose around his face, but he didn't look unkempt. No, he looked sleek, fashionable, and his dark hair shimmered under the lobby's crystal chandeliers.

His lips shone, and silver highlighted his eyes, the understated makeup accentuating his sharp, androgynous features.

Rev's deep indigo suit, moulded to his body, featured constellations embroidered in silver thread on the lapels.

Instead of a shirt and tie, he'd chosen a black mesh top with a low-cut neckline, and a silver belt that held his skinny, high-waisted trousers up, co-ordinated with a silver buckle on his shiny black loafers.

He was fucking gorgeous.

Rev stopped when he caught me staring, and the visible lines on his skin pulsed the colour of marmalade. He raised his hand in an awkward wave, and I offered a warm smile, hoping to put him more at ease.

It didn't, because he stood there like a statue, hand still raised as he glanced between the ballroom entrance and the bar.

I sighed.

Time to take a more direct approach.

"You coming over or what, rookie?" I called out, and the words echoed off the high ceilings.

I didn't intend for my voice to carry that much, but the acoustics in here were next level. It worked, though, spurring Rev into action. He dropped his hand and strode through the lobby, glaring in a way that made my dick take interest.

Down, boy.

"You're such a barbarian," he grumbled, climbing onto the stool beside me. Our knees brushed, and I swear a shock of electricity flew up my thigh and straight to my groin. "Can't take you anywhere."

"I had to get your attention, Revvy," I teased. "You were standing there like a right melon."

"I was not."

The bartender stopped in front of us. "What can I get you?"

Rev angled his face towards them, and I studied his sharp jawline, decorated with unique markings that trailed down his torso.

His button nose turned up ever so slightly, pierced with a tiny purple stud and a silver hoop through his septum. And when he asked for a martini, my gaze dropped to Rev's pillowy lips. The bottom one was a touch fuller than the top, giving him a natural pout that wasn't fair.

In my lap, my hand curled into a fist, grounding myself before I did something stupid, like lean in and catch his lower lip between my teeth. Or deck the bartender for looking at him.

Calm down, Kai. It's his job, for fuck's sake.

I'd only had two drinks, so I couldn't even blame my rampant thoughts on the booze.

"Kai?" I blinked, realising I'd zoned out while staring at Rev. He frowned back at me. "Do I have something on my face?"

He lifted a hand to his cheek, about to rub his skin, but I caught it and guided it to my knee. His palm rested there, warm and hesitant. I placed my hand over Rev's, his delicate fingers soft against mine. He didn't resist, and when I gave his hand a gentle squeeze, he intertwined our fingers.

I didn't look down. I didn't know what the fuck I was doing, or why I wanted to hold his hand. If I didn't look, I wouldn't have to acknowledge what was happening.

But Rev looked, and his small fangs sunk into his lip, the same way I wanted to. My skin felt hot under my suit, and I wanted to pull the collar away from my neck.

I didn't. I hardly breathed, not wanting to disrupt our quiet little bubble.

"You look good, rookie," I whispered.

Rev's skin flared yellow with hints of lilac, and butterflies fluttered in my chest. I rubbed my thumb across the luminescent lines on the back of his hands. "You too, hotshot," he whispered, eyes locked on where we touched.

When he looked up, we were closer than I thought, leaning in like two magnets of opposite poles, drawn to each other. The diamonds in his eyes swirled like snowflakes in the wind. Staring into the voids, I realised how easy it would be to fall among the stars.

I opened my mouth, unsure of the words that might come out.

But we'd never find out.

"Kai!"

Rev and I straightened up as Jax's voice echoed through the lobby, putting an appropriate amount of distance between us. Our hands disconnected, returning to our respective laps, and I hated how empty my palm felt.

We both sipped our drinks, avoiding eye contact now that the bubble had burst, the real world flooding back in.

"There you are." My teammate slapped me on the back, cheeks flushed and eyes sparkling. How many drinks had he had? "You good?"

I nodded, glancing at Rev, who was finishing his martini. He picked up the skewer and raised it to his mouth, tongue wrapping around the olive garnish.

"Yep," I croaked, eyes returning to Jax. "Having a drink with the rookie."

Jax turned his attention to Rev and smiled. "Bloody hell, Rev. You clean up well."

His mouth twitched, the lines on his skin lit with yellow. "Thanks, Jax. Nice shirt."

He had no idea how long it had taken Jax to settle on that damn shirt, so it was the right thing to say. Jax's face lit up like a supernova, and I could've kissed Rev for it.

"We need to sit down," Jax informed us, looking back towards the ballroom. "They're serving dinner."

"Okay, let's go."

I grabbed my drink and climbed down from the stool, holding my hand out to help Rev do the same. He didn't take it right away, just stared at my fingers like they might be dangerous. I was about to drop my arm, convinced he wouldn't take it.

But he slotted his hand in mine and stepped down, releasing it to dust non-existent lint from his jacket.

He looked up at me, whispering, "I guess I'll see you in there."

Jax still heard, though, and he placed a hand on Rev's shoulder, urging him to walk between us. "I already checked the seating plan. You're at our table, with Zylo and Saelix."

"Oh, okay then."

We entered the ballroom together, and as we drifted through the crowd, Rev's tail flicked back and forth. With a hand on the small of his back, I guided him through the sea of guests. With so many already sitting at the tables, it didn't feel as busy, but there were still a lot of people.

Something brushed my arm, and when I looked down to see what it could be, Rev's tail was wrapping itself around my wrist, holding it in place. I bit my lip to stop myself from smiling, and followed the bounce of Jax's dark curls in silence.

Zylo and Saelix were already there when we arrived.

Zylo was wearing a traditional black tuxedo, his beefy arm wrapped around his partner's thin shoulders. Saelix stood out in a fuchsia blazer, unbuttoned to reveal his bare chest, and a pleated pumpkin-coloured skirt that ended mid-thigh.

"Kai!" Zylo bellowed, drawing the other guests' attention. He rose from his seat to wrap me in a hug, gasping when he caught sight of Rev just behind me. "And look who you brought with you."

He released me in favour of pulling his teammate into a tight embrace. Rev grimaced—classic—but I didn't miss how he leaned into Zylo's chest, just for a second, like he secretly wanted it.

Saelix offered his own hugs, and Zylo pulled out the seat next to him for Rev. Name cards indicated who sat where, and I was happy to find myself sitting across from the rookie. Ailor and their partner, Velen, were also at our table, along with Tavoris and his wife, and Sam.

"Alright, mate?" I said, shaking his hand while taking my seat. "No date tonight?"

"No." Sam pouted, resting his elbows on the table. "Ailor said there were no seats left."

"Gotta put a ring on it, my guy," Jax cut in from my other side. "Then they have to let you bring 'em."

"He's gotta find someone to put a ring on first," I added. Before tacking on, "And a cock ring doesn't count."

As the three of us tumbled into fits of childish laughter, the hairs on the back of my neck rose.

Looking across the table, I caught Rev watching me, only half listening to whatever Saelix was saying. Lifting my half-filled glass to my mouth, I sent him a flirty wink over the rim. He rolled his eyes and turned back to the conversation, but with his hair up, he couldn't hide the way his ears twitched, and his skin shimmered pale pink.

Dinner passed in a quiet flurry of fleeting glances from Rev, winks from me, and the occasional smirk, traded like secrets across the table.

There were six courses, and every dish was a lesson in the art of torture as I watched Rev's purple tongue curl around his fork. Every smack of his lips and moan of approval made my dick harder. So much so that if I were to stand up, I'd be taking the table with me.

While Rev finished his sorbet, I considered sneaking away to the bathroom to find some relief, but the emcee's voice cut in, announcing the start of the award presentations. It meant a shitload of long speeches, but at least I'd have something to look at that wasn't Iskari food porn.

Lunvara hobbled onto the stage, aided by the CRF's vice president, a middle-aged human woman called Denise. The old man grabbed the microphone and began speaking at a pace that aged us all by a century.

It took about ten minutes for him to reach the end of his sentence, and I was glad when Denise took over. In contrast, she hurried through her lines with fleeting glances at the bar, like she needed a drink—or ten.

"Tonight is about more than just trophies," she started, eyeing the sea of guests. "It's a celebration of the people behind the vehicles. The drivers who risk everything, the teams who build brilliance. The engineers, strategists, pit crews, and every person who pours their heart into making the Astro Space League so great.

"So far this season, we've seen speed redefined, limits tested, and outstanding performances that remind us why we love racing. We've watched rookies prove their worth and veterans reaffirm their legendary status, and witnessed unforgettable moments on the track that we'll replay for years."

I glanced at Rev, who was watching Denise like everyone else.

Call me sentimental, but as Denise highlighted all the things that made the ASL fantastic—the passion, the innovation, the risk-taking—I realised I was wrong about the rookie.

I'd accused him of trying too hard to prove his worth among the professionals. Called him a wannabe who should've stayed in the underground league.

But Rev had belonged from the moment he arrived at the paddock. He hid his emotions from the world, but behind the mask, there was a fiery determination that burned in his eyes. His desire to leave his mark on the league was unmatched, because he wasn't in it for fame and fortune.

His intentions were altruistic, using the opportunity to bring recognition to an entire group of people. A group that had struggled more than I realised because of circumstances beyond their control. He didn't want the Iskari to suffer anymore. He wanted to set new expectations, eliminate prejudice, and take them into a new age of independence.

All the while, he was carrying the burden alone, fighting tooth and nail in every race.

So yes, I was wrong. So very wrong.

He had moments of recklessness, but his brilliance shone through. And when he caught me staring *again*, his soft smile set my chest aflame.

"You've shown that racing is as much about character as it is about crossing the finish line first," Denise continued. "And before we hand out the awards, let me say this. Whether you're walking away with recognition tonight or not, you've given us something to cheer for. You've kept the spirit of racing alive, and for that, the Cosmic Racing Federation thanks you."

Applause rippled through the room, and Lunvara took a seat on the stage, ready to hand the awards to Denise.

Zylo won Veteran of the Year, and Jax and I won Best Duo. I was lucky enough to also win Fan Favourite and Driver of the Year. For the fastest and most consistent pit stops, Vortex Racing won Best Pit Crew, while Zenith received the Tech Innovation Award for vehicle upgrades.

The guests celebrated each one with enthusiasm, but the relief was palpable when there was one award left on the table.

"This final award is extra special," Denise announced. "The award for Standout Performance is about more than a single race. It celebrates the driver who didn't just meet expectations, but obliterated them, and this year, that honour goes to a name I think we'll hear for a very long time.

"From the moment they took the wheel, they showed us what it means to race with raw instinct, precise control, and a level of adaptability beyond what we often see in the league. More than speed, it's about style, guts, and heart. It's about showing up to one of the most competitive leagues in the galaxy as though they were born to be behind the wheel.

"So, for the first time, the winner of this award is a rookie. This season isn't just the best rookie season the ASL has ever seen; it's the kind of season that forges legends. That's why I am honoured to present the award for Standout Performance to Revvak Arathiel."

For a moment, the room held its breath, the weight of the words sinking in. Then everything shifted.

The applause was deafening, and Zylo, Saelix, and Tavoris stood from their seats, followed by every Zenith team member in the room. Everyone else followed their example, including me, until the only person still in his seat was the winner himself.

Rev sat frozen, wide-eyed, the luminous lines on his skin cycling through every colour in the spectrum. When our gazes met, the stars in his eyes swirled as if they were on the brink of colliding, ready to spark a cosmic explosion. His expression was a storm of awe, disbelief, and terror, like he couldn't believe it was *his* name they'd called.

He needed something to ground him, and he stared at me like I was the only solid thing in his world right now. I didn't hesitate, circling the table to reach his chair. I held out my hand, and his trembling fingers curled around mine. With a soft tug, I helped him stand and drew him against my chest. He rested his head against my shoulder, exhaling rapid puffs of air against my neck.

People were staring, but I didn't care. Let them think whatever they wanted, because the only thing that mattered was Rev, and he could take all the time he needed.

I dipped my head and whispered in his ear. "You've got this, little comet."

"Promise?" There was a tremble in his voice, the kind that only comes when someone is trusting you with the softest part of themselves.

Whatever defences I had left around Rev dissolved in that moment.

"I promise."

He swallowed, throat clicking, and nodded once. Then he straightened up and pulled his shoulders back, his face transforming into his usual mask of composure before my eyes.

He left the cradle of my arms, but before he walked away, he squeezed my hand in a silent thank you. The only trace of nerves was in his tail, which lashed once, twice, then curled around his thigh as if to hold itself still.

He climbed the steps to the stage and shook the hands of Denise and Lunvara before accepting the award. Stepping up to the microphone, he kept his eyes down towards the empty dance floor.

"Thank you," he began, his quiet voice projecting across the room. "I didn't expect to receive this award—or any award. I never would've made it to the league without the team taking a chance on me."

He glanced up at Tavoris and Zylo. "I wouldn't be here without Tavoris, and I wouldn't be half the driver I am without Zylo."

Zylo beamed and brushed a tear from his cheek, while Saelix rubbed circles on his back. Tavoris's eyes were glassy, and he reached for his wife's hand, smiling proudly at Rev.

"Because of who I am—*what* I am—I've been called a lot of things in my life. Freak. Weirdo. Reckless." His eyes flicked to me, mouth twitching as he fought a smile. "But certain people in the league made me better, even when I refused to admit it. Thanks to them, I no longer feel like an intruder, a fresh-faced rookie terrified of making a mistake."

His skin shimmered a brilliant shade of purple, like the deep glow of an amethyst. "Thanks to them, I feel brave."

And then he smiled.

Wide, heartfelt, and unfiltered.

It was so beautiful, so pure, that my heart skipped a beat. I exhaled when he looked away, realising I'd been holding my breath.

"And yeah, I race for me, but I also race for the Iskari. I race for those who others have marginalised and made to feel like outsiders. Every time I step onto the track, I carry my people with me. Their hopes. Their fire. Their strength." He turned the award over in his hands. "This win isn't just mine. It's ours."

Everyone clapped as Rev descended from the stage.

But he didn't return to the table. The sound of roaring applause followed him through the doors into the lobby.

I didn't think; I just moved.

Jax called my name, but the growing distance between us drowned out his words. The party was still going, but none of it mattered. I had somewhere else to be. Someone to be with.

I found Rev in a shadowed hallway, eyes closed, breathing deeply as he leaned against the wall. Hiding his breakdown in the comfort and safety of his own company.

And I realised . . . I didn't want Rev to be alone.

But more than that, I wanted to make sure he never felt that way again.

FEELING HOT UNDER THE HELMET

Kai

"Rev?"

He didn't move, didn't open his eyes. If it weren't for the way his chest continued to rise and fall, I'd have thought Rev was a mannequin. He clutched the award to his abdomen, knuckles blanched. Sharp crystal edges dug into his skin, and it had to be painful, but it was like he couldn't feel it.

It was obvious he was overwhelmed, trying his best to process what had happened. He was *feeling*, something he tried so hard not to do, and he refused to do it in front of others.

True to the stray I likened him to, he'd vanished for a while, needing space, needing to shake off the feeling of being watched from every angle. He wasn't used to being seen, far too good at blending into the background, despite being so different.

On the stage, he'd allowed his emotions to shine through, his smile so happy and proud. And now he was experiencing the aftermath, the storm of emotions in his head and heart.

But I was here, and I refused to let Rev carry it all alone.

"Rookie?" I wrapped my hands around his, and the contact interrupted the steady cadence of his breathing.

His eyes opened, black holes that had made me uncomfortable in the beginning—dark and endless, threatening to drag me down into depths so deep I'd never resurface. But now I'd willingly fall into the blanket of stars I was becoming so fond of.

"There you are," I whispered, smiling as I brushed a thumb over his knuckles.

"Kai?" Rev's voice cracked, the word barely a huff of breath. If the corridor weren't so silent, I wouldn't have heard it. But standing so close, I heard the tremble—the pleading, like he needed to escape the spiral.

He was ecstatic about his win. I'd seen it in his eyes when he made his speech, the way the colours danced across his skin. Two things he couldn't hide no matter how well he masked.

Events like these were a lot, even for the biggest extroverts. I was always exhausted when I returned to my hotel room, my social battery depleted. Had I stayed in the ballroom tonight, it would've been the same.

Except now it wouldn't be, because this year was different.

I wasn't in the ballroom, dancing terribly with Zylo, or challenging Sam to a drinking game. I was in a quiet hallway with someone who'd been a pain in my ass just a few short weeks ago. A man who'd tilted my world on its axis the moment I bowled him over in the paddock.

From the very first scowl, I knew Rev was bound to bring chaos. I just didn't expect that chaos to bring us here.

We were still rivals and always would be as long as we were on opposing teams. Hell, even if we were teammates, we'd still try to best each other.

But things weren't straightforward anymore, because we weren't *just* rivals. I had no idea what we were, but whatever it was, I . . . well, I liked it.

As gently as I could, I removed the award from Rev's grip and placed it on the floor beside us. Flipping his hands over, palms up, I rubbed my thumbs over the angry-looking indents left behind.

But our eyes stayed glued to one another, and Rev exhaled, long and weary. "It's too much."

Three words that could've meant so many things. The party we'd left behind. The pressure of his goal. The league. Stars, maybe he meant whatever *this* was.

I didn't ask him to clarify, just said, "I know."

His mouth opened, but the words didn't come, so he gripped the lapels of my blazer, balling the expensive material in his fists. Rev pulled me forward, eliminating the minute distance between us, and my hands hit the wall on either side of his head. It was the only thing that stopped me from crushing him. But the glitter in his eyes swirled in a way I'd seen twice before.

Once in the locker room, and once in the dim hallway at Nebula.

They screamed that this was what he wanted. What he needed.

I relaxed my arms and leaned in, crushing his back against the wall. We were flush against each other, from our chests down to our toes, and his breath left him in a slow, contented sigh.

I lowered my head, brushing my nose along his jaw, inhaling the sweet smell of apples mixed with something entirely Rev. I wasn't sure what it was, but I imagined it was what the stars smelled like, and the combination made my mouth water.

"What do you want, little comet?" I rasped, pressing my lips against his skin.

His tongue poked out, trailing along his lips. My eyes shifted, drawn to the movement like a moth to a flame.

"I want you to kiss me."

The words went straight to my dick, which was already half hard in my trousers, but I didn't dive right in.

We'd kissed in the locker room, but heat and spontaneity had taken the lead. I'd slammed my mouth against his without hesitation, and Rev hadn't pushed me away. He'd melted against me, swept up in the rush of desire.

But he hadn't initiated it either, and I had to wonder . . . would he still have wanted it if I hadn't taken the lead?

Now we had the chance for a do-over, an opportunity to do things right, and I couldn't let it be another spur-of-the-moment decision.

A moment he'd regret.

I hesitated, studying him. I searched Rev's face for something, anything that told me this was what he wanted. That *I* was what he wanted.

Because along the way, Rev had wormed his way under my skin like a parasite. Like a fever I couldn't shift. He'd always be a pain in my ass, but it turned out that I liked it. Liked the way he pushed me, fighting back when my ego got the best of me.

He wasn't a thorn in my side, he was something more, and I needed to know he felt the same.

Rev tightened his grip on my jacket, his eyes locking with mine. Within them, the glittering particles swirled, certain and unshakable. The tension wound tight in my chest loosened, unravelling thread by thread, until the weight of the moment settled heavy and undeniable between us.

And with a low growl, he whispered, "Kiss me, Kai."

So I did.

Once again, we came together in a clash of lips and teeth, desperation seeping from our pores as we fought to devour one another. Rev's hands slid up to my shoulders, to my neck, fingers pressing against my pulse, like he wanted to feel the rapid-fire beat of my heart.

I slipped a hand from the wall and into his hair, fingers tangling as I pulled the messy bun loose, letting it tumble in waves past his shoulders. My fingertips brushed against his scalp, and his chest vibrated with a purr-like sound. But with a light tug on the strands, it morphed into a moan that set me aflame.

I pulled Rev's head back, changing the angle so I could kiss him deeper. Our tongues clashed, battling for dominance, just like we did so often on the track. I could taste the sharp tang of the martinis he'd drunk, a mix of briny olive and the crisp bite of gin.

When I pulled back, Rev chased my mouth with a whimper, so I took his bottom lip between my teeth. With a hard bite, I sucked it into my mouth, and Rev moaned, loud and wanton. His body slumped against my chest, the bulge in his trousers pressing against my own.

Something squeezed my thigh, and when I broke the kiss to look down, I saw his tail wrapped around my limb, tugging me even closer. The shift brought our bodies flush, and the friction between us sent a spark through me, igniting every nerve.

"Fuck," I hissed, resting my forehead against his.

I rolled my hips, and Rev whined, his mouth hanging open.

"*Kai,*" he gasped, panting breaths tickling my lips.

His ears twitched, the markings on his skin pulsing with a delicious shade of rosy pink. Hooded eyes gazed up at me, lips swollen, jaw slack as his chest heaved. His hair was loose and knotty, a messy dark halo that contradicted the pale complexion of his pearlescent skin.

A single kiss had wrecked Rev, and he'd never looked more gorgeous.

A door slammed down the hall, reminding us we were dry-humping in a public corridor.

"Come with me."

I stepped back, holding out my hand. Rev nodded, taking it without hesitation. Dipping down to grab his award, I caught the way he diverted his attention from my ass, and I winked. "Like what you see, rookie?"

"Fuck off, Mercer," he grumbled, but his lips curled in a shy smile.

After tugging him down the hall, I released him upon arriving in the lobby. Not that it mattered. Anyone with a single brain cell could look at us and know what we were up to. Our swollen lips, flushed cheeks, and obvious boners were a dead giveaway.

But holding hands was intimate, and would invite questions neither of us were ready to answer.

Rev followed me to the lift, and I pressed the button to take us to my floor. His eyes stayed glued to the tiled floor, while I watched the numbers tick down on the screen beside the doors.

From the corner of my eye, I spotted Jax leaving the bathroom to the left of the reception desk. His curls were wild, like someone had tugged on them, and the shirt he'd ironed within an inch of its life was a mess—half untucked, buttons misaligned, and hanging out of his trousers like he'd dressed in a rush.

I was about to call his name, forgetting I was trying to keep both Rev and myself unnoticed, but the bathroom door opened again, and who should stroll out in a similar state but Valen fucking Dray.

Yeah... no way I was touching that with a ten-foot pole.

When the lift opened, Rev and I stepped inside. I ignored the two supposed mortal enemies crossing the lobby, each of them looking freshly fucked.

Jax looked over as the doors began to close, and I raised my eyebrows at his dishevelled state. He didn't react, aside from a quick glance between me and Rev, neither of us looking much better. Jax's expression mirrored my own—bemused and all too knowing.

Seemed like weird things were happening all over the place tonight.

The closing doors left Rev and me in silence as we ascended, leaving the lobby noise behind.

My room was on the twentieth floor, and as we passed the twelfth, we still hadn't said a word. Rev had hardly moved, eyes locked on the mirrored walls surrounding us, and I worried that he was second-guessing things. That maybe he was uncomfortable, feeling pressured into something he didn't want to do.

But when I opened my mouth to ask, Rev grabbed my hand and silenced me with a reassuring squeeze.

It said he still wanted me—still wanted whatever this was—and that was enough for me to sprint from the lift when the doors opened on the twentieth floor.

I dragged him along behind me, heart beating harder with every door we passed.

2014... 2015... 2016...

2017.

My room.

Pressing my watch against the sensor, I exhaled a shaky breath before opening the door and pulling Rev inside.

The room was basic, furnished with a king-sized bed, two side tables, a cuck chair, a dresser, and a flat-screen TV on the wall. The bathroom had a double sink and a shower that was big enough for two.

Rev dropped my hand and walked further into the room. His eyes shifted from my open suitcase under the window to the small pile of clothes I'd left on the chair.

As he gazed around the room, I walked to the side tables, placing his award on the wooden surface. The cool-toned overhead light seemed too bright for the atmosphere we were going for, too clinical, so I opted for the softer lamplight instead.

As I circled to the other side of the bed, I felt Rev's gaze on me. It was hot and unblinking, like prey mesmerised by the predator it couldn't bring itself to flee, and my body shuddered with anticipation.

With the lamps on, I switched off the main light before turning to look at him.

He stood stock-still, worrying his bottom lip between his teeth. At first glance, he looked nervous, but I noticed the way his hands clenched into fists at his sides, his tail lashing back and forth with a sharp, audible swish.

The bulge in his trousers was the most obvious sign of how he was feeling. Stiff and unwavering, pressing against his zipper as though trying to break through the tight fabric.

"That looks painful," I said, and I saw the way his cock twitched beneath his skinny trousers.

When he responded, there was a slight tremble in his voice. "What are you going to do about it?"

What I *wanted* to do was leap across the room like a crazy person and take him. Push him down on the bed, shed his clothes, and taste him from head to toe.

But I forced myself to remain calm and wait. I needed to make it last.

Besides, they say good things come to those who wait . . . and I wanted really, *really* good things.

I took slow, measured steps as I approached him, stopping right at his side. My chest pressed against his shoulder, and I raised my hand to trail a single finger over his trapped cock. The touch was feather-light, but his breath hitched as I stroked up and down.

When his hips bucked, I abandoned his cock, continuing my journey upwards.

"Kai," Rev croaked, wetting his kiss-swollen lips with his tongue.

The image of that tongue wrapped around my cock almost made me blow, and I started running through my times tables before I came in my boxers.

One times six was six. Two times six was twelve. Three times six was . . .

"What are you going to do to me?" he asked.

I exhaled into the crook of his neck, watching goosebumps ripple to life along his pulse point. Dragging my finger up his chest, the thin mesh of his shirt bunching under my skin, I whispered, "I'm going to take you apart." My finger trailed over to his nipple. "I'm going to touch you, taste you, *devour* you."

Rev whimpered as I rubbed the sensitive nub, the friction of his shirt adding an extra layer of sensation.

"I won't stop until you're writhing beneath me, moaning my name, brainless with pleasure and begging for more."

I leaned in, dragging my tongue along his throat, tasting the clean heat of his skin beneath the salt of sweat. The mix was intoxicating, and my cock throbbed, thick and restless.

My lips parted as I latched onto his neck, sucking hard until a deep purple bruise bloomed on the tender curve where it met his shoulder. He whined, hand shooting out to grab my hip. I released him with an audible pop.

"Do you want to fall apart for me, little comet?"

Rev's skin glowed a shade of hot pink, and he bobbed his head up and down.

"Please," he mewled, trembling as he clung to me.

Wrapping my fingers around the back of his neck, I pulled him towards me, crushing our lips together in a messy kiss. Rev turned into my embrace, scrambling to remove my clothes with desperate, shaky hands. I followed suit, the two of us pulling at jackets, shirts, and zippers until we were in nothing but our underwear.

I pressed him back until his thighs bumped the bed, then gave a firm push, hard enough to send him falling onto the sheets. I didn't follow. Not yet. I stood there, savouring the view, my gaze devouring him like a promise.

Legs splayed wide, the tip of his cock peeked out from under the waistband of his boxers. It was flushed a delicious shade of indigo and already leaking precum. The sight made me salivate, hungry for a taste of him.

I palmed my cock through the fabric of my boxers, the pressure sparking heat low in my gut, a rough pulse shooting straight to my balls. Rev groaned, propping himself up on his elbows, his gaze locked on my hand.

"Take them off," he ordered.

I smirked at his boldness, not ready to end my teasing. "Say please, rookie."

Things between us might've shifted, but my urge to provoke him hadn't.

I wanted to light the fuse. To rile him up and piss him off before dragging moans from his throat, his fire burning itself out in pleasure.

And never one to disappoint, Rev scowled, glare simmering with equal parts irritation and heat. He shifted onto his knees and crawled across the bed, his tail dragging along the sheets behind him. His hand moved for my waistband, but I caught his wrists first, holding them tight enough to leave marks.

Rev wriggled, attempting to free himself, but I yanked him forward, and he collided with my bare chest.

"Don't worry, baby," I whispered, our foreheads pressed together. "I'll have you begging before we're done."

"Don't count on it, starboy."

With a shove, Rev landed on his back with a yelp, and his glare melted into something hotter as I pushed my boxers down. My cock sprung free, smacking my stomach with a wet slap, the tip slick with precum. I allowed myself one rough stroke, just to take the edge off, and placed a knee on the bed.

Releasing my cock, I crawled up his body and knelt between his legs. Rev's breathing stuttered as I removed his boxers, and when I settled on my stomach, my face hovered over his dripping cock.

This was my first opportunity to get a good look at it, since our last encounter had been fast and furious.

It was uncut, and darker compared to the rest of his periwinkle skin. Thinner and slightly shorter than mine, there was still more than enough to fill my throat. Both his cock and balls were hairless, and I revelled in the way those delicate markings I craved trailed down every inch of his shaft. They ended right at the tip, pulsing pink beneath my gaze.

Unwilling to wait any longer, I trailed my tongue up Rev's length and sucked him down to the root.

"Fuck!" he yelled, tail smacking against the bed.

Rev buried his fingers in my hair, tugging at the strands like he wasn't sure whether to push me off or pull me closer. I pulled up, sucking the tip while he tried to bury himself deeper in my mouth. I laid an arm over his stomach, forcing him to stay put, and stroked his frenulum with my tongue.

He whimpered, hips twitching in short, desperate jerks beneath my weight.

"Kai," he whined, and I released his cock, dipping my tongue into his slit to scoop up his warm, salty precum with hungry lips.

"Ready to beg yet?"

"No," Rev snapped. Then he used his hands in my hair to push my head down.

I obliged, but not for long. My head bobbed in a steady rhythm, and I dragged my tongue over a vein on the underside before releasing him once again. He growled, shuddering when I blew warm air over his wet cockhead.

"You know what I want," I replied calmly, a complete contradiction to the heat burning me inside out. "You know what you have to say."

Swallowing his length once, twice, before pulling off again, I watched with smug satisfaction as it dropped to his stomach with a dull thud.

Rev released my hair and slammed his fists into the mattress.

"Kai!" He choked on a sob, eyes wild and cheeks flushed.

Sweat beaded along his hairline, the long strands tangled from rolling his head over the mattress. His skin flared deep magenta, bright enough to rival the bedside lamps. His chest heaved, and he gazed down at me in silence.

And when he breathed out a trembling, broken, "Please," it felt like a choir of angels filled the room.

I groaned, nuzzling the crease between his thigh and groin, scraping the soft skin with my stubble.

"So good for me, little comet."

Rev had given me what I wanted, and now he deserved a reward.

I dived in, taking him deep, and gagging as he hit the back of my throat. The sheets crumpled in his fists, and the sound of his ragged breathing and rough pleading was a symphony that made me feral. Hollowing my cheeks, I sucked hard enough to make him curse. I dragged a hand over the soft skin of his thigh, his balls, and pressed my thumb against his taint.

When I released his cock and sat up on my knees, Rev whined, reaching out for me. He was so fucking needy, I couldn't stop myself from crawling up his body and claiming his lips to reassure him.

The kiss was devastating, leaving me panting for breath as we broke apart.

"I need to be inside you, baby," I murmured, tracing my tongue over his lips.

Rev nodded, looking so dazed that I wasn't sure he understood the words.

I reached for the bedside table where I had stashed a bottle of lube, meant for a solo session but now destined for something far more thrilling. Before I could grip the drawer handle, Rev touched my forearm, so I glanced down.

He caught his lip between his teeth, his eyes darting away from mine.

"I . . . I-I'm . . . I've never . . ." Rev stammered, his delicate lines glowing a soft burnt orange.

I knew what the unspoken words meant.

Rev was a virgin, and he trusted me enough to let that vulnerability show.

Butterflies beat against my ribs when I cupped his cheek, brushing his lips with my thumb. When he looked up, I gave him a soft smile.

"We don't have to go all the way to have a good time, rookie." I hoped the familiar nickname would anchor him, a steady thread of stability in such a fragile moment.

He returned my smile with one of his own, grateful and almost shy. I dropped a quick kiss on his lips and reached for the drawer.

But he stopped me again, so I asked, "What's wrong?"

"What are you doing?"

My brow creased, but I brushed my nose against his. "Getting the lube so I can make you scream."

Rev swallowed and cleared his throat. "You, um . . . y-you won't need it."

He pushed at my chest, creating space until I was looming over him on my knees. Then he raised his legs, placing his feet flat on the mattress before taking my hand in his. He moved my hand lower, avoiding his dick, until it rested between his cheeks, directly over his hole.

I wheezed, the breath punched out of my chest.

"What the . . ." I looked up, eyes wide with shock.

I was also very curious.

Rev's smooth crease was already slick. The substance felt like lube, but it was warm and more viscous. Rubbing a finger through it, I circled his hole, feeling it twitch under my ministrations. I used my free hand to spread his cheeks, enjoying an unobstructed view of his glistening pucker as it pulsed, winking at me.

"Iskari are... different from humans," he muttered, gasping when I increased the pressure against his hole.

The tip of my finger breached the slippery rim with little resistance, and he released a breath, melting into the mattress. I watched, enraptured, as I sank my finger further inside his hole, past the first and second knuckles.

"Different how?" I asked, pulling back until only the tip remained. Then I slid back in, repeating the motion in a steady, teasing rhythm.

He didn't answer my question, just moaned, "More."

I removed my finger, hushing his needy mewls, and lowered myself back down onto my stomach. With his cheeks spread wide, I inhaled something sweet and warm like toffee, mixing with his mouthwatering apple scent.

I replaced my finger and repeated my question. "Different how, rookie?"

When I added a second finger, Rev hissed at the stretch. My hand paused in its movements, allowing him a moment to adjust, and when he rolled his hips, fucking himself on my fingers, I resumed thrusting. With a crook of my fingers, I located his prostate, making Rev cry out as the muscles in his ass flexed around them.

He tried to speak, but I wasn't making it easy, and his breaths stuttered with each thrust.

"I-Iskari have evolved over t-time. With our n-numbers so l-low... *fuck*... the men can c-carry children." He groaned when I pegged his prostate, chest rising and falling rapidly. "It means we... we... *shit*... it means we c-can make our own l-lube."

Well, good fuck.

My brain froze, then slammed into reboot. Did that mean Rev could get *pregnant*?

As a twenty-eight-year-old professional racer, kids weren't on my radar just yet. Yet while I pumped my fingers deep inside Rev's virgin ass, my mind drifted, imagining little Kais with black eyes gleaming and tails flicking as they ran wild.

Stars, it was a struggle not to yank my fingers free and slam my cock inside him. The caveman in me ached to fill him to the brim with cum so there'd be no question whether one of my swimmers had found its mark.

Breeding kink unlocked—and something to explore at a later date.

A familiar burnt-orange glow drew me out of my haze, and Rev looked up at me, concern flickering across his face.

"We can stop," he whispered. "Y'know, if it's too . . . weird."

It made my heart ache.

He'd told me—*showed* me—something so personal, and I'd remained silent. Sure, it was different, but it wasn't weird. It was a good thing. A *great* thing, that made my cock leak into the sheets beneath me.

But he didn't know that, so I had to tell him. Had to show him like he'd shown me.

I dipped my head, laving my tongue over his balls. They were heavy, pulled up tight and in need of release.

"Little comet," I murmured, breath thick with desire. "What you just told me . . . fuck, that might be the hottest thing I've ever heard."

I trailed my tongue down to Rev's hole, stroking his rim while my fingers continued to thrust. His slick on my tongue tasted like the sweetest ambrosia, fit for the gods, and a deep groan rumbled from my belly.

"The next time I see this ass, I'm going to stuff you so full of cum, you'll be dripping for days."

I rubbed his prostate again and again, and Rev sobbed, back arching off the bed. His thighs twitched, his hole gripping my fingers like it wanted to suck them deeper. His tail wrapped around my wrist, tugging my fingers as deep as they could go, and his head flipped back and forth like a madman.

"Do you want that, little comet?" I purred. "Want me to fuck you? *Breed* you?"

"Fuck, Kai... yes... shi—*please*!"

By the fucking stars.

I stopped playing around. I needed to taste his cum, and I needed it an hour ago. Swallowing his shaft, I choked as his cock high-fived my tonsils. But I wasn't a quitter. Taking a deep breath through my nose, I relaxed the muscles, letting his cock burrow deep into my throat. I probably looked obscene, with my neck bulging in the shape of his prick. Spit leaked down my chin, and the lack of air made my head spin, but I held it there and squeezed his hips, encouraging him to thrust.

Rev caught on, fucking into my throat while my fingers pummelled his hole.

"Shit," he panted. "Fuck, oh *god*. Kai... I'm... I'm g-gonna..."

As the edges of my vision darkened, his cock twitched on my tongue. I swallowed, the muscles in my throat squeezing his cockhead.

"*KAI!*"

He exploded in my mouth, flooding it with the salty, heady taste of his cum.

I swallowed as much as I could, but some spilled from the corners of my mouth. Rev trembled with aftershocks, limbs twitching so much it made the mattress shake. I licked him clean, pulling off when he complained of oversensitivity, and flopped down beside him.

My dick was on a hair trigger, so I grabbed my cock, expecting to get myself off while Rev recovered.

But before I could even think of stroking it, Rev shot up, throwing his leg over my body. He straddled my hips, hair mussed and sticking out every which way. His eyes shifted between my pulsing cock and my face.

I trailed my hands up his smooth thighs, pink light dancing over his skin. "What are you doing, baby?"

He gripped my dick in his fist and started pumping it with loose fingers.

"Can I taste you, starboy?" he purred, looking down at me through those long lashes, with sultry eyes that made my heart race.

Stars, he was a vixen, a predator . . . and now *I* was the prey.

"I'm all yours, baby."

The stars in Rev's eyes seemed to glow, and he lay down between my legs, mirroring my earlier position.

He glanced up at me, chewing on his lip, and whispered, "I won't be very good."

His voice quivered, betraying the nerves hidden beneath that sexy front. I brushed a hand through his knotted hair, fingers caressing his scalp, and he leaned into the touch. He melted like a tiny kitten craving pets, looking so damn adorable I half wished I could snap a photo.

"Whatever you do will be perfect," I reassured him. Then quickly tacked on, "Just watch the fangs."

He grinned, wide enough to flaunt his sharp little canines. Then he clacked his teeth, pretending to deliver a teasing little nip.

It was unexpected, surprising, and this new side of him made me laugh.

But it morphed into a groan when he stuck out his tongue, licking along the underside of my shaft.

He gripped the base to hold it steady and took the tip in his mouth. It took everything in me to hold still, to not thrust too deep and choke him. The last thing I wanted to do was embarrass him. I worried if I did, he'd never want to do this again—with me or . . . anyone else.

Something dark and possessive bloomed behind my ribs at the thought of someone else's cock near his mouth. So I gripped his hair tighter, as if to remind him he was *mine*. For tonight.

Rev opened his mouth, resting the tip of my cock on his tongue, testing it. Sealing his lips around it, he dipped up and down, taking more of my length with every pass. He compensated for what wouldn't fit by massaging the base with his hand, and he gagged once or twice, but soon got the general gist of it.

His movements were sloppy and uncoordinated, but what he lacked in experience, he made up for in determination. He sucked me with an eagerness that had my back rising from the mattress, fists tugging his hair until the strands pulled at his scalp the way he liked.

As requested, Rev was careful with his teeth, but now and then, the ridge of his fangs grazed the side of my cock, and the sensation caused a blazing fire to rage through my groin.

"Fuck, baby," I groaned, pumping into his mouth with shallow thrusts. "Your mouth is so good."

The praise made him hum, the vibrations feeling incredible as he dared to take me deeper. When he gagged, it almost sent me over the edge.

He looked like a wet dream—chin covered in spit, a steady stream of tears leaking from his dark eyes. His hand stroked the coarse hair on my thighs, and he cupped my balls, squeezing them while he devoured my dick.

"Shit," I panted. "I'm c-close, Rev. Fuck, I'm so fucking close."

He gazed up at me, eyes glowing with determination. His skin glowed midnight blue as he squeezed my balls again and sucked me as deep as he could. And when his throat twitched, trying to stifle a cough, I couldn't hold on anymore.

Bright colours exploded behind my eyes as I tumbled over the edge, ropes of cum firing from my cock and straight into Rev's mouth. He pulled off, choking as he tried to swallow, but the sight just made me cum more, painting his lips and cheeks with my load.

I swear I blacked out, and when I came to, I watched Rev wipe his cock with the rumpled bedsheets. It was wet with fresh cum, so he must've rutted against the mattress while sucking me off.

I patted the space beside me. "Come here."

Part of me worried he would run now that the storm of sexual tension had subsided.

But he didn't, he just crawled up my body and plopped down at my side. He laid his head on my chest, draped an arm over my stomach, and wrapped his tail around my calf.

His skin pulsed the colour of amethysts, and I wanted to ask what it meant. I'd only seen it once before, and while I thought every colour he glowed was gorgeous, this one was my favourite.

Instead, I kept my mouth closed, and Rev didn't say a word.

We didn't speak. Didn't need to right now.

We shifted until we nestled beneath the quilt, tangled in each other, and drifted into a deep, dreamless sleep.

Twice throughout the night, we woke and exchanged orgasms, communicating in kisses, grunts, and moans until the planet's two moons made way for the light of dawn.

When I woke up for the last time, I was alone in the bed.

Rev's clothes were nowhere to be seen, and the award, which I'd left on the bedside table, was absent. At some point, he'd erased any sign that he was ever here, but when I buried my face in his pillow, the soft, unmistakable scent of apples clung to the fabric.

Rev might've fled, too scared to face whatever was growing between us in the harsh light of day, but the memory of him, of what we'd shared the night before, was stitched into every thread.

And no amount of running could undo it.

WRITTEN IN THE STARS, SCRAMBLED BY GRAVITY

Rev

I'd made it to twenty-four before having sex, and the second time it happened, I'd become a douchebag who disappeared while the other person slept.

Waking up with my head tucked into Kai's neck, his arms holding us chest to chest and my tail curled around his ankle, had filled me with a quiet joy. Tired, considering we'd got off twice more throughout the night, but still . . . content.

I'd lay in bed for what felt like hours, committing every detail of Kai's face to memory. We'd been so desperate to fall into bed, we hadn't even bothered to close the curtains, and the sun had streamed through the windows, casting him in a gentle golden glow.

Face relaxed in sleep, he'd looked soft, precious, a man born to bask in the sunlight. Faint freckles decorated the bridge of his nose, and a silvery scar cut through the arch of his right eyebrow. Stubble that I'd thought was a simple brown shone with blonde and auburn highlights, and the memory of those coarse hairs rubbing against my thighs sent a flare of heat through my groin.

Tucked away behind his ear was a single tattoo. The number forty-two—Kai's racing number.

It was small and delicate, inked in a serif font and easily hidden by his messy hair. But I'd got close enough to see it. Kai had *allowed* me to get close enough to see it . . . and that sparked the panic that twisted in my belly.

And without considering how Kai might feel waking up alone, I'd fled.

Fear pressed down on me until I couldn't breathe, like a sudden wave sweeping me under and pulling me down. It was fear of what this . . . this *thing* between us was becoming. Fear of what it meant now we'd crossed that line not once, but twice.

What had started as a stupid rivalry was shifting into something deeper, something heavier.

It had become something more, at least for me. I hadn't considered why Kai had booked a hotel room, too busy gagging for a taste of his cock. For all I knew, this was his annual routine. Just a bed to fuck whoever caught his eye at the party, and I was just the lucky winner.

I didn't know Kai, not really. Not beyond the track.

But part of me wanted to.

I wanted to know what had driven him to the ASL, how he'd got that scar on his face. I wanted to know about his dreams, about his childhood and his family. I wanted to know *everything*, and I feared this meant more to me than to him.

It was enough for me to run.

That was two weeks ago, and now the award I'd tucked away stared down from the shelf in the living room, more accusation than accolade. It should have made me proud, but it reminded me of my vanishing act. It made me feel like a twat, because I hadn't even messaged him, too scared to reach out and apologise.

What if he acted like the night had meant nothing, like my leaving had saved him the trouble of kicking me out in the morning?

So instead of doing the right thing, I stayed silent.

But I hadn't heard from Kai either, and I couldn't tell if it hurt or not, which made me feel like a bigger twat. I had no right to feel hurt, because I was the one who'd left.

Except it only made me spiral more, convinced I was just another notch on his bedpost, a story to brag about over a beer.

Did getting blown by an endangered species earn some serious lad points?

Today's race loomed, and I was terrified of bumping into Kai. If I saw him, I'd either act like a bumbling idiot or go full postal and sprint in the opposite direction.

There was no in-between.

Avoiding him had been easy so far. I'd holed up in the garage or ducked around corners whenever I heard his voice. Zylo called me jumpy, but I passed it off as nerves, which wasn't too much of a stretch.

Starfall Traverse was a new experience, and like Horizon Rings, an anti-gravity track. I was thankful there were only two, because I much preferred the feel of tyres gripping the ground over flying blind through open air.

The track wove through a giant asteroid belt, with massive rocks that exploded on impact, constant meteor showers to dodge, and rogue comets threatening to destroy your thrusters. It needed perfect timing and sharp precision.

Considering the risks I took, they weren't my strengths, and I wasn't feeling confident.

This, combined with my Kai-induced anxiety, meant I was heading into the race on edge.

Practice was rough, my times slow and shaky, and qualifying hadn't been much better. So now I was starting on the back foot in twelfth on the grid, my worst starting position all season.

"You'll be fine, Revvy," Zylo said as we walked from the shuttle park.

Just like Horizon Rings, the paddock was on a levitating platform a short distance from the track, while a few grandstands hovered a safe distance away.

"Thanks," I muttered.

He laid a hand on my shoulder, giving it a squeeze.

"In my rookie season, I qualified dirt last for this track. Ended up finishing the same way on race day." He stared at the mass of floating rocks in the distance. "Took me a few seasons to get my head around it."

I scoffed. "Like I believe that. You're good at everything."

"Greatness takes time, kid." He laughed, ruffling my hair. The small bun at the back of my head came loose, so I slapped his hand away with a small smile. "Besides, you're doing pretty well for yourself, mister standout performance."

The reminder of my award, the one that made me think of Kai, wiped the faint smile I'd mustered right off my face.

Since he had the eyes of a hawk, Zylo noticed.

"It's okay, Rev," he reassured me, oblivious to the true source of my anxiety. "It doesn't matter whether you finish first or last. You deserve that award more than anyone else in the paddock."

Zylo was always full of compliments, but this one hit differently.

I'd tried to keep everyone at arm's length, but Zylo had slipped through my defences. He didn't let my general standoffishness faze him. Instead, it only encouraged him to try harder, to act like a mentor, even if I never let it show just how grateful I was for his attention.

He was always so open with me, and something made me want to return the favour.

Maybe Kai was rubbing off on me more than I'd thought.

Could the ability to be more open, more honest, spread through sex? Like some bizarre sexually transmitted disease?

"Zylo." I stopped walking and stared at his chest, not ready to look at his face.

"You okay?"

"Yeah. Yeah, I'm okay. I, uh . . . I just . . ."

My tongue felt too big for my mouth, the ability to form full sentences escaping me. Fucking hell, was it so hard to be vulnerable?

Stars, the thought of it made me shiver, and I worried I'd break out in hives before I was done.

"Rev—"

"No," I cut him off. "Just let me . . ."

I took a deep breath, exhaling and counting down from five. The tension in my shoulders eased, and I felt brave enough to meet his eyes. "Thank you, Zylo. Thank you for everything."

The man's eyes widened, as surprised as I was by the words pouring out. He opened his mouth, no doubt to say something, but I was on a roll now, so I pushed ahead before the bravery could fizzle out.

"Since I joined Zenith, you've been nothing but kind to me, even when I came off as a bit of a dick."

The last part was a murmur, but he still caught it, giving me a look that said, *"A bit?"*

"I appreciate the advice, the help during training, and the reassurance. Everything." I dropped my eyes to the gravel beneath my feet, returning to my usual state of awkwardness. "I couldn't have asked for a better mentor than you, Zylo."

He said nothing at first, and the stretching silence was making me uncomfortable, worried I'd offended him or something. But when I glanced up, Zylo smiled bigger than I'd ever seen, and his golden eyes glistened under the floodlights.

"Are you—"

Before I could finish, Zylo pounced. He swept me up in a bear hug, crushing me against his bulky frame.

"Oh, Revvy!"

My face was smushed against his pecs, and I could hardly breathe. He seemed so happy, though, and the risk of a few broken ribs was worth it.

My vision grew fuzzy, so I patted his side until he dropped me back onto my feet. His tears had spilled over as he held me, and he wiped them away with a sniffle.

"You're such a sap." My grimace was half-hearted at best, making Zylo chuckle.

"You're a good kid, Rev. I haven't had a teammate for a while. Not since..." He trailed off at the mention of Xander Korr, his deceased mentor. Now Zylo was mine, and I was glad to have him. "If I had to have anyone, I'm happy it's you."

His comment stunned me into silence, and to my horror, my eyes burned.

I was not about to cry in front of Zylo.

I'd been vulnerable enough, damn it.

Instead, I stayed silent, but for Zylo it was more than enough.

"Am I interrupting something?"

We turned to see Kai standing outside the Nexus shuttle, grinning as he watched us. It wasn't his usual cocky smile reserved for race weekends. This one was softer, more affectionate—like the smile he gave me when I'd admitted to being a virgin.

And the sight of it made the panic I'd held at bay surge forward, shattering the calm I'd found during my moment with Zylo.

One overwhelming feeling replaced another. So instead of acting like a mature adult with his wits about him, I sprinted in the opposite direction.

Looks like I'd chosen to go postal.

I continued to avoid Kai until it was time to race.

When he walked out of the garage, I went inside. I engaged the crew in pointless conversation about the weather—in space. And in one particular fit of creativity, I turned my back on him.

But Kai being Kai, I had a feeling he wouldn't let this slide. A feeling that proved right during the fifteenth lap.

"You're avoiding me," he said over the radio.

I knew I could ignore him, a fact Kai knew too. I could switch the drivers' radio off, only responding to my team on the Zenith channel.

But that would be petty, so I opted for the next best thing.

Lying.

"No I'm not?" My voice trailed up at the end, like it was a question.

"You're a terrible liar, Revvy," he replied, and I cursed myself. "Your face hides your feelings, but your voice gives it away."

I sighed, because while I'd expected Kai to call out my odd behaviour, I didn't want to discuss it on the drivers' radio.

"We can't talk about this here, Kai."

"Why not?" He replied.

"Because I don't want to give the league and the fans a front-row seat to my dirty laundry."

Kai chuckled. "We're not on the drivers' radio."

"Um, yes we are."

"No," he explained. "It's a private frequency."

I looked at my wheel, surprised to find it set to a channel I'd never seen before. "How did you do this?"

"I paid a member of the Zenith crew to set it up for me," he replied, and I could picture his smug expression. "It was the only way we could talk since you literally turned your back on me."

I winced. "Who'd you pay off?"

"I'll tell you later. There are more important things to discuss right now."

"I'm a little busy, Kai," I snapped, and this time it wasn't a lie.

I'd been stuck in twelfth since we started, and I was struggling to catch up to the driver in front.

He sighed, and I wilted a little under the weight of his disappointment. "Rev, talk to me. Why are you avoiding me?"

"I'm n—"

"If you say you're not, I will turn around and shove your car into an asteroid."

A surprised laugh burst out of me, and Kai whispered, "I like it when you laugh, Revvy." I could imagine his fond smile, the one that'd sent me running earlier. "Please talk to me."

"I . . ." I trailed off, unsure of what to say.

I'd already opened up once today. Did I have the energy to do it again?

It was a sad thought, but I wasn't used to letting people in. Whenever I did, it ended the same way—disappointment. I became a little more hollow after giving away a piece of myself I'd never wanted to lose.

I only showed my true self, unmasked, to my family, because they never asked for anything in return. To them, I wasn't a freak because I was different. I wasn't a novelty for people to gawk at. My family never made me feel like I was anything less than worthy, just as I was.

Except, Kai hadn't either, had he?

He challenged me and pushed back, but never because of my species. We clashed because we were both stubborn, both driven to win. Despite that, he'd shown me his softer side, steady and kind when I'd crumbled at the dinner, never asking for anything in return.

When he'd made me fall apart under his expert hands, he hadn't expected me to reciprocate.

It was my choice to throw myself at his dick, and I'd fucking liked it too.

"I was scared." The words were so quiet I worried he hadn't heard me, and I didn't want to say them more than once.

"Why?" he asked, like it was that simple to explain.

Didn't stop me from blurting, "I saw your tattoo."

"You've got marks all over your skin, and a little artificial ink scared you off?"

"Don't take the piss, Mercer." My hackles rose as I slipped into defence mode.

If I got angry first, it wouldn't hurt as much when he inevitably started mocking me.

"I'm not, Revvy," he replied, voice soft and steady. And because I was a total simp for him now, it soothed me. "I'm just trying to understand."

"I know. I just . . . I . . . *ugh*."

If this whole "being open" thing was going to become a habit, I'd need to practice in front of a mirror. Maybe get lessons from Zylo.

"Take a breath, rookie," he ordered, and I did. "Now tell me what's going through that brilliant mind of yours."

"I got close enough to see your tattoo, Kai. A piece of you that nobody would know was there, not unless you wanted them to. And you . . . wanted me to. At least I think you did."

"I did," Kai replied. "I wanted you to be close to me."

Before I could reply, a rogue meteor whizzed past my front wing. The force tilted my vehicle to the side, throwing me off balance.

"Fuck," I hissed, turning my wheel the opposite way, attempting to right myself.

"You okay?"

"All good. I just—mother*fucker*!"

The incident gave the person behind me—a rookie from the Vanguard team—the perfect opening to overtake.

"Rev!"

"Someone overtook me," I grumbled, trying to catch up. "It's fine."

"I thought something had happened!"

"You worried about me, hotshot?" I asked, attempting to ease the tension.

"Of course I was worried about you, dickhead. I care about you, for fuck's sake."

"You . . ." The word caught in my throat, shaky and small. My chest felt tight. "You c-care about me?"

"Yes, Rev, I care about you," Kai snapped. "Stop deflecting and tell me why you ran away."

"You're the one who brought up your feelings!" I shot back, not at all deflecting.

"Rev, I swear on the fucking stars—"

"I'm scared I was nothing more than a body to warm your bed, okay?!" I shouted. "I woke up, saw that damn tattoo, and wondered what the hell was happening to us. Because somewhere along the way, you stopped just annoying the hell out of me—which, for the record, you still do. I just want to kill you a little less than I used to.

"You were supposed to be nothing more than the cocky bastard who lived to piss me off. But being with you, waking up with my head on your chest and having you hold me like it meant something terrified me, Kai. Because to me, it did mean something. No, it meant *everything*, and I didn't want to be the fool if you didn't feel the same.

"So I ran. I ran before you could wake up and confirm my fears. In my mind, I thought I was making it easier—for you, for me. I was protecting myself, because as much as I want people to think so, I'm not infallible."

I panted, chest heaving.

"I'm fragile, just like everyone else. The only difference is that I hide it better."

My eyes burned, mirroring the anger that consumed me from the inside out. But I wasn't angry with Kai. I was furious with myself for bottling it up, for lacking the courage to speak like the adult I believed I was.

Now it had exploded like a shaken soda can, and the pressure was too much. I'd blown up, dragging Kai down as collateral damage, and he was going to hate me for it.

I sat in silence, alone with the hum of my engine and the roar of the thrusters. I wanted to say his name, to plead with him to speak, but fear held me back. I couldn't face the dreaded confirmation.

The radio crackled. "Rev, I—"

I didn't hear what he said because the team radio kicked in, overriding the other frequencies. Kai's voice cut out, replaced with the frantic voice of my engineer, Kileen.

"Rogue meteor heading straight for you, Rev. We missed it on the radar. You need to—"

Something hit the side of my vehicle with such force my helmet smacked the glass dome covering the cockpit.

"Shit!"

My vision swam, and when it cleared, the world was spinning. Not from a head injury, but because my vehicle had veered off the race line, crossed the track boundary, and plunged straight into the surrounding asteroid belt.

"Rev, are you okay?" I heard Tavoris ask, but I didn't respond. I was too busy shaking off the fog in my brain, white-knuckling the wheel.

I hit the button for my backup thrusters, the ones meant to stabilise the vehicle, but nothing happened. An insistent beeping filled the cockpit, and that made my stomach drop.

The asteroid hadn't just clipped me; it had obliterated the thrusters on the right side. The left ones were still firing, but with nothing to counterbalance them, all they did was spin me wildly, making the damage worse with every sickening rotation.

I fought between trying to stop the spinning and not throwing up inside my helmet. If this is what the Tilt-a-Whirl felt like at the theme park, I was glad I'd missed out as a kid.

Slamming the button to kill the thrusters, I powered down everything but the radio, hoping it would stop the dizzying spin.

It didn't.

Another comet struck with a deafening crash, throwing me sideways.

I barely had time to see the mass of rock looming beside me before we collided. The impact shattered the asteroid into a thousand shards, debris pelting my vehicle like bullets. It chipped the glass above my head, while metal shrieked and bent. A large chunk slammed into the side panel, crumpling it inward.

Pain exploded through my lower leg, white-hot and blinding, like fire tearing through my nerves. I screamed, but it sounded distant, like it belonged to someone else.

The vehicle stopped spinning, leaving me hanging in deep space, surrounded by debris.

My hands clenched the steering wheel, but I couldn't feel them. Couldn't feel anything except the buzzing in my head. Shock was setting in, my body beginning to tremble, and all I could do was sit and wait for the medical shuttle to arrive.

My team talked, saying words I couldn't comprehend. I was too busy drifting away in my head, floating somewhere I could just relax for a while, ignoring the shitshow going on around me.

And at the edge of it all, Kai's voice crackled over the radio. Calling my name, over and over. Like maybe if he said it enough, it would bring me back to him in one piece.

OUT OF THIS WORLD & INTO YOUR ARMS

Rev

The medics returned me to the paddock and sent me to the nearest hospital for stitches.

The crumpled metalwork had tried to take a chunk out of me when it jabbed me in the side. It wasn't so deep that it would cause permanent damage, but it looked gnarly when I saw the shredded leg of my racing suit, sticky blue-black blood covering my calf.

The doctors insisted it looked worse than it was. That despite the volume of blood, the laceration hadn't hit anything important. It was basically a giant paper cut—stinging like a motherfucker, even though the damage wasn't substantial.

Two hours in the hospital and thirty-six stitches later, the team shuttle dropped me off at home.

Zylo, Tavoris, and Kileen had been in touch, but all I could muster was a cursory, "I'm fine, stop worrying." Anything else was too much energy, and I was desperate to crawl into bed.

Kai had reached out while I was waiting for the doctor to sign off on my discharge.

> Annoying Prick
>
> Are you okay?
>
> I saw the footage, and it looked fucking rough. You were bleeding a lot . . .
>
> No one will give me an update, and I'm going out of my mind.
>
> Zylo said they took you to the fucking hospital. Did you hit your head? Is your leg okay???
>
> Please, Rev. I need to know you're okay.

I hated that I'd worried him, so the plan was to reply as soon as I got home.

It didn't seem like he hated me, if his frantic messages were anything to go by. He might change his tune once he found out I was okay, but I had to push aside my confusion, my fear. The curt response reserved for everyone else wouldn't cut it with Kai, because he deserved more than that.

He deserved more from me.

I arrived at my apartment on the fifth floor, ready for a peaceful night and a long hot shower.

So imagine my surprise when I reached my door to find it unlocked, and buzzing around my apartment like they owned the place were my Mum, Dad, and Grandma.

"*Zyli!*" Mum tackled me before the front door had closed. "I'm so glad you're okay."

She stepped back and gripped my shoulders, analysing me from head to toe. Her eyes welled up when she saw my calf, where the raised leg of my sweatpants revealed a thick white bandage, speckled with blood.

"It's fine, Mum," I whispered, lips ticking up in a reassuring smile.

She didn't look convinced, but she nodded all the same.

She led me from the hallway into my open-plan living and kitchen area, where Grandma was cooking up a storm. The mouthwatering smells permeated the air, and my stomach rumbled, reminding me I hadn't eaten since this morning. Dad lounged on the leather sofa, watching an old series of *Love Planet*—his guilty pleasure.

"There's my wounded soldier!" he bellowed, holding his big arms open.

I limped over, letting him pull me into a bear hug, before plopping down beside him. And if I tucked myself further into his side, enjoying the feel of his arms wrapped around me, that was no one's business but my own.

Dad and I rested our feet on the coffee table, and I looked up at Mum.

"What are you doing here?"

"We saw the footage, *zyli*." She plucked a microfiber cloth from the pile of cleaning supplies stacked up near the kitchen. The markings on her skin pulsed sky blue, revealing her concern. "Nina called and let us know you were okay and were at the hospital, but with the race still going, there wasn't time to update us."

"You know what your mum's like," Dad cut in with a playful wink. "She dragged us straight here, convinced you were coming home one leg short."

"Like you weren't concerned he had a concussion," Mum snapped, hands on her hips.

Dad chuckled, squeezing me tighter. "Of course I was worried! How am I supposed to live the high life as the dad of a pro racer if his head's too banged up to race?"

I nudged him in the side. "Don't worry, Dad. No need to give up on your aspirations yet."

"Let me look at my grandson," Grandma demanded, rounding the kitchen island to approach us with the natural air of seniority she carried.

She perched on the sofa cushion next to me and reached out a hand, brushing the loose strands of hair away from my face. I winced when she touched the hard lump on the left side of my forehead, caused by my helmet.

"Look at your pretty face," she muttered, taking in the bruised skin. "All knocked up."

"You make it sound like I'm disfigured," I grumbled.

She tutted and narrowed her eyes.

"You're lucky you weren't! Look at your leg." She gestured to the bandages. "That's going to scar, *va'tari*. You need to be more careful!"

"I was being careful," I shot back. "Last I checked, I can't control the galaxy's asteroids."

Grandma pinched the tip of my ear between her surprisingly strong fingers, tugging my face closer to hers.

"Watch how you speak to your elders," she scolded, giving my head a little shake. "I'll let you off because you're tired and hurting, but remember, you're never too old for a spanked behind."

I dropped my gaze in shame, shrinking into my dad's side when she released me.

Her threats were never empty, and the vision of her coming for me with that heavy wooden hairbrush she loved was enough to put me in my place.

"Sorry, Grandma," I mumbled, pacified when she leaned in and brushed my cheek with a soft peck.

The lines on both our skin flared sunshine yellow, signifying our love and care for one another.

"I love you, my little supernova."

I smiled. "I know. Love you too."

She kissed me once more before standing up from the couch. "Go and shower, *va'tari*. You smell like antiseptic, and it's making my nose burn."

"Could also be the food you're cooking," Dad quipped.

Grandma glared at him, while Mum slipped away to dust a set of shelves that were already spotless.

"I will spit in your dinner," she hissed, turning on her heel and storming back to the kitchen.

"Good luck with that one, Dad."

We shared a conspiratorial grin. Dad had been winding Grandma up my entire life, and while she acted like he was the bane of her life, we all knew it was for show.

Dad helped me up from the sofa before turning back to *Love Planet*, and I limped towards my bedroom, dropping a peck on my mum's cheek as I passed her.

"Do you need any help, *zyli*?" she asked, and I shook my head, closing the door behind me.

I sighed, leaning back against the wood. I loved my family to death, but even I could admit they were a lot.

Showering was awkward, since I couldn't get the bandages wet, and I ended up precariously balanced in the walk-in shower, bad leg hanging out of the open door. It left the tiled floor a little wetter than I'd have liked, but it was worth it to feel clean after everything that had happened.

By the time I hobbled into the living room, dressed in a baggy T-shirt and some pyjama bottoms covered in cartoon race vehicles—a birthday present from my parents two years ago—I was dead on my feet.

I curled back into my dad's side, only half listening to the new episode he'd started while I showered. Mum and Grandma joined us, the latter handing me a bowl filled with the traditional Iskari stew she saved for when someone was ill.

I wasn't sick, but I was feeling worse for wear, so I appreciated the warmth from the secret combination of spices she used. Even Mum didn't know what was in it, and when she tried to recreate it, it never tasted quite the same.

I was falling asleep into my almost empty bowl when a knock at the door startled me awake. Mum jumped up from her seat to answer it, but I waved her off, placing the bowl on the coffee table.

"Don't worry, I'll get it."

"You need to rest, *zyli*."

"Need to keep moving so I don't go stiff."

When I opened the door, I wished I'd let her answer it instead.

Standing on my doorstep, holding a bright bouquet and a stuffed black cat, was Kai. I frowned while he stood there, wide-eyed. We said nothing for a moment, just stared at one another, taking everything in.

I leaned against the doorframe, relieving some of the weight off my injured leg.

"Kai," I said, and he blinked back to awareness, shoving his offerings into my hands.

An array of floral scents filled my nose, and I eyed the fluffy cat toy. The cat toy's ugliness was almost cute; its black fur stuck out as if it had been electrocuted. The huge purple eyes stared into my soul, and it held a sign between its oversized paws that read, *"You had me at meow."*

I glanced up at him, one eyebrow raised, and he scratched the back of his neck. His cheeks flushed a satisfying shade of red.

"I saw it and, uh, I thought of you, y'know?"

"Right." I used the bouquet to cover the lower half of my face, hiding my shy smile. "What are you doing here?"

"I wanted to make sure you were okay," he explained. "I got your address from Zylo—"

"That man is a walking data protection lawsuit," I muttered, rolling my eyes.

"Yeah," Kai chuckled. "He wanted to come with me, but I persuaded him not to." He shifted from one foot to the other. "I didn't hear from you, and I was worried. I . . . I just wanted to check on you."

"Sorry," I replied, my skin glowing bright orange. "I was going to text you, but I got distracted with—"

"Who is it, *zyli*?" Mum called, interrupting our awkward exchange.

With Kai's surprise drop-in, I'd forgotten I already had company, and now I wasn't sure what to do.

Beyond my family, I'd never had visitors, so I wasn't sure of the social etiquette. Did I tell him to go home? Invite him in and introduce him to my family?

I didn't have time to decide, because Mum appeared, beaming at Kai.

"Oh, hello!" Her skin flickered with golden light. "You're Kai Mercer, aren't you?"

I watched, mesmerised, as Kai shook off the awkwardness and transformed into his usual charming self.

He smiled back at Mum, holding out his hand. "I was the last time I checked. You're Rev's mum?"

"Yes, I am." She took his hand in hers, then spotted the gifts in my arms. "Oh, they're lovely. Are they from you, Kai?"

His cheeks burned brighter than the red lights on the track. "I wanted to make sure Rev was okay," he explained, eyes shifting to me. "I didn't mean to interrupt."

"You're not," I replied, trying to reassure him.

"Sorry. I'll leave you to it—"

"No," I blurted, a little louder than I meant to, startling Mum and Kai. "You don't need to go."

Kai bit his lip, and Mum picked up on his uncertainty.

"I'll take these for you, *zyli*." She removed the gifts from my hands and smiled at Kai. "There's plenty of food if you're hungry, Kai? Rev's grandma cooks enough to feed an army."

I could see him struggling with an internal debate, and when he looked at me, I nodded, trying to let him know without words that he was welcome to stay.

Whatever he saw in my face put him at ease, and he returned Mum's smile with a charming one of his own. "That would be great, Mrs Arathiel. Thank you."

"Please," she called over her shoulder, disappearing into the main living area. "Call me Mina. Mrs Arathiel makes me feel like an old woman."

"What's wrong with being an old woman?" Grandma retorted, while Dad muttered a quiet wisecrack in response.

I didn't hear what he said, but I couldn't miss the grunt he made when Grandma no doubt whacked him.

"Welcome to my home, I guess," I said with a shrug.

Kai followed me as I limped down the hallway, his hand resting on the small of my back, just above my tail. The heat of his palm seeped through my T-shirt, warming me to my core, and my tail wrapped around his wrist, a place it seemed to favour these days, like it was trying to keep him close to me.

He leaned in close and whispered in my ear, "Nice PJs, rookie."

"Fuck off, Mercer." My grumble was half-assed, and I sent a small, shy smile his way.

When we entered the main room, Dad and Grandma turned their heads towards the fresh addition. Dad smiled and opened his mouth to speak, but Grandma beat him to it.

"Oh look, it's the asshole."

Kai and I froze, and an uncomfortable silence filled the room. We turned to stare at one another, wearing matching expressions of surprise. My skin pulsed with a mix of burnt orange and sky blue.

"I am so sorry," I squeaked.

Kai remained silent. I was about to give Grandma an earful, wooden brush to the backside be damned, when his face crumpled.

And then he laughed.

It came from deep within his belly. A joy-filled cackle that flooded the open space of my apartment as he bent at the waist, hands resting on his thighs. From the corner of my eye, I could see my parents watching on with open mouths, probably wondering if Kai was losing it.

Had Grandma broken him?

I was wondering whether he'd cracked, when he straightened up and rubbed his stomach muscles. Tears tracked down his cheeks, and he wiped them away before looking at me.

"I can see where you get it from," he wheezed. "It's fucking cute, Revvy. You're so fucking cute."

That strange amethyst glow flickered between us, dancing across my skin. It was the one that only ever showed up around Kai, and I couldn't remember the last time it had burned red with irritation.

In my periphery, I caught Grandma eyeing my skin with a knowing smile that shifted into a smirk as she looked back at Kai.

"Well then, Mr Mercer. Come and take a seat." She gestured to the empty chair beside her as if she owned the damn place. "It seems we have a lot to learn about you."

Kai shrugged, then crossed the room and sat down. I shook my head, a small smile tugging at the corners of my mouth.

Fucking families.

I was ashamed to admit that I didn't know all that much about Kai beyond what I saw on the track. I felt bad that he was at the centre of my family's inquisition, but it surprised me to learn what I did.

"My mum raised me on her own," he explained when Dad asked about his family. "She took me to Karting for Kids, and that's how I got into the sport. I'd like to say it was because I found an old kart I was obsessed with . . ." He smiled, resting a hand on my thigh. "But I was a hyper little shit, and I think she just wanted some peace on the weekends."

Everyone laughed at that, even me. I could picture Kai as a child, running amok and driving his mum up the wall.

His smile turned sad. "Growing up, we were close. Not so much now."

I gripped his hand in mine, wanting to comfort him. Kai was so full of joy, the sadness looked almost wrong on his face, and I wanted to take it away.

"We talk when we can, but I'm busy with the league, and she's travelling the galaxy. I bought her a house after winning my first championship, just to say thanks for the sacrifices she made."

"I'm sure she appreciates everything you do for her, Kai," I said, eyes fixed on our joined hands.

He gave mine a gentle squeeze. When I looked up, the sadness was gone, replaced with a lopsided grin. "Thanks, little comet."

Heat flooded my cheeks while my skin glowed amethyst. A quick glance around the room revealed my family's eyes on us, watching a little too closely. I cleared my throat, slipped my hand from his, and shifted in my seat.

The conversation turned to lighter topics, and then Mum asked him about me.

"What are the other drivers like, Kai? Are they being nice to Rev?"

"Mum," I groaned, hiding my face in my hands.

She made it sound like I was the new kid at school, wanting to know if I was being bullied. Kai found it hilarious, slinging his arm around my shoulders and pulling me closer. I inhaled his scent—leather and cardamom—and I had to force myself not to glue my face to his neck.

I was already embarrassed enough, and I refused to make things worse.

But then Kai's fingers traced slow, absent patterns along my bicep, and I leaned into his side without thinking.

"They're great," Kai confirmed, putting Mum at ease. "Everyone thinks Rev's brilliant. He's putting some of the veterans to shame."

I groaned louder, whipping Kai's legs with my tail when he laughed.

We settled into a game of Monopogalaxy, where Grandma bankrupted us all and Dad threatened to flip the board if someone sent him to jail again.

Watching them bicker between themselves, I could see where my own competitive streak came from, and considering Mum was busy trying to calm them both down, it wasn't from her.

Noise filled the living room, but it didn't bother me as much as I thought it would.

I was used to it just being the four of us. My family. I had never brought a friend home, especially not someone I was sort of in a relationship with.

Not that this was a relationship.

I wasn't sure what this was. But seeing the way Kai joined in, slipping seamlessly into their dynamic, made something warm spark in my chest. It was like he'd always belonged there.

Grandma served bowls of *luzari'eth*, and Kai enjoyed it so much he had seconds, *and* thirds. He rivalled Dad in the volume of food he could put away, and he won Grandma over when he gushed about her cooking. She fell head over heels when he asked if there was any leftover stew, because he wanted to take some home.

When my family announced they were leaving, I was exhausted.

Kai helped Mum sort the dishes in the kitchen, and Dad kissed me goodbye before leaving to start up their shuttle. It left just me and Grandma on the couch, and I had some questions that needed answering.

I shuffled along the cushions until we were side by side. "Grandma?"

"Yes, *va'tari*?"

"I think something's wrong with me."

She frowned, looking me up and down. "What do you mean?"

I traced the markings on my forearm with my finger. "I've been glowing a funny colour. It's like . . . amethyst."

When she didn't reply, I glanced up, horrified to see her eyes glisten. "Oh, stars," I croaked. "Is it bad? Am I dying?"

She took my hands in hers, the skin fragile, almost paper-thin. But her touch grounded me while I panicked about my untimely death.

"No, *va'tari*," she soothed. "You're not dying."

"Then what does it mean? It keeps happening, and I'm confused."

She cupped my cheek.

"It's not a bad thing, my darling. Not a bad thing at all." Her gaze flicked towards the kitchen. "It's something beautiful, I promise. But you're not ready to hear it yet."

"What do you—"

"I'll tell you when you're older."

I scowled. "I'm twenty-four."

When she flicked me on the tip of my nose with her talon-like nails, I yelped. "Listen to your elders, Revvak."

I huffed, my bottom lip poking out like a baby. "Yes, Grandma."

Mum and Grandma gave me a million hugs and kisses, and Mum asked at least five times if I wanted her to stay. She left when I reassured her I'd call if something was wrong, and then it was just me and Kai in my living room.

We stood in awkward silence, looking everywhere but at each other.

Kai cleared his throat, running a hand through his hair.

"I'm glad you're okay, rookie." Then he jerked his head towards the hallway. To the front door. The exit. "I should go."

"You don't have to," I rushed out, and Kai's eyebrows flew up towards his hairline, so fast I thought they might take flight.

He stepped towards me, arm twitching like he wanted to reach for me . . . but he didn't, and to my surprise, I felt disappointed. I wanted Kai to touch me. I wanted him to pull me against his chest and kiss me senseless, just like he'd done so many times before.

When I didn't scowl or step away, he took another step, and when his arm twitched, he didn't fight it. He brought his hand to my face, brushing some strands of hair behind my ear. The gesture was so tender it made my mouth dry.

When my tongue poked out to wet my lips, Kai's eyes followed the movement.

"Kai," I whispered, worried that my voice could break the quietness between us, as if the moment was delicate like glass.

He lowered his head, lips inching closer to mine, and I rose onto my toes to meet him, but pain shot through my leg, sharp enough to make me hiss. He pulled back at once, eyes dropping to my legs, where I was leaning hard on the right to spare the injured one.

"You're in pain," he stated, and despite his tenderness, I rolled my eyes.

"That'll happen when metal takes a slice out of you."

Instead of snapping back, he snickered. "You're such a brat."

He dragged a hand down his face, and before I could come up with an appropriate retort, Kai was in motion.

He wrapped an arm around my back, dipping lower to hook his other arm behind my knees. In one fluid motion, he swept my feet off the floor. I squeaked, throwing my arms around his neck, and he cradled me against his chest.

"What are you doing, Mercer?" I snapped.

"I'm carrying you. What's it look like I'm doing?"

His cocky smile used to make my blood boil, but now, surrounded by his warmth, it sent the butterflies in my chest into a frenzy.

"I'm not a damsel in distress." My traitorous tail betrayed the cool front I was trying to maintain, curling around his hips and giving them a squeeze.

"No, you're definitely not," he deadpanned, swatting me on the ass. "Where's your bedroom, rookie?"

I smirked. "Why? Planning to haul me off and claim your spoils in bed?"

My fingers curled into the short hair at the nape of his neck, giving them a light tug. He shivered in response, eyes still dark from our almost kiss.

"You have no idea how much I want to ravage you, little comet," he replied, voice a deep rasp that went straight to my dick. "But not tonight."

I opened my mouth, ready to demand he put me down, to cover my embarrassment over his rejection.

But before I could, he leaned down, kissing the tip of my nose.

"You look knackered, Revvy." Like he'd commanded it, my mouth stretched wide with a yawn. "I'm taking you to bed, where I'm going to hold you all night. And tomorrow, I'll take care of you. Got it?"

Speechless, I could only nod, my mouth hanging open.

He asked again where my bedroom was, and I pointed down a different hallway. "Second door on the right."

"Good boy."

Kai carried me deeper into the apartment. In my bedroom, he set me down in the middle of the bed, then switched on the lamp.

"Painkillers?"

"In the cabinet above the sink," I replied, pointing at the door to my en suite.

He disappeared into the bathroom, returning with a plastic cup of water and two strong painkillers in the palm of his hand. He handed them over, ordering me to take them, and when I'd swallowed them, I showed off my empty mouth just to be childish. He took the cup and left it on the bedside table.

As I shifted on the bed, pulling back the covers to slide underneath, Kai started undressing. I paused halfway, watching as he stripped down to his boxers, the soft lighting emphasising his washboard abs. He caught me eye-fucking him, and I couldn't even pretend to be ashamed.

The man was a snack, and he knew it.

"Eyes up here, baby."

I had to rip my eyes off his body like Velcro, and he chuckled darkly.

I lifted the quilt so he could slide in beside me. He shifted me until I was lying on my side, facing away from him, and his chest was against my back, and the heat from his skin made it feel like I was lying in the sun.

But instead of shying away from it, I basked in it, pressing myself as close to him as possible. It meant that the hard line of his cock slotted between my ass cheeks, and I was annoyed I was still wearing my pyjama bottoms.

When I started squirming, Kai thrust his hips forward, and the sensation made me whimper.

"You're making it fucking hard to be a gentleman, rookie," he groaned, burying his face against the back of my neck.

"Who said you need to be a gentleman?"

I rolled my hips against him, but before I could take things further, Kai placed a heavy hand on my hip, halting my movements.

"Not tonight, baby," he insisted, pressing his lips against my nape, leaving behind the softest kiss. "We're going to sleep, and tomorrow we're going to talk."

I stiffened, remembering how we'd left things before I crashed.

The way I'd exploded, blurting out my fears in a waterfall of word vomit. How convinced I was that he'd hate me, despite the way he'd desperately called my name on the radio, begging me to answer him.

Sensing the sudden change in mood, Kai dragged his hand from my hip to my stomach, rubbing in small circles. The action was calming, soothing my anxious heart, and I relaxed back against him.

"At least with an injured leg you can't run away in the morning," he quipped, giggling like a schoolboy when I kicked him in the shin. "Close your eyes, Revvy."

Like he'd pulled my fatigue to the surface, my eyelids felt heavy and I allowed them to close, blanketed by the warmth of his larger body, the smell of cardamom and leather soaking into my sheets.

Just as my consciousness slipped away in favour of sleep, he whispered, "I'm not going anywhere, little comet."

And throughout the entire night, Kai kept his promise.

FULL THROTTLE, ZERO INHIBITION

Kai

My skin felt too tight, and the molten heat pooling in my groin set my body on fire.

I peeled open my eyes, only to find the darkness remained, and I realised after a second that my face was buried in Rev's hair. Colorful hues shone from the strands, splayed out on the pillow in the early morning sun.

Some of it had found its way into my mouth, which was less than pleasant, but not enough to make me complain. I could complain about the lead pipe tucked between my bedmate's ass cheeks, though.

Stars, forget the hair. I wanted something else in my mouth.

Rev's dick, in case that wasn't clear.

All night, I'd held him close, my arm around his waist and his tail around my calf. My skin was damp with a thin layer of sweat thanks to the combination of the covers and our body heat.

But that wasn't enough for me to let go. I'd promised him I wouldn't go anywhere, and I wanted to keep my word.

Even if I was ready to bust a nut.

I recited the phonetic alphabet in my head, trying to calm myself down because I couldn't bear to disturb him. He looked so peaceful, face smoothed out in sleep. It wasn't the same as his usual mask, which was blank and refined with sharp edges.

Now he looked soft, mouth open as he drooled on his pillow, little fangs poking out to say hello.

He scooted backwards, pressing his ass flush against my groin. The added pressure made a groan slip out before I could stop it, and his tail tightened around my leg. His breathing remained steady, and I assumed he was still asleep.

I knew I was being played when he pressed against me a second time. And a third.

"What are you doing, rookie?" I slid my hand under his T-shirt, enjoying the cosy warmth of his soft skin.

Rev hummed, reaching back to thread his fingers through my hair. "Just checking you're awake."

"You *know* I'm awake."

I thrust against his backside, and his fingers gripped my hair as he moaned, pushing back against me. I was dying to feel his body against mine, with no barriers between us.

Dragging my hand up his chest, I continued rolling my hips, fingers circling his nipple. I pinched the sensitive bud, and Rev's hips bucked as he whimpered. He fisted my hair until it stung, adding an extra layer of enjoyment.

It was exhilarating, knowing I could make Rev writhe like this. Knowing I could rip away his facade and make him lose control.

Releasing his nipple, my fingers drifted down to his stomach. I stroked along the waistband of his pyjama bottoms, and he trembled in my arms, moving his hips forward to coax my hand lower.

Leaning in, I teased the shell of his ear with my teeth.

"We still need to talk, little comet." I nipped his earlobe, making him shudder. "Don't think I've forgotten."

"Of course you haven't," he huffed. "Can it wait?"

I cupped his cock through the cotton fabric and squeezed. Rev chewed his lip, trying to stifle his moans.

I couldn't have that, so I rubbed my thumb over the tip, teasing him until I felt the growing wet patch on his crotch. He whined my name, trying to increase the friction, but every time he moved, I loosened my grip.

"You'll talk to me if you want to come, baby."

He rolled his head on the pillow, staring up at me through a mess of dark hair. His eyes were wild, the inner stardust swirling.

"I've already said everything," he panted. "It's your turn to talk."

Releasing Rev's cock, I sat up, pressing on his shoulders until he lay flat on his back. I positioned myself between his legs and pushed his T-shirt up to his armpits. His tail thumped against the mattress, matching the rise and fall of his chest, and when my thumb brushed his nipple again, he gasped, arching into the touch.

"Tell me again."

"Kai, please."

I pressed my lips against his stomach, tongue dipping into his belly button. "Come on, baby. Tell me."

"I . . ." He trailed off with a swallow, and my eyes shifted to watch his Adam's apple bob in his throat. "I'm scared, Kai."

He shivered when I kissed his ribs. "Scared of what?"

"Of whatever this is." I rewarded Rev's honesty by pulling his nipple between my lips. When I sucked, he squirmed, hands flying to my head.

"I don't know w-what we're doing or w-what this is. I just know it m-means something, and I . . . *fuck*, Kai . . . I just . . . I don't want to be just another f-fuck. Not to you."

I leaned forward and pressed a kiss to his chin. Then I covered his body with mine, mindful of his injured leg, hoping the weight would anchor him while he flayed himself open for me. I stroked his side, fingertips dancing over his ribs.

"Is that what you think this is? Just a casual fuck?"

He nodded, then shook his head, before nodding again. He settled on a weak shrug.

"I don't know," he whispered, wrapping his tail around my waist.

"Oh, Revvy." My hand cupped his cheek, and his eyes fluttered closed when he leaned into the touch, ears twitching against the pillow. "I don't know how to tell you this, but I'm obsessed with you."

The markings on his skin shimmered pink, and when he opened his eyes, I saw the beautiful galaxies I wanted to drown in. He pursed his lips, trying to fight a smile, but it broke through anyway, and it left me breathless.

"Like a stalker?" he teased.

I pinched his cheek. "I mean, I'm not gonna tap into your calls or climb through your window at night—"

"You'd have your work cut out for you, since I live on the fifth floor."

"You don't know what I do in my spare time," I protested. "I have great upper-arm strength."

Rev giggled, nuzzling my palm.

"Anyway, what I'm trying to say is, you consume me, rookie." His breath hitched. "After that very first scowl, you wriggled deep into my mind, like those giant sandworms on Ithara—"

"Are you calling me a worm?"

I groaned, dropping my face onto his chest. "You're so difficult."

"Sorry, starboy. I'll be good," Rev snickered, running his hand through my bedhead. "You were calling me a worm?"

I glared, but his teasing smile, a novelty he rarely shared with others, made my heart flutter. And I melted for him faster than an ice cube in the sun.

"I'm falling for you, Rev."

His eyes widened, mouth forming a perfect circle. His skin glittered with pink and gold light. "You . . . y-you're . . . what?"

"I'm falling for you," I repeated. "I don't know how we got here, because we didn't hit it off in the beginning."

Rev scoffed, because that was the understatement of the year.

"You mask yourself around others," I continued. "Wielding indifference like a shield to keep them at a distance. But even when I thought you couldn't stand me, you let little pieces of yourself slip through. I saw the *real* you, Rev. The man behind the curtain."

He swallowed, processing what I'd said. But unlike before, he didn't interrupt, sensing I had more to get off my chest.

"Your interview was where I got to know you, even if you didn't really want me there. I learned just how incredible you are, and since then, you've only proved me right. I wish the rest of the world could see it too, but I'm a selfish bastard at heart, and I'm glad you save that part of yourself for me."

Brushing a hand through his hair, my fingertips grazed over his scalp. Rev's eyes grew wet, glassy, and his tail squeezed my torso, urging me to continue. I knew he was overwhelmed, but he needed to understand my feelings before we could move forward.

"I want to be your safe space, rookie. The place you can rest when the shield gets too heavy. To be your quiet haven when the world gets too loud. And I want to see you glare at everyone else, sexy and broody, knowing you save the rare smiles for me.

"Somewhere along the way, you became *everything* to me, little comet. And I'll gladly feel the burn if I get to hold you close."

Rev said nothing. Stars, was he even breathing? The silence dragged on, and I worried I'd read this all wrong. That I'd ruined whatever I thought was blooming between us by opening my big mouth.

We'd bared our hearts to one another, something that was obviously new to Rev. He spent ninety-nine percent of the time locked up tighter than a vault, but today he'd been cracked open. And I'd added my own feelings to the mix until the contents were overflowing.

So how would he react?

He had already run once before, and just because he was injured and we were in *his* bedroom, I wouldn't put it past him to do so again.

And then he sat up. So suddenly that I had to scramble to my knees. I just avoided a broken nose and another mouthful of hair.

Rev cupped my cheeks, soft fingers caressing my jaw.

"Do you mean it?" he whispered, dark eyes staring deep into my soul, sparking a fire that warmed the cavern beneath my ribs.

Desperation laced his hopeful expression; he wanted—no, he *needed*—my words to be true. The fact that he doubted me broke my heart for him, because he deserved so much more. Someone who would never make him feel like he had to face the world on his own.

I wanted to be that person.

My hands rested on top of his, keeping him right where he was. He pressed his legs against my thighs, and his tail curled around my forearm, as though he needed to touch every part of me to know this was real.

I'd reassure him. Every damn day if he'd let me.

But now felt like the perfect time to begin.

"Every word, baby."

He tightened his hold on my face and pulled hard enough that we ended up a tangle of limbs on the bed. He wheezed as I landed on him, but it didn't stop him from smashing his mouth to mine.

We met in a clash of teeth and lips, pure passion and fire. The kiss consumed me, and I didn't know where Rev ended and I began. It felt like he was devouring me, taking pieces of me for himself, locking them away behind his walls.

I'd give him every one of my breaths if it made him fucking smile.

He wrapped his arms around my neck, clinging to me, nails digging into my skin. I gripped his hips, feeling the sharpness of his bones below his skin.

He was slim, dainty, almost fragile in appearance. But appearances could be deceiving. Rev was as nimble in life as he was behind the wheel, and I knew he could tackle me to the bed in an instant if he wanted.

He was an enigma, surprising everyone he met.

I just hoped he would never stop surprising me too.

Sliding my hands under his T-shirt, I dragged it up his body to reveal his pearlescent torso. When I pulled back to remove the offending material, Rev chased my lips with a whine. His lips were swollen, eyes burning with lust. The marks on his skin pulsed, and I chuckled.

"Feeling needy, baby?"

"Yes," he said on an exhale. "Kai, I-I want you to . . . I want . . ."

I pressed my forehead against his, the tips of our noses squished together. "What do you want, Rev?"

I had a feeling, but I needed him to say it.

"I want you to fuck me."

The words echoed through my head on repeat.

Rev wanted me to fuck him.

He wanted *me* to be his first.

I searched his face for any evidence of doubt. "Are you sure?"

He released my shoulders to grab the hem of his T-shirt, tugging it over his head. "I want you, Kai. So take me."

He didn't have to ask twice.

I trailed kisses along Rev's jaw, dropping to his neck, his chest, and his stomach. I dragged his bottoms as far down as I could, sitting up to pull them the rest of the way off. Rev laughed as I tossed them over my shoulder, uncaring where they landed.

They could've gone straight out the window for all I cared, because he was bare beneath me, and my mouth was watering for a taste .

"I'm going to get you ready for me, little comet." I gripped the outside of his thigh. "Then I'm going to fill you with my cock."

Rev whimpered, gripping his bedsheets. His tail curled around itself before unravelling, repeating the motion like it didn't know what to do with itself. His skin shimmered with colour, a gorgeous rosy pink.

"Please, Kai."

His cock twitched, leaking precum that pooled on his stomach. I couldn't resist laving my tongue over the silky skin, and his sweet musk exploded on my tastebuds.

We groaned in unison.

"Turn over for me, baby. Let me prep you."

He flipped onto his stomach, burying his face in the pillows. The position put the round globes of his ass in my face, so I dipped my head and nipped his rump with my teeth. He gasped, rubbing his cock against the sheets.

"On your knees."

Chest down, ass up, Rev was a vision.

The view of his slick, shiny hole made me salivate. His tail coiled around his thigh, and with no reason to delay, I dived between his cheeks, dragging my tongue over his pucker. He cried out, jerking forward before pressing back against my face, and I wrapped my hands around his thighs, burying my face in his crease.

I switched between sucking his hole and prodding it with my tongue, and as his rim softened, I stiffened the muscle and breached him. His slick was as sweet as I remembered, and I couldn't get enough, thrusting my tongue in and out as he writhed against me.

"Oh, fuck, Kai... *yes*."

My finger slid in next to my tongue, thrusting in and out. When he fucked himself easily on the single digit, I replaced it with two, then three.

"You're doing so well, baby," I praised, kissing his ass cheek. Crooking my fingers, I searched for his prostate, and when I found it, Rev squealed.

"Oh my... *fuck*, Kai! There... r-right th—oh... yes, there!"

"I can't wait to get inside you."

His tail squeezed his thigh, the pressure leaving the skin beneath a dusky violet.

"Kai, I'm ready. So ready. *Pleasepleaseplease*, shit, *please*, f-fuck me," he babbled.

"I've got you, little comet."

I removed my fingers, watching his hole twitch with the desperate need to be filled. He moaned my name into the pillow, and I shushed him, licking the base of his tail.

"On your back. I want to see your face when I get inside you."

With a gentle touch, I prompted him to roll onto his back, bringing us face to face. "Hurry, Kai," he begged, fuchsia dancing over his skin. "I need you."

Assuming Rev, like any other grown man, kept his supplies in the bedside table, I reached for the top drawer. But my stomach sank when I slid it open and found it empty.

"Fuck."

He propped himself up on his elbows. "What's wrong?"

"There are no condoms."

I felt all sorts of stupid. He might not need lube, but he still needed protection. The man could get pregnant, for fuck's sake.

Rev was a virgin, though, so why would he have a drawer full of condoms?

Moments like this were supposed to be special and planned in advance. Unless you were me, the guy who lost his virginity in a quick tryst behind the local cinema at sixteen.

Rev bit his lip. "We don't need them."

I jerked my head toward him so fast I almost gave myself whiplash. "What?"

"Well, I'm a virgin." He shrugged. "Do *you* need one?"

I knew what he was asking, and I shook my head. "I was tested before the season started."

His lips curled in a wry smile. "Dry spell?"

"Yes, if you must know," I replied haughtily. "But I don't think we need to discuss that right now. Do you?"

"Problem solved, then."

"But what about . . . ?" I trailed off, wondering how to ask. "You know . . ."

"Pregnancy?" Rev asked. "I'm on birth control, Kai. Have been for the last two years. Y'know, just in case."

"They do birth control for men?"

"Iskari aren't the only species with men who can get pregnant, Kai." He raised an eyebrow. "Did you sleep through biology class?"

"I mean, sort of?" I mumbled. "It was boring."

"Well," he said, voice dripping with sarcasm. "Sometimes when a man and another man really like each other—"

"Alright, I get it," I cut him off, glaring while he snickered.

Rev nodded at my cock, which had flagged during our conversation. "Are you sure you know where to put it?"

"Of course I fucking do," I snapped.

"Crack on, then." He flopped down onto his back, curling his legs up to show off his hole. "Breed me, starboy."

Fuck, I was done with waiting. Now that he'd given the green light, I was ready to bury myself inside him.

I gave Rev one more kiss and grabbed a spare pillow.

"Lift up." When he did, I placed it underneath his hips. "Hands behind your knees, baby. Pull your legs back towards your chest."

"Okay," he breathed, his voice trembling, so unlike the teasing tone he'd worn just moments before.

I notched my cock against his hole, adding the slightest bit of pressure. "Bear down and try to relax, okay? It might sting a bit, but I'll go slow."

He nodded, nibbling his lower lip. His skin shifted to a burnt orange glow, flushed with a hint of pale pink.

I stroked the soft skin of his thigh. "I'll take care of you, little comet."

And he whispered, "I trust you, Kai."

I thrust my hips forward, sliding him onto my cock until the tip nestled just inside. Rev hissed as his rim stretched to take me in, and I paused, giving him a moment to adjust.

Jaw clenched, I bit out, "You okay?"

He was hot inside, tight and unyielding. His muscles twitched, his hole constricting around the head of my cock. Rev breathed in and out, his eyes closed and jaw clenched. Sweat gathered on my forehead as I forced myself to stay still, to wait for him to be ready.

Then he nodded, telling me to move.

Rev's erection had flagged with the intrusion, so I gripped it in a loose fist and stroked. He moaned, and as his muscles softened, I eased in a little further.

After half of me was inside, I withdrew slightly, and then began gentle, measured thrusts, sinking deeper until I was fully sheathed. I paused, my eyes fixed on his hole stretched around my pulsing length.

On my next thrust, he opened his eyes, the small galaxies glowing as he looked at me. He released his legs and wrapped them around my waist, lifting a hand to trace my cheekbone with his finger. Then it curled behind my head, pulling me down to meet his lips.

The kiss was tender, filled with the words we couldn't say.

Thank you for giving me this.

Thank you for trusting me.

Thank you for letting me in.

I broke the kiss, whispering, "Are you okay?"

Rev gazed up at me, dazed, his tail wrapped around my calf. When he rolled his hips experimentally, I groaned.

"Move, Kai," he replied on an exhale.

So I did.

I settled into a steady rhythm, careful not to go too hard and hurt him. But stubborn as ever, Rev moved to meet my thrusts.

"I won't break, Kai," he growled, digging his nails into my skin. "Give it to me. *Breed* me."

Gritting my teeth, I changed the angle of my thrusts, pegging his prostate. I smirked when he cried out.

"You want me to fill you, baby?" Drops of sweat fell from my nose, landing on his collarbones. "Want me to stuff you full of cum?"

"Yes! Fuck," he mewled, back arching off the mattress. "Do it, like you promised."

My thrusts grew harder, pushing deeper. I grabbed Rev's legs and pushed them back until he was folded like a pretzel under me. I pulled out until just the head of my cock stayed buried inside, then slammed back in with fierce force.

The impact knocked the air from his lungs, and his hands flew back to slam against the headboard, using the leverage to push hard against me.

"Fuck, rookie," I gasped.

My balls slapped against Rev's cheeks, sweat tracing cold lines down my back. The heavy scent of sex hung thick in the air, while the wet rhythm of skin against skin became our soundtrack. His skin pulsed in shades of pink—soft bubblegum fading into deep magenta—so bright it almost blinded me.

My climax raced toward me like a vehicle tearing around the track, but I was desperate for Rev to cross the line before I did.

"Touch yourself, little comet," I demanded. "I need you to come for me."

Instead of using his hand like I expected, his tail slid over his abdomen and curled tightly around his shaft. Precum leaked from the slit, lubricating his own personal cocksleeve, and my brain short-circuited.

"Fuck," he gasped. Rev tilted his head back, the muscles in his neck straining as I continued pegging his prostate. "Oh god, I . . . I-I'm—shit . . . *Kai*!"

He exploded, my name on his lips as cum burst from his cock. It covered his tail and his stomach, and some even hit his neck. I wanted to lick him clean, but I was too close. So close to falling into oblivion.

"Kiss me," Rev ordered, just able to breathe, curled in a ball while I pounded his hole.

The feeling of our lips meeting set me off, his wet tongue rubbing against mine. My hips stuttered, and my cock pulsed, flooding his ass as my orgasm hit me like a comet, the impact huge and earth-shattering.

My body went numb, and I released Rev's legs, collapsing on top of him. My weight crushed him against the mattress, my face tucked into his neck, but Rev didn't complain, just waited patiently for my breathing to even out. He wrapped his arms around me while I lay there like a dead weight, too exhausted to move.

"Fuck me," I wheezed.

"Give me five minutes," he mumbled, voice slurred.

I laughed into his neck. "Did you just make a joke?"

He huffed, smoothing his hands down my back. "I can be funny."

"Could've fooled me."

A hard smack on the ass made me yelp, and my hips bucked forward.

He groaned, mumbling, "Sensitive."

"Sorry."

I heaved myself off him, catching his slight wince as my cock slipped out. Gripping his knees, I spread his legs, watching the cum drip from his puffy hole.

My cum.

Stars, I wanted to scoop it up and push it back inside him.

But I didn't.

I lowered my head to drop a kiss on his hip, and Rev sighed. Rising from the bed, I walked into the en suite, rooting through the cupboards for something I could use to clean him. Settling for a soft hand towel, I wet it under the tap and returned to the bedroom.

Rev hadn't moved, still sprawled out on his mattress with his legs and arms spread wide. Even his tail was still, not fidgeting like it usually did.

He blinked up at me when I perched beside him, and I helped him lift his legs. Then I tenderly cleaned his hole, his stomach, and his tail in silence.

I didn't know what to say, unsure how to sum up something that was so . . . perfect.

And if I said the wrong thing, would he freak out? Would he get up and run?

I didn't want him to, not after we'd shared so much. Seeing him throw up the walls I'd managed to dismantle would kill me.

"Thank you."

Rev's words were quiet, delicate enough to vanish on the breeze. He looked up at me, cheeks still flushed, his mouth curved in a tender smile. And I returned it, lowering myself to press a soft kiss just above his belly button.

I tossed the cloth in the hamper he kept in the corner, and slid into bed beside him, covering us with his duvet. Rev curled into my side, using my chest as his pillow. His lips brushed my pec as he nuzzled the skin, and I wrapped my arms around him.

"Are you okay?"

He raised his head and smiled, happiness making him glow with quiet radiance. "I'm perfect, starboy."

I leaned in to whisper against his lips. "Me too, little comet."

Me too.

FLY THE RED FLAG

Rev

The next six weeks were . . . pretty good.

On the track, things were the same as always. Lots of bickering, plenty of insults, and the same old rivalry.

But after the race ended, we'd spend time together. We were getting to know each other, finding out what made the other tick. Every few days, Kai would show up at my apartment, and sometimes I even went to his.

We'd order in, or I'd teach him simple recipes—he might have been great at racing, but in the kitchen, he was hopeless. After that, we'd put something on SpaceFlix and argue over which characters were the hottest.

At night, we'd crawl into bed, tangled up in each other until we collapsed in a sweaty heap.

Kai was insatiable—not that I was complaining. One night, we fucked so many times that I walked bow-legged for days afterwards. He had the audacity to call me a "space cowboy," like it wasn't his fault I was in that state.

Fine, maybe it was my fault too.

Since we'd admitted our feelings, everything had changed, and it felt great.

I smiled more... laughed even. Kai had offered to be my safe space, and saying yes felt as natural as breathing. I kept up the stony-faced facade in public, but with Kai, I could let my guard down and be myself.

It made me feel lighter than I had in a long time, like the weight of the galaxy wasn't crushing down on me as much as before.

Even my family noticed the difference. My parents commented that I seemed happy when I walked through their door to visit—visits that included Kai more than once. I'd been nervous at first, unsure about showing him where I grew up, but he'd already met my family, and once Grandma started begging me to bring Kai over for dinner, I gave in pretty quickly.

Before long, it became a regular thing.

Every Wednesday, Kai watched *Love Planet* with Dad, gossiped with Mum, and gorged himself on Grandma's food.

Their first meeting might've been rocky, but now I was pretty sure she adored him more than the rest of us combined. She treated it like her own personal mission to fatten Kai up with every Iskari delicacy she could think of.

And every time he moaned and sighed over whatever she set in front of him, Grandma beamed, declaring how lovely it was to have "someone who truly appreciated her cooking."

Meanwhile, I was stuck hiding an inappropriate boner under the table, thanks to the downright pornographic sounds coming out of his mouth.

And don't even get me started on the way he licked his cutlery clean.

On one of our weekends off, I took him to another underground race—just as spectators this time. He loved experiencing it from the crowd's perspective, pointing out all the ways it differed from the more structured ASL. And when Al crossed the finish line in first place, Kai cheered so loudly I feared for my hearing.

But now we were back at the paddock for the eighth race of the season.

Two races remained, and Kai was leading the championship. He wasn't untouchable, though, and Zylo was close behind him. Despite the small gap,

Kai felt utterly sure of his ability to win a fourth championship. I was sitting in fifth place, just behind Dray in fourth and Jax in third.

It wasn't the podium finish I'd hoped for, but I was still the highest-ranking rookie in league history, and that had to mean something.

Winning was great, but I had something more important to race for. If I could end the season shining a positive light on the Iskari, that would be enough.

The championship meant something different to Kai, though.

At first, I'd assumed he just craved the spotlight, but now that I knew him, I understood it was about his legacy. About proving he was still the best, even under the weight of everyone's expectations.

The countdown to the end of a driver's career started when they sat behind the wheel for the first time. And it only got worse when you won, because when you made it to the top, the only place left to go was down.

Kai faced relentless scrutiny, fans and media circling like vultures, ready to tear apart every choice he made. Always wondering if this would be the season his reign at the top ended.

Zylo had gone through the same after winning consecutive championships. Now he was one of the greats, a veteran in the sport, but no one expected him to win, not anymore.

Kai wasn't ready for that. He'd been in the league for five years, and in his mind, he had many more seasons ahead of him. And every season meant another chance to win.

He didn't just compete against the others, he competed against the version of himself everyone expected him to be. And somehow he made it look effortless, like racing through the stars at breakneck speed was the only time he felt free.

Kai was used to dominating the track. Nobody could touch him—but I had, and he hadn't known what to do with that. So he'd lashed out, and I'd pushed back, sneering at him for being what he was—a cocky showboat. Mix the two together and we'd formed a rivalry fuelled by ego, assumptions, and enough resentment to blow like a supernova.

Funny how much a bit of communication could change things.

I was reading on the frosty grass outside the paddock, soaking up the minimal sun Krythion offered when Kai found me.

He bounded over with a smile on his face, eyes covered by his favourite pair of aviators. His unzipped racing suit pooled around his hips, and the thermal underlayer left little to the imagination.

He crossed his legs at the ankles and dropped to the ground with a smirk. "Like what you see, rookie?"

My ears twitched, the lines on my skin pulsing burnt orange. I'd tried to mask my staring with my sunglasses, but I was still caught.

"Fuck off, Mercer," I replied, returning to my holo-reader.

"Whatcha reading?"

He reached out and tapped my screen. It flipped the book to the next page, and I batted his hand away.

"A book."

"Wow, that was so enlightening," he deadpanned. "You should be a life coach with the wise words that come out of your mouth."

I raised an eyebrow. "I prefer things that come *in* my mouth."

Kai blushed and cleared his throat, and I snickered as he shuffled around to adjust himself. I had no doubt he was thinking of the night before, how he'd fucked my mouth while my head hung over the edge of the bed.

Except now, so was I, and it took everything in me not to squirm like he was.

"Come on," he croaked. "Tell me what you're reading."

I sighed as if he was annoying me, but I was just as grateful for the distraction.

"It's a gay romance about two best friends. One's a werewolf, and the other is a wolf shifter. They're in love, but the werewolf doesn't realise it yet."

"What's a werewolf?" he asked.

"A guy who turns into a wolf."

"And what's a wolf shifter?"

"A guy who turns into a wolf."

"So . . ." His head tilted to one side, thinking about it. "What's the difference between a werewolf and a wolf shifter?"

"Read it and find out," I replied, leaning in to flick him on the knee.

Kai closed the distance, his sunglasses slipping down his nose. "I could think of something a lot more fun we could do."

My cock perked up, but I couldn't have him thinking I'd give in so easily. I wouldn't be me if I let Kai get what he wanted right away, just because he asked.

I pursed my lips and hummed. "I'm not sure I'm in the mood."

He brushed his nose against mine, breath warm against my cold lips. "I could get you in the mood, Revvy. I know all your hotspots."

I realised it might look like we were kissing, right here on the icy grass of the paddock. The gap between our mouths was small, and if I pushed forward just a smidge, they would meet. If anyone looked this way, it'd be clear that something was happening . . . something between us.

We hadn't told anyone what was going on. Hadn't discussed it. It was so new, so fragile, that we were happy keeping it between ourselves.

Only Jax gave the slightest inkling that he knew. He never said it outright, but based on the occasional wink he sent my way, I was sure he'd guessed.

"My book's pretty good," I replied.

"I promise what I've got in mind is better than your book."

"You're all talk, starboy."

Kai winked, standing up far more gracefully than his tall frame should allow. "I suppose I'll have to show you, then."

He held out a hand, and I decided I'd teased him enough.

He helped me up, dusting dirt from my ass. It was far more thorough than he needed to be, but I let him have his moment because I liked the feel of his hands on me.

He led me through the paddock, still holding my hand. Our joined hands drew curious looks, but Kai didn't care, he just marched forward like a man on a mission, dragging me along behind him. His legs were longer than mine, so one step for Kai was about three for me, and I was practically sprinting.

When we stopped in front of a nondescript door, my chest was heaving.

"Where . . . are . . . we?" I panted, glancing around.

He led me between some buildings and around a corner, ending up in an area that looked reserved for the cleaning crews. With the race starting in just under an hour, it was no surprise there was no one here; they were all getting ready for the grid.

He pulled on the door handle, and pleased to find it unlocked, he swung it open and tugged me inside. Cardboard boxes, mop buckets, and metal racks full of cleaning supplies surrounded us.

"Do I want to know how you stumbled onto this?"

"I found it in my rookie year," he replied, smiling proudly.

"Bring all your groupies back here?" I muttered.

The thought of Kai being in here with different men and women was a slight boner killer. I wanted to push past him and walk right back to the paddock.

His smile dropped as he registered the change in mood, and he prowled towards me until my back hit one of the racks.

"I come here when I need a bit of quiet time," he replied, voice low and laced with danger. "Why? Are you jealous, rookie?"

"No," I lied.

"I'm not the player you're making me out to be." He leaned in close, and I shuddered when his lips tickled the shell of my ear. "Besides, there's only one person I'm interested in, even if they drive me insane."

His hand wrapped around my waist, and he placed a kiss on the crook of my neck.

"We don't have long, little comet, and I want to see you come." Kai used his free hand to unzip my suit. "You look so beautiful when you come for me."

He slipped the fabric off my shoulders, and the top of my suit gathered around my hips. Then he dropped to his knees, tugging it down to my ankles. My cock tented my red boxer briefs, and my tail thumped against the racks behind me.

My skin shimmered fluorescent pink, bathing the room in a rosy glow.

"Look at you," he crooned, eyes locked on my erection. "So needy for me. Does it hurt?"

His words made me whimper, and when he glanced up, I nodded.

Kai licked from the base of my shaft to the tip, his tongue dragging along the fabric of my underwear.

I gasped, knees threatening to buckle as my fingers curled around the shelf by my hips to support my weight. He dragged my underwear down to mid-thigh, and my suit was around my ankles. I was trapped. Kai's eyes, dark and full of heat, looked ready to burn me from the outside in, and I didn't want to stop him.

Without warning, he opened his mouth and sucked me down to the root. The feel of my cock at the back of his throat made me cry out, and my legs trembled.

"Fuck!"

Kai swallowed around me, and his face grew redder as my dick cut off his oxygen. When he pulled off with a pop, gasping for breath, a string of saliva connected his lips to my cock, and his eyes were glassy and wet.

Before I could utter a word, he dived back in.

My head dropped back onto my shoulders, knocking against a plastic bottle of cleaner. Kai's head bobbed up and down, massaging my shaft with his tongue, and I released moans and strings of gibberish.

When I mustered the energy to look down, his eyes were on my face, tears streaming down his rosy cheeks. He patted the inside of my thighs, and I adjusted my stance, opening my legs as wide as my restrained legs would allow. His finger brushed my slick hole, and my hips jerked forward, pushing my cock deeper into his throat.

Kai moaned, and the vibrations felt amazing along my length.

He pulled off and rasped, "Fuck my face, baby." Before returning his attention to my cock.

With the green light to move, I thrust inside his mouth, just as his finger slipped past the tight ring of muscle.

"Shit." I gripped his hair in a tight fist. "Oh f-fuck, Kai."

I rocked between thrusting deeper into his throat and grinding back against his finger, nearly falling apart each time he pressed against my prostate. My orgasm barrelled towards me, and my balls tightened, ready to explode.

I moved faster, battering Kai's tonsils with my cock. And just when I thought I couldn't take any more, Kai slid a second finger into me, nailing my prostate with perfect precision.

That was all it took.

I came hard, spilling into his mouth, thick pulses shooting straight down his throat. He swallowed what he could, but it dribbled down his chin, mixed with his saliva. He swallowed with a loud moan.

He suckled the tip of my cock, while my thighs trembled, knees threatening to buckle. I hissed when I grew too sensitive, and Kai released me, wiping his mouth with the back of his hand.

He smacked his lips as if he'd just eaten an ice cream. "Delicious."

I chuckled, brushing my fingers through his messy hair. "You're such an idiot."

Stars, I wasn't sure how I was supposed to race now he'd sucked my soul out through my dick, but at least I was relaxed.

He pulled my boxers back into place, and dragged my suit up to my hips. When he climbed to his feet, his knees popped.

"Getting old, Mercer," I teased, and he growled, nipping the tip of my nose.

"Not too old to make you scream, baby."

A laugh tumbled from my mouth, so he silenced me with a kiss. The taste of myself on his tongue made me shiver, and I cupped the bulge at his crotch, feeling the heat of him against my palm.

"Rev," he moaned as I stroked him, slow and teasing.

Then my watch pinged, and I let my hand fall away.

"Wait, what . . ." Kai's voice faded, confusion clear in his eyes as I slipped my suit over my shoulders and zipped it up.

I brushed a few stray hairs behind my ears, pressed a kiss to his parted lips, and walked past him toward the door.

"What's happening right now?"

I opened the door, letting the sunlight fill the dim interior.

His hair stuck up in every direction thanks to my hands, his pupils blown wide until his eyes looked as dark as mine. His cheeks were flushed, lips swollen, and his voice carried a gravelly edge, courtesy of my not-so-gentle use of his throat.

His boner tented the tight fabric of his suit, and I felt sorry for him.

But it was the perfect chance for payback. To make him suffer for all the times he'd driven me up the wall, even if things between us were better now.

"We've got a race to catch, hotshot," I said, my tone far too cheerful for the situation. Especially when Kai looked miserable and horny.

"You can't be serious."

"Deadly, Kai. Now, chop chop, or you might miss lights out."

I shot him a wink, turned on my heel, and strolled out, leaving him alone in the cupboard, tousled, breathless and far too turned on.

A few yards away, I heard him yell through the door.

"I can't believe you're making me race with a fucking boner!"

I cackled the entire way back to the garage.

Eclipse Spire was a bastard of a track, but at least we had wheels on the ground.

Set on Krythion, a frozen rock in the shadow of a binary star system, the course cut through jagged peaks and winding ravines. Light and darkness switched without warning as the two suns constantly eclipsed one another, plunging sections of the track into pitch blackness before flooding them with blinding light.

The stretch of road twisted through narrow caves slick with black ice, and crumbling rock spires lined the edges like sentinels, ready to fall under the slightest breeze. If the sudden light shifts didn't fuck you over, the falling debris or icy patches might.

It was shorter than some of the other tracks, so we were doing seventy laps rather than the average fifty.

Each one was a constant fight. We had to adapt to every change in light, dodge other racers in claustrophobic tunnels, and pray the next blind corner didn't end with a rockslide.

Up until lap sixty-one, the race had been mostly straightforward, marked by just two major incidents.

The first happened on lap three, when a rookie lost control speeding over a patch of ice and took out another racer. The second occurred on lap forty-two, when Dray swerved to avoid a falling rock but ended up crashing into the ravine beside the road.

According to Zylo, two incidents was a low number for this track. During qualifying, he'd told me the highest he'd ever seen was eleven, and only four drivers had crossed the finish line that day.

So yeah, while it'd been tough, and my rear wheels had lost traction more than once, I was feeling pretty positive.

Kai checked in a few laps ago, but we'd both agreed beforehand that we wouldn't speak too much. We didn't want to distract each other on such unstable terrain.

The race seemed to stretch on forever, and my body felt like lead. The shifting light gave me a headache, and even under multiple thermal layers, I was freezing.

I was in sixth, while a driver from Pulse was up ahead in fifth, a five-second gap between us. Cassiopeia from Nebula Shifters was behind me, a little too close for comfort.

I shot into the mouth of the cave just as the light vanished. Total darkness swallowed the tunnel, and I cursed under my breath. Even with Iskari eyes, I was almost blind, with no way to tell if it would last five seconds or five minutes.

The only thing I could rely on now was instinct, and the low, creeping growl of Cass's engine behind me.

She'd been tailing me too close for too long; I could feel her hovering at my rear like a shadow with teeth. My fingers twitched over the comms button. I was tempted to snap at her to back off, but the drivers' radio was public and I didn't want my request to be misinterpreted by anyone listening in.

Dray might not care who heard, but he wasn't trying to improve the reputation of an entire species.

So I said nothing. Just clenched my jaw and kept going, waiting for a sliver of light at the tunnel's end.

Cass veered right. I caught a flicker of motion and realised too late that she was trying to overtake. In a tunnel this tight, with zero visibility, it was suicidal.

Kai called me reckless, but this? This was plain stupid.

Screw it. I hit the comms button.

"Cass, what the fuck—"

A sharp crack snapped on my left, and my dash lit up red.

Damage to the left wing. Shit. I'd drifted too close to the wall, too busy clocking Cass's dumb move to react in time.

Heart pounding, I yanked the wheel to the right, hunting for space. No jolt. No impact. Maybe I'd cleared her.

Then came the screech.

Tyres shrieked through the dark, ricocheting off stone like a scream.

My stomach flipped.

The light surged back, blinding and brutal, just in time for me to catch Cass slamming into the wall.

The impact crumpled the metal, folding her front end like foil. Tyres shredded and spun, bouncing loose. Her engine gave one tortured growl before it blew. Fire swallowed the wreckage, the blast lighting up the cave like a supernova.

My breathing turned shallow, and my heart hammered against my ribs. I wanted to scream. To puke. To stop.

To run into the fire and drag her crumpled body out myself.

The cave wall split where she'd hit it. A jagged crack tore upward, racing the length of the ceiling as I neared the exit, and I just made it through.

Then the roof gave way.

Rock crashed down behind me, swallowing Cass's vehicle in a deafening roar.

I slammed on the brakes. My seat caught my spine like a punch, but I didn't feel it. Couldn't. I stumbled out of the vehicle, ripped off my helmet, and let it hit the ground.

Air.

I needed air.

But no matter how hard I sucked it in, my lungs stayed hollow. My head spun, ears ringing with phantom brakes and the crunch of metal.

My brain was still trapped inside that collapsing cave.

The radio hissed in my helmet, Kileen and Tavoris firing questions I couldn't answer. I wasn't ready to relive it. I'd seen crashes before; they were a dime a dozen in the underground circuit.

But never a death, never up close.

Tears blurred my vision, sliding down my cheeks in silent streams. I didn't lift a finger to stop them.

Didn't think I deserved to, because I was alive and Cass was dead.

So I let them fall.

The camera drones closed in, circling me like hawks ready to strike. I should have wanted to hide my face, to mask the raw emotion written there plainly for all to see.

But I didn't care.

Let them film it.

Let them broadcast me dropping to my knees on the frozen ground, eyes fixed on the mountain of rock sealing the cave shut.

Let them capture every sob that racked my chest as I knelt there, alone in the ice and silence.

For the first time since I was a kid, I let the world see me break.

DON'T GO BRAKIN' MY HEART

Kai

The officials called a red flag, bringing the race to a complete halt. Drivers were directed back to the pit lane with no explanation, only instructions to wait for further information.

There'd been an incident, that much was certain, and given the history of past seasons, it had only been a matter of time before something went wrong on the track. Finishing a race with just two minor incidents at Eclipse Spire was unheard of.

I was the first back to the pit lane, followed by Jax and Zylo soon after.

"Any idea what's happened?" Jax asked.

I tossed my helmet onto my empty seat. "Nope. Must be bad, though."

Crew members hurried up and down the pit lane, readying for the drivers' return. But the team principals clustered around a CRF official, their grim expressions doing little to ease my anxiety.

One by one, drivers returned to the pit, pulling in from both ends rather than just the usual entrance.

"Must be a blockage on the track," Jax observed.

"Rockslide maybe?" Zylo added.

"A rockslide wouldn't cause this level of pandemonium."

"It would if someone was hurt," I muttered.

Zylo and Jax talked among themselves, while I looked over everyone's heads, trying to spot my favourite scowling face. With every driver who returned before him, my unease deepened.

I was just about to check Zenith's garage, worried I might have missed him, when Sam walked past, his face pale.

"Sam," I called out.

He looked over at the sound of his name, changing course to approach us. His hair was messy, like he'd run his hands through it.

"Everything alright, mate?" I asked.

"No." He looked wound tight, like a spring about to go off.

"What's going on?" I kept my voice low, and Jax and Zylo huddled in closer.

"It's bad, man," Sam said, eyes haunted. "Like, seriously fucking bad."

"Is someone hurt?" Jax asked, frowning.

"Worse," Sam mumbled, his voice breaking at the end.

"Fuck," Zylo muttered, panic sharpening the edge of his voice. He glanced around the pit lane, likely searching for the same thing I was. "I can't see Rev."

Zylo had already lost a teammate in the past, and I knew he had a huge soft spot for Rev. But this time, he wasn't the only one feeling frantic.

Rev wasn't my teammate, but he was so much more than just another driver in the league.

Jax placed a comforting hand on Zylo's shoulder. "I'm sure Rev's fine."

Then he turned to me and nodded.

I hadn't told him what was happening between me and Rev, but I'd be foolish to think he didn't already know. After all, we'd grown up together, and Jax knew me better than I knew myself.

He'd also seen us at dinner, and there was no hiding the way I'd been looking at the rookie over the past month.

"It's not Rev," Sam confirmed.

My shoulders slumped in relief, and I knew I should've felt guilty. I didn't want to lose anyone in the league, but knowing it wasn't Rev went a long way towards calming me down.

"Do you know what happened?" Zylo asked.

"The live feed caught it," Sam replied. "The footage is already doing the rounds on InSTARgram."

The three of us checked our watches, ignoring Sam's half-hearted protests that we should wait for the officials' word.

Deep down, he knew just as well as we did that there was no point. Before they could even decide what to say, all the drivers would watch the footage online.

"I've got it," Jax piped up, and with a few taps, the hologram hovered above his wrist.

I recognised Rev's car right away, with Cass hot on his tail. My breathing picked up, and I glanced up at Sam.

"I thought you said it wasn't Rev."

"It's not," he breathed out, hollow and broken.

I returned to the footage just as Rev entered the cave at turn ten, with Cass too close given the track conditions. The drones surged ahead, and as darkness fell, the feed switched to night vision.

All seemed normal until Cass's vehicle crept to the right.

Jax's eyes grew wide, saying what we were all thinking.

"She's not doing what I think she's doing, is she?"

I watched on in disbelief, because Cass, a seasoned driver, couldn't be thinking about overtaking Rev in the narrowest cave on the track. The angle of the cave walls made it impossible for two cars to drive alongside each other without hitting the rock.

But it looked like she was chasing the impossible—idiotic, even—trying to wedge herself in beside Rev.

I wasn't sure what happened next, but Rev swerved to the right, into Cass's path. The sudden movement made her lock up, and I didn't need the audio to know how loud her tyres screeched as they smoked.

It took less than a second for her vehicle to hit the wall head-on and explode, while Rev's vehicle rode on, exiting the cave just as a waterfall of rock buried Cass's vehicle and the drones along with it.

"What the . . ." Jax trailed off.

"Cass . . ." Zylo's voice cracked, his face as shattered as his words.

Over the years, he and Cass had become close, and true to his nature, Zylo cared for everyone in the league.

When the footage cut off, anger took root in my chest, replacing my earlier panic.

Cass's decision to overtake was stupid. But Rev's choice to swerve into her path, cutting her up and causing her to lock up, had been idiotic.

I'd called him reckless from the start, and I'd seen how he raced in the underground circuit, where rules were nonexistent and outlandish manoeuvres were encouraged. He'd taken the Hessirian out without even flinching.

"If you wanna play dirty, you've gotta be prepared for others to do the same."

I didn't think he'd bring that attitude to the ASL. And fuck . . . I'd warned him.

Told him he could hurt someone.

Could kill someone.

And now, the unthinkable had happened.

The medical shuttle pulled into the pit lane, and the door opened, revealing a catatonic Rev, staring into space. His void-like eyes were puffy, ringed with a deep purple that matched the tip of his nose.

Had he been crying?

His hair hung loose around his face, messy and tangled, as if he'd dragged his fingers through it over and over, gripping in frustration.

Worst of all, the marks on his skin were dark, void of colourful light.

The logical part of me tried to be reasonable, begging me to comfort him while he was in distress. I wanted to pull him into my arms and ask if he was okay. To whisk him back to his apartment before wrapping him up in blankets. I'd even encourage him to binge that werewolf book he'd told me about.

But my rage was too potent, growing inside my chest like a beast.

It didn't want to be logical right now, and it didn't want to comfort him.

No, it wanted to be set free, and damn the consequences.

I stepped towards the shuttle, and Jax, being the observant fucker he was, had spotted the tension in my shoulders, my clenched jaw.

"Kai." He gripped my bicep. "Take a minute."

I should've taken his advice. Taken a minute—or ten—to calm down.

But I shook my head, eyes locked on the Iskari. Rage choked my voice, but the words threatened to erupt anyway.

I ripped my arm out of Jax's grasp, ignoring his impatient sigh, and stormed towards the shuttle.

"This isn't the time, man." He tried again, but still I ignored him.

Medics tried to speak to Rev, to coax him out of the shuttle. But he didn't react, so I pushed past them, turning a deaf ear to their protests, and stopped at the open door.

"Rev."

My voice seemed to rouse him from sleep, and that alone should've told me everything. It should've made me see how much he needed me, should've quieted the beast clawing inside my chest. It should've let the part of me that cared for him rise up and do the right thing.

But the beast was louder, and even the fresh tears spilling from his eyes couldn't silence it.

"Kai," he whimpered, voice cracking as a sob escaped him.

The marks on his skin bloomed amethyst, pulsing with quiet beauty. He threw himself out of the shuttle and slammed against my chest, causing me to stumble back a few steps. He wrapped his arms around my neck, clinging to my suit while he wept against my shoulder.

Beneath the rage pulsing through my veins, my heart ached.

Rev would never let anyone see him like this, not in his right mind. He'd never allow anyone to perceive him as weak. But he wasn't thinking clearly, not now. He clung to me as if I were his only anchor in the storm, breaking apart in full view of everyone.

It didn't change what had happened, though, so my arms hung limply at my sides, even as my fingers twitched with the need to hold him.

The heartless beast resisted, and the sounds of his pain only made me angrier. Who was he to cry when he was the reason for this?

Why should he feel upset when it was his fault that we'd lost one of our own?

"I told you not to be reckless, Rev." My voice shook, as I barely hung onto the part of me that didn't want to explode at him.

The crying stopped, and his breath hitched as he tried to control himself, gazing up at me. The galaxies in his eyes were dim, like a dying star on the cusp of burning out.

"W-What?"

I scanned the crowd, catching the way their eyes clung to us. The curiosity was thick in the air.

Look at the champ and the rookie all over each other.

Are they friends?

Are they fucking?

Rev didn't notice, and that should've told me everything. The man who preferred to vanish into the wallpaper wasn't flinching under the weight of a hundred stares.

Even though fury twisted in my chest, the part of me that still cared—still ached—wanted to protect him. I wouldn't call him out in front of nosy onlookers. This was between us.

I shoved past the medics, ignoring their protests.

Past crew, drivers, officials. Everyone inching closer to eavesdrop.

Past my best friend and Rev's teammate, who followed anyway—close enough to intervene, but far enough back not to pry too much.

Rev stuck to me the whole way, walking backward, clutching my chest like it was the only thing keeping him upright.

If only I weren't about to rip it out from under him.

Once we were far enough from prying eyes, I gripped his shoulders and pushed him back.

"I warned you what would happen if you were reckless."

"K-Kai," he stuttered with a hiccup, looking up at me with wet eyes. "It w-wasn't my fault. I—"

"Then whose fault was it, Rev?" I hissed through my teeth.

The beast was done waiting patiently for Rev to pull himself together.

The anger in my chest detonated, a blazing atomic force threatening to reduce anyone who came too close to nothing but ash.

"You were so stupid out there!" I snapped, the words sharp and unforgiving. "You swerved in front of Cass and pushed her into the fucking wall!"

"I didn't. I s-swear I didn't!" He was pleading, desperate for me to believe him. "It wasn't l-like that—"

"I've seen the footage, Rev." I jerked my head to the side, in a fierce gesture towards the onlookers. "We've all seen the footage."

"Kai, stop it," Jax said from somewhere behind me.

But I ignored him, because I was on a roll. So why not finish?

"You pulled a reckless fucking move, and someone's dead. Cassiopeia is *dead*."

"Kai." Rev's shoulders slumped, his legs trembling. I wondered if they'd buckle, unable to hold him up under the weight of his pain. Before, I would've caught him if they did. But right now, I couldn't be sure. "Please, y-you have to believe m-me."

"Don't you get it? That could've been you." I raked a hand through my hair, not even caring when my fingers snagged a knot. "*You*, rookie. What if you'd been in Cass's place? What if you were still in that cave instead of standing here in front of me?"

"Kai—"

"You could've died, little comet," I whispered, voice catching on the nickname I usually said with a smile.

I swallowed hard.

"Your team would've lost you. *I* would've lost you." The heat of tears burned down my cheeks. "I just . . . I can't believe you were that reckless."

Rev's own tears streamed unchecked, while snot clung to his upper lip. He was a mess, a heartbroken mess.

Even so, all I could feel was my pain. My own near loss. Like his hurt didn't matter next to mine.

"The footage is clear as day," I bit out. "I told you, if you drove like you were still in the underground, you'd kill someone. And look what's happened."

Zylo joined us, stepping up beside his teammate and wrapping an arm around his shoulders. "That's enough, Mercer."

And it should've been enough.

But I wasn't done.

I looked down at Rev, the beautiful, infuriating Iskari I was falling for. I stared into those dark eyes I'd memorised, the ones I used to find comfort in.

But this time, I let my face go slack.

No anger. No softness. Just blank.

"I thought I could handle this," I said, voice low and stripped of feeling. "Handle you. But if this is what it's going to be . . . if it means watching you come that close to dying . . . I don't know if I can do it."

I saw the moment he shut down. The second every raw feeling he'd bared to me vanished back into his chest, like he was locking away a part of himself. Pulling away from me in the quietest, most heartbreaking way.

His face transformed from agony to indifference. He didn't wipe his tears away, didn't clear the snot from his nose. He left them there like war paint, reminding me of the pain he'd felt, the hurt I had added to.

And for the first time in what felt like forever, the lines on his skin blazed a deep red.

"Thank you for sharing your true feelings."

His voice was wooden, lifeless, mirroring my own. Only the flicker of red on his skin suggested he felt anything at all.

Seeing it made the anger fizzle out, leaving behind a curling trail of smoke, the only evidence of my carnage. Dread settled in my stomach like a stone threatening to drag me down.

What the fuck had I done?

"Rev—"

He held up a hand, silencing me. "You've said enough, Mercer."

Then he turned and walked away.

Past his teammate, who reached for him. Past the curious onlookers, all trying to make sense of what they'd seen but not heard. He held his head high, as if I hadn't just crushed the remnants of his already bruised heart.

Like I hadn't just torn down everything we'd built over the last six weeks.

When he disappeared into Zenith's garage without looking back, the only thing left in his place was regret.

Because I knew . . . I'd just made the biggest mistake of my life.

STEER CLEAR OF HEARTBREAK

Rev

It had been three weeks since Cass's funeral, and five since the accident. I had stayed in my apartment almost the entire time, living in my pyjamas and glued to the sofa.

Mum and Dad called every day, and I managed to string together a few words. Their worry became clear when they started dropping by unannounced, just to make sure I hadn't drowned in the shower or starved in front of the TV.

I would've had to step into the shower to risk drowning in it. But I let myself rot, only dragging myself to the bathroom for a quick splash at the sink whenever Mum complained she could smell me from the kitchen.

I had no energy for anything else—cooking, cleaning, even eating felt like too much. Mum and Grandma batch-cooked meals in their apartment, bringing them over several times a week until my fridge was overflowing.

They wouldn't leave until I'd eaten at least one meal, and I couldn't bear to disappoint them, so I forced each bite down, even though every mouthful tasted like ash on my tongue.

Others checked up on me too.

Tavoris, Zylo, Saelix... even Jax sent a message or two. I replied once or twice, just enough to let them know I was alive, that I was holding it together. But they didn't have to know how far from the truth that was.

Most nights, I stayed awake, haunted by Kai. Wanting to forget him, yet unable to stop thinking about him.

Physically, I was avoiding him, but my mind refused me any form of respite.

Kai kept trying to talk to me, of course he did. Persistence was one thing he never lacked.

On the day of the crash, I'd holed up in my bedroom, breaking down beneath the blankets. Then the doorbell rang—Kai, pressing it over and over and pounding on the door. He looked terrible. Hair stuck up in every direction, like he'd run his hands through it, and his T-shirt was inside out.

But he hadn't looked angry anymore, and I told myself that was the only reason I let myself listen to the audio.

"Rev, please open the door." He stopped banging and rested his head against the door. "I know it wasn't your fault, but I was angry, upset, and so fucking wrong. I've seen the rest of the footage, watched it from every angle. I know it wasn't your fault."

Kai sighed, thumping his head on the wood once, twice, three times. "I didn't mean it, Rev... that I couldn't handle you. I was just... terrified. So fucking scared of losing you." His voice cracked. "And now I think I've lost you anyway."

He took a steadying breath and spoke again. "Please open the door. You can scream at me if you want, call me every insult under the sun. Hell, punch me right in the jaw if that's your jam."

When I still didn't answer, he looked into the camera, eyes glistening with unshed tears. "I was such a fucking idiot, little comet. I'm so sorry."

He stayed for another five minutes, eyes flicking between the door and the camera as if he knew I was watching.

But I never answered.

Just watched him walk away, with a piece of my broken heart in his pocket.

I wanted to chase after him, grab his face and kiss him—maybe even throw a punch just because he said I could—then kiss him again, hard enough to steal our breath, forcing us to gasp for air.

But I held back. Not after he'd turned his back on me. This time, he'd come back, but what about next time?

What if I slipped up, crossed a line he couldn't forgive? When Kai decided once more that being with me was more than he could bear?

I'd shatter.

It was safer to stay alone. Less risk, less pain, less chance of getting hurt.

I was always an outsider. People stared at me like I was some kind of sideshow, whispered behind my back, and mocked me for being different.

As a kid, I'd tried to make friends—to let people in—but the moment a bully called me a freak, they would all disappear, choosing the easy way of fitting in over standing by the kid whose skin glowed like a torch.

In the end, I was always alone.

The only people I trusted to stick around were my family. But on the worst days, irrational thoughts crept in. Thoughts that maybe they stayed only because we were bound by blood, not because I was someone worth keeping.

Deep down, I knew it was ridiculous.

Of course my family loved me. I could murder someone, and Grandma would offer to help bury the body, Mum would scrub the crime scene spotless, and Dad would have the getaway shuttle ready.

Kai was the wildcard.

He'd told me he was falling for me, and truth? I was just as fucked up over him, even if saying it out loud made me want to throw up.

We'd had six weeks of something real, maybe even perfect, but at the first hurdle, we hit the ground so hard it knocked the wind out of me. Like that stupid three-legged race all over again, except this time, Kai's rock-hard abs weren't there to catch me.

I didn't know which cut deeper. The doubt in his eyes when I said Cass's death was an accident, or the weight of him saying he couldn't handle me.

So I shut Kai out.

I ignored every call, every message, every knock at my door.

Though it wasn't easy, since he'd showed up on my doorstep every night since the incident. He was relentless. Part of that maddening charm I both loved and hated.

But with every knock, every flower, every quiet gift he left behind, Kai made it clear I still mattered. That even if I'd closed the door on him, he hadn't forgotten me. And no matter how hard I tried to push him away, I held onto that.

Because I wasn't ready for the day he stopped trying.

It wasn't about being materialistic or needing yet another bouquet to join the growing collection stuffed into glasses and mugs on my kitchen island.

It was about what the silence would mean. That Kai had given up. That he'd stopped caring, stopped trying. That he was giving me what he thought I wanted. What *I* thought I wanted.

A life without him in it.

The idea of living a life without Kai made my chest ache, so much so that I'd considered going to the hospital once or twice, just to get it checked out.

But even with the pain gnawing at me, I still couldn't face him at Cass's funeral.

I hadn't wanted to go at all, not even after the CRF cleared me, ruling the crash an accident.

New footage had surfaced from alternate angles, clips that hadn't aired during the live broadcast. Together with the video of me falling apart outside the cave, it was enough to exonerate me. Enough to silence the trolls and stop the threats flooding my inbox and comment sections.

But none of it brought Cass back. And none of it made me feel any less hollow.

In the end, it was Mum who got me there, though it took a lot of heavy lifting.

She dragged me off the couch, shoved me into the shower, and dressed me like I was a kid again, fixing my hair until I looked presentable. Then she flew me to the crematorium on Cass's home planet and waited outside in the shuttle park, promising to take me home when it was over.

I offered my condolences to Cass's wife and family, and they assured me they didn't blame me.

Still, I couldn't bring myself to speak to the other drivers, not when it meant getting closer to Kai. I wasn't ready to meet his eyes. Zylo had spotted me and made to come over, but Saelix stopped him, like he understood I needed space.

I took a seat at the back of the crematorium, alone, only half listening to the service. I kept my gaze fixed on the photo of Cass smiling down at us from the top of her coffin, because if I didn't, my eyes would gravitate to Kai, sitting between Jax and Valen.

Jax noticed me just as the service ended. He nudged Kai and pointed my way, but I didn't wait to see what happened next.

I slipped out before anyone could reach me, glimpsing Kai's face falling just as I climbed into Mum's shuttle.

After that, the only time I left my apartment was to compete in the penultimate race at the Void Loop, where I came in dead last. My head and heart weren't in it, and it showed.

Tavoris and the team had said little about my performance. They knew I didn't need the reminder. I was already beating myself up enough.

And now, with my standing knocked down to eighth in the championship, the damage was more than just emotional.

So here I was, drowning in my pity party on the couch.

The same one I'd been glued to for weeks.

Mum and Grandma had dropped off their food delivery, and Kai had made his daily gift run. I expected to be left alone for the night, so I jumped when my watch buzzed with an incoming call.

I frowned at Nina's name on the screen. She rarely called me unless it was to do with something press related, and even then she preferred to speak in person.

"Hello?"

"Rev!" she chirped, her voice way brighter than I felt. "How are you doing?"

"Fine." I kept it short, knowing Grandma would flick my ear for being rude.

But I didn't have the energy to talk. I just wanted to zone out to another episode of *Love Planet* and crash in bed.

"Are you sure? Did you contact the grief counsellor like I suggested?"

Nina had sent me the name of a local counsellor after the accident. But every time I thought about reaching out, I'd chastised myself for needing help.

I wasn't grieving; I was wallowing. So why did I need to speak to someone?

"I'll take your silence as a no." She sighed. "Look, I can only imagine what's going through your head, but I think it'd do you good to speak to someone."

"I know," I replied, even if I disagreed.

Talking about my *feelings* was the last thing I wanted to do, and the idea of taking a deep dive into my head was enough to make my stomach hurt.

"Just promise me you'll think about it, okay?"

"I will."

"Okay, well, I have a reason for calling," she said, paper rustling in the background. "The Governor of Intergalactic Relations got in touch, and they want to meet with you."

"What? Why?"

"You've made it clear since day one that one of your main reasons for joining the ASL was to bring attention to the Iskari."

"Right . . ."

"Well, you've caught the GIR's attention. Now they want to meet and talk about it."

"Caught their . . . wait, what?"

"They want to talk to you about the Iskari, Rev. And I think this could be what you've been hoping for."

With everything that had happened over the past few weeks, I'd almost lost sight of why I started this journey. I should've felt guilty, but my guilt-o-meter was already maxed out. I just didn't have any room left for more.

"When?" I asked.

"Tomorrow."

"Tomorrow?!" I squawked.

"Their office called half an hour ago. Apparently another meeting was cancelled," Nina explained. "I know it's short notice, but this might be your only shot. They're set to leave for a diplomatic mission, so if we pass this up, it could be months before they're available again."

Fuck. My mind was spinning, and the one person I wanted to talk to was the exact one I was running from.

I couldn't wrap my head around why the GIR, the very person who might make my people's dreams come true, wanted to meet me.

Maybe they'd seen the accident and would tell me to get fucked.

"Rev?"

Could I even do this?

I'd been fighting for Iskari recognition from the start, and if Nina was right, this might be my only chance.

Damn it, why did Kai have to be such an asshole? And why was I so damn stubborn?

No matter. It didn't matter.

Like always, I was on my own, and I couldn't bear the thought of letting my people down. I shook my head, cleared my throat, and focused back on Nina.

"Okay," I said, sounding way surer than I felt. "Let's set it up."

NOT OVER TILL THE CHECKERED FLAG WAVES

Rev

Talia Monroe was a plump woman in her mid-forties. She had a warm smile and a general air about her that screamed "motherly." It was the opposite of the cold professionalism I'd expected of the Governor of International Relations.

We met in the conference room of a hotel in downtown Zyphar, just like when I'd done my tell-all interview all those months ago. I was surprised to see only the two of us there. I'd expected an entourage of security personnel, but she'd given them the afternoon off.

In the corner, her insectoid Sylphian assistant, Sirellka, perched with practiced stillness, antennae twitching, ready to record every word. Nina had come with me, but we'd agreed it would be better for her to wait in the lobby. She assured me she'd be nearby if I needed anything, so I left her to work in peace at the hotel bar.

"Would you like a drink, Revvak?" Talia asked. "Tea?"

She poured a stream of dark liquid from a metal teapot into her mug, stopping just before the rim. There was just enough space for a splash of milk.

"No, thank you, Ms Monroe," I replied. "And please, call me Rev."

"In that case, you can call me Talia," she said with a smile, adding two spoonfuls of sugar. "Sorry this was so last minute. My schedule's all over the place. Galaxy life, you know?"

I wrung my hands under the table. "I'm sure it gets tiring."

"But not as tiring as yours, I'd bet." She took a sip of tea. "Jumping from planet to planet, all that pressure and adrenaline . . . I think I'd be a wreck by the end of the weekend."

She wasn't wrong.

The crash after a race weekend hit hard. I'd learned to manage it better as the season went on, but in the beginning I was just the way Talia described—exhausted, jittery, sometimes shaking for days. The weeks between races had felt like a blessing.

Talia set her mug on the table.

"I'm sure you're busy preparing for the last race, so I won't keep you long." Her tone shifted, and she folded her hands in front of her. We were getting down to business. "The plight of the Iskari has been on my radar since I first took this position."

"How long ago was that?"

"Ten years."

"If you care so much, why has it taken so long for you to meet one of us?"

The words slipped out before I could stop them.

I slapped a hand over my mouth. I stood by what I'd said, but there would have been a better way to say it. I hadn't meant to be so blunt. I glanced up, expecting Talia to be furious. She was a governor, and I'd snapped without thinking.

But she wasn't angry, and she didn't scold me for my boldness. Instead, she smiled, her eyes soft with a quiet sadness.

"I'm so sorry—"

She held up a hand, cutting off my apology. "I understand your frustration, Rev."

"Can I speak freely?" I asked, forcing diplomacy into my voice.

There was so much weighing on me, but I feared my words might sound harsh. I couldn't afford to ruin this chance; this moment might be everything for the Iskari. Still, silence wasn't an option. I had to speak my truth.

"Of course."

"I'm not sure you can understand." I fiddled with a loose thread on my T-shirt, trying to keep my voice steady. "You're human, which means you've got it easier than most of the galaxy's species. Plus, you're a governor."

Talia placed her hands flat on the table.

"You're right," she replied. "I am a human, so my life differs greatly from yours. But . . ." She glanced at her watch. "Maybe it's better if I just show you."

Sirellka's fingers stilled on the keyboard as Talia rose from her chair, her footsteps soft against the floor. She opened the conference room door, slipping into a hushed conversation with someone in the corridor.

When she returned, she wasn't alone, and I was surprised to see who had joined her.

This man was an Iskari. If I had to guess, he was also in his mid-forties. When our eyes met, his so similar to mine, the lines on his skin flared sunshine yellow, a sign of warmth . . . happiness.

"I haven't seen that colour since before your mother passed away," Talia gasped, taking the man's hand with a smile.

Was this . . .

"Rev, I'd like you to meet my husband, Tharek."

The man, Tharek, reached across the table. "It's great to meet you, Rev."

Yellow flickered across my skin when I clasped his hand, offering a brief shake, and I cast a sheepish look at Talia.

"I'm sorry. I didn't expect—"

"Bah." Tharek waved me off with a deep laugh that reminded me of my dad. "Don't worry. No one ever does, am I right?"

I nodded, still shocked another Iskari was in the room.

Meeting one you weren't related to was a rarity, and in the course of a few months, I'd met two. More if I included the brief interaction with Korvi's parents when they'd picked him up from KFK. I mean, what were the odds?

"I hope you can see why I have such a vested interest in a better life for the Iskari," Talia explained, leaning in to kiss her husband's cheek. "If not for Tharek, then for our children."

"You have kids?" I asked.

Talia tapped the screen of her watch, and the image of two teenagers hovered above her wrist. "Rina and Xiveth are big fans of the ASL, especially this season."

My skin shimmered orange and violet, but the longer I stared at the picture, the more I realised.

"They don't look human at all."

Sirellka nearly dropped her tablet, and I realised too late how rude that sounded. But in this case, curiosity beat politeness, and to my relief, Tharek threw his head back and laughed. Even Talia let out a quiet snicker.

"You're right," Talia replied. "We used an Iskari donor, and Tharek carried them to term. With the numbers so small, we wanted to do what we could to add to the population."

Knowing that Talia had let her husband carry their children and had chosen a donor over using her own genes, just to protect the future of the Iskari, made my eyes burn.

"That's incredible."

Talia stared lovingly at the twins. "*They* are why I've spent ten years campaigning for the Iskari."

"It's not that I don't appreciate your efforts," I started, shifting in my seat. "But nothing's changed."

"I agree. But I don't have sole authority for passing changes through the Intergalactic Government."

Tharek picked up the teapot, pouring his wife another cup of tea with the easy familiarity of a couple who had been together for years. She smiled at him, a quiet warmth passing between them, then she turned back to me.

"That said, your presence in the ASL, along with your honesty about the Iskari's situation, has influenced the conversation in meaningful ways."

"In what way?"

Nerves twisted my stomach into knots. I was terrified she was about to say I'd undone ten years of hard work, and that now, any chance of change was slipping further away.

"We've started the process, Rev."

"I'm sorry, what?"

I leaned back in my chair, gripping the arms until they creaked. Talia didn't look at me like I'd ruined everything, and Tharek was grinning from ear to ear.

Could it mean . . . ?

"As of yesterday afternoon, the IGG has agreed to recognise the Iskari once more."

I could've sworn my heart stopped. My breath hitched and then rushed out in a gasp.

For a long moment, I was still. Too stunned to move or even think straight. The weight of those words sank in, and disbelief fought with a rising wave of hope. I blinked hard, as if that would make it all more real.

Deep inside, I felt something I hadn't allowed myself in years—relief.

Finally, the fight was turning in our favour.

"Things won't change overnight, but it's happening. The Iskari will have equal rights, and a better future for all generations." She reached across the table and covered my hand with hers, her touch steady and warm. It was a quiet promise that I wasn't alone, not anymore. "You should be proud of yourself."

And despite recent events, I *was*.

Everything I'd hoped for was happening. It would take time, but just knowing it was underway was enough. A wave of calm washed over me as I pictured my family safe and my dreams fulfilled.

To be like everyone else.

To feel like I belonged.

We spent the rest of the meeting discussing the next steps.

Talia requested that Tharek and I, along with other Iskari volunteers, have regular meetings with the IGG. It would ensure that everything was being done to improve Iskari lives and also keep us in the loop.

Nina joined us, as well as an IGG publicist, and together we agreed on a statement to be released to the press ahead of the last race. Then we commemorated the moment with a nice group photo. I even smiled.

I left the hotel feeling dazed. Nina offered to drive me home, but my parents' apartment was only a short walk away. It was the first time I'd left the house in a while, and Zyphar's sun was shining, so I decided to enjoy the walk.

Strolling down the busy streets, locked in my head, it was the perfect opportunity for me to process what had happened. To think about what was going to change.

And to wallow in what I missed.

Kai was the first person I wanted to call, even before my family. I wanted to celebrate with him. I wanted to share my happiness, to let him see it and feel it with me.

In my mind, he would be so excited that he would come straight to my apartment. He would hold me in his arms and tell me how proud he was, how glad he was that it had happened. Then he would kiss me breathless and take me to bed, where we would celebrate each other until we passed out, tangled and smiling.

But I hadn't spoken to him in weeks, still set on avoiding him.

So I didn't call.

I told myself it made more sense to share the news with my family first. They were the ones I should celebrate with, not Kai.

Grandma was in the apartment alone, my parents using their afternoon off work to go grocery shopping.

Seeing me, freshly washed and out in the wild, surprised her. I'd just settled on the couch when she shoved a bowl of noodles in my face and pecked me on the cheek.

"You're looking skinny, *va'tari*." She tutted, sitting down beside me. "Don't think I haven't noticed the amount of food still in your freezer."

"Sorry, Grandma," I mumbled through a mouthful of food.

It was the first time in weeks that food had flavour, that it wasn't just a lump of mush in my mouth. After today's success, the noodles tasted like heaven, and it wasn't long before the bowl was empty.

Grandma took it from me with a smirk, coming back with a second portion. And because I was ravenous, I devoured that too, before settling back in my seat with a smile.

"Why are you in such a good mood?" Grandma plucked a crochet hook from her pocket and reached behind the sofa for a ball of yarn.

The sight made my chest hurt.

When Kai had started coming over, Grandma had taught him how to crochet. He'd taken to it like a duck to water, and every week, they'd sit and work together, chatting about everything and nothing. Grandma had given him his very own hook and a bag of yarn, and an unfinished scarf was stuffed down the side of my couch.

I couldn't bring myself to bin it, because every time I saw it poking out from between the cushions it reminded me of him.

Kai hadn't cared when I'd teased him about his new hobby. He'd just insisted it made his fingers nimbler, which apparently could help him on the track.

"Everything's changing for the better, Grandma."

Her fingers stilled. "What do you mean?"

I told her everything, recounting the meeting and explaining the changes that were coming for the Iskari. She was crying by the time I'd finished, and we clung to each other on the couch. She even called my parents, telling them to drop whatever they were doing and come home right away.

But not before they picked up the ingredients for *luzari'eth*.

It was a day of celebration, after all.

"I'm so proud of you, *va'tari*," she whispered, brushing loose hairs behind my ear. I leaned into the touch, loving the comforting feel of her familiar hands. "But something's still bothering you, isn't it?"

I sighed, because Grandma was right, and I hated it.

On the surface, I had everything I wanted. A loving family, my dream career, and a hopeful future.

I should've been happy.

And I was.

Despite that, I felt incomplete.

"You miss Kai."

"I do." A lump clogged my throat, and my voice cracked. "But he walked away, and I can't let him do it again. I . . . I'm too scared."

"My darling." She pulled me closer, and I rested my head on her bony shoulder.

"Everyone walks away. They leave because I'm a freak. I'm too much, too different." I choked back a sob. "B-But Kai didn't. He saw me, all of me, and he s-stayed. He told me I w-was safe with him, that I . . . I could trust him."

The words caught in my throat.

"But then he said he couldn't h-handle me. And it hurt so m-much worse than all the others, because . . . because . . ." I broke off, trembling.

"Because you love him," Grandma whispered.

I couldn't say the words. They were too big—too painful, because he wasn't around to hear them.

But they were true.

So fucking true, my heart should be bursting.

I'd never been in love before, and somehow I'd fallen hard for Kai. But he was nowhere to be found, and instead of joy there was only this deep, aching pain that felt like it was crushing me from the inside.

Stars, was *this* why I'd been so miserable?

I told myself again and again that I'd be better off without him. I thought shutting him out would protect my heart from the agony of losing him again.

But it only made the pain worse. Because losing him once was unbearable, and the idea of losing him twice felt impossible to survive.

Grandma placed a kiss on the top of my head. "Remember the colour you asked me about? Well, I think it's time I told you what it meant."

I sat up, using my sleeve to wipe away some tears and snot. Despite the mess, Grandma took my hands and held them in her lap.

"If you're about to tell me it means love," I said with a shaky, self-deprecating laugh. "I think that might actually break me."

"You've seen the colours of love with your parents, *va'tari*. It's not the same, is it?"

"Okay, so what the hell does amethyst mean?"

The moment might have been tender, but that didn't stop Grandma from reaching over and giving my ear a sharp pinch.

"Watch your mouth," she scolded, and I winced, muttering an apology.

"Right," she said, settling back. "It'll make more sense if I start with our history."

"I already know our history."

"Not everything, you don't," she huffed. "Now listen."

I sat up straighter, just to avoid another flick of her long nails.

"Before Iskanya's destruction, amethyst lights shone across the planet. It was a symbol of community, of being connected to each other. And the lights were amethyst because that was the colour the Iskari's marks glowed when they found their home."

Her words hit me like a wave. My heart caught in my chest, and my stomach twisted with the weight of it.

"We seldom see it anymore. Our community broke apart and scattered, causing the sense of connection to fade. And how can we feel like we belong anywhere, when everything that once tied us together is gone?"

"So, if that's the c-case," I stammered. "Then why . . ."

"Why do you see it with Kai?" She smiled at me with that soft, knowing look. Like the answer had been there all along. "I think you already know, *va'tari*."

"Because I . . . I b-belong with Kai." My breath caught on a sob. "I found my home. My . . . my s-safe place."

"A sense of belonging is so much more than love," she replied, cupping my cheek. "What you have with Kai is beautiful."

"But he left me, Grandma," I croaked. "I can't let him do that again."

"What did he say to you, *va'tari*?" She asked, brushing a tear from my cheek with her thumb.

My mind reeled back to the moment everything fell apart.

To Kai, furious and afraid, lashing out with words that had carved into me like a blade.

"If it means watching you come that close to dying . . . I don't know if I can do it."

"He said . . ." I began, my voice fragile. "He said he couldn't handle me."

"I didn't mean it, Rev . . . that I couldn't handle you."

Kai on my doorstep, night after night, with flowers and dumb stuffed animals whose awful puns still lived rent free in my brain . . .

"I can't bear to be without you."

"I'm not lion when I say you're my everything."

"I'm pawsitively yours."

Kai, calling my name in desperation. Still hoping I'd turn back, even after I'd already walked away.

"I was just... terrified. So fucking scared of losing you."

Oh my god.

"And now I think I've lost you anyway."

My breath caught, and I felt the world shift under me.

I was so engrossed in my hurt I didn't notice the truth staring me in the face.

Kai had been scared—scared of losing me—and I'd mistaken that fear for rejection.

He hadn't walked away. I had.

And through it all, despite how much I pushed him away, he'd never stopped hoping I'd come back. He kept choosing *me*. And maybe... just maybe... that meant I was someone worth choosing after all.

"Oh, fuck." I sprang up from the couch, turning to the woman who'd just turned my world upside down. "Grandma—"

"I'll handle your parents," she interrupted, a knowing smile tugging at her lips. "Go get your boy, Revvak."

"Thanks, Grandma."

I moved to the door, fingers already stretching toward the handle.

"Oh, and *va'tari?*" I paused and glanced back.

Her smile had turned wicked. A grin that promised trouble.

"You tell that boy, if he ever hurts you again, I'll cut off his balls and cook them in that stew he loves so much."

"Uh. Okay. I'll... pass that along."

I made a mental note never to cross her. Ever.

Then I bolted out of the apartment, pounding down the stairs two at a time, and bursting onto the street, I sprinted like my life depended on it.

Grandma was right again.

I had a boy to get to, and nothing was going to stand in my way.

ON THE RIGHT TRACK

Kai

"Kai."

My eyes came back into focus to see a "game over" screen on the TV. I must've zoned out, falling deeper into my head than I realised. I couldn't even remember where we'd gotten up to in the game before we'd lost.

We'd been playing *Grand Rift Turbo* in my living room for hours—Jax's idea, his way of dragging me out of my slump.

It hadn't worked as well as he'd hoped, since we'd lost one of the easiest missions in the game. I'd played it loads of times and could smash it with my eyes shut if I wanted, but my heart wasn't in it, my mind too busy thinking about pearlescent skin, a prehensile tail, and void-like eyes.

Glancing at my watch, I was happy to see it was only four o'clock. That meant I hadn't missed my daily grovelling sesh on Rev's doorstep.

I tried to keep to the same time every day, keeping my fingers crossed today would be the day he'd open up. But so far, it'd been nothing but apologising to the wooden door until my voice was hoarse.

I knew his neighbours were sick of me. Sick of me interrupting their dinner and trashy TV with my knocking, ringing, and begging.

The Hessarian from two doors down had burst into the hallway last week, telling me in no uncertain terms to fuck off if I didn't want my ass kicked. He'd changed his tune when I pulled out a raggedy Nexus ball cap and offered to sign it, and I hadn't seen him since.

I'd sign a thousand hats for every resident in the place if it meant I could still get to Rev's door, could still whimper at the wood like a lost puppy waiting for its owner.

I kept coming back each day with a fresh bouquet, blooms that mirrored the shimmering colours of his skin. I emptied the local gift shop of all the stuffed animals it had. Something about the cheesy love notes spoke to me.

I knew Rev would pretend to hate them, but beneath the act, he was a man who loved soft things and an even softer touch.

Sometimes he was there when I stopped by.

The doors weren't thick, and I could hear him shuffling around the hallway. The doorbell also had a camera, so recordings of my whiny ass begging for forgiveness were uploaded onto the cloud somewhere, just waiting to be leaked to the world.

I didn't care, though. All I cared about was Rev, and how guilty I felt for the things I'd said.

Every time I returned, the previous day's delivery was missing. He might have thrown them down the rubbish chute, but I hoped he'd kept them, knowing I was thinking of him. Knowing that despite my twattish behaviour, I hadn't given up on him . . . on *us*.

I just hoped he hadn't given up on *me* yet.

"So, when did you and Rev go from mortal enemies to whatever weird thing you've got going on now?"

He asked the same question every time he came over, and every time I dodged it by stealing shuttles, robbing banks, and shooting strangers—for fun, of course. All acceptable in the game, and ideal for bleeding out the heartbreak I couldn't say aloud.

"I don't know what you're talking about."

"Bollocks," he retorted, restarting the mission we'd lost.

It involved stealing a modified hoverbike from a courier and delivering it to a chop shop before the Unified Space Enforcement could trace the bike's signal.

"I saw you in the lift together. If the sex hair hadn't given it away, the massive boner you were sporting would have."

I knocked the courier off the bike with our shuttle, and Jax's character hopped onto it. I side-eyed him as I tailed him through the Nebula slums.

"It wasn't just me with a boner, though, was it?"

"Nope," he bit out, narrowly avoiding an old woman walking her cat down the street. "We're not going there."

"Funny how *you* can avoid the topic of feelings, but I can't." The on-screen map flashed red and blue, and sirens wailed in the background.

"I've let you avoid the topic for weeks." He took a right turn, using a back street to avoid the nearby USE shuttles. "Also, you're the one who used the F-word, not me. So tell me. Why are you in a funk?"

"I'm not in a funk."

"Yesterday you cried watching *How to Lose a Guy in Ten Galaxies*."

"You know I'm a sucker for chick flicks!" I argued, braking hard as a bus cut me off. "That means nothing!"

"Kai," Jax sighed.

He paused the game and turned to face me. I threw my controller down on the couch but refused to meet his eyes, though I could feel them burning a hole in my skull. The patient motherfucker would wait me out, because I was always the one to crack first.

But I was a different man now, and I could stay strong.

For about thirty seconds.

"I just . . ." Dragging a hand down my face, I reclined further into the couch with a groan. "I don't know when it happened, just that it did. I can't stop thinking about him, Jax. And him not talking to me?" My head fell back, and I stared at the ceiling, eyes burning. "It's tearing me apart."

I blinked hard, fighting back the tears. I might drive fast cars, but there's nothing wrong with a good cry. It's cathartic, and I'd die on that hill.

"I was a prick," I whispered, voice cracking.

"You were," Jax agreed. "But emotions were all over the place. It hit all of us hard, Rev most of all."

I flung my hands into the air. "Exactly! He'd just gone through hell, and I stormed in like a Thraxian in an antique shop to kick him while he was down."

"Kai, it wasn't that—"

"You didn't see him when they opened the door, Jax." I continued as if he hadn't spoken. "He was like a zombie; the lights were on, but no one was home. Then I say his name, and he throws himself at me, like . . . like . . . like I'm his saviour or something!"

I stood up and started pacing in front of the couch. "And what do I do? I tell him it's his fault that Cass is dead."

"I don't think—"

"Yeah, I'm in a funk. Yeah, I'm in my feelings. In fact, right now, I'm feeling pretty damn shit. But I fucking deserve it, Jax. I deserve for him to ignore me, because I'm the worst person in the galaxy. In fact, I wouldn't be surprised if he never speaks to me—"

The doorbell cut me off mid-rant, reminding me to take a breath. A frantic knock followed, and I stared at the door as if it were a black hole.

Neither Jax nor I moved, and I was about to ask if I'd imagined it, when the doorbell sounded again.

"Are you gonna get that?" Jax asked.

"I don't know."

I didn't know who was at the door, but whoever it was, I didn't want to see them. It wouldn't be who I was hoping for, and I couldn't set myself up for disappointment. So when the doorbell chimed *again*, Jax rose from the couch and stalked past me with a put-upon sigh.

"I'll get it, then."

I didn't answer. I just watched in silence as Jax opened the door a crack, clinging to hope like a fool, even knowing it was useless.

"Can I help—oh. Hello."

When Jax stepped aside, revealing the mystery knocker, my breathing stuttered. My heart beat against my ribs like a champion boxer, because there on the doorstep was Rev.

He wore tight jeans and a clingy T-shirt, dark with sweat at the collar and under his arms like accidental tie-dye. He had twisted his hair into its usual messy bun, but damp strands clung to his temples and cheeks. He gripped the doorframe on both sides, flushed and breathless, like he'd just sprinted to get here.

But he wouldn't have done that, not for me. Not after what happened.

I didn't move at first, too stunned and convinced it was a dream.

Endless black eyes stared at me over Jax's shoulder, and I wanted to shove my teammate aside and pull Rev into my arms. I was desperate to hold him against my chest, sweaty body be damned, and inhale the scent of apples that clung to his skin. I wanted to breathe him in until I was dizzy, to make him roll around in my sheets so they carried his scent.

Because if he left me again, at least some part of him would still be here.

Jax cleared his throat, his eyes flitting between the two of us.

"Well, I, uh . . . I'll see myself out." He slipped past Rev, exiting through the door. But before he left, he placed a hand on the rookie's shoulder. "Good to see you, Rev."

"You too," he wheezed, though his eyes stayed locked on mine.

"Are you okay?" I took a careful step towards him, not wanting to scare him off. It was the first time I'd seen him in weeks, and I'd hate myself if I ran him off just as he'd arrived.

"Had to . . . see you," he panted, stepping over the threshold and allowing the door to close behind him.

The sharp click of the latch carved through the silence like a knife, and he fiddled with the hem of his T-shirt, busying his hands as though he was nervous.

It was laughable, because why would he be nervous? If anyone should be shitting themselves, it was me. I was terrified that he'd walk out of my apartment and I'd never see him again—at least not like this.

Of course I'd see him at the track, but he'd been skillfully avoiding me, and I couldn't stand the thought of that continuing for the remainder of my career.

Having him here felt like a dream I didn't want to wake from.

After weeks apart, just being near him again was everything. I noticed the dark circles under his eyes, the way his jeans hung a little looser than before. I wanted to ask if he was sleeping. If he was eating. Fuck, just looking at him made me want to make his favourite meal and watch him eat until he was full, even if I burned half the kitchen trying.

There was so much I wanted to say and do, but I didn't know where to begin. My mouth was dry, my tongue feeling too big for the small space, but the silence was growing awkward, tense, so I cleared my throat.

"Honest question," I said, catching the way he jumped at my voice. "On a scale of one to 'go to hell,' how badly did I fuck this up?"

His brow furrowed, and I expected a barrage of angry words. But then his lips twitched, and a sudden laugh bubbled out of him, the sound verging on hysterical.

He slapped a hand over his mouth, eyes widening like it surprised him.

Fuck, every time I heard it, I was surprised too.

"I've missed your laugh, Revvy."

His fingers curled into a loose fist against his mouth, eyes glassing over with tears. "Kai," he whispered, voice unsteady and soaked with emotion.

I didn't want him to crumble if I couldn't hold him, not again. So I held out my hand, hoping he'd take it. When he did, the weight I'd been carrying on my shoulders for weeks melted away in an instant.

For the first time since the day it all went to shit, I felt like I could take a full breath.

"Let's sit down, yeah?"

His eyes fell to the point of our connection, and as I led him to the couch, he chewed on the skin around his thumb. I put the game controllers away and took my usual spot. Rev perched beside me, leaving a slight gap. The distance hurt, but it was smaller than I'd expected, and he hadn't let go of my hand.

He went to speak, but I cut him off. I had things to get off my chest, and it needed to be done before he had the chance to end things. Before he could run away and disappear altogether.

"I'm so fucking sorry," I said, dragging our joined hands into my lap like an anchor. "What I said that day . . . I didn't mean a word of it."

My voice shook as I kept going.

"Yeah, we were all on edge, and sure, emotions were high, but that doesn't excuse any of it. You went through hell, and instead of being there for you, I made it worse."

I looked down, breath catching, gripping his hand tighter.

"I care about you, Rev. More than I've ever known how to say. You're everything to me, and the thought that I made you feel like you weren't, that I might've wrecked this . . . fuck. I'd give anything to take it back."

"Kai—"

"I was a fucking idiot," I said, cutting him off before he could argue. "A real asshole for saying I couldn't handle you. There's nothing about you that needs handling. You're incredible, even if you do scowl like it's your full-time job."

I let out a shaky breath, my voice softening.

"But you're perfect to me, rookie. Just as you are. And if you want to walk away, I won't stop you . . . but please don't. Don't give up on us. I'll do whatever it takes to fix this, to be someone who deserves you. Just . . . please don't leave me. Not like this."

Rev's free hand landed on top of our entwined fingers. I was too scared to look, but when I did, I saw his tears. They made me panic, so I continued rambling.

"I don't know if I deserve you, but I'm begging you to let me try. Let me prove that you're worth fighting for, because losing you would break me in ways I can't bear to think about."

He stared at me, astonished, like he'd never expected my apology. Or maybe he had, but not like this, and that shattered something inside me. Stars, I'd drop to my knees and grovel at his feet if it showed him just how sorry I was. Sorry for what I'd said, for shutting him out when he'd needed me the most.

"Kai," Rev said again, shuffling closer and eliminating the gap.

He leaned in and cupped my cheek, delicate fingers tickling the hairs on my jaw. He was so close, I could taste the sweetness of his breath, and all I wanted was to taste him.

"I'm sorry too."

"Wait." I gripped his wrist, feeling his rapid pulse under my thumb. "Why are *you* sorry?"

His skin glowed orange, and he worried his lip with a fang. "You didn't ruin things. I thought I was injured, but I misjudged the situation. I . . ."

Rev exhaled, shaking his head like he was trying to get his thoughts in order. Then he straightened up, looking me right in the eye, gearing himself up to say something important.

"I've always felt alone."

"But—"

"Kai." He shot me a glare, but there was no spark. More habit than heat. "As much as your obnoxious personality has grown on me—"

I started to argue, but his lips found mine, stealing the words—and the breath—straight from my mouth.

"Like I was saying," he murmured with a smirk. "You're growing on me like a rash. But I need to get this out, so with all due respect, please shut the fuck up."

I nodded, because if it meant he'd kiss me again, I'd never speak another word. For at least an hour.

"You already know parts of my story," Rev said, his fingers tracing a slow line along my jaw. Not to comfort me, but maybe to soothe himself. "I've never had real friends, never had a relationship. I've never let anyone in, not really. Because in the end, everyone left."

He paused, eyes distant. "Sometimes it was subtle, and sometimes they just... drifted. But mostly, it was because being close to the freak—the rare, endangered Iskari—was only fun for a while. I was a curiosity. A conversation piece. And when the novelty wore off, so did their loyalty."

His voice softened to something almost bitter. "I think I stopped expecting anything different. People always found a reason to disappoint me, so I stopped trying. And yeah, I was lonely. Not that I'd ever admit it out loud.

"As you like to remind me, I've got a scowl for every occasion, and everyone just assumes I'm grumpy. But that's the point," Rev sighed. "It's easier to keep people at a distance. If they can't get close, they can't let you down. They can't decide one day that you're not worth the trouble and walk away."

His mouth twitched, almost a smile but not quite.

"Then this absolute prick shows up—loud, cocky, and so damn sure of himself. Tells me I'm gonna hurt someone if I keep driving like I've got a death wish. But he stuck around. Even when I pushed back, even when I was impossible, he kept coming back. Maybe just to piss me off, but maybe..." The lines on his skin flickered a beautiful shade of yellow. "Maybe he saw something in me worth staying for."

"Was this absolute prick handsome, at least?" I leaned in, resting my forehead against his.

Rev laughed, lighter than I'd ever heard it. Like he was shaking off years of weight he'd carried alone. I soaked it in, this fragile closeness blooming between us.

He was letting me in.

"He was very handsome, even if he was a bit of a tosser," he mumbled, pressing a soft kiss to the tip of my nose. I preened, even as I rolled my eyes at the backhanded compliment. "It felt good getting close to you, Kai. For the first time, I had someone to turn to. Someone who saw *me*, not just my rarity. And I liked it. I liked it more than I ever expected. I gave you all of my firsts, because how could I not?"

He paused. "Then everything fell apart. You were kind of a dick, yeah, but looking back, I get it. That day was hell for all of us. We were scared, angry, and grieving. But the thing is, you didn't walk away. I did."

His voice softened, and his tail curled around my wrist. "You were the one calling after me. The one who showed up at my door every single day, like a very charming, obsessive stalker. Yet I ran away, and not for the first time. Because when it comes to you, Kai Mercer, I'm ridiculously smitten, and that scares the shit out of me."

I slid my hand up his thigh to his hip and gave it a firm squeeze. My chest swelled with something fierce and warm when the markings along his skin lit up with a vibrant amethyst glow.

"At first, I convinced myself it was all your fault," he continued. "That you'd disappointed me, like everyone else. But thanks to some wise words from a very old woman—don't tell Grandma I said that, because I know you like to gossip—I realised I was wrong."

He shrugged.

"Maybe it was trauma, maybe it was my own messed up way of protecting myself. I ran because I thought it would hurt less to leave than to be left behind. But the thing is, Kai . . ."

His hand moved from my jaw to the back of my neck, anchoring me there in his orbit.

"I'm so fucking in love with you it aches. Not just in my chest, but in my bones. In the breaths I can't take when you're not around. Every day without you feels like drifting through space without a tether. I never imagined I'd miss your relentless teasing, or that cocky smile. Stars, even your ridiculous ego that only just fits in the room."

I laughed, my cheeks aching from the sheer force of my grin, even as his words washed over me, raw and real.

Rev leaned back, and I found myself lost in the twin galaxies of his eyes, captivated and willing to be held prisoner forever.

"You said I was like a comet," he continued. "But you're the fucking *sun*. You burn brighter than anything else in my sky, and I'm done hiding in the shadows. I want you to drag me into the light."

Rev took a deep breath and exhaled. "I love you, Kai, and if you'll have me, I'm yours—fire, flaws, and everything in between."

HEART OVER WHEELS

Kai

I stared in silence as shock held me in a tight fist.

"I love you, Kai, and if you'll have me, I'm yours."

Rev told me he loved me. No sarcasm, no jokes, no sharp edges. Just honesty, raw and real, and threaded with affection.

And I just stood there, staring at him like a complete pillock.

Rev's touch vanished as he leaned back, the distance leaving me cold. I wanted to grab his hands and press them anywhere on my body, just to feel him, to be sure he was real.

But I didn't move. Didn't speak.

Terror gripped me. Not at what he'd said, but at the chance this could all be a dream. That he wasn't really here, hadn't said he loved me. If I so much as shifted, the moment might crack apart and reveal itself as nothing more than a cruel, beautiful illusion.

"Um . . ."

He pulled away, uncertainty written all over his face. I saw it. The flicker of doubt. The quiet unravelling. He questioned himself, questioned whether he'd said too much, and whether I felt the same.

Regret settled over his features like a shadow creeping into sunlight, dimming what should have been a beautiful moment.

And when the light in his eyes faded, it jolted me back into motion.

"It's okay if it's not w-what you want . . . if I'm not what you—*Kai*!"

I lurched forward and grabbed his hips, pulling him into my lap.

He landed straddling my thighs, clutching my shoulders for balance. His wide eyes searched mine, uncertainty clinging to him like a foul smell. His tail thudded against the couch, and his skin shimmered with shifting colours—orange, blue, gold, pink. His knuckles were white as he clutched my shirt, terrified I would vanish.

He'd thrown himself at me before, and instead of giving him the safety he needed, I'd pushed him away.

I must have done something good in a past life, though.

Saved orphans from a fire. Pulled a star from the sky. Something.

Because this storm of a man, all quiet thunder and guarded walls, loved me.

Of everyone in the galaxy, he chose me. Even after the mess we'd made at the start, even after the hurt I'd caused, Rev still reached for me.

And I would never push him away again.

"Kai . . ." he whispered, body vibrating in my lap.

The stars in his eyes swirled with anticipation, a mix of nerves and longing. I gripped the back of his neck and pulled him closer until I could feel his sweet breath on my lips.

"You're everything to me, rookie. All I could ever want." I placed my hand on his chest, on top of his thundering heart. "I was miserable without you, and I'm sorry for hurting you. Sorry for every time you felt alone or unwanted. For every time you watched from the sidelines, wishing you could belong."

A single tear slid down his cheek, and I brushed it away with my thumb, pressing a soft kiss to the damp skin.

"I promise to be your safe space, the place where you can drop the mask and just be. I want to know every version of you, even the one the world never sees.

You're the center of my galaxy, Revvy, and I would gladly revolve around you for all time."

Rev inhaled sharply. His fingers followed the curve of my brow, my nose, and my lips, as if memorising every line.

"I love you so much, little comet," I whispered. "If you ever want to run, you can. But I'll catch you every time, and I promise I'll always bring you back to me."

Rev pressed a tender kiss to the tip of my nose. Then he smiled, bright and glorious, his skin glowing my favourite shade of amethyst. "I'll always come back to you, Kai. I belong with you."

He was stunning when he was happy, and I made a silent promise to ensure he stayed that way, for as long as he would let me.

"Can I kiss you now?" he asked.

Cupping his face, I pulled him close, and my lips brushed his in a teasing caress as I replied. "You never have to ask."

Like every time we'd kissed, we collided in a storm of fire and passion. Both of us were desperate, wanting to make up for the time apart.

Given the matching stiffies we were sporting, I'd say Rev was as happy to get the show on the road as I was.

He dipped lower, pressing our groins together, and when he rolled his hips, the friction made my eyes roll back into my skull.

"Fuck," he whimpered, finding his rhythm. "I missed you."

"I missed you too," I panted between kisses.

I needed him more than I could stand, and it was only the dizzy ache of breathlessness that made me pull away. Not that I regretted it. From here, I had a perfect view of Rev's flushed cheeks, kiss-bruised lips, and the unmistakable bulge pressing against his skinny jeans.

I needed more. Needed to see him, every inch.

I tugged his T-shirt over his head, letting my hands linger on his skin before peeling off my own. With a grin, I coaxed him onto his knees.

His tight jeans earned a muttered curse as I struggled to get them off, yanking and shimmying as though I were in a fight I was losing. He wobbled with every pull, laughter bubbling from his lips as he clutched my shoulders to stay upright.

By the time I got them off, I was sweating like we'd already gone three rounds.

"Loose clothes only from now on," I groused.

He giggled, then kissed me breathless while I made quick work of my joggers. We both groaned when our bare cocks pressed together, the sound echoing off the wall-to-floor windows.

One day I'd have him against that glass, legs wrapped around me while I took him hard and slow, but right now the need was too sharp, too urgent. I couldn't imagine moving from this spot, not when I was so desperate to be inside him.

I gripped the curve of his ass, guiding him into motion, and with every roll of his hips, I met him with a thrust. I was so wound up it didn't take long before I was teetering on the edge of release.

Rev's thighs trembled as he climbed higher with each movement. His tail coiled tightly around my calf, the squeeze sharp enough to sting but not enough to pull me out of the moment.

I didn't want to come yet, not without feeling his ass around my cock. But it felt so good—damp skin pressed together, his hot breath warming my cheeks—I couldn't stop.

When Rev rose to his knees, putting his stomach level with my face, I was grateful for the reprieve.

"Had to stop," he wheezed, running his fingers through my hair. "Didn't want to come."

"You did good, baby," I replied, and the lines on his skin pulsed gold.

He pulled hard on my hair. It made me hiss, but the sting did wonders for calming me down. I pressed a kiss to his stomach, just below his belly button, and dropped my gaze to his cock.

It stood straight up from his groin, twitching with need and dribbling precum. Pearly droplets dripped onto my chest, and I was dying to remind myself of the taste.

Swiping a finger through the mess, I sucked it into my mouth, and groaned as his salty flavour burst on my tongue. Different shades of pink danced across his skin, and his tail flicked back and forth, whipping my legs.

"Fuck," he breathed, ears twitching, endless eyes flaring with heat.

I looked up at him, a slow smirk tugging at my lips.

"Good thing we've got all night."

Then I took the tip of his cock into my mouth, dipping my tongue into his slit.

He squealed, hips jerking as he tried to push deeper. I caught his hip in one hand, holding him firm, a silent command to stay still. My grip was tight, hard enough to bruise his soft periwinkle skin, and the idea sent a delicious thrill down my spine.

My free hand slipped between his legs, knuckles brushing his balls before sliding into his crease. He was already slick, and he squirmed when my finger circled his hole.

He moaned as I slid a single finger inside him, his body yielding with effortless grace, and he tipped his head back, lips parted in a breathless gasp.

"Oh god."

I stayed still, letting him adjust to the sensation. When he whimpered, "More," I began a slow, deep thrust. He moved with sharp, uneven motions, so I added a second finger, scissoring them to stretch his tight muscles. My fingers found his prostate, and a fresh burst of precum coated my tongue as I stroked the sensitive gland.

By the time he was writhing on three fingers, I was close to losing control. Watching him arch over me, riding my fingers and moaning like a porn star, brought to life the image I'd dreamed of all those months ago.

He was a wet dream made real, and I was the lucky one living it.

I released his cock and growled, low and dangerous.

"You look so good taking my fingers, baby." His sweet, oily slick dripped from his hole, tracing slow rivulets down my hand. The wet slap of every thrust only made me harder, and I couldn't wait any longer. "Gotta be inside you."

Withdrawing my fingers, I brought the glistening digits to my mouth and sucked them clean. The taste of him made my head spin. Then he lowered himself onto my lap, pressing my cock to his entrance. Ready.

But when he locked eyes with mine and whispered, "Fuck me," how could I say no?

Rev bore down, and the head slipped through the first ring of muscle with a soft pop. My head fell back against the couch, a moan escaping me. Just clear-headed enough, I grabbed his hips, holding him back from taking me all at once.

"Careful, Revvy," I bit out as he sank lower. "Don't want to hurt you."

"Need you, *solvenari*."

I didn't know what the word meant, but the way he whispered it, reverently and breathlessly, made my chest ache. It sounded precious, like a secret I was lucky to hear. With Rev, it could have also meant "idiot."

But stars, I wanted it to mean "*mine*."

When his ass hit my thighs, I held him down. I knew he was desperate to move, but he needed a moment to adjust. And if I was being honest, so did I.

Rev leaned in for a kiss, and we used the opportunity to slow down, to take a breath and reconnect.

He nibbled my bottom lip, catching it with his fang, and the taste of copper mixed with our saliva. It stung, but when he licked my lip, swallowing the taste of my essence, it only made me thirst for more.

He broke the kiss and wrapped his arms around my neck. His eyes were wet, overflowing with a mix of fear and adoration.

"I love you, Kai."

I kissed him again, because when it came to the rookie, I would never get enough.

"I love you too, Rev."

He rose on his knees, most of my cock slipping free, and with that, the time for sentimentality ended. Now, it was all about pleasure.

When he dropped down hard, I cried out, and he kept going, again and again. I stayed still, hands cupping his ass, guiding his rhythm. This was Rev's show, and I was his captive audience.

I slid my hand up his chest and pinched his nipple, hard. "You're so fucking beautiful, baby."

He whimpered, skin flushing a scorching hot pink. He sped up, sweat slicking his hairline and dripping down his trembling torso.

"Kai." He moaned my name like a prayer. "More."

I pushed against his chest, urging him to lean back and shift the angle. His hands gripped my knees, and his tail curled tight around my ankle for balance. With every thrust, my cock hit his prostate, and his head lolled back.

"Fucking *hell*," he sobbed towards the ceiling.

Rev's thighs trembled with a mix of pleasure and exhaustion, and my balls drew up tight. I couldn't hold on much longer, and judging by the sounds he was making, neither could he.

I planted my feet on the hardwood floor and gripped his hips. When I thrust upwards, driving deep inside him, he screamed. His nails dug into my legs, and I could have sworn I felt a warm trickle of blood slide down my skin.

"Kai! I—shit . . . oh m-my *god* . . ." he babbled.

"You gonna come for me, little comet? Gonna mark me as yours?"

"Yes!" he cried, cheeks wet with tears. "I need to c-come, *solvenari*. Please let m-me come!"

He reached for his cock, but I slapped his hand away, and he groaned in frustration.

"Come for me, baby," I snarled. "Just let go."

He was so close, right on the edge. I knew if I hit the right spot with my next thrust, he'd—

"*KAI!*"

With no friction to his cock, he erupted, his cum splattering my chest and stomach, scorching my overheated flesh. His skin glowed magenta, so bright it almost blinded me, and his mouth hung open, silently screaming through his orgasm.

"Look so pretty when you come." I slammed into him with a grunt. "Gonna fucking breed you, baby. Fill you with my load and mark you, inside and out."

He whined as I ravaged his hole. Then he clenched tight, and my cock jerked, my release crashing over me like a meteor. I roared, eyes squeezed shut, spilling inside him until it overflowed, warm and slick, dripping down my shaft and into my pubes.

It felt like I blacked out, seconds passing like hours before I came around, relaxing into the soft couch. My softening cock fell from his hole, a mixture of cum and slick pooling in my lap.

"Remind me to clean my sofa," I murmured, eyes and limbs heavy with exhaustion.

Rev laughed and slumped forward, resting his cheek on my shoulder. The mess was smeared between us, but I didn't care. All I cared about was the man in my lap.

The rookie who'd become my everything.

Before I could get too comfortable, I lifted Rev from the couch, still cradling him in my arms. He was dozing, but the movement stirred him awake, and he clung to me like a koala, limbs wrapped tight, while his tail traced slow, soothing strokes along my thigh.

I carried him through my bedroom to the en suite, where I lowered him onto the counter. He squeaked when his skin hit the cold marble, and I gave him a quick kiss as an apology. Ducking into the shower, I turned on the water, and when it was warm enough, I helped him down and ushered him under the spray.

I stepped up behind him, sliding under the large rainfall showerhead, and he hummed, resting his head against my chest as I grabbed a soft washcloth and drenched it with shower gel.

My mind buzzed with satisfaction, knowing I'd filled him up and now he'd carry my scent for a little while.

Fuck, if I were a dog, I'd piss on his leg.

"What are you doing?" he asked as I scrubbed his arm.

"Taking care of you, little comet."

It wasn't our first shower together, but before, it had always devolved into another chance to get off.

This time felt different. It was about taking care of him, tracing every curve, line, and contour of his body, and making sure he was safe and happy.

I washed every part of him, from his face to the very tips of his toes. He flushed when I scrubbed the more intimate areas, even though I'd had his cock in my mouth less than thirty minutes before.

I chuckled when the markings on his skin flickered, and I realised I'd never asked, even though I'd been desperate to know.

"What do the colours mean?"

His eyes grew wide, and for a moment I worried I'd offended him. I opened my mouth to apologise, to say it didn't matter, but he rested a hand over my heart, his lips curling into a small, gentle smile.

"I didn't mean to react like that. It's quite . . . intimate for the Iskari, so no one else knows."

"You don't have to—"

"No, I want you to know," he cut me off. "I'm glad you asked, Kai."

He exhaled, psyching himself up.

Opening up was still new for him, and I knew old habits wouldn't break overnight. I'd give him all the time he needed.

"The colours represent our emotions." He paused, searching for the right words. "We wear our emotions for everyone to see, but only Iskari know what they mean. It's a vulnerability, in a way, letting the galaxy know how we feel at all times. So we keep it a secret between those who understand . . . a way to protect ourselves."

He gave a small, rueful smile." Like, you don't want every person walking down the street to know you're pissed off at your job or jealous of an ex-lover. Hell, even horny, because that would be embarrassing."

I snorted and tucked a lock of hair behind his ear.

"Thanks for telling me," I said with a smirk. "Let me take a wild guess . . . Does that fiery red I always see mean you're madly in love with me?"

Rev raised an eyebrow and flashed a mischievous grin. "Sure, let's go with that."

I washed his hair, and he repeated the process on me with the same amount of care. After drying off, Rev braided his damp strands, and I led him to my bed, not bothering with clothes. When we slipped under the covers, I thanked the gods that Jax had made me change the sheets that morning.

Rev curled into my side, one arm draped over my stomach. His tail lay still behind him, telling me just how tired he was.

My eyes grew heavy, and I was just drifting off when the rookie opened his mouth. "I have something to tell you."

He opened his mouth to speak, but a yawn overtook him, so wide his jaw gave a soft, audible click.

"You can tell me after we nap," I said, giving him a squeeze.

But because he was a stubborn little shit, he didn't care that he couldn't keep his eyes open. "I'm too excited, Kai. I have to tell you now."

I chuckled as he yawned again. "Go on, then."

He launched into a story about meeting with Talia Monroe, and the more he talked, the wider my eyes got.

Not just because the governor had an Iskari husband, but because Rev's people were going to be recognised. His determination had paid off, and the Iskari were going to be seen.

Most importantly, they were going to stand as equals.

"I . . . am . . . so . . . proud . . . of . . . you . . ." I said, punctuating each word with a kiss to his cheeks, his nose, his eyes, his forehead, until I reached his lips.

"I didn't do much," he mumbled, skin glowing burnt orange mixed with violet.

"You did *something*, baby." I stroked his soft jaw. "That's more than most would do.

"I'm just glad things will be better for my family," he murmured, sleep taking him. "I've been saving part of my salary to buy them a bigger apartment, so they won't have to waste money on rent anymore."

"That sounds great, little comet." I pressed a kiss on his forehead, and he sighed. "I'm sure they'll appreciate it."

Talking about the Iskari reminded me of the word he had said earlier. I'd assumed it was in his native language, and now I was desperate to confirm he hadn't called me an asshole, or something equally insulting.

"You called me something before," I said, glancing down at him. Rev looked up, eyes heavy with exhaustion. "Sol-vay-nerry, or something like that?"

I butchered the pronunciation, and he knew it, because he giggled, low and sleepy.

"*Solvenari*," he corrected, the word slipping off his tongue like silk. It gave me goosebumps, and my cock twitched.

Not the time, Kai.

"What does it mean?"

"It means 'solar flare,'" he replied, yawning as he nuzzled into my chest. "Because you're blinding, magnetic, and impossible to look away from."

My throat tightened, and my eyes prickled. It was more beautiful than I'd imagined.

"Also," he added in a drowsy mumble. "You're hot as fuck."

I barked out a laugh, helplessly in love.

I couldn't get enough of him, and I'd spend forever making sure he knew it.

"I fucking love you, little comet."
"I love you too, *solvenari*."

ALL'S FAIR IN LOVE & TRACK LIMITS

Kai

I was being insufferable, and I knew it.

I'd been bouncing off the walls like a kid on E-numbers for days, and I was surprised Rev hadn't walloped me yet. He'd come close, and in the past, he wouldn't have hesitated to smack me upside the head.

But instead of choosing violence, Rev would just take a breath and give me one of those tight, pained smiles. I figured he spent a lot of time screaming into a pillow when I wasn't around, but hey, that's what growth looked like.

I couldn't help it, though.

Every year, I was far too excited about the end of the season. I performed to the best of my ability in every race, and when my points reflected that, it hyped me up to the point of insanity. Jax was used to dealing with my insane ass, but this year, that responsibility had fallen to Rev, and my teammate was more than happy to hand over the baton.

It was a good thing he'd already said he loved me, because there were no fucking takebacks.

Now the big day was here. The final race of the season, and the day I'd take home my fourth championship.

Rev had laughed when I showed him the space I'd cleared for the trophy.

"Feeling confident, hotshot?"

But he wasn't laughing later that night. Not when I backed up every bit of that confidence—slowly, thoroughly, and with no room for doubt.

I went into today's race at the top of the table, but that didn't mean I could relax.

The gap between me and Zylo was razor-thin, and one mistake could cost me everything. If anything went wrong, the championship was his, so I had to bring everything—every ounce of focus, every drop of speed.

Today, it was first place or nothing.

Rev was in eighth, and I'd told him how impressive that was, especially for a rookie. It was the highest finish for a first-timer in league history, and he had every reason to be proud. He wouldn't take the win, but he lit a fire under me.

He pushed me, challenged me, shook me up in all the right ways. And I made sure he knew just how much of a prize that made him.

Instead, he poured all his energy into hyping me up, and there was no one I'd rather have in my corner. In another life, maybe he would've felt bitter, but with a brighter future on the Iskari's horizon, he remembered why he'd chased the ASL dream to begin with.

Trophy or not, he was proud to have been part of it, and I was proud to finish out the season by his side.

Every driver dreamed of winning the championship, but I knew Rev had years ahead of him in the league, and he'd be keeping me on my toes the whole way. With a little more experience and a lot less chaos, he could steal that title from all of us as early as next season.

And as his rival, I'd be right there, ready to fight him for it every step of the way.

These days, though, we had much better ways of dealing with the tension.

Arriving at the paddock, race prep was already in full swing. Crew members darted back and forth as always, but there was an extra buzz in the air, a charged anticipation you could almost taste.

As we walked to the team garage, Jax nudged my side. "You ready?"

I looked over the top of my favourite aviators and smiled. "Always."

I was grateful when the morning flew by, and an hour before the race, I was feeling pumped.

Rev had slept restlessly beside me before leaving early to travel with Zenith, but not before I'd blown the nerves out of him.

Veilbreaker Circuit was the league's most legendary and demanding track.

It carved a jagged path across a volatile tectonic fracture zone, the ground beneath shifting and groaning as if warning us to stay alert. That's why they saved it for last.

I'd never seen anyone die on those twists and turns, but I knew just how quickly things could go wrong, and how unforgiving the track could be.

Ailor had seen a driver get roasted like a chicken when superheated steam erupted from one of the track's geothermal vents, and every year he reminded us to be careful. I'd given Rev the same heads-up, and he'd promised to play it safe and make it to the finish line in one piece.

I'd been edging him for an hour at that point, but I was almost a hundred percent sure he meant it.

Okay, ninety-five percent.

I spotted Zylo in front of Zenith's garage, going over his vehicle with the crew. Rev's was there too, but I couldn't see him, and I frowned.

He was a stickler for doing his own checks.

"Have you seen Rev?" I asked while Zylo fiddled with his steering wheel.

"Not since our team meeting," he replied. "Everything okay?"

"I just wanted to make sure he was okay."

Zylo's expression turned oddly serious. "Don't mess with him, Mercer," he warned. "Not after what happened with Cass."

We hadn't told our teams about us yet, wanting to enjoy each other in peace until the season was over. Only Jax knew. After how I'd left things with Rev in front of Zylo before, it wasn't surprising he felt protective.

"Everything's fine." I gave him a reassuring smile. "Better than fine. I swear."

Zylo grinned like he'd just won a prize, flashing those sharp teeth. There was a wicked glint in his eye, and I half wondered if Rev had spilled the beans.

"Saelix was dead certain something was going on between you two, but I just thought you liked to piss each other off." He threw his head back and laughed, the sound booming like he owned the whole paddock. "Looks like I owe him a blow job after all."

My jaw hit the floor. His brutal honesty left me speechless.

After a beat, I just gave his arm a solid pat.

"Good talk, man," I muttered, and Zylo's laugh followed me into the garage.

As the crew rolled the vehicles out to the grid, I realised I still hadn't spotted Rev, so I asked Tavoris.

"Kai Mercer," he said with a grin. "No room for you here if you're thinking about jumping teams."

I laughed with him, but I was glad to know he was happy having Rev around. "Not this time, mate. I was just wondering if you'd seen Rev?"

Tavoris glanced at his watch and frowned.

"Not for a while. Kileen!" he called to one of the engineers. "Have you seen Rev?"

The engineer shook their head. "Nah. He said he was going to the bathroom, but that was a while ago."

"Can I check on him?" I asked, and Tavoris raised his eyebrows. "I just want to make sure he's okay. No funny business, I swear. He . . ." I hesitated, not wanting to reveal too much without Rev's permission. But I was worried, so he could deal with it. "He means a lot to me."

Tavoris's mouth curved into a smile. "I had a feeling."

So much for being subtle.

"Go on," he said, nodding towards the open garage. But just as I stepped forward, he held out a hand to stop me. "And keep your eyes off the screens, yeah? Gotta preserve a little mystery."

"You got it."

I marched through the garage before he could change his mind, eyes fixed straight ahead. Curiosity tugged at me, and loyalty to Nexus whispered that one little peek wouldn't hurt. But I behaved. I stopped only once to ask a crew member where the bathrooms were.

I found Rev curled up at the far end of the room, arms wrapped around his legs, head resting on his knees. The lines on his skin flickered lime green, and his breaths came short and uneven. I crossed the tiled floor without hesitation and dropped down beside him, slipping an arm around his shoulders and pulling him close.

Black eyes peeked up at me through the curtain of hair falling over his face.

"Kai?" he croaked. "What are you doing here?"

"I was worried about you, rookie," I said, giving his shoulder a gentle squeeze. "Hadn't seen that pretty face in a while, and you know I go into withdrawal."

He smiled, but it didn't reach his eyes. He sniffled and leaned down to rub his nose against his sleeve. That's when I noticed the glassiness in his eyes, the tension in his shoulders. He looked nothing like the relaxed guy who'd left my apartment that morning.

"What's going on, Revvy?" I asked, keeping my voice low.

Sound bounced like hell in these cramped bathrooms, and right now, anything louder than a whisper felt like it might spook him.

He wouldn't look at me. Just dropped his head back onto his knees, his voice muffled against his racing suit.

"I don't think I can do it, Kai."

My heart skipped. I didn't think he meant us, not after everything we'd shared. I didn't ask, though. This wasn't the time to project my own fears. I had to trust he was in this the way I was.

Most of the time, I did.

It would take time for both of us to believe, deep down, that the other wouldn't run. But we'd get there. I loved him too much to let him go, and I was sure he felt the same.

"What do you mean?"

"The race," he mumbled, and I let out a quiet breath of relief.

Alright. This, I could handle.

"Of course you can, baby," I said, pulling him in closer.

I slid an arm under his legs and eased him into my lap until he was lying sideways, his body resting against mine. He tucked his head into the crook of my neck, nuzzling under my chin like he was trying to lose himself in the warmth of my skin.

At least now he couldn't hide behind his knees.

"I don't think I'm ready," he whispered, lips brushing my neck. His fingers tightened around the front of my racing suit. "I'm not good enough."

"You're more than ready." I slipped my fingers under his chin, tilting his face up to meet mine. "You're one of the best rookies this sport has ever seen, and not just because of some title. You've earned your place out there. You've been on that podium more than once already, which is more than most drivers can say in their entire rookie season."

"But I—"

"You're incredible, little comet. Don't think about what happened this season, okay? Think about the race ahead." I pushed some loose hair behind his ear. "And the way I'm gonna fuck you against my windows after I've claimed my win."

Rev giggled, and the sound sent a warm burst through my chest. This time his smile was wide and real. He gave my chest a soft punch. "Of course you're so sure you've already won."

"One of us has to have a winning mindset, baby. Might as well be me," I shot back with a wink.

"Still gonna fuck me if you lose?"

I gasped, feigning shock as I glared down at him. "We do not speak of such things!"

"You've got this, *solvenari*," he reassured me, leaning up to kiss me.

When we pulled apart, I gave his hip a gentle pat and urged him to stand. He watched me with curiosity as I tapped my watch, and when an upbeat pop song filled the room, he raised an eyebrow.

"What's happening?"

"Don't pretend you don't like it, rookie," I teased, holding out my hand. "I heard you singing along in my shuttle."

"I did not," he scoffed.

Still, he took my hand and let me pull him close.

"We're gonna dance it out, baby."

Moving from side to side, Rev looked at me like I'd grown a second head.

"Excuse me?"

"We're gonna dance it out," I said, gripping his hips and pulling him into a sway. "Shake out the nerves, dance like no one's watching, and get ready to race."

"You're insane, you know that?"

"But you love me anyway."

"Don't know why," he mumbled. I couldn't resist slapping his ass, and he yelped.

"I've seen you dance, rookie. It's about time I got my turn."

I pushed him away and grabbed one of his hands, pulling him into a quick spin. He chuckled, so I did it again before dragging him back against my chest. One hand settled at the small of his back while the other held our joined hands high as we swayed back and forth like a couple during their first wedding dance, only more exaggerated.

I cranked up the music, loud enough to fill the entire garage.

But as Rev loosened up, singing and spinning on his own, his skin flickering in a rainbow of colours while he waved his arms, none of it mattered.

Seeing him happy and free felt better than any championship trophy.

When the song ended, we collapsed against each other, breathless and flushed. Our cheeks burned as we leaned in at the same time and shared a soft kiss, and I felt Rev's lips curl into a smile before he pulled away.

"Okay," he said on an exhale, his lithe frame relaxed. His eyes sparkled, the stardust swirling like a fresh snow globe. "I'm ready."

"You're damn right you are."

I took his hand and led him through the garage to where our teammates waited on the grid.

And right up until the moment we climbed into our vehicles, Rev held on tight, never letting go.

The track was kicking my ass, just like it did every year.

But this time, my mind kept drifting to a certain rookie who'd clawed his way into fourth place. He was miles ahead of Jax in fifth, and my teammate had already grumbled about not being able to close the gap.

Rev might not have a shot at winning, but he was pushing hard enough to snag one more podium before the season wrapped up.

Zylo was in second. He'd been riding my ass for the last five laps, and I couldn't lie; it rattled me. With only two laps left, there was no way I was going to screw this up now.

"I might have to dust off my trophy shelf if you keep this up, Mercer," Zylo cackled over the radio.

"Fuck off, old man," I shot back, making him laugh even harder.

I was sure the producers running the livestream were loving our little soundbites, but I was more worried about Zylo inching closer in my wing mirror.

On top of that, I was sweating buckets inside the cockpit, and part of me wished I was driving in just my boxers.

Veilbreaker Circuit was a track that hugged the planet's massive shifting fault lines, skimming volcanic ridges and plunging through sulphuric canyons. It was a hot, stinky ride, and one I was relieved to be almost done with.

There was also sulphur fog. Thick, yellow, and a nightmare on the lungs if you got caught in a cloud while driving around the track. The smell of eggs would cling to your hair and skin for fucking days, and given I had some plans that involved Rev and me, naked and writhing against each other, I wanted to avoid any turnoffs.

The track looked straightforward on the surface. A simple ride, right? Wrong.

Large cracks could open up anywhere if the fault lines shifted, leaving cavernous pits that were tricky to navigate if you weren't paying close attention. To make matters worse, bursts of steam hotter than the fires of hell could explode through the asphalt with no warning.

Chunks were already missing from the road around turn three, forcing at least three drivers from different teams out of the race. One of the Vanguard drivers had also lost the back end of their vehicle when steam erupted at the worst possible moment, sending them into the wall.

Whoever had thought it was a good idea to build a track over a river of lava and geothermal vents was a fucking psychopath.

"My grandma drives faster than you."

I snorted as Rev's voice crackled through the drivers' radio. It was followed by a colourful string of curse words from Dray, who must have been overtaken.

"Since when can your grandma drive, rookie?" I chimed in.

"She can't," he fired back. "That's what makes his driving even more embarrassing."

"Oh, fuck you, you snarky little twatwaffle," Valen fumed, which made the two of us snicker like schoolboys.

"Nice of you to join us, Revvy." Zylo's voice came through, happy to see his teammate up in the top three. I couldn't blame him, because I wanted Rev on the podium with me just as much.

Rev slipped in behind Zylo like a shadow, just visible in my wing mirror. Whatever nerves had plagued him earlier were gone. His movements were sharp now, purposeful.

Whether he meant to overtake or box Zylo in, I couldn't say. But I didn't mind. Even if his team came before me out here, I couldn't help the swell of pride I felt at the fire he brought with him.

"Gonna give me a hand and take out your teammate, rookie?"

"I'd rather take you out, hotshot."

"That can be arranged, boo," I shot back, making a smoochy sound with my lips. "See me after the podium."

"Can you two keep it in your pants?" Dray groaned. "I swear I'm gonna puke in my helmet."

"So that's what the smell is," Rev retorted. "I thought it was the sulphur smoke, but it turns out it's just Dray."

Dray was mid-curse when the gravel behind Zylo burst open in a violent hiss of steam.

A car shot through it like a missile, spinning end over end before crashing down on its roof, skidding in a hail of sparks to the track's edge.

Another engine howled through the plume a beat later, tyres screaming as a sleek green vehicle tore past the wreckage and slipped in behind Zylo.

My stomach plummeted.

That was Dray's car—still racing, still whole—which meant the wreck wasn't his.

"Fuck!"

"Kai!" Zylo's voice cut through the radio, sharp and urgent. "Can you see anything?"

He was right behind me. If he couldn't see through the steam and choking black smoke, then neither could I. But one thing was certain. Rev wasn't standing there watching.

He hadn't climbed out of the wreck.

Zylo thundered past, engine roaring, and that's when I realised I was easing off the throttle. My grip had slackened. I stared at the nightmare unfolding in my wing mirror, desperately praying for Rev's lean silhouette to emerge from the smoke.

But it didn't.

The smoke only thickened, curling higher into the sky, lit from within by the flicker of flames. My chest tightened. When Dray tore past, I made the only choice I could.

I pulled off the track and powered down.

Sam's voice crackled in my ear, asking me what I was doing. Before I could respond, Zylo cut in over the radio.

"What's going on, Kai?"

"You go on, Zylo," I muttered. "I'll get him."

"Kai, I—"

"Don't worry, man."

I didn't blame him for not stopping. Teams trained drivers to continue driving unless they were physically unable to. To leave the accidents to medics and officials. That was the rule.

But Rev wasn't just a teammate. He was more than that. And I'd be damned if I left him scared and alone, waiting in the wreckage.

"Take care of him, Kai," he mumbled with a sniffle.

"Win this for him, old man."

One by one, the other drivers streaked past, their engines screaming as they fought for the podium I'd just abandoned. My shot at a fourth championship evaporated with every blur of colour that passed me by.

But none of that mattered now.

Because somewhere behind me, a car was on fire. Rev's car.

I unstrapped my seatbelt and launched myself from the cockpit. My boots hit the gravel hard, and I ran—heart hammering, lungs burning, ignoring the stewards shouting after me. I didn't stop. Not when smoke curled above the wreckage like a warning. Not when fear clawed at the edges of my mind, whispering worst-case scenarios I refused to believe.

Winning meant nothing if I couldn't celebrate with Rev by my side.

The man I loved.

The man who meant everything.

And I would burn the whole damn track down before I left him behind.

I scanned the track, eyes sharp for cracks or another jet of steam ready to rip the road open. No way was I getting flattened before pulling off my super heroic rescue.

The buzz of drones closed in, their lenses tracking my every move. My image was likely all over the livestream, since drivers didn't abandon races for their rivals.

But screw the headlines. Let Ailor chew me out later.

Rev was worth it.

"Rev!" I shouted, my voice muffled inside the helmet, praying it would still cut through the chaos. "Rev!"

Smoke swirled around me, thick and disorienting, but my visor held strong. I pressed forward into the smoke, each step pulling me closer to the rising heat. Then I saw it—Rev's vehicle, flipped, flames licking up the chassis like hungry teeth.

A gust of wind tore through, scattering the smoke just enough to reveal him. Rev lay on his stomach, half hidden beneath the wreck, blood trailing from a gash at his hairline. His helmet lay beside him; the visor was cracked. Fingers clawed at the dirt, scraping for purchase as he tried to crawl through the narrow gap beneath the burning machine.

"Rev, fuck," I hissed.

His eyes snapped up as I sprinted over, wide with pain and fear. "Kai!" he gasped before coughing violently.

I dropped to my knees beside him, gravel biting through my race suit.

His breath came in ragged pulls, chest hitching with each inhale like his lungs couldn't quite catch up. Sweat clung to his skin, his bun half undone, loose strands matted to his forehead. I reached out and swept them back, my fingers brushing the warm stickiness of blood.

He winced.

A shallow cut marked the bridge of his nose, angry and red, and fresh crimson smeared his split lower lip, as if he'd clamped down during impact.

"Hey," I croaked. "You with me, baby?"

"Absolutely . . . peachy," he panted, managing a weak smile. "But I think I'm stuck."

I sprang to my feet and stepped in front of him, leaning down to grab both his hands. His skin was slick with sweat and grime, shaking with effort.

"Hold on to me," I said, voice firm but low as I tightened my grip. "I'm pulling you out."

He gave a sharp nod, jaw clenched, and locked his fingers around mine. His grip turned bruising, knuckles blanching white against the dirt-smudged contrast of my gloves.

I braced myself, boots grinding into the gravel, and pulled with everything I had.

A harsh scrape tore through the air, fabric catching, tearing. But what froze me was the choked sound that followed. A strained, breathless cry wrenched from his chest.

I stopped cold, heart thudding, terrified I was doing more harm than good.

"Shit," I breathed. "Are you alright?"

"Yes," he breathed, dropping his head to the ground. But when he rolled his shoulders with a sharp wince, guilt hit me hard.

I scanned the vehicle's undercarriage, eyes darting over warped metal. The frame was crumpled, but maybe . . . maybe I could lift it. I wouldn't need to move the whole thing, just enough to give him space. To unhook him from whatever had him pinned.

The heat radiated off it in waves, shimmering in the air between us. I could feel it even through my suit, as if I were standing too close to a forge. I stepped towards it, hands flexing in preparation, about to grab hold of the metal.

But before I could touch it, a hand clamped around my ankle. I froze. Rev's trembling fingers could barely maintain their desperate hold on my boot.

I looked down and met his eyes.

"What are you doing, Kai?"

"Gonna get you out, baby," I said, shaking off his hand.

I stepped over him, planting my feet on either side of his thighs so I faced the vehicle. The flames surged, spreading along the vehicle, so we had to move fast.

"Rev, I'm gonna try to lift it. Crawl out as much as you can, alright?"

"Are you crazy?!" he squawked, twisting to glare at me.

"Crazy about you, rookie." I grinned and winked, but Rev just shot me a hard look. "No time to waste. When I say go, start shimmying."

"This is idiotic, Kai," he huffed.

But he knew we had no choice. With a resigned breath, he flopped back onto his stomach, arms reaching forward, bracing to drag himself free.

"On three." I crouched low, sliding my hands beneath the vehicle's edge. The metal seared through my gloves, jagged shards scraping raw against my skin. Pain flared, but it was nothing compared to what was at stake.

"One . . ." I bent my knees. "Two . . . *three*!"

I heaved with all my strength, pushing the side of the vehicle just an inch off the ground. Rev seized the moment, wriggling free and dragging himself clear of the wreck.

I let the metal drop and rushed to his side, helping him to his feet. He flinched as soon as he put weight on one leg, a sharp hiss escaping through his teeth.

That was when I noticed the tear in the fabric along his thigh, just above the knee, blood smeared beneath it. The cut was long but shallow. Painful, but not life-threatening.

Still, it made my chest clench.

"Shit, you okay?"

"Yeah," he gritted out, limping forward on his bad leg. "Just stings a bit."

"Fuck that. This was supposed to be heroic."

I slid one arm behind his back, the other under his knees, and he let out a startled squeak as I lifted him off the ground. His arms curled around my shoulders, eyes narrowing as if I'd lost my mind.

But as I carried Rev away from the burning wreck, through the choking smoke and into fresh air, his frown softened. He eased my helmet off, letting it fall to the ground as we walked. His fingers tangled in the damp hair at the nape of my neck, pulling me closer.

Our lips met, slow and tender, like time had stretched just for us.

He pulled back to whisper, "Thanks for saving me, *solvenari*."

I held him close, soaking in the way he looked at me as though I was his whole damn universe. The lines along his jaw shimmered with a perfect amethyst glow, and I leaned in to kiss him again, not giving a single shit about the drones hovering nearby.

We stayed like that until the medical shuttle pulled up beside us. Only then did I let him down, helping him steady himself as the medics moved in. They checked him over, cleaned his cuts, and bandaged his leg.

When they were done, he turned to me with a grin that made my chest feel too full. "A race winner and a hero. Not a bad look, hotshot."

He looked so damn pleased, like the idea of me taking the championship meant everything if he couldn't. But I already had everything I needed right here, in one marginally banged-up piece.

I slid an arm around his shoulders and pulled him in, pressing a soft kiss to the top of his head.

"I didn't win, baby. I pulled out to come and get you," I explained. "Pretty sure Zylo took it in the end."

His head snapped up, galaxies swirling fast in his eyes. He didn't speak right away, and I figured he'd be glad his teammate had clinched both the race and the title.

Instead, he exploded.

"What the hell, Kai?!" He smacked me hard in the chest, and I stumbled back with a grunt.

"Wha—"

"Why would you give up the damn race? Why would you throw away the championship for me?!" He shoved me again, eyes blazing. His skin lit up with a deep crimson I recognised too well. "You could've won, and now you're going to resent me for it, and—"

He kept going, words tumbling out in a furious mess. But I was stuck on one thing.

You're going to resent me.

As if I ever could.

Didn't he get it? I didn't care about the title, not if he wasn't there to share it.

I'd won before. Alone. But since Rev crashed into my life, I couldn't picture racing without him. Couldn't imagine the league meaning anything without his voice in my ear and his hand in mine.

"Fucking hell, Kai. I can't believe this! Why would you—"

"Because I love you, you idiot!" I roared, silencing him.

His chest was still rising and falling with anger, but when I cupped his face and pulled him in, he slumped against me like his fight had drained away. The red glow on his skin faded, replaced by a shimmer of soft gold, pink, and amethyst.

"You're everything to me, Revvy. If I haven't made that clear, then I'm saying it now. I'd give up every championship if it meant keeping you safe. There'll be other races, other wins, but if you're not there with me, they'll mean nothing."

I pressed my forehead to his, breathing him in as the medics started moving again, scrambling to get the shuttle ready.

"I'd give it all up again in a heartbeat, as long as you're still by my side."

"So," he murmured, eyes locked on mine, his breath brushing my lips. "What you're saying is . . . if I want the championship, all I have to do is threaten to quit and you'll hand it over?"

I laughed, deep and unfiltered. Full of relief and joy. Rev joined in, his skin lighting up the space between us. We leaned into each other, shaking with laughter, grinning like idiots.

Looking at us, you'd never guess one of us had just crawled out of a fiery wreck, and the other had pulled off a rescue dramatic enough to go down in ASL history.

And yes, for the record, that legend was me.

"I love you, little comet."

"I love you too."

When the medics told us it was time to go, I helped Rev settle into the back of the shuttle. As it began reversing toward the pit lane, the fastest route back, I reached out and grabbed the driver's shoulder.

"The race is over, yeah?"

"Yeah," they said. "They're waiting for you two so they can start the ceremony."

"Think we can follow the track and cross the finish line in the shuttle?" I asked.

"Are you sure?" Rev squeezed my hand, eyes hopeful.

I kissed his nose and glanced at the driver, waiting for their answer.

"Don't see why not," they said with a grin.

So we followed the track, dodging cracks in the asphalt and bursts of steam from the vents. I hit the button to lower the back window, pulled Rev onto my lap, and we waved to the crowd as we neared the finish line.

And when we crossed it, we did it the only way that felt right.

Together.

FAST TRACK TO FOREVER

Rev

My eyes should have been on my teammate as he accepted his championship trophy. But I was drawn to the man beside him, standing in second and grinning like he'd won something greater.

That smile wasn't for the crowd.

It was for me.

Kai's gaze locked with mine, warmth and quiet joy radiating from him. He lifted his silver trophy and blew me a kiss, and I felt heat rise to my cheeks. The drones caught the way my skin flushed in soft shades of pink, but nothing else mattered.

Seeing him there, proud and glowing, was a victory all of its own.

Plus, Kai was hot in general.

Sue me.

He lowered the award and pointed at me, then at the podium where he stood. I imagined his voice in my head.

Next year, rookie, this will be you standing right here.

But I was never one to settle for second best, not if I didn't have to. So I shook my head and pointed at myself, then at the spot where Zylo stood.

I'll be in first, hotshot.

He winked at me, and when I gave him a wide, unfiltered smile, he blew me a kiss.

Zylo had won the championship after Kai dropped out to save me. A part of me still worried he might resent me later on, that his loss would cause a rift between us, but Grandma would have my ass if she knew what I was thinking, because Kai wasn't like that.

We both knew there was more to life than the ASL, even if that was sometimes easy to forget.

The time for running was over. Kai loved me, and I loved him. I just had to trust in what we were building together. After years of feeling like an outsider, I knew it would take time.

But with Kai by my side, I felt like I belonged, and that was better than anything.

Ceremony over, the press and cameras pulled the drivers in all directions, but they surrounded Kai, Zylo, and Jax—who'd come in third—far longer than the rest of us.

I was busy too, especially now that news of what was coming for the Iskari had broken.

The sky had darkened by the time we wrapped up.

I leaned against the wall outside Zenith's garage, watching as Kai strolled over, a skip in his step and a casual sway to his hips. The end of the season prompted most crews and drivers to head home early, ready to celebrate before the paddocks were cleared tomorrow.

The vehicles were lined up outside their teams' garages—including my blackened heap. They looked stunning under the fading light, but my eyes focused on something far better looking.

Kai approached with a wry smile I could no longer resist.

"Well, look what we've got here," he said, stopping just in front of me. There was barely an inch between our chests, and he planted one hand on the wall beside my head, caging me in.

Luckily for him, there was nowhere else I'd rather be tonight—or at any other time.

"There's that cocky grin I know so well," I mused, tracing a finger over his cupid's bow. "Well done on at least one win, hotshot."

Kai might not have won the driver's championship, but Nexus still took it for the constructors, thanks to his and Jax's combined points.

"I won something much better than a championship, rookie," he said, voice low.

He leaned in, pressing his lips against mine, and I slid my hand up to his neck, holding him close. When he licked along the seam of my lips, begging for entry, I opened up. Our tongues met, dancing and exploring each other's mouths, and Kai swallowed the sound of my moans, as if keeping my pleasure just for himself.

Just how I wanted it, now and always.

Before things could get too intense, Kai pulled back, breaking the kiss. I wasn't ashamed when I followed his lips with a quiet whine. I would never tire of kissing Kai, the way he consumed me with something as simple as his mouth on mine.

And thankfully, I wouldn't have to.

"So," he panted, eyes half-lidded, the hazel erased by his blown pupils. "What's next, rookie?"

"I seem to remember someone promising they'd fuck me against some windows," I teased.

Kai's grin turned wolfish as he leaned in, dropping one last kiss on my lips before grabbing my hand and pulling me away from the wall. "You gonna light up the city for me, little comet?"

"That depends," I replied. "You gonna make a wish on me?"

Kai laughed, pulling me close so his arm draped around my shoulder, his warmth seeping into my skin. "My wish already came true, baby," he said, eyes locked on mine. "I got you in the end, didn't I?"

We strolled through the paddock together, the planet's oversized sun dipping below the horizon behind us, its last warm rays brushing our backs like a gentle farewell for the season.

Kai led me towards the shuttle park where a single vehicle waited, the driver already inside, ready to take us home.

It didn't matter whether we were heading to Kai's place or mine—though I was looking forward to being fucked against his windows.

Home wasn't a single spot anymore.

And thanks to a cocky pro racer who loved to rile me up and drive me crazy every day, I no longer felt like an outsider looking in.

No, what I felt now was pure love and happiness. At least whenever Kai was near. I reserved my scowls for everyone else these days, and my smiles belonged to him.

Kai was my home, and with him around, I knew I'd never feel alone again.

EPILOGUE

Kai

A look through the window showed the change from deep space to hazy yellow skies as we entered Ithara's atmosphere. A giant moon filled the horizon, bright enough to provide daylight for twenty hours a day, all year round.

The planet was nice, with its wide open spaces and miles of grassland, but other than some cool animals on the ground and in the sky, there wasn't that much to see. Not beyond the capital of Luminara.

Though maybe I was biased, because nestled on the outskirts of the city was my favourite place—on this planet, at least. As the shuttle descended through Ithara's dust clouds, long cracks in the ground came into view, causing my heart to pump a little harder.

Like every year, I was excited for the season ahead. And just like every year, Jax said, "Welcome home, bud."

But this year . . . yeah, this year felt different.

In the past, my heart had always been wherever the race was, and I'd often dreaded the six months of the off-season before training for the next season began. But my home wasn't a racetrack anymore, or even the Astro Space League.

Now my home was a certain Iskari, waiting for me in the shuttle park.

We stepped off the shuttle, and I walked straight over to my love.

Rev greeted me with a wide smile, then masked it with his usual blank expression as he nodded at Jax. Butterflies fluttered in my chest, because even after all these months together, he still saved every single smile just for me.

"Miss me?" I asked, pressing a kiss to the top of his head as we made our way towards the paddock.

Jax raised an eyebrow. "Didn't you see him a few hours ago?"

It was a new season, and I still couldn't raise a single fucking eyebrow. Rev had tried to teach me after I begged for hours on end, because he had it down to a fine art, but he gave up after my fortieth failed attempt, declaring I'd have to settle for looking like I was having an aneurysm.

That didn't stop me from practicing in our bathroom mirror.

Daily.

Rev had moved into my apartment two months ago. I'd always thought we'd move into his place whenever the time came, because his was cosier, a proper little nest, and since he was such a homebody, I figured he'd prefer the space he knew so well.

But something had changed his mind, and when I'd tentatively suggested moving in together, he'd said yes and started packing up his things.

I wasn't sure, but I thought it had something to do with the floor-to-ceiling windows in our living room. I'd fucked him against them more times than I could count, and with how often I caught him gazing at them, it became a regular thing.

We'd gone through so much glass cleaner from wiping away bodily fluids, I was considering buying some shares in the company. Maybe I'd present them to Rev as a gift for his birthday.

His parents had moved into Rev's old apartment, while his grandma stayed in their family home.

When the last season ended, the IGG officially recognised the Iskari as equals. There were still changes to be made, some of which would take years to complete, but a few of the most important had already taken effect.

Rev's parents now received a respectable wage from their jobs, with employers no longer able to underpay them just because of who they were. We'd tried to convince them to find better paying jobs, but both were happy where they were. They'd been there a long time, were good friends with their colleagues, and enjoyed the work they did.

His grandma received a pension now, and no longer had to rely on selling herbal creams on Astrazon. Rev had bought the apartment from their landlord as a gift for her, ignoring her protests when she refused to accept the deed.

She gave in when he batted his lashes at her, because no one was immune to that look.

She'd also started a new crochet business, and whenever we stopped by during the week, I helped her create some stock. As a result, my fingers were more nimble than ever, and I was damn sure Rev's prostate was grateful.

Overall, the Iskari's situation had improved. Rev met up with Talia and her husband often, and we'd even attended their twins' sixteenth birthday party. Both he and other Iskari volunteers attended regular meetings with the IGG, ensuring the ongoing changes remained positive, and so far everything was going well.

Jax and Rev chatted while we walked through the paddock. I hadn't seen much of my best friend during the off-season. He'd been busy with something he wasn't sharing with me. But I wasn't about to pry. Not yet.

I hoped he'd tell me soon, though. Otherwise I'd have to stick my nose in, despite Rev's warnings to stay out of it.

When Zenith's garage came into view, I spotted Zylo talking to one of the crew. He caught sight of us as we got closer and broke off the conversation, hurrying over to greet us.

"Revvy!" Zylo boomed, as if we were miles away instead of just a few feet.

He swooped in and wrapped Rev in a bear hug, lifting my boyfriend off the ground. He squeezed so hard I thought I heard Rev's ribs creak, making me wince in sympathy. I'd have to kiss them better later. What a shame for me.

"How was your off-season, Zylo?" Jax asked, and Zylo launched into a romantic story about proposing to Saelix after thirteen years together.

Rev and I had already heard the story straight from Saelix, since we'd ended up seeing Zylo quite a bit during our time off.

Despite Rev's usual aversion to people, he'd made it clear that he wanted to get to know his teammate better. So we'd met up with the couple often, whether for dinner at their home in Zyphar or drinks at a cocktail bar on Solveth.

On one memorable night, I'd got my chance to bump and grind with Rev on the dance floor, before heading home and fucking him against the shower wall.

Fuck you, Dray. This guy was mine now.

As Tavoris and Ailor emerged from their respective team garages, our conversation drew to a natural close. It was time to get to work.

Zylo and Jax were the first to peel away, heading off to meet with the strategists and start planning for the season ahead. But Rev and I lingered, stealing a few extra seconds together, even though we'd end up in the same place by day's end.

"Ready for another year, rookie?" I asked, voice low and just for him.

Rev arched a sculpted brow. "I don't think you can call me that anymore, Mercer."

Oof. Surnames. That meant one thing. Competition mode. And fuck, I loved it.

"You'll always be a rookie to me, baby."

He trailed his fingers up my chest, slow and deliberate, stopping at the base of my throat. "Maybe this year you'll be calling me a winner, hotshot."

"Over my dead body," I said with a grin. "I already gave up one championship for you. This year, I'm taking it back."

His lips curled, black eyes gleaming with mischief. "Wanna make this weekend a little more interesting?"

The openness in his expression was still such a novelty, something I never wanted to take for granted. He could have asked me to do just about anything, and I would've said yes.

Stars, he could suggest I streak down the pit lane with a furry tail lodged where the sun doesn't shine, and I'd agree without blinking.

Still, just to be safe, I said, "What've you got in mind?"

His grin turned wicked, and the markings along his skin lit up in a shade of teal I recognised as playful. Mischievous in the best kind of way.

Over the past few months, he'd walked me through what each colour meant, explaining their shifts with shy patience. And every time a new one appeared, especially when he was flustered or turned on, I felt like I'd unlocked some rare treasure.

It was incredible watching him grow into himself, especially when I thought back to our first meeting last season. Back then, he'd been colder than a moonlit crater. But now, he was unfurling like a flower stretching toward the sun.

At least around me.

He still wore his scowl like armour in front of everyone else, chasing people off with a single glare. But in private, when it was just us, he lowered his walls and let his real self peek through. And damn, he was such a goof when he wasn't trying so hard to stay guarded.

"How about a bet?" he said, casual but sly.

"Alright, rookie. I'll bite," I replied, already intrigued. "If I win today's race, you're going to dress up in the prettiest pair of lace panties I can find . . . and let me tear them off with my teeth."

His skin flushed a vibrant pink, glowing like embers, and I swear I felt his cock twitch against my thigh. "Alright, hotshot. You're on." Then he tilted his chin up, all faux innocence and smug confidence. "But if I come out on top . . . I get to *top you.*"

The words hit me like a sucker punch to the gut, stealing the air from my lungs, and my cock jerked hard in my jeans, pressing against his stomach. He noticed. His smirk said it all—wicked and victorious.

"It's on, then," I said, though it came out more croak than confidence. My voice cracked on the last word, so I cleared my throat and gave my head a quick shake.

Now wasn't the time to be thinking about how good he'd feel inside me.

"I'll see you at the finish line," I added, smirking. "When you come in second."

"Thems be fightin' words, Mercer." He narrowed his eyes in a mock glare, the corner of his mouth twitching like he was holding back a grin.

I stepped closer, closing the last inch between us until we were nose to nose."I'll fight you when we get home, little comet. No doubt about that."

His skin deepened to a dusky pink, starlight spinning fast in his eyes. "You promise?"

"I already cleaned the windows," I said with a wink.

Rev snorted and slapped my chest, laughter bursting out of him before he could stop it. "You're such a twat."

"And you love me anyway."

His smile softened as he reached up, fingers brushing my cheek in a touch that still made my heart skip. "Yeah. I do."

"Rev!" Tavoris called from across the paddock, just as Sam stepped out to check on me.

"Coming!" Rev called back, though his eyes never left mine.

"Time to get to work, baby," I murmured, low enough for only him to hear.

And he reached up, pulling me down into a soft kiss laced with so much love and quiet promise it made my heart thud hard against my ribs. Like every time was the first time.

"I love you, *solvenari*," he whispered. "See you at home."

Then he turned and walked away, disappearing into Zenith's garage to begin the long months ahead.

I stayed there for a moment, watching him go.

Home wasn't four walls or a familiar stretch of racetrack. Home was the man who'd just walked away, carrying half my heart in his hands.

The only difference now?

Rev always came back to me.

And this time, I'd be right here, waiting to catch him when he did.

THE END

AFTERWORD

Thank you for reading Hyperspeed!

Dray and Jax are up next in a second-chance romance with an accidental wedding, forced proximity, and fake husbands with benefits.

Afterburn
Astro Space League Book 2
Coming in early 2026

ACKNOWLEDGEMENTS

I'd dreamed of finishing a book for years, but none of my WIPs ever stuck. These boys did, and in less than two months, I had a first draft.

While they say it takes a village, this story took a city.

Jemma, thank you for being my compass. You got me to the finish line—yes, pun intended—and I'll never stop being grateful for your guidance, love, and friendship.

Leo, your art gave life to this universe. From characters to worldbuilding, Hyperspeed wouldn't shine half as bright without your vision and constant support.

Eryn, Ronan, Al, and Tiff, my beta legends. Thank you for your brilliant notes and chaotic commentary. Quinn, for the check-ins, the hype, and the sanity-saving chats in the early hours. Sam, thank you for your eagle eyes and sharp edits. You made Hyperspeed stronger in every way.

To Jamie, my partner, thank you for loving me through the chaos, listening to all my space rambling, and for taking the dog out so I could write—I love you.

To Paige, Chloe, and Dad (who still shouldn't be reading this). You believed in me, even when I didn't.

And to you, the reader. Thank you for picking up my debut. I poured my heart into this story, and it means the world that you're here to read it.

ABOUT THE AUTHOR

Lily James is a UK-based author with a soft spot for beautiful, heart-stealing queer romance. A lover of swoony stories, she's especially fond of tales where complicated men fall hopelessly for each other. She lives in the West Midlands with her partner and their chubby dog, Winston—who definitely has main character energy.